ALSO BY MARGARET BROWNLEY

A Match Made in Texas
Left at the Altar
A Match Made in Texas

The Haywire Brides
Cowboy Charm School
The Cowboy Meets His Match

Christmas in a Cowboy's Arms anthology

The Cowboy meets his Match

MARGARET BROWNLEY

sourcebooks
casablanca

Published by Sourcebooks Casablanca, an imprint of Sourcebooks
P.O. Box 4410, Naperville, Illinois 60567-4410
(630) 961-3900
sourcebooks.com

Printed and bound in Canada.
MBP 10 9 8 7 6 5 4 3 2 1

What men call accident is God's own part.

—PHILIP JAMES BAILEY

1

Haywire, Texas
1886

THE MOMENT EMILY ROSE STEPPED OFF THE TRAIN, SHE knew she'd made a terrible mistake. It wasn't just the heat pressing down on her like a thick, wet blanket. Nor the dust that clogged the throat and stung the eyes. It wasn't even the relentless flies.

Rather, it was the feeling of dread that settled like a lead weight in the pit of her stomach. One look at the sorrowful excuse for a town, and the trouble she'd left back in Boston seemed like a tea party in comparison.

The dark-skinned driver set to work tossing her baggage into the rear of the hotel omnibus with reckless abandon.

"Oh, do be careful with that," she cried, grabbing her bandbox out of his hand.

Shooting her an exasperated look, the driver reached for her carpetbag and hurled it into the compartment with the rest of her baggage. Since her belongings commanded all available space, the other passengers were forced to carry their travel gear on board.

One matronly woman glared at Emily, her beak-like nose flaring. "Some people have no consideration for others," she grumbled, her voice loud enough to gain the attention of those still standing in line.

Emily apologized and offered to help the passenger with her valise, but the woman would have none of it. Instead, she made quite a show of lugging her single satchel up the steps of the omnibus, grunting and groaning and complaining like an old crow.

Emily disregarded the woman's theatrics, but it was harder to ignore the curious stares directed at her stylish blue traveling suit. She had been so anxious to make her escape, she'd not thought about clothes. The last thing she needed was to call attention to herself. Had she been thinking straight, she would have purchased something more sedate like a simple gingham or calico dress, though she doubted such a thing could have been found in all of Boston.

The same was true of the plain cloth bonnets locals seemed to favor. Her own felt hat, stylishly trimmed with feathers, now seemed hopelessly out of place.

Sidestepping a pile of horse manure, Emily boarded the omnibus, her bandbox in hand. She pulled a handkerchief out of her sleeve and wiped off the dusty leather seat before adjusting her bustle and sitting.

The driver took his seat and waited until the last of his passengers had boarded before shaking the reins and clicking his tongue. As if to protest the heavy load, the two roans snorted as they plodded forward, scattering more dust with their heavy hooves.

Emily fanned her heated face with the soiled handkerchief and gazed out the glassless window.

Compared to Boston's sturdy redbrick buildings, the adobe shops with the false fronts and rough-hewn signs looked like they could be blown away with one good gust of wind.

No cobblestones lined the thoroughfare. Instead, a bumpy dirt road wound through town, flanked by wooden sidewalks.

She looked for the drugstore owned by the man she'd traveled all this way to marry but didn't see it. Instead, they passed a general store, a bank, a gunsmith, and a leather shop, but no ladies' hat or dress emporiums. A sign reading *Haywire Book and Sweet Shop* gave her a flicker of hope. The selling of books suggested that maybe the town wasn't as primitive as it appeared.

Emily reached into her purse and pulled out the dog-eared letter that had been carefully tucked inside. Unfolding it, she reread the simple instructions written in bold handwriting. She was told to check into the hotel. A driver would pick her up at four o'clock sharp and drive her to the courthouse. Her betrothed would meet her there to exchange vows.

She chewed her lower lip and forced herself to breathe. Never had she imagined herself a mail-order bride. But then neither had she dreamt she would be forced to leave Boston in shame, with hardly a penny to her name.

Her only hope was that her soon-to-be husband was as kind and caring in person as he appeared to be in his letters.

She checked her pendant watch, grateful that she'd remembered to adjust it to local time at the train station.

The omnibus turned onto a bewildering series of winding, pretzel-like streets before pulling up the drive leading to the Haywire Grande Hotel. Judging by the weathered facade, the only thing grand about the hotel was its size.

Emily's stomach knotted. Whatever fate had in store for her couldn't be any worse than what she'd left behind. While the thought did nothing to lift her spirits, it did help calm her pounding heart. Refolding the letter, she returned it to her purse. Moments later, she stood in the blazing sun and waited for the driver to unload her luggage.

"Will that be all, ma'am?" he asked. His sudden politeness could only mean he expected a generous gratuity.

"Yes, thank you." She handed him twice the number of coins she normally would, more out of guilt for commanding so much space than gratitude.

While a bellhop arranged her luggage onto a wooden handcart, she glanced again at her watch. In just two hours, she would be married to a man she had never set eyes on—a total stranger.

Now that she'd seen the town, it seemed that she was about to exchange one prison for another.

Chase McKnight paced the floor of the judge's chambers. Where was she? His bride should have been here by now.

The dark wooden paneling and teak desk reflected his gloomy thoughts. Never had he imagined a wedding day as bleak and unsettling as this.

There were three men in the room, counting Chase. Judge Gray sat behind the desk, waiting to perform the wedding ceremony. Chase's uncle occupied the single chair in front of the desk, ready to serve as a witness. With their dark suits and serious expressions, they could just as easily have been attending a funeral.

Chase wished to God he'd never agreed to this marriage. He'd met the bride-to-be but once, years ago when they were both in their early teens. Still, what choice did he have? What choice, for that matter, did the lady have?

Now a widow with three small children—two boys and a girl—she lived in the next county. He'd heard that she regularly attended church, was a hard worker, and had accepted her lot in life with grace and goodwill. If his memory served him right, she wasn't that bad to look at either. But that wasn't the point.

He glanced at his uncle. "Maybe she's not comin'." It would be disastrous if she didn't show, but who could blame her? He was as much a stranger to her as she was to him, with a less-than-stellar reputation.

"Relax. She'll be here," his uncle said, though his drumming fingers belied the calmness of his voice. Uncle Baxter was a large, pompous man who resembled his brother—Chase's father—in size, but not disposition. He was a hard-nosed businessman whose relentless ambition had driven more than one woman away. "She needs this marriage as much as you do."

Chase sincerely doubted that, but now was no time to argue.

Judge Gray reached into his vest pocket for his watch and flipped the case open with his thumb. As round as he was tall, the judge had a long, white beard and white hair. Faded gray eyes peered from behind tortoiseshell spectacles.

"She better come soon. I've got another wedding in fifteen minutes."

Chase balled his hands at his sides. He longed to shrug off the frock coat and boiled shirt. As a cattle rancher, he wasn't used to such formal attire. Why weddings required such a getup was one of the mysteries of life.

Discomfort turning to irritation, he glared at his uncle. "I don't know why I let you talk me into this." There had to be another way.

Uncle Baxter leaned forward and snubbed his cigar in the copper ashtray on the judge's desk. "You know what your father's will said. The first son to marry gets the ranch. Do you want your brother claiming what's yours?"

"*Step*brother," Chase gritted out through wooden lips.

The mere thought of losing the ranch was like a knife to his heart. It wasn't just a spread; it was a family legacy. The Rocking M Ranch had been founded by his Scottish grandparents. It was Grandpapa McKnight who had taught Chase everything he knew about cattle and ranching. By the age of twelve, Chase could ride, rope, and shoot as well or better than any man.

The judge checked his watch again. Chase's uncle's gaze sharpened, and his mustache twitched, but he said nothing.

Chase paced the floor and punched his fist into his left palm. When his uncle had first approached him with the idea of marrying the widow, it had sounded like the perfect plan. It wasn't easy being a rancher's wife, and few women could handle the demands. Cassie Decker had grown up around cattle. That alone would make her an asset.

Had things gone according to plan, not only would the marriage have saved the ranch and Chase's family legacy, but it would have helped a woman and her small children. Now, the plan seemed bound for failure.

A clamor made Chase stop pacing and turn. "Why'd you bring that?" he asked, tossing a nod at his uncle's shotgun on the floor. "I said no violence."

"Think of this as insurance." His uncle reached for the shotgun and tapped the floor with the gunstock. "If your stepbrother gets wind that you're here, there could be trouble. I don't aim on letting anything go wrong."

Chase pinched the bridge of his nose. Something had already gone wrong. The bride-to-be had apparently suffered a case of cold feet. "Maybe I can get a bank loan." He resented having to pay his stepbrother to save the ranch. But if his bride didn't show, he might not have a choice.

His uncle discounted this idea with a shake of his head. "No bank is gonna give you a loan, and you know it. Not with the economy the way it is."

"I'll think of somethin'."

"If there was another solution, we'd have thought of it by now." His uncle slipped a hand in his waistcoat pocket and pulled out his gold watch. "You better start praying that the lady shows."

The judge's unkempt, bushy eyebrows rose and fell. "You have ten minutes."

Chase took a seething breath and continued pacing while his uncle kept checking the time. After another couple of minutes, he stopped. "Whether she shows or not, I'm not givin' up."

Uncle Baxter grimaced. "You may have to," he said, surprising Chase. It wasn't like his uncle to admit defeat. "It's a shame for it to end this way. The ranch meant everything to your father."

Chase's nostrils flared. "If it meant so much to him, then why did he put such a stipulation in the will?"

How his father's second wife had persuaded him to write such a will was a puzzle that continued to haunt Chase. Her son, Royce, had never put in an honest day's work in his life. Drinking, gambling, and womanizing were more his style.

"There're some things that are out of a person's control," his uncle said cryptically.

Chase's gaze sharpened. "What things?"

A look of uncertainty crept into his uncle's expression. "Just…things."

There was something his uncle wasn't saying, but Chase was too incensed to pursue it.

The judge's voice floated across the room. "If your bride doesn't show in the next couple of minutes, I won't have time to marry you. The next wedding party is due to arrive momentarily."

Chase sucked in his breath and started for the door.

"Where are you going?" his uncle asked. "There's still time."

Chase whirled around. "Marrying the lady was your idea, and I should never have agreed to it." Lord knew he had enough on his plate without taking on an unwilling bride.

"Now listen to me—"

"No, you listen to me." Chase was shouting now but didn't care. "If I lose the ranch, I lose the ranch. But at least I won't be tied to a loveless marriage!"

He turned toward the door just as it flew open. The widow had finally arrived, and she was decked from head to toe in full bridal regalia.

2

EMILY STARED AT THE TWO MEN WHOSE VOICES HAD
been loud enough to be heard in the hall. She guessed
that the younger man was Jake Garvey, the druggist
she'd come here to wed, but she couldn't be certain.
Please don't let the groom be the one with the shotgun...

Whichever he was, the groom had sounded as
reluctant to marry her as she was him, and that was
odd. He'd been so persuasive in his letters, so com-
mitted to making a life with her, so perfectly charming
and kind.

If she hadn't known it before, she knew it now.
Coming to Texas had been a mistake. How foolish of
her to think that marrying a stranger would solve her
problems.

Since neither man seemed anxious to say to her face
what had been said before she'd walked in, it appeared
it was up to her.

"I...I changed my mind," she said, grateful for the
veil that covered her face. Instead of sounding bold
and sure of herself as she'd hoped, she hardly recognized the uncertain voice as her own. Dear God, if she

didn't marry the man, how would she ever support herself? She had no skills. At least none that would earn a living in a town such as this.

She cleared her throat and knotted her hands at her sides. "I-I can't do this," she said. Her decision could mean sleeping in doorways and eating bread crumbs, but at least she wouldn't be tied down to a man who didn't want her.

"I can't marry you," she said, her voice stronger this time. There had to be another way; there just had to be.

The silence that followed her outburst was broken by a previously unnoticed third man in the room—a man she suddenly realized was the judge. "Five minutes."

The older man with the shotgun opened his mouth to speak, but the younger man interrupted. "If that's how you feel…"

"I-I think it's best." Casting a nervous glance at the man with the gun, she added, "Please accept my apologies." Anxious to make her escape, she picked up her voluminous skirts and hurriedly left the room.

Outside the courthouse, shouts and mass confusion greeted Emily and stopped her in her tracks. What had moments earlier been a calm and peaceful town was now mass confusion. Men, women, and children ran down the middle of the street, screaming.

A man on a horse raced by, waving his hat and yelling, "Clear the way. Clear the way!"

The wooden-plank boards beneath her satin slippers began to vibrate, then violently shake. Startled, she clutched at the railing. It felt as if the world was coming to an end.

A thick, roiling cloud of dust headed her way, and terror held her in its grip. Just as the cloud reached the courthouse, the dust gave way to thundering hooves, bawling cries, and clashing horns.

Emily's jaw dropped, and her eyes rounded. She'd heard of cattle stampedes, of course, but had never witnessed one. Even her wedding veil couldn't keep the dust from clogging her mouth and stinging her eyes. Unable to see or even breathe, she squeezed her eyes shut and clung to the railing until her fingers ached.

Someone grabbed her by the arm and dragged her back into the courthouse. Grateful for the relatively clean air, she gasped, and her chest heaved. The reprieve lasted for only as long as it took for her vision to clear. The first thing that greeted her startled eyes was the shotgun the man held at his side.

Her horrified gaze traveled upward to the gun owner's face. It was the older man with the mustache.

"I'm here on behalf of my nephew," he said. It was necessary for him to shout to be heard over the thundering hooves. "I'm hoping you'll reconsider and wed him as promised." When she failed to respond, he continued. "Given your, shall we say, dire circumstances? It would be to your advantage to go through with the wedding."

Emily's breath caught in her chest, and her stays pinched her ribs. Was that a threat? And if so, how did this man know of her difficult situation? She'd not written a word in her letters about her true circumstances or why it was necessary to leave Boston.

Aware suddenly that he still cupped her elbow, she pulled her arm away. "He doesn't want to marry me."

He held a ring-laden hand to his ear. "What?"

Lifting her voice over the commotion outside, she repeated herself. "He doesn't want to marry me."

"Ah, so that's the problem. You overheard our... discussion." Shifting the shotgun to his left hand, he took her by the arm and steered her down the hall. She tried pulling away, but that only made him tighten his hold. "Trust me, my nephew didn't mean what he said. When it appeared that you wouldn't show, he was just trying..."

"What?" She could hardly hear for the turmoil outside.

He stopped and released his hold on her. "I said, my nephew was trying to save face," he repeated, his voice louder this time. "A man doesn't like to be jilted by his bride. But I do believe marriage is best. For you, especially."

His meaningful look gave her pause. It certainly sounded like a threat. And if so, then he wasn't bluffing; he knew her true identity. But how?

Outside, the cattle kept running; their pounding hooves echoed the hammering of her heart. She dragged air into her mouth and tried to breathe.

Apparently taking her silence for consent, he crooked his right elbow. His demeanor suggested he'd made some sort of conquest. "Shall we?"

Feeling trapped both physically and emotionally, Emily hesitated.

"You won't be sorry," he coaxed.

She was already sorry, but there didn't appear to be much she could do about it. Alone in a strange town with hardly a dime to her name, she didn't have much in the way of options. She only hoped that the man's nephew was as kind as his letters suggested.

With more than a little anxiety, she slipped her arm through the offered elbow, and together, they walked to the judge's chambers.

Neither the groom nor the judge appeared to hear them enter the room. Instead, their attention remained riveted on the mass confusion outside the courthouse window.

The uncle tapped the floor with his shotgun to get their attention. "Let's get this wedding over with." His deep voice barely penetrated the clamor that seemed even louder in this room than in the hall.

Both men turned. The man she was here to marry stared at her with raised eyebrows. "Are you sure you want to go through with this?" he asked.

Emily opened her mouth to say something, but the older man by her side answered for her. "She's sure." He shot her a warning look, as if daring her to disagree.

The judge shook his head. "No time," he said with a glance at his pocket watch.

"There's time," the uncle insisted. "Traffic is blocked. No one can leave or enter town. The next wedding party has been delayed." His eyes gleamed with triumph. "It seems that providence has inter-vened on our behalf."

The judge shrugged. "All right then." He raised his voice. "Let's get on with it." Turning, he opened the room's second door and made a motion with his hand. A thin, pasty-faced man entered the room and was introduced as the court clerk.

"Now that we have our second witness, I believe

we're ready." The judge pointed to where he wanted the bride and groom to stand.

Glancing through her thick veil at the man she was about to marry, Emily balked. Sympathetic eyes met hers, and he extended his hand, revealing the same kind nature shown in his letters. "Shall we?" he mouthed.

Swallowing hard, she placed her hand in his, and he tightened his grip. He was quite tall, and she barely came up to his shoulders. Unlike the other two men in the room, he was clean-shaven, and she caught the pleasant smell of bay-rum aftershave. His hair was trimmed neatly and fell short of his collar.

Appearance-wise, he was everything she could hope for in a husband. That alone was a surprise. She tried to equate this man with his letters and couldn't. He'd written he wasn't much to look at, and that had turned out to be anything but true.

The modesty he'd shown on paper hardly seemed to match the strong, confident man leading her across the room. Skin bronzed by the sun and wind and blue eyes brimming with intelligence, he flashed her a reassuring smile.

This man could probably have any woman he wanted. How odd that he would turn to a marriage broker to find a wife! Matrimonial ads were for the desperate, like her, or the lonely, and it was hard to imagine this man being either.

He drew her to the place in front of the judge and released her hand. "It'll be all right," he said, speaking directly into her ear. His breath sent warm shivers down her neck.

Despite his reassurances, it was hardly the kind of wedding day she'd envisioned, and it wasn't only because of the stranger by her side. Thanks to the ongoing stampede, the building shook with worrisome creaks. The windows rattled like old bones, and the floorboards trembled beneath her feet. She gave the swinging gaslight a nervous glance before turning her attention to the judge.

The noise from the cattle all but drowned out the judge's voice, and she could hardly hear what he said. She glanced over her shoulder at the uncle standing behind them. He held his shotgun ready, as if to bar the door should she try to escape.

Mouth dry, she looked away and tried to make out the judge's muffled words.

Only when he looked directly at her did she whisper, "I do."

After they'd exchanged vows, the groom slipped a plain gold band around her ring finger. It felt like a shackle.

The noise outside gradually died down. The building stopped shaking just in time for the judge to make the final declaration. "By the authority granted me by the state of Texas, I now pronounce you man and wife. You may kiss the bride."

With a look of uncertainty, the groom turned to her, and she stiffened.

He reached for her veil, and her heart jolted against her ribs. *Oh no!* He was going to kiss her. She hadn't allowed herself to think about the physical side of marriage, but now that it crossed her mind, she began to panic and pulled back.

The groom dropped his hands to his sides. Tilting his head with an apologetic look, he accepted her rejection without comment.

Meanwhile, seated at his desk, the judge handed the groom a pen. He dipped the nib into a bottle of ink and scribbled broad strokes on the page before handing the pen to her.

Accepting the offered pen from the man who, in the eyes of the law, was now her husband, Emily fought to hold her hand steady as she signed her name. She then handed the pen to the clerk, who scribbled his name beneath hers and then moved aside so the uncle could sign.

Just as the judge finished signing the registry, the door flung open, and a second bride entered the room.

The heads of three small children peered from behind her white calico skirt.

"Sorry I'm late," the newcomer said, sounding breathless as if she'd been running. "I couldn't find Bobby's shoes, and by the time we found them, the driver had already left the hotel, and the stampede—" Her gaze lit on the shotgun pointed straight at her, and she stopped talking with a gasp.

Muttering a curse, Emily's new husband slapped at the muzzle. "Put that thing away," he snarled angrily. He waited for his uncle to lower the gun before apologizing. "Sorry about that," he said. "He thought you were someone else."

Lifting her young son in her arms, the woman's gaze swept the room. Her eyes bored into Emily before finally lighting on the groom. "Chase? What... what is the meaning of this?"

Emily frowned. Who was this woman, and why was she calling Jake *Chase*? She felt her new husband stiffen by her side.

"Cassie? Cassie Decker. Is that you?"

"Of course it's me," the woman said, removing her veil with her one free hand. She then pointed a finger at Emily. "Who is that?"

The groom whirled about to face Emily, his face grim. "That's what I want to know. Who in blazes are *you*?"

His voice made Emily flinch, and her mind scrambled in confusion. How could he ask that question of her after they had just exchanged vows? "I'm…" She lifted her veil. "I'm your wife."

The groom stared at her with a blank expression, and for several moments, no one uttered a sound. "Your name?" he grated out at last. "Your name."

Confused, Emily stared at him, not knowing what he asked of her. "I'm Mrs.—"

"Your maiden name!"

"Emily…Emily Rose." She had dropped her real name, Fields, and used her middle name instead—a precautionary measure. She doubted that anyone in Texas would recognize the name Fields, but she didn't dare take chances.

The groom reared back to glance at the registry she'd signed as if to check the legitimacy of her claim.

A sick feeling washed over her. "Y-you're not Mr. Garvey? Mr. Jake Garvey?" she stammered.

A dark look crossed his face. "I'm Chase McKnight, and I was supposed to wed Mrs. Decker here." He tossed a nod at the other bride, who stood clutching her son and gaping at Emily with an openmouthed stare.

The uncle pulled a handkerchief from his pocket and mopped his forehead. "Oh boy."

McKnight's eyes bored into Emily. "How do you know Garvey?"

Before she could explain, another man rushed into the chamber. "Sorry I'm late." He brushed the dust off his trousers and shirt. Unlike the other four men in the room, the newcomer was casually dressed in black trousers, plaid shirt, and vest.

"Those blasted cattle…" Clamping his mouth shut, the man stared at the uncle's raised shotgun. "What's going on?" His gaze swung between the two brides. "I'm looking for Miss Emily Rose from Boston."

The full impact of what had happened finally sank in, and Emily felt her knees threaten to buckle. "I-I'm Emily R–Rose." Or at least she was until a few minutes ago.

"Well now," the newcomer said, his face bright with approval. He hung his thumbs from his suspenders and added, "I'm Jake Garvey, and I reckon a man couldn't ask for a purtier bride." Grinning, he glanced at the others. "I'm a lucky man!"

Struck speechless, Emily covered her mouth with both hands and stared over her fingertips with horror-filled eyes.

A druggist by trade, Mr. Garvey's face lacked McKnight's rugged countenance. His arms appeared to be too long, his face too narrow, his clothes ill-fitting. But what he lacked in appearance, he more than made up for in eagerness.

No one seemed to know what to say, and a stunned silence filled the room.

At last, the judge cleared his throat. "I'm afraid there's been what you might call a bit of a hitch."

The druggist afforded the judge a questioning look. "What kind of a hitch?"

With a toss of her head, Mrs. Decker set her son down. "That's what I want to know."

The judge shot the widow a look of apology. "Well, it's like this." He eased his hefty bulk into his groaning chair. "The lady—Miss Rose here—is already spoken for."

The druggist cast a look in Emily's direction before turning back to the judge. "What do you mean, 'spoken for'?"

McKnight answered for the judge, his voice rough. "He means she's married to me."

Mrs. Decker's face turned the same creamy white as her dress. "You…you're already married?" she asked, her voice hollow with disbelief.

Looking like he'd been shot, the druggist reared back. "Whoa, now. That can't be right. Miss Rose here sent me a letter agreeing to be *my* wife."

Everyone started talking at once. Emily stared in bewilderment at the angry faces around her. Even the judge jumped into the fray, vehemently denying any wrongdoing. Clutching at their mother's skirts, the wide-eyed children stared at the battling adults, the youngest with his thumb in his mouth.

Mrs. Decker shot an angry glance at Chase. "How could you make such a mistake?"

"That's what I want to know," Garvey said, looking to Emily for an answer.

Wringing her hands, Emily shook her head. "I-I thought you were him."

Mrs. Decker scoffed. "That's a likely story. They don't even look alike."

Emily and Chase took turns trying to explain how such a mistake had happened, but their words fell on deaf ears. Neither Mrs. Decker nor the man Emily was supposed to have married could be placated.

Hands at her waist, Mrs. Decker glared at Chase McKnight. "If you didn't want to marry me, why didn't you just say so?" Scooting her children out the door, she left in a huff, with Mr. Garvey close behind.

Chase started for the door, but his uncle waylaid him. "Let her go. She's too upset to hear anything you have to say. Wait till she's had time to calm down."

Chase hesitated for a moment before giving a reluctant nod. Jaw clenched, he spun around and slammed his fist on the judge's desk. "Fix this!"

Emily turned toward the desk, hoping for a speedy solution to their problem, but her hopes were dashed the moment she set eyes on the judge.

Looking befuddled, he ran a finger inside his collar and grimaced. "Well, I…"

Chase's uncle shook his head. "There's no time. Your stepbrother—"

"I don't care," Chase seethed. "I want this fixed! Now!"

With a glance at the clerk, the judge drew a handkerchief out of his pocket and dabbed at his sweaty forehead. Replacing the handkerchief, he cleared his throat. "I'm sure this isn't the first time something like this has happened." The judge's hollow laugh was met with scowls. Growing serious, he reached for a leather-bound book and thumbed through the pages.

"Ah, here we are," he said, sounding relieved. "Annulment." Adjusting his spectacles, he quickly scanned the page. "This should only take a few minutes. You just have to answer a few questions." Finger holding his spot, he looked up and asked in all seriousness, "Why do you want an annulment?"

Chase reared back. "Why? Because I married the wrong woman, that's why!"

"Yes, yes, yes, I know that." The judge stabbed the page with his finger. "But that's not listed here as legitimate grounds for annulment."

The uncle jabbed the muzzle of his shotgun on the floor and placed both hands on the butt. "What *are* legitimate grounds?"

The judge's finger moved down the page. "Bigamy, for one." He looked up. "Are either of you married?"

"Yes, we're married," Chase said, his voice thick with impatience. "To each other!"

The uncle stared straight at Emily. "I think he's asking if either one of you is married to someone else."

Emily's eyes flashed him a look of disdain. If it wasn't for him and his veiled threats, neither she nor Chase would be in this predicament. "I'm not married. Or at least I wasn't until a few minutes ago."

The judge checked the book again. "Okay, forget that. Are either of you underage?" The judge had directed the question to her.

"I'm twenty-two," Emily said.

"Twenty-six," Chase said.

The judge's finger moved down the page again. "Are either of you related to the other?"

Chase shook his head. "Absolutely not."

The judge peered at them over the frame of his spectacles. "Are either of you"—he cleared his throat—"unable to consummate the marriage?"

Emily's face flared, and Chase threw up his hands. "This is getting us nowhere."

The judge held up the palm of a hand. "Now hold on. There's more." He glanced at the uncle's shotgun. "Were either of you coerced into the marriage?"

Emily felt a flicker of hope, but before she had a chance to answer in the affirmative, the door flew open. A man stormed into the chambers with a bride in tow, and he looked fit to be tied.

The uncle stepped in front of the new arrivals, his shotgun raised in a threatening pose. The newly arrived bride gasped and fell back.

"Sorry, Royce," the uncle said. "You're too late. The will said the first one married will have full ownership of the ranch." He tossed a nod at Emily. "Meet Mrs. Chase McKnight, your new sister-in-law."

3

CHASE GUIDED THE HORSE AND WAGON SLOWLY through town. Though the cattle had been somewhat contained, thick clouds of dust still hung in the air like heavy fog. The dust blocked what little daylight was left and stung the eyes.

He felt bad, real bad. Felt bad for the widow, Mrs. Decker, and her three children. He'd never meant to let them down. But he also felt bad for Garvey, who had arrived at the courthouse expecting to wed. Chase felt especially sorry for the stoic figure by his side, his accidental bride.

Had Royce not arrived with his own bride-to-be, Chase's unfortunate marriage would have been nullified. But when things got ugly, the judge ordered all parties out of his chambers. That left his marriage intact, Royce still single, and the future of the ranch secure. At least for the time being.

Chase studied the stranger who was now his wife. Still in her wedding gown, she'd discarded her veil, allowing him an unhindered view of her face. Hair the color of corn silk was pulled to the top of her head and cascaded down her back in lush, shiny curls. Lashes as thick as Spanish lace framed her expressive blue eyes. Skin yet untouched by the Texas sun or wind stretched over the delicate bones of her face as white and smooth as fine porcelain.

Though she held a handkerchief over her mouth to keep out the dust, she somehow managed to look like a force to be reckoned with. Shoulders back, body rigid, she never passed on an opportunity to shoot visual daggers at him.

Still, for all her bravado, he sensed an inner vulnerability that brought out his protective nature.

"Sorry, ma'am," he said. "'Bout what happened, I mean." His apology failed to ease the tension or earn him any favor. All he got in return was a glare that would do an angry bull proud.

Not that he blamed her for feeling the way she did. This mess was partly his fault. If he hadn't been so anxious or so rushed, he might have noticed that the woman behind the veil was not the woman he was supposed to have wed.

True, both women had blond hair and were near the same height, but that was where the similarities ended. The sun had turned Cassie's skin the color of leather. Hard work had made her as brawny as any man. In contrast, his new bride's slender form and gentle curves were bound to wilt beneath the rigors of ranch life. Her soft, white hands looked more suited to soothing an infant's brow than hauling hay or roping a calf.

His uncle and that blasted shotgun hadn't helped either. Uncle Baxter had made things worse. A whole lot worse. Easterners depended on lawyers to settle disputes, not shotguns. Was it any wonder that the woman by his side wanted nothing more to do with him or his uncle?

Then there'd been the stampeding cattle. Had it not been for all the noise and confusion, her Boston accent would have given her away. As it was, they had hardly been able to hear each other.

She struck him as somewhat of a puzzle, and he couldn't help but be curious. The way she spoke suggested she'd come from good stock and probably had much in the way of book learning.

He didn't know much about fashion, but never had he seen a finer wedding gown. It was hard to imagine that much lace could be found in all of Texas. The way the soft fabric hugged her tiny waist and slender hips suggested it had been made special for her and wasn't one of those hand-me-downs worn by most local brides.

Why a looker like her would have to resort to setting herself up as a mail-order bride was a puzzle. What was wrong with the men in Boston? Why would she settle for a simple druggist in a small western town when she could probably have any man she set her cap for back home?

She was a puzzle, all right, in more ways than one. She sat as far away from him as the buggy seat allowed and looked ready to fight him at the least provocation. No surprise there. It was only after much persuasion on his part that she'd agreed to let him drive her to the hotel.

That was turning out to be more of a challenge than he'd imagined. The cattle had created havoc in the town. Wagons had been overturned, and bales of hay and produce were scattered everywhere. Frightened horses milled around looking for a means of escape. Goats and sheep darted around stranded wagons and carriages. Finally, traffic stopped altogether.

Spotting the sheriff, Chase lifted his voice. "I'm trying to get to the hotel."

"No chance of that," Sheriff Keeler yelled back. "Least not till Fisher rounds up his cattle."

Chase shook his head. Fisher again. He should have known. The fool Englishman knew nothing about raising cattle, and this hadn't been the first time his stock had run rampant through town. "How long do you think that'll take?"

The sheriff shrugged, and his mustache twitched. "Beats me. My guess is that we'll be lucky if we clear the mess up by morning."

Chase glanced at his passenger. Hands clenched on her lap, she greeted the news with a look of dismay. She was new in town and probably didn't know anyone.

"I'll take you to the ranch," he said. "You can spend the night there."

"I'll get off here," she said.

"And do what?"

"Walk."

He glanced down at her wedding dress and dainty white slippers. "You could get trampled. Those cattle are already spooked. It won't take much to start another stampede."

"I'll take my chances."

Before she could follow through with her foolhardy

plan, Chase snapped the reins hard, and his horse surged forward. Startled, the lady fell back against her seat.

"Stop!" she cried. "I said stop!"

"Sorry, ma'am, I can't do that." He drove the wagon in a circle at the wide intersection called the Dead Line, which separated the respectable part of town from saloons and gambling halls. Chickens, goats, sheep, and an occasional steer scrambled out of his way as he headed for the ranch. "Like it or not, you're my wife, at least for the time bein'. As such, I'm responsible for your safety."

Holding on to the dash railing, she glared at him. "I'm not your wife!"

"The law says you are. Until it says otherwise, you're under my protection."

"I was coerced into this marriage, and that's what I intend to tell the judge tomorrow."

"Coerced?"

"Yes, coerced!" She folded her arms across her chest. "Your uncle made me go through with the wedding. He even held a gun. What else would you call it?"

Chase grimaced. "The gun was for protection. He wouldn't have harmed you."

"Oh no? Then what do you call forcing me into this…this marriage?"

Chase blew out his breath. "Again, you have my heartfelt apologies. Like I said, you can spend the night at the ranch. We'll sort the rest out come mornin'."

Narrowed eyes met his, and he could see the wheels turning in her head. The stubborn look on her face gradually yielded to an expression of wary acceptance.

It would soon be dark, and she knew as well as he that her choices were limited.

"We're married in name only," she said. "That's all."

"If you're worried about me claimin' my husbandly rights, you can put your mind at ease. I've never had to beg a woman for favors, and I don't aim on startin' now."

She narrowed her eyes and studied him with bold regard. "Long as we understand each other."

"Oh, we understand each other just fine." Even in the shadows of dusk, he could see her bristle with indignation. She might have a small rope, but she sure did throw a large loop.

Unable to resist the temptation to see just how much starch she had in her corset, he added, "You lock your bedroom door, and...just in case you get any untoward ideas, I'll lock mine."

His answer came in the shape of a well-placed fist on the side of his face. Rubbing his sore cheek, he stared straight ahead. The woman was a regular spitfire. He'd best watch his step.

4

FOLLOWING A RESTLESS NIGHT, EMILY STOOD IN FRONT of the cheval mirror. "What a mess you got yourself into this time!"

Since her luggage was still at the hotel, she'd slept in her petticoat. She didn't even have a hairbrush, and her hair looked like a rat's nest. But that was the least of it.

How could she have married the wrong man? Of all the crazy things. Chase McKnight looked nothing like the man she had imagined from Garvey's letters. She should have known something was wrong.

Palms on her forehead, she tried to think. The wedding—and everything that had happened after— was a blur. If it wasn't for the unfamiliar room and the gold wedding ring on the dresser in front of her, she would have thought the whole thing a bad dream.

This was no dream. The ring was real, as were her new surroundings. What a nightmare! Her only hope was to get her current marriage quickly annulled so she could marry the right man. That is, if he would still have her. The look on Garvey's face last night hadn't been encouraging, but maybe today he would be more forgiving. Or at least more understanding.

Her spirits lifting somewhat, she reached for her watch. Normally an early riser, she was shocked to see it was well after ten. It had taken forever to fall asleep, and even then, slumber had come in fits and starts. It wasn't just the strange, oversized four-poster bed that had made her feel small and insignificant and, more than anything, vulnerable. It was also the stillness of the night. Never had she known such quiet. It was almost morbid.

In Boston, the sound of clip-clopping hooves and iron wheels on cobblestones was constant and sounded at all hours of the day and night.

Boston. Surprised to feel a wave of homesickness for the town that had caused her so much pain, she turned from the mirror. That was when she noticed her luggage piled up inside her door. Someone had taken it upon himself to fetch her luggage from the hotel and enter her bedchamber while she was still asleep. Mr. McKnight?

As relieved as she was at not having to appear in front of the judge in her wedding gown, she couldn't help but worry. Mr. McKnight knew she had no intention of staying. So why would he go to all the trouble of retrieving her belongings? Unless…

The thought of being held against her will filled her with horror. Running barefooted across the room, she ripped the door open. It wasn't locked. Breathing a sigh of relief, she quietly shut the door and slumped against the cool, smooth wood.

Maybe Mr. McKnight was just being thoughtful.

So far, he had been a gentleman and had seemed as eager to set things straight as she was. Feeling better, she crossed the room to take care of her morning ablutions. It was easier to face life's challenges when looking one's best.

After filling the porcelain basin with water and washing her face, she picked out the plainest dress she owned. The rust-colored print brought out the golden highlights of her blond hair. The dress molded around her small waist and trim hips and fell into a modest bustle in back. Lace trimmed the square neckline and sleeves.

She'd worn the dress in the past when shopping and visiting friends. Never could she have imagined that one day, she would wear it to end a marriage.

After finishing her ablutions and arranging her long, blond hair into a tidy bun at the back of her neck, she stared at the wedding dress tossed carelessly on a chair. The opulent gown reminded her of everything she'd come to Texas to forget. She should have burned it along with all the other reminders.

Sighing, she turned. She was reluctant to leave the safety of the room, but she was anxious to take care of business. The sooner her marriage was annulled, the sooner she could wed the man she was supposed to wed and get on with her life. With that in mind, she quietly cracked open the door. Silence greeting her, she stepped into the hall.

It was but a short distance to the staircase. She'd been too tired from her journey and too overwhelmed by her disastrous wedding to take much notice of the ranch house the night before. Now it commanded her full attention.

The stairs led down to a large masculine-looking room filled with oversized leather furniture. Used to the lavishly furnished rooms back home, Emily found the ranch house stark, almost cave-like in appearance. No heavy draperies or curtains adorned the windows that stretched from baseboard to ceiling. Instead, the windows had been left bare, allowing for panoramic views of sparse land and rolling hills. Never had Emily been able to look so far and see so little until coming west.

Pulling her gaze away from the windows, she studied her surroundings. Framed photographs adorned the upright piano, most of the subjects looking as grim as the decor. The only embellishments on the painted white walls were steer horns and antlers and the stuffed head of a snarling wild cat.

Shuddering, she followed the smell of coffee through a large dining room with an oak table that could seat twelve. An open door led to a barn-size kitchen.

She was greeted by a man with a broad face and a wide smile. His long, white hair was brushed from his forehead and tied at his neck with a length of rawhide.

"Ah, you must be the new Mrs. McKnight," he said, drying his hands on his apron. "I'm the chief cook and bottle washer. The boys call me Cookie."

Encouraged by his friendly face, she allowed herself to relax. "Nice to meet you, Cookie. But please, call me Emily."

"Emily, uh?" His face grew serious. "The boss told me about the little mix-up."

She regarded the cook with a look of curiosity. "Marrying the wrong person hardly seems like a *little* mix-up."

He shrugged. "Maybe not, but I have to say, you sure are a sight for sore eyes. You don't look like no rancher's wife I've ever seen."

Not sure if he meant it as a compliment, she wrinkled her nose. "Is that coffee I smell?"

"Well now, ma'am, there's coffee, and there's what is known as my famous son-of-a-gun coffee. You won't find better. That I'll guarantee you. Would you care for some chow to go with it?"

Emily shook her head. Last night, the housekeeper had brought a bowl of stew to her room, but she'd been too upset to eat, and her nerves were still in a tangle. "Just coffee for now."

Cookie turned to the cookstove and reached for the coffeepot.

It was a large kitchen with tall windows, a brick fireplace, and a wood-burning stove. An icebox stood next to an open door leading to a well-stocked pantry. Beneath rows of shelves lined with canned goods were large sacks of flour and rice.

A bowl filled with plump, black berries and four empty pie plates were spread across the butcher-block counter.

Following her gaze, Cookie nodded. "Picked those dewberries fresh this morning. I reckon they'll make some mighty fine pies."

Emily had never heard of dewberries, but if the berries tasted as good as they looked, they would make fine pies, indeed.

"I'll bring you your coffee on the veranda, if you like."

"Thank you, but this will do." Despite its barn-like

size, the kitchen appeared to be the friendliest room in the house.

Emily sat at the table and reached for the *Haywire Dispatch*. Sipping her coffee, she scanned the headlines. The coffee was every bit as good as the cook had promised. The paper, however, was a week old, so there was nothing about the stampede. The main news story was about a desperado tracked down by the Texas Rangers.

She was just about to turn the page when a smaller headline caught her eye. It read, BOSTON BUSINESSMAN SENTENCED TO PRISON.

Dear God, no! Never in her wildest dreams had she imagined such news showing up in a small-town newspaper so far away from home. The article gave few details except to say that her uncle had been sentenced to prison for cattle fraud.

Fields & Fields had been started by her father as a loan company with a fine reputation. But under her uncle's leadership, the company had also ventured into other moneymaking schemes, some legal, most not. His latest scam was to convince Eastern investors to sink thousands of dollars into what he touted as the new gold—cattle.

No cattle had ever been purchased with investors' money. Had prices not dropped, her uncle's scheme might never have been discovered. When investors tried to bail out, there was no money to pay them.

His company had also purchased small ranches in Wyoming and Montana at low cost and resold them at great profit. This was done by making buyers purchase the same herd at least twice. This was easily accomplished. Cattle were simply driven around a hill two or even three times during census, making it appear that a herd was larger than its actual size.

The months that followed her uncle's arrest had been a nightmare of publicity and scorn. Though she'd known nothing about his business practices, Emily had been forced to testify against him. The prosecutor had used her college degree to discredit her.

"Surely, an educated woman would recognize unsavory practices in a family business," he'd said, casting doubt on her testimony.

Her uncle's property had been seized, leaving her without a roof over her head and precious little money to her name. No one wanted to hire Harry Fields's niece, so there was no way to support herself.

Answering a mail-order bride ad had been an act of sheer desperation. She'd hoped that Texas offered a far-enough escape from her uncle's shadow. Now, seeing the article in the newspaper, Emily wondered if such a thing was possible.

Stomach churning, she took a hasty sip of coffee and tried to convince herself that her secret was safe.

So far, everything had gone according to plan. Except, of course, for marrying the wrong man. That she hoped to quickly remedy.

At first, she'd thought Baxter McKnight's veiled threats related to her background. That had turned out not to be true. He'd thought she was Mrs. Decker. Last night had been one misunderstanding after another.

Thank goodness she'd thought to drop her surname, Fields, and use her middle name instead. Nothing could be done about her Boston accent, but she could tone down her clothes so as not to call undue attention to herself.

Confident that her true identity was secure, she finished the last of her coffee and stood. A movement caught the corner of her eye, and she jerked her head around. A tiny mouse scampered along the baseboard, mere inches from her foot.

With a cry of alarm, she leaped onto a chair and screamed to high heaven.

5

CHASE HAD JUST RIDDEN UP TO THE RANCH HOUSE
when he heard the scream. "What the—!"

Quickly dismounting, he tossed the reins over the
hitching post, bounded up the porch steps, and burst
into the house.

He raced through the dining room and came to a
skidding stop just inside the kitchen door. There he
found his new bride standing on a chair, waving her
arms and screeching like a train whistle.

He glanced at Cookie, who simply shrugged and
said, "She saw a mouse."

The woman was making so much noise, it was necessary to read his cook's lips. A mouse? The woman
who had thrown an ironclad punch at him was now
carrying on over a danged mouse?

Taking quick action, he grabbed her around the
waist and lifted her off the chair. He then slung her
over his shoulder and carried her from the room.

"Let me go," she cried, struggling in his arms.
Failing to earn her release, she punched him on the
back with pounding fists. She was a regular tiger, but
fortunately light in weight.

He was tempted to dump her on one of the leather chairs in the parlor, but spotting his housekeeper's young daughter, he changed his mind at the last minute. Instead, he hauled her all the way to his private office. There he lowered her to the floor.

Bristling like a wild hog, she pulled away from him. With an indignant toss of her head, she straightened her skirt and yanked on a sleeve. Without all the ruffles and lace of her wedding gown, she looked even smaller in stature than she'd appeared the night before. It wouldn't take much of a norther to blow her away.

She continued to be a puzzle. A looker like her wouldn't normally have any trouble roping in any man she wanted. What she lacked in physical size, she more than made up for in pluck and spirit. When she wasn't glaring at him, her eyes shone with keen intelligence. When she wasn't spewing angry words, her mouth looked soft and supple.

So why would such a woman choose something as risky as being a mail-order bride? Why, for that matter, had she even come to Texas?

Oh yes, the lady had secrets. Secrets that could very well work to his advantage. That is, if he played his cards right.

"You can relax, ma'am. I doubt that the mouse had murderous intent."

She gave the baseboards a quick glance before turning to him with doubt-filled eyes.

"If you don't mind, I need someone to drive me to the courthouse."

Biding his time, he took his seat behind his desk and considered how best to earn her trust. Last night, he'd impetuously wanted to get their marriage annulled. This morning, a cooler head prevailed. Leaving the marriage intact would save the ranch and might even benefit the lady.

Now that she'd seen the ranch house and the kind of life he could provide, he hoped she would be more receptive to the idea than she might have been the day before. Or at least listen to what he had to say.

"About our marriage," he began in a tentative voice.

She studied him with an odd combination of determination and uncertainty. "We don't have a marriage."

"Legally, we do." Assured that he had her full attention, he continued, "It might be beneficial to us both to leave things as they stand. At least for the time bein'."

An incredulous look crossed her face. "Surely you're not suggesting that we stay...married?" She made it sound like he'd proposed robbing a bank.

He splayed his hands. He hadn't wanted to go into detail, but she had the right to know what he was asking of her and why. For that reason, he gave her a short version of the ranch's history. "Unfortunately," he added through gritted teeth, "my father's will stipulates that the first of his two...sons to marry inherits the ranch."

Regardless of the will's wording, Royce wasn't his father's biological son and had no right to the ranch. None!

"I don't see what the problem is," she said. "You are the first one married. The ranch is yours."

"For now. However, to keep it, I have to stay married for a full year."

Her eyes widened, and she stared at him with a look of horror that quickly turned to dismay. "You...you want me to stay here on this…this…" She drew in her breath. "This ranch f-for a year?"

He tried not to take the combination of horror and dismay on her face personally. It was foolish to expect a lady like her to see the advantages of ranch life. It might not seem like much through her eyes, but it was his whole world and the only one he'd ever wanted.

He clasped his hands on his desk. "I don't know what your story is or why you left Boston, but I suspect you're runnin' from somethin'."

She lifted her chin. "What makes you think that?"

"It's been my experience that only three things bring folks to the Lone Star State: wealth, health, or a ruined reputation. You don't strike me as a gold digger, and you don't look sick. So that leads to only one conclusion."

He studied her face to see if there was any truth to his suspicions. The trapped look in her eyes was all the confirmation he needed.

"You didn't kill anyone, did you?" Taking her shocked look as a no, he continued. "Did you rob a bank?"

"Certainly not!" she said, her eyes flashing.

"Hmm." More intrigued now than curious, he decided to leave his questions for another time. "Whatever it is you're runnin' from, you'll be safe here at the ranch. I give you my word. In return, I ask that you remain my wife for the full year."

Her eyes narrowed, and a shadow of indecision fleeted across her forehead. "What happens after… that time?"

Her query gave him a measure of hope. At least she was thinking about it. "You then give me the gate."

She stared at him. "The gate?"

He sighed inwardly. He'd forgotten that Easterners required everything spelled out in precise language. "A divorce," he said.

"Oh."

Since she appeared not to like the idea of a divorce, he added, "If'n you prefer, we can have our marriage annulled after the year is up." When she made no response, he continued. "After our marriage has been properly dissolved, I'll see to it that you have enough ballast to start a new life."

She frowned. "What...does that mean, exactly?"

He raised his eyebrows. Not only was she unsuited to ranch life, it appeared that the two of them didn't even speak the same language. "It means you'll have enough money to start a new life."

Her forehead creased. "Why would I help you? Your uncle—"

"My uncle has nothin' to do with it. This is strictly atwixt you and me."

For a long moment, she didn't say anything. "You're forgetting something," she said at last.

"Oh?"

"I'm promised to Mr. Garvey."

He rubbed his upper lip. "Under the circumstances, I doubt that Garvey harbors any illusions of you keepin' that promise."

She stiffened. "That's for him to decide."

He sat back in his chair and studied her. "Are you sayin' that you still intend to follow through with your promise to him?"

"If he'll still have me."

"He's as much a stranger to you as I am."

"That's not true," she said. "I got to know him quite well through his letters."

"Apparently not well enough. Otherwise, you wouldn't have mistaken me for him." He bit his tongue, but it was too late. Judging by the closed look on her face, his glib comment had defeated his cause.

"My mind is made up," she said, her voice cool. "I'm asking the judge for an annulment."

"On what grounds?"

"On the grounds that I was coerced."

He rubbed the side of his still-sore face. The lady might be small, but she could sure deliver a punch. "If you were coerced, why am I the one who got hit?"

She looked momentarily unnerved but quickly recovered. "I was referring to your uncle," she said. "He threatened me."

"Threatened you?"

"Not in so many words. But his meaning was quite clear. Or at least it seemed so at the time."

"My uncle thought you were someone else. We both did, and for that, I apologize. But I can assure you my uncle's bark is worse than his bite."

She regarded him with eyes as cool as a wintry day. "Either I claim coercion or"—she lifted her chin—"I tell the judge our marriage was not…consummated. Those are our only two options."

His eyebrows shot up. The lady sure didn't mince words. "The judge is more likely to believe that my uncle threatened you than me bein' unable to perform my husbandly duties."

Something flickered across her face, but he couldn't

decide if it was disdain, reproach, or curiosity. "Very well," she said. "Then it's settled."

Maybe in her mind, but not his. He cleared his throat. "I'd be mighty obliged if'n you would leave things as they now stand. At least temporarily." He hated begging, but she gave him little choice. "Like I said, I'll make it worth your while. Moneywise, that is."

"Sorry," she said, and she actually sounded like she meant it. "But I'm already promised to another." The eyes meeting his begged him to understand.

"I guess our business is complete then," he said, his voice ringing with a note of finality.

She arched an eyebrow. "So, you agree to the annulment?"

He shrugged. "It's not like you're givin' me a choice."

She looked uncertain. "Don't you have to sign or something?"

"I'll stop by the courthouse later."

Relief crossed her face, but still, she lingered.

"Is there somethin' else?" he asked.

She hesitated, and two red spots colored her cheeks. "About the mouse…"

He frowned. "Go on."

"As a child, I was accidentally locked overnight in a cellar overrun with mice. I'm afraid I allowed my childhood fears to get the best of me."

Curious as to why she thought it necessary to explain, he shrugged. "Other than givin' Cookie a scare, I'd say no harm was done."

They stared at each other for a moment before she turned away. Hand on the doorknob, she shot a glance over her shoulder. "When can I expect my ride?"

"I'll have my foreman pick out a hoss for you."

"A…a horse?"

"You can leave it at the stables in town when you're finished. Just let me know where you want your luggage sent." Something in her face made him frown. "Something wrong?"

"I—" Clearing her throat, she turned to face him. "I don't know how to ride."

He reared back. "You're not serious." He had practically been born in a saddle and couldn't imagine life without a horse.

She lowered her lashes, and her cheeks turned red. "I-I know how to drive a horse and buggy. Even a carriage." Her lashes flew up. "B-but never found the need to ride a horse."

"Never?" He shook his head. What a strange one she was. She could hint at his manhood—or invented lack of it—with hardly a falter, but a subject as benign as riding a horse had her stammering like a schoolgirl. "I can't imagine such a thing. Not ridin', I mean."

"That's probably because you were never required to ride sidesaddle."

"Sidesaddle, huh?" Of course. He should have known. A lady like her… "I think you'll find us more *civilized* out here," he said wryly. "We don't expect our womenfolk to do anythin' so ludicrous as to ride half-cocked." When his attempt at humor failed to bring the hoped-for smile, he added, "I can take you to town myself. But that would mean you havin' to ride on the back of my hoss."

"What about the buggy you drove last night?"

"I rented it in town for my weddin'. One of my

men used it to retrieve your luggage and has since
returned it. We've no need for such contraptions out
here. The most we have is a chuck wagon, which has
no room for passengers, and a freight wagon. The
buckboard is in for repairs."

Her face dropped in dismay. Feeling sorry for her,
he added, "I'll send one of the boys to town to rent a
four-wheeler."

"If you don't mind. I'd be…most grateful."

Oh, he minded all right. He needed his men on the
ranch, working. Still, he was partly to blame for the
woman's plight. The least he could do was help make
things right.

"Anythin' else?" he asked.

She shook her head. "No, thank you. That will be
all." She started for the door and stopped. "I'm sorry
for hitting you."

"I've been hit worse," he said.

She turned her head to look at him over her shoulder. "Have you now?"

"Yes, and some might say I was deservin'."

"In that case, you must consider yourself a very
lucky man, Mr. McKnight."

"Lucky?"

"Not everyone gets what he deserves."

He couldn't be sure, but he thought he detected a
dent in her guarded demeanor, but it was gone in a
blink. Shoulders back, she left the room with far more
dignity than when she'd entered.

Staring at the closed door, Chase sat back in his
chair with a frown. Too bad the lady was so hell-bent
on dissolving the marriage. She would have saved

him a world of trouble. No sooner had the thought occurred to him than he changed his mind.

A woman scared of mice and who couldn't ride would be more trouble than she was worth. Still, she would have livened things up a bit, that was for sure.

His gaze found its way to his grandfather's daguerreotype. The grainy picture had been taken years ago when his grandfather was about the same age as Chase was now. The man in the photograph looked more like a country parson than the man who had fought off rustlers to save the ranch. That was the least of it. Through the years, his grandfather had also lost cattle to disease, droughts, and wildfire.

Chase didn't want to think that Grandpa McKnight had it easy. But nothing had threatened the ranch more than a single sentence on a legal document. *The first son married will have full ownership of the ranch, providing the marriage lasts a full year.*

6

THE CHORE OF DRIVING EMILY TO TOWN HAD BEEN assigned to a wrangler by the name of Big-Foot Harry. A tall man with bear-size limbs, he had craggy skin with the same rough surface as a peach pit.

The moment Emily settled onto the seat of the four-wheel buggy, he clicked his tongue, and the sorrel mare shuffled forward. A second horse tied to the back of the rented vehicle belonged to the driver and would provide transportation back to the ranch.

It was hot and muggy, and Emily felt sticky all over. It was hard to know what had the worse influence on the lungs—the sunbaked dust or the unforgiving reek of cattle. Did anyone ever get used to the horrible smell? Feeling as if she would gag, she pulled a monogrammed handkerchief from her sleeve and held it in front of her nose and mouth.

It wasn't just the smell that bothered her—it was also the desolation. She couldn't imagine living in such a place by choice. Only a hermit could relish such an existence.

If that wasn't bad enough, her head still rang with the sound of the ranch owner's voice. *You didn't kill anyone, did you?* he'd asked. Good Lord. What must he think of her to ask such a question?

Leaving the ranch, they drove under an iron arch attached to two massive poles. The words *Rocking M Ranch* were engraved on the metal bar in large letters.

"Is…is all that land part of the ranch?" Emily asked.

"Sure enough is," Big-Foot Harry said with a nod. "All the way past them there hills. It's what we Texans call a braggin' ranch. 'Course the boss don't believe in braggin' none. Gotta respect a man like that. Know what I mean?"

Emily wasn't at all sure what he meant, but since he seemed to expect an answer, she nodded anyway. It seemed strange to respect someone for simply not bragging.

Oh, how she missed the lush, green lawns of Boston and the nearness of neighbors. Before her world had come crashing down, the nights had been filled with parties, theater, and concerts. She'd had her choice of beaus, and everyone had predicted a bright future for her. In Boston terms, that meant a suitable marriage. Never had she imagined anything like her current bleak circumstances.

"What do people do here to pass the time?"

Big-Foot Henry cast a puzzled look her way. "Do?"

"You know, for entertainment."

"Well now, let's see. We tell stories, and Kansas Pete plays the fiddle. Sometimes, we just sit around a campfire and watch the stars do their thing."

Emily studied him with curiosity. If watching the stars was his idea of excitement, she would sooner twiddle her thumbs. "Doesn't sound very exciting."

"If it's excitement you want, I reckon you came to the right place. The cattle provide about all the excitement a body can take." He continued, "Once a year, the town holds a rodeo. That gives us a chance to show off our ridin' and bulldoggin' skills. Do you have anythin' like that where you come from?"

His question gave her pause. "You mean do we have bricklaying contests? Or banker competitions to see who can turn down the most loans?"

He threw back his head and laughed. "I guarantee you won't see any bankers at our events."

She laughed too. "Have you lived here in Haywire all your life?"

"Not yet, ma'am, but that's the plan." He arched an eyebrow. "I have to say… I never thought I'd see the day that the boss would commit holy matrimony. Certainly not to a lady such as yourself."

Seated primly on the horsehair seat, her face shaded by her feathered hat, Emily blinked the dust out of her eyes. "We married by accident," she said.

"Is that so?" Big-Foot Harry made a funny sound with his mouth. "Never heard of such a thing. Marryin' by accident, I mean."

"The stampede caused a lot of confusion."

"Guess that explains it then," he said with a shrug. "Confusion and weddin's just seem to go together. Fisher and his crazy cattle sure have caused a lot of bedlam in this town. Would you believe the fool man fenced his property with *smooth* wire? Plain wire's fine for sheep, but bobbed wired is the only thing that will hold in cattle."

He spit out a stream of tobacco. "Everyone has the

right to be a fool, but if you ask me, Fisher's abusin' the privilege." As an afterthought, he added, "First time I heard his cattle causin' an accidental weddin' though…"

A chatty type, Big-Foot Harry seemed to welcome Emily's silence as it gave him full rein to fill the space with his own voice. For that, she was grateful. She didn't feel like talking. She had too much on her mind.

Somehow, she had to convince Mr. Garvey that she had every intention of keeping her promise to marry him. If he refused to live up to his side of the bargain, she'd be in a fine pickle. Staying in her current sham of a marriage and living on an isolated ranch was out of the question. With no means of transportation, she'd be stuck in the middle of nowhere for a full year and dependent on Chase McKnight for her every need. Even the town of Haywire was preferable. At least there, she could get around on her own and maintain some independence.

The buggy wheels hit a rut, and her thoughts scattered. They had reached a rough patch in the dirt road, and it was all she could do to keep from being bounced out of her seat. That and trying to breathe commanded most of her attention. Neither the rutted road nor the dust seemed to bother Big-Foot Harry, and he just kept jawing away like an old woman.

"Next time those dang cattle run rampant," he said with a shake of his head, "I best take cover. The last thing I need is to accidentally find myself with a wife."

He'd interrupt himself on occasion to point out various landmarks along the way. "That's the Buttonwood ranch," he said. "You better watch out for Mrs. Buttonwood. She makes everyone's business her own."

He was still talking as they drove into town. It was hard to believe, but compared to the isolation of the cattle ranch, Haywire didn't look half as bad as it had when Emily first arrived. Most of the damage caused by the cattle had been cleared away. Save for a few chickens and a goat, there were no other loose animals running around.

Spotting the Haywire Pharmacy, Emily gathered up her purse. "You can drop me off here," she said.

Big-Foot Harry tugged on the reins, and the buggy rolled to a stop. "Nice meetin' you, ma'am." He tossed a nod to the back of the buggy. "Want me to leave your belongin's at the hotel?"

Unsure of what kind of reception awaited her, she anxiously eyed the front of Garvey's shop before answering. "Yes, thank you." She stepped to the ground, careful to avoid a pile of dung. "Stay away from stampedes."

He laughed. "Will do. Will do." With that, he clicked his tongue and drove away.

Emily hated to see him go. His friendly chatter had been oddly soothing. Feeling very much alone, she moistened her lips and studied the drugstore with a worried frown. After last night's fiasco, would Mr. Garvey still want to marry her?

Smoothing down the front of her dress with a gloved hand, she forced herself to breathe. Her only hope was that Garvey displayed the same courtesy toward her now as he had in his letters.

A riot of jingling bells greeted her as she pushed the door open and walked into the drugstore. A strong medicinal smell assaulted her nose. There seemed to be no subtle odors in Haywire.

She spotted Mr. Garvey immediately in the back of the store, sweeping the floor. He looked up and appeared neither surprised nor pleased to see her.

He simply leaned his broom against the counter and stepped over the pile of broken glass as if she were just another customer. Today, he appeared taller than she remembered but still failed to measure up to McKnight in height. He also lacked McKnight's robust physique and sun-bronzed complexion. Instead, Garvey's shirt and trousers hung loosely from his lanky frame, and his pale skin stretched over hollow cheeks and a narrow nose.

Surprised, even dismayed, to find herself comparing him unfavorably to McKnight, Emily tried to remember the speech she had rehearsed.

"Dang cattle," he muttered by way of a greeting. "Cost me big in inventory. Lucky they didn't start a fire."

Emily eyed him with more than a little concern. The fact that the cattle had also cost him a wife didn't seem to merit mention.

Save for the broken glass, the rest of the store was neatly organized and well stocked, offering every possible remedy for whatever might ail a person. An assortment of sundries, including fancy soaps, perfumery, and fireworks, was also on display.

Emily's gaze fell on the broken glass at his feet. "Is there anything I can do to help?"

Mustache twitching, he looked her over, his gaze lingering a moment on her feathered hat. Only then did he turn down her offer with a shake of his head.

"That's all right, ma'am. Wouldn't want to mess up your purty clothes."

She gripped her purse with both gloved hands. "I just want you to know that what happened was a mistake." She drew in her breath. "I fully intend to keep my promise to marry you. That is, if you'll still have me."

For the longest while, Garvey studied her and said nothing. His unhurried demeanor was no more than what she had expected. His letters had been neatly written, with no crossovers or ink smudges. He seemed just as careful in person, his every move thoughtful and precise. His ill-fitting shirt and trousers were nonetheless neatly pressed; his dark hair was cut collar-length and parted in the middle.

"Don't know how it is in Boston, ma'am," he said, his voice gentle and unassuming. "But here in Texas, it's against the law for a man to have hisself two wives. I reckon the same applies to a woman with two husbands."

"Oh no! I didn't mean... Soon as I leave here, I'm heading straight to the courthouse to straighten out the mess." She gave an indignant nod. "I have grounds for an annulment." When he failed to comment, she continued. "The marriage was a mistake and should never have happened. I thought he was you."

Hooking his thumbs around his red suspenders, he studied her from the tip of her hat to the toe of her polished high-button shoes. "The bigger mistake might have been hitchin' up with me."

She drew back. "Why...why would you say such a thing?"

"I'm just a pharmacist."

"I'm well aware of that," she said. That was one of the things she'd found so appealing about him.

Chemistry had been one of her favorite subjects in school, and she'd thought she could be an asset to him. She also liked that he had downplayed the importance of what he did and found his modesty refreshing. Most men tended to exaggerate their circumstances, making themselves sound more successful than they were. "You made that quite clear in your letters."

"Then you know McKnight can give you a better life than I can."

She frowned. "On a cattle ranch?" The mere thought of living in such a godforsaken place made her shudder.

His gaze sharpened. "That's where the real gold is."

She drew herself to her full height. "Had I cared about money, I wouldn't have agreed to marry you in the first place."

"Had I known the kind of lady you were, I wouldn't have asked you to."

Hearing censure in his voice, she stiffened. "And… and what kind of lady am I?"

"The expensive kind." He let that sink in for a moment before adding, "Most of my customers can't afford to pay me." He shook his head, his face suffused with regret. "Sorry, but I can't afford to give you fancy clothes or…" He lifted his eyes to the ceiling. "I can't even offer you a proper home. I live upstairs. You'd be much better off with McKnight."

Emily stared at him in disbelief. "That's it?" she asked. "You take one look at me and decide I'm a…a…a gold digger?"

He shook his head in protest. "Oh, no, ma'am. I never said that. Never even thought it. It's just… I can see you're a fine lady, and I'm just a poor druggist." He pulled his hands away from his suspenders and dropped them to his sides. "Let's not make this any harder than it already is."

Not wanting to give up so easily, Emily's mind scrambled. "I-I don't understand. I knew what I was getting into. You were honest in your letters, and I was honest with you." Or as honest as she dared to be. She hadn't told him everything. How could she?

"Yes, but when you said your uncle was a business-man, I had no idea…" His gaze traveled the length of her again. "Naturally I thought you were equally impoverished and used to living a simple life."

"I don't deny that my uncle was once a wealthy man, but"—she searched for words—"recent circum-stances changed all that. I now have no money of my own. Not even a dowry."

"That's why you'll be better off married to McKnight. He can give you the life you're accus-tomed to."

"I sincerely hope not!" she exclaimed. The kind of life she'd had in Boston had come at a price too high to pay. She would gladly live in insolvency if it meant being able to once again hold up her head.

He returned to his broom and began sweeping the floor with more vigor than the job demanded. The set look on his face told her his mind was made up. Trying to convince him otherwise would be a waste of time.

Whirling around to leave, she thought of something and stopped. "I shared some things in my letter that I would prefer no one else in town knew." She glanced back over her shoulder with a beseeching look. She'd not told him everything, but enough that an enterprising person might be able to figure out the rest.

The broom stilled in his hands. "What thangs?" he asked.

"About my uncle being a businessman." Since marriage was now out of the question, she hoped to land a job as a governess. If word of the scandal got out, no one would hire her. "I don't want people to get the wrong idea."

He stared at her with furrowed brow. "Not sure I understand, ma'am."

She debated how much or how little to say. "They might think I have no need for a job."

His gaze traveled from the tip of her fancy hat all the way down to the hem of her tailored skirt. "Don't worry. Your secret's safe with me."

"I'm truly sorry for the way things turned out," she said and meant it. She could hardly blame him for feeling the way he did.

She glanced around the shop. It was modest by Boston standards, but glass vials were lined neatly on the shelves behind the counter and sundries carefully arranged. "You have a fine place here, and I think you would have made a fine husband."

Since there was nothing more to be said, she left. Walking along the boardwalk, she felt as if all eyes were upon her. Feeling like Hester Prynne in *The Scarlet Letter*, she imagined a sign hanging over her head reading, *Disgraced*. She could almost hear the wind whispering in her ear. *For shame.*

The moment Chase spotted his fence rider galloping toward him like a bat out of hell, he knew there was trouble. As owner of one of the largest cattle ranches in the Hill Country, he had trouble imagining a day without some sort of problem, but the rider's haste suggested this was more serious than a distressed cow or stuck calf.

Chase stepped off the veranda to greet his man. He was in no mood to deal with yet another crisis. Not today. Not when his mind was on other things—like how to save the ranch.

For all he knew, the judge had already granted an annulment. At least Miss Emily Rose would have gotten what she wanted. If that were true, then the ranch belonged to Royce. Or would.

Billy Wilder pulled his horse to a quick stop in front of him. At age twenty, he was the youngest cowhand. As such, he was given the thankless job of riding the fences. He was the most reticent man Chase had ever met and doled out words like they were pieces of gold to be given out sparingly. The other cowhands jokingly called him Gabby.

"Fence cut. North end," he yelled.

Chase blew out his breath. "How many we lose this time?"

"Fifty. Maybe more."

Chase cursed beneath his breath. This was the third time in as many months that he'd lost cattle! It wasn't just the cattle thieves that gave him trouble; it was also the advocates for an open range—the fence cutters, as they were called.

"Gather up the boys and follow their trail."

With a nod of his head, Gabby headed back in the direction he'd come.

Chase spun around and headed for the stables. Could this day get any worse?

7

AFTER LEAVING GARVEY'S SHOP, EMILY WALKED TO THE
courthouse, only to learn more bad news. The clerk
informed her that the judge had been called out of
town and wouldn't be back until Friday. That was
three days away.

Leaving the courthouse, she wandered along Main
and tried to decide what to do. What little money she
had left would have to last, so staying at the hotel more
than one or two nights was out of the question.

Looking for a reprieve from the heat, noise, and
curious eyes, she stepped into the relative coolness
of Gordon's General Store. The air was thick with
the mingled smells of plug tobacco, leather, and
coffee. Counters were piled high with bolts of gingham and other dry goods. Pots and pans hung from
the rafters, along with a wide selection of lanterns,
oilcans, and tools.

Barrels filled with pickles and crackers were
arranged about the store, along with bins of sugar,
flour, and beans.

A bespectacled man greeted her from behind a

counter that displayed knives, mouth organs, and pocket watches. "Haven't seen you around these parts. I reckon you're new in town."

"Yes, yes I am," Emily said.

"Mack Gordon."

"Emily…" Recalling with a jolt that her legal name was now McKnight, she fell silent.

A lady did not introduce herself by her Christian name, but if the shopkeeper thought her ill-mannered, he kept it to himself.

"Well, howdy do, ma'am," he said in a full Texas drawl. "What can I do you for?"

"I'm looking for employment."

He raised his eyebrows. "'Fraid I can't help you there," he said. "I'm not lookin' for anyone to hire."

"Actually, I'm looking for employment as a governess," Emily explained.

In a small town like Haywire, the general store proprietor probably knew everyone and was privy to everything that happened there. Certainly, he would know if someone needed a governess. At least, that was what she was counting on.

Gordon pushed his spectacles up his nose. "Well, ma'am, it's like this," he said, drawing out his words beyond endurance. "We already have a governor. Name's Ireland. Far as I know, we're not lookin' to replace him yet. And certainly not with someone of a female persuasion."

Before Emily could explain that she didn't want to run the state, an elderly woman dressed in widow's weeds walked up to the counter and set her basket next to the cigar display. "She means she wants to tutor," the woman said, rolling her eyes. "Men!" She held out a gloved hand. "I'm Mrs. Peters."

Surprised that the woman so freely offered her hand to a stranger, Emily shook it. "Please call me…Emily."

"Nice to meet you, Emily. You must be from the East."

"Ah…yes," Emily said, not wanting to mention Boston by name.

"Unfortunately, you've come to the wrong place. I'm afraid the citizens of Haywire wouldn't know what to do with a governess if they had one."

"I see…" Emily's already low spirits spiraled another notch lower. "Do you know of an opening of any kind? I'm a hard worker."

Mrs. Peters gave her a once-over with a dubious look. "Hmm. Let me think." After a moment, she brightened. "Do you sew?"

"I do stitchery."

The woman discounted this with a shrug of her shoulders. "Don't we all?" She tapped a finger on her generous chin. "What other skills do you have?"

"I speak French and play the harp."

"Oh dear." Mrs. Peters's expression dropped in dismay. "I think you'll be hard-pressed to find a harp in town. As for speaking a foreign language, I don't know anyone who speaks French locally. German, but not French."

"What about that other foreign language she speaks," the store proprietor added helpfully in his same slow way. "You know, An-glish."

Emily blinked in confusion. "You don't speak English here?"

The store owner gave a mischievous grin. "Nope! Here, we speak Texan."

Mrs. Peters rolled her eyes. "Don't listen to Mack. He's just pulling your leg. Have you no other skills?"

Surprised that the woman would use a crude word like *leg* instead of the more socially accepted word *limb*, Emily tried to think how to answer her. "I'm quite good with numbers. Perhaps I could work as a bookkeeper. Or...or secretary. I'm slow on a typing machine, but accurate."

The woman looked less optimistic than Emily had hoped. Mr. Gordon just looked baffled.

Mrs. Peters cleared her throat. "Most folks around here like to keep their own books. As for typing machines..." She shook her head and patted Emily on the arm, her face suffused with sympathy. "Sorry we aren't more help. But if I hear of anything, I'll let you know. Where can you be reached?"

"Uh...I'm not sure. For now, I'm staying at the hotel."

"Very well. I'll ask around."

"Thank you. You're very kind."

Thanking them both, Emily left the shop. Pausing, she glanced up and down the boardwalk, reading each sign in turn. Almost all the shops were male-oriented, but there was the Feedbag Café, a bakery, and the candy shop. She knew nothing about baking and even less about candy-making, but the café offered possibilities. How hard could it be to wait tables?

Chase rode up to the ranch house and dismounted. He'd ridden into town to report the theft of his cattle, for all the good it would do him. A rash of cattle rustling had plagued the county in recent months. Not only had the thefts stymied the local sheriff, but they'd also baffled the Rangers.

But that wasn't the only thing that had put him in a bad mood. He'd stopped by the hotel hoping to talk to Cassie Decker, but she'd already checked out. Feeling bad for letting her down, he'd sent her a telegram that he wanted to talk to her. There had to be something he could do to make amends.

There had been one bright spot in his day. He'd learned the judge was out of town. That meant he was still married, at least for now, and the ranch was still his. It might only be a temporary reprieve, but it gave him time to think up another plan.

Blast it all! Who was he kidding? The only way to save the ranch was to satisfy the requirements of his father's will.

After tying his horse, Rebel, to the rail, Chase walked to the side of the house and rolled up his sleeves. Hanging his hat on a hook, he lowered his hands into the rain barrel all the way to his elbows. The cool water offered a welcome respite from the dust and the heat but did nothing for his dark mood.

He plunged his head all the way into the water, as much to curtail his troubled thoughts as to cool down his heated body.

It had been an especially warm winter and was an even warmer spring, with very little rain. That meant a bleak summer ahead.

Lifting his dripping head out of the barrel, he sputtered and reached for a towel. He wiped his face dry and blinked the water out of his eyes. The sound of footsteps on gravel told him he wasn't alone. Thinking it was one of the cowhands with news about the rustlers, he turned. Much to his surprise, he found himself staring into the big, blue eyes of his accidental bride.

Without so much as a howdy-do, she tossed her head and regarded him with a narrowed gaze. "What happens after the year is up?"

He glanced at the horse and buggy he'd failed to notice earlier. He needed a full moment to make sense of her words. "So, have you given up on an annulment?"

"The judge is out of town until Friday," she said. "So again I ask, what happens at the end?"

Chase stared at her with wary regard. Was she really thinking about staying in the marriage? "Like I told you. Either we stay married, or you give me the gate…eh…divorce," he said, keeping his voice neutral. He didn't want to scare her off a second time.

He couldn't tell by the look on her face if it was the married part or a possibility of divorce that she found distasteful. True, divorce was still looked down upon by most folks, but it was gradually becoming more acceptable. The only grounds necessary were incompatibility of temperament, which made a divorce easier to attain than an annulment.

Hanging the towel to dry, he plucked his Stetson off the hook. He raked his fingers through his still-dripping hair before donning his hat. "What happened with Garvey?"

She moistened her lips. "I decided that perhaps I had acted a bit too…hastily."

He shook his head. "So he turned you down, did he?"

She lifted her chin. "Mr. Garvey is…no longer in a position to take on a wife."

"Ah. So you decided to come crawlin' back here." He didn't mean to give her a hard time, but the whole situation had put him in a bad mood.

She stood straight and refused to wilt beneath his steady gaze. "I am not crawling back. I simply want to know what I would be letting myself in for, should I decide to stay."

He considered her query. "Like I said earlier, if'n you stay, I'll make certain you'll have enough ballast to start a new life after the year is up."

She hesitated before asking, "As your wife, what would my…duties be?"

He rubbed his chin. Ah, now they were getting down to business. "The usual. I'd expect you to run my household and oversee my social obligations. Of course, you'd also help with the beeves."

"Beeves?"

He frowned. "Cattle."

When the puzzled look remained on her face, he explained. "There are certain times of the year that things get hectic around here, and we need all the meat hooks we can get." Her frown told him he'd lost her again. "All *hands* are needed," he said by way of explanation.

His easygoing manner belied his growing concern. Ranch life was tough. He'd known big, brawny men to break beneath its rigorous demands. What chance did a dainty lady with baby-soft hands and creamy-white skin have of surviving such a life?

"Have you ever cared for livestock?" he asked. "Cows? Goats…?"

She shook her head. "I had a cat once."

"A cat?"

"And a bird."

He stared at her, incredulous. Of all the women he could have married, he doubted there was one less suited to ranch life. "I don't think this will work," he said. "You stayin' here, I mean."

"Why not?" she asked, her eyes ablaze.

"No offense, ma'am, but this life isn't for everyone."

She lifted her chin. "You said it would be for only a year."

"A year's a long time if you're somewhere you don't want to be."

She studied him for a moment. "I'm willing to give it a try if you are."

It was a tough decision. He needed her every bit as much as he suspected she needed him. Still, everything told him it was a bad idea, and he couldn't help but worry about her welfare and safety. If something happened to her…

He was just about to send her away when the sudden look of desperation in her eyes made him change his mind. "If you insist on stayin', there's not much I can do about it. But don't say you weren't warned."

She accepted his decision with a nod. "About my duties as your wife…"

The sudden flare of her cheeks told him that it wasn't the difficulties of ranch life that worried her. Or even the cattle.

"The will states that it has to be…a *real* marriage." Reminded that only a short while ago, she had threatened to tell the judge he was unable to perform his husbandly duties, he couldn't help but add, "And I can assure you, that would not be a problem."

He paused to both weigh her reaction and gather his thoughts. Here they were, discussing the intimate side of marriage, and he didn't even know what to call her. *Missus* sounded too formal, but her Christian name suggested a familiarity neither of them were ready for.

The color drained from her face. "By a real marriage, you mean—"

"It'll have to look that way publicly," he hastened to assure her, "but privately, I shall…respect your wishes." It wasn't the kind of marriage he'd envisioned or even wanted, but beggars didn't always get to be choosers.

"You mean if I don't want—"

They stared at each other for a full minute. In the short time he'd known her, he'd seen her scared, angry, indignant, and proud, but nothing had affected him as much as the vulnerability now showing in the depths of her long-lashed eyes. A protective surge rushed through him, followed by guilt for giving her such a hard time. As difficult as it was for him to admit needing another's help, there was no getting around it. If she stayed, she would be doing him a huge favor.

"I know I'm not the man you planned on marryin'," he said. "But I promise to do right by you." When she showed no sign of lowering her guard, he continued. "All I'm askin' for is a year. If'n for any reason you wish to end the arrangement before the time is up, I'll not stop you from leavin'. I'll even pay your way back to Boston, if'n that's what you want. In return, I ask only that you act like a real wife to me in public. No one must know about our private arrangement."

"Why a year?" she asked.

Chase drew in his breath. The unresolved hostilities with his pa still festered like an open wound. He'd hoped to earn his father's forgiveness, but now it was too late. Even on his deathbed, his father had not uttered the words Chase had longed to hear.

"My father had the notion that a man wasn't settled until he had a wife to support." Not wanting to go into detail, Chase gave her the least complicated answer he could think of. "Guess the marriage stipulation was his way of makin' sure his heir stuck to business and did right by the ranch."

She mulled over his words with a thoughtful frown. "Didn't he know how much this ranch means to you?"

Surprised that she knew that much about him—knew what even his father hadn't known—Chase was momentarily speechless. "I once gave him reason to doubt me," he said after a long moment. "Doubt my loyalty to the ranch."

"I see," she said.

He raised an eyebrow. "So, what do you say?"

She lifted her chin, and this time, the eyes meeting his were as bold as a charging bull's. "If I agree to stay, do I have your word that you will not try to claim your physical rights as a husband?"

He studied her with keen interest. Never had he met a woman of such extremes. One moment, she appeared vulnerable, and the next instant, she looked ready to fight him tooth and nail. "You have my word," he said. "And I trust that I have your word that you won't get jealous, should I assert my husbandly rights on another?"

He wouldn't, of course. Due to his father's will, he had to take this sham of a marriage seriously. He also happened to believe that marriage, even one as precarious as this one, deserved fidelity. Still, he couldn't resist challenging her as she'd challenged him.

Much to his chagrin, she didn't blink an eyelash. "You wouldn't risk the ranch for a meaningless dalliance," she said, her expression daring him to contradict her.

It irritated him that he was still trying to figure her out, and she already had him fully pegged.

"Should you demand…marital privileges, our deal is off," she added with meaning. "Do I make myself clear?"

Confound it! The woman was beginning to sound like a Philadelphy lawyer. Still, she was offering him a chance to save the ranch, and he'd be a fool not to take it. "Oh yes," he said tersely. "Quite clear."

"So?" she asked, taking the bull by the tail. "Do we have an agreement?"

"Depends," he said, studying her.

She narrowed her eyes. "On what?"

"Whether I can trust you to ride for the brand."

"I told you, I don't ride."

Not used to having to explain himself, Chase tried

not to let his irritation show. "'To ride for the brand' means to put the ranch first and foremost. Long as you're here."

She hesitated. "If that's what you want," she said at last and held out her hand like a man accustomed to closing lucrative business deals.

The woman continued to amaze. She might be afraid of mice, but there was definitely more to her than met the eye. As much as he hated to admit it, Chase was intrigued—and that was what worried him. Not only was she as unpredictable as the weather, but she was unlike any other woman he'd ever met. Their marriage might not be a conventional one, but neither would it be dull. His only hope was that they made it through the next twelve months without killing each other, as unlikely as it seemed.

He grasped her offered hand in his and wondered how something so small and delicate could have delivered such a hard blow to his right cheek. "Deal."

8

CHASE'S LARGE HAND SWALLOWED HERS LIKE A WHALE swallowed a minnow. Feeling momentarily disconcerted by the sheer power of him, Emily pulled away. Not wanting to let on how his size and strength intimidated her, she swallowed her insecurity and stared at him with a boldness she didn't feel.

He stepped away from the rain barrel. "Since we're now official, I'll show you around." Without waiting for her to agree, he started across the yard and obviously expected her to follow.

Dressed as he was for work, his spurs jingled, and his holster creaked beneath the weight of his firearm. A red kerchief was tied loosely around his neck, and his ever-present Stetson rode firmly on his still-wet head.

Like a man on a mission, he pointed out the stables, the bunkhouse, and other outbuildings, including a root cellar, the blacksmith/farrier works, and the icehouse.

Walking by his side, Emily fanned her heated face with her hand. The relentless sun didn't seem to bother her escort, and it was all she could do to keep up with his long strides. It wasn't just her straight skirt that hampered her movements. Her shoes, made of thin Moroccan leather with paper-thin soles, were better suited for a Bostonian tea party than a romp around a cattle ranch.

Chase stopped by a fence in the shade of a sprawling sycamore and hung his clasped hands over the wooden rail. The fence surrounded one of several pastures, each serving a different purpose. "Are you okay?" he asked, his eyes keen and assessing beneath the brim of his hat.

He sounded genuinely concerned for her welfare, but Emily still felt shy and unsure of herself in his presence, though she did her best to hide it. Somehow, she sensed he respected strength.

"I'm fine," she said brusquely. It was bad enough that she had to depend on him for her very survival. The last thing she wanted was his pity.

She joined him at the fence, careful to keep a safe distance between them. Could she trust him to keep his end of the bargain? Legally, he had every right to demand full privileges as her husband. For that reason, she was acutely aware of his strong masculine presence. He oozed virility in a way that no other man of her acquaintance ever had. How long could such a man be satisfied with a marriage in name only?

The air quivered with heat, and the distant outbuildings looked like they were underwater.

"I didn't know Texas was this hot," she said, dabbing at her wet forehead with a dainty lace handkerchief.

He glanced at her. "Doesn't it get hot in Boston?"

"Yes, but not in March," she said. "It's even been known to snow as late as May or June."

"Sure glad I'm not raisin' cattle there. Hard enough to raise 'em here."

She studied his strong-chinned profile. It seemed that he measured everything by how it would affect his ranch.

"Hey, Rusty," he called to the wrangler exercising one of the horses. "How 'bout bringin' Daisy out so my wife can get acquainted with her?"

Emily stiffened at the word *wife*. Though legally he had every right to call her that, it still sounded strange and unfamiliar. She'd always hoped to marry for love. To keep herself for that one special man. Crazy as it seemed, she still hoped to fulfill that dream, though her chances now looked slim if not altogether impossible.

She waited for Rusty to move out of earshot. "What should I call you?"

The question seemed to confound him, and he took a long time to answer. "My name's Chase," he said at length. "Call me that." He studied her. "And I'll call you Emily."

Something in the lazy way he said her name, the way he stretched it out as if reluctant to let it go, made her catch her breath. "That sounds so…informal. In Boston, many married couples refer to each other as Mr. and Mrs. At least in public."

The corner of his mouth quirked upward. "Like I said, we're much more civilized out here."

They both looked away just as Rusty walked out of the stables leading a gray-and-white horse by a rope. From a distance, Rusty had looked older—probably because of his slow walk, which had just a touch of swagger. A closer look revealed he was somewhere in his mid to late twenties. The ginger hair beneath his wide-brim hat explained his name.

Chase ran his hand along the horse's neck. "This here is Daisy. You'll enjoy ridin' her."

Emily kept her distance, her stomach clenched tight. "I...I told you, I don't ride."

Chase's eyes narrowed. "And I told you that your duties would include helpin' with the cattle. You won't be much good to me on foot."

Emily swallowed hard. "But...she's so...tall."

His hands stilled on the horse's neck. "This here pony is only fourteen and a half hands."

Emily frowned. "Hands?"

"That's how we measure hosses." Bending his thumb to his palm and holding his fingers together, Chase showed her the proper way to measure a horse. "Most people workin' with horses don't have a tape measure handy, but we all have meat hooks." He finished by running his hand along the horse's neck. "Trust me, she's gentle as a lamb."

As if to agree, the mare dipped her head and nuzzled Chase's vest pocket. "Sorry, Daisy. I don't have any treats for you today."

"Want me to saddle her up?" Rusty asked.

"Yeah, why not?" Chase said. "While you're at it, saddle my hoss as well." He locked her gaze in his. "My bride and I will take a ride."

"You...you want me to ride?" she gasped.

He dismissed Rusty with a nod before answering. "It's the only way I can show you the rest of the ranch."

"I told you I don't ride."

"I guess we'll just have to ride double then."

"I'm sorry…"

He turned his head to meet her gaze. "You'll have to ride on my hoss with me."

The mere thought of sitting in the same saddle as this man brought a flush to Emily's face, and her nerves tensed. To hide her discomfort, she crossed her arms and lifted her chin. "I don't ride horseback. Period."

He turned to face her square on. "Well, ma'am, it's like this. Either you learn to ride, or you better plan on livin' like a hermit. What few vehicles the ranch owns are needed for work. I'm not fixin' to send one of my boys into town to rent a four-wheeler every time you get the notion to giddy-up somewhere."

Emily dropped her hands to her waist and stared up at him with grim determination. It wasn't just that she couldn't ride. Horses scared her, and for good reason. As a child, she'd been bitten by one and still had a scar on her thigh to prove it.

"I'll walk to town, if need be," she said.

His eyebrows shot up. "Walk?" He laughed. "Do you have an idea how long that would take you?"

Emily lifted her chin, eyes flashing. "I'm not getting on that horse!"

His jaw clenched. "Like it or not, you're gonna have to learn to ride. As my wife, you'll be expected to accompany me to the gospel mill," he said, his uncompromising voice leaving no room for argument or even discussion. "We'll also be expected to attend certain social affairs."

She blinked. "What's a gospel mill?" she asked.

Chase's eyes widened. "You're kiddin', right? They don't have places of worship in Boston?"

She drew in her breath. This married life was beginning to be more complicated than she'd imagined. Just figuring out the language was turning out to be a full-time job.

"We have *churches* in Boston," she said. "And I made it clear there were certain things I would not do."

"The only thing you made clear is that you would not share my bed."

The mention of his bed unnerved her, but she refused to back down. "You can add horseback riding to the list."

"I'll do no such thing! Learning to ride is for your own good."

She glared at him. "I agreed to your terms. It's only fair that you agree to mine!"

"You agreed to playin' your role in public." His eyes blazed. "And that includes wearin' my ring."

She quickly covered her bare left hand with her right. "I-I—"

"Oh no!" He groaned and shushed her with a finger to his mouth. "Looks like we have company," he said beneath his breath. He squinted against the sun. "I'm afraid you're 'bout to meet my nosy neighbor, Mrs. Buttonwood."

Recalling Big-Foot Harry's warning, Emily followed Chase's gaze to the horse heading their way.

Chase slipped a possessive arm around her shoulder. Startled, she looked up at him. "We're newlyweds, remember?" he said and turned her to face their guest.

Even as she felt a pleasant jolt at his touch, Emily bristled at the ease with which he pretended their sham of a marriage was real.

"A new bride would be expected to smile," he added, his warm breath tickling her ear. Heat that had nothing to do with the sun coursed through her veins. Fearing her knees would buckle, she steadied herself with a hand on the fence.

Mrs. Buttonwood brought her black gelding to a stop in front of them and dismounted. The horse stood a full head taller than Daisy.

Emily felt Chase squeeze her shoulder. Taking the hint, she swallowed her irritation and forced a smile.

Mrs. Buttonwood greeted her in kind. "I went to the house, and your housekeeper said I'd find you here." She gave Emily a quick once-over. "Now aren't you two the lovebirds?"

Accustomed to the sidesaddle riders back home, Emily was surprised at the woman's masculine command of her horse, as well as her manly attire.

Chase moved his arm away from Emily's shoulder. "Nice to see you, Mrs. Buttonwood."

"Yes. Well, I wanted to meet the new bride." Switching the reins from her right hand to her left, Mrs. Buttonwood afforded Chase a playful punch on the arm. Turning to Emily, she nodded approval. "So, you're Cassie."

A moment of awkward silence followed before Chase spoke. "Actually, my wife's name is Emily."

"Oh?" Mrs. Buttonwood looked confused and then curious. "I could have sworn that I heard that your new bride's name was Cassie." Falling silent, she waited for an explanation and, when none came, remembered her manners. "By the way, I'm Helen Buttonwood. My husband and I own the ranch down the road a piece."

Since Mrs. Buttonwood was considerably older, Emily bobbed her head. "Pleased to meet you," she said politely.

Mrs. Buttonwood's eyes widened. "Oh my! Aren't you the lady? Please call me Helen. And do let me see your ring."

"Well, I—" Emily hid her bare hand in the folds of her skirt.

"It's being resized," Chase said as smoothly as if he'd rehearsed it.

Mrs. Buttonwood looked momentarily alarmed. "Oh. I do hope it'll be ready by next Saturday."

Chase frowned. "What's next Saturday?"

"I'm planning a little get-together. You know, to help celebrate your wedding. Nothing outlandish, of course. Just a small gathering with a few neighbors. You didn't think we'd let an occasion like this pass unnoticed, did you?" Without waiting for a reply, Mrs. Buttonwood directed her next comments to Emily. "This is the most important occasion in a woman's life, and men act like it's no big deal. Everyone will want to meet you. You will come?"

Fortunately, Chase answered, relieving Emily of the need to do so. "My new bride and I haven't had a chance to discuss how and when I would introduce her to our neighbors."

"Problem solved," Mrs. Buttonwood said, undaunted. "So, do I hear a yes?"

"I'd rather we wait for a couple of weeks," Chase said, and Emily didn't miss the challenge in the look he gave her. "That will give my wife time to get used to her new role."

"Oh…I see… I understand," Mrs. Buttonwood said, though it was clear by the disappointed look on her face that she didn't. "But do tell. How did the two of you meet?"

It wasn't a question Emily was prepared to answer. How did one explain marrying the wrong man—a stranger—by mistake?

"We would love to tell you the full story, but we're fixin' to take a ride," Chase said smoothly. "I want to show my bride the ranch."

Mrs. Buttonwood's gaze lit on Emily's dress, her expression changing to alarm. "You're riding dressed like that?"

Emily glanced at Helen's plain divided skirt and no-nonsense man's shirt. "Well, I…"

Mrs. Buttonwood didn't give her a chance to finish before assailing Chase. "How could you think about taking her horseback riding dressed in her Sunday-go-to-meeting best? Why, she'd have to lift her skirts to unprecedented heights just to mount."

"I'll tell you what," she continued without stopping to take a breath. Her social invitation had been declined, but she apparently had no intention of being turned down a second time. "I'll have one of my hands ride over later today with appropriate riding attire." She stepped back and visually inspected Emily's figure. "Such a tiny thing," she said with a shake of the head, as if Emily's small stature posed a problem. "But I'm sure I'll find something to fit you."

"That's very kind of you," Emily said. "But I don't want you to go to any trouble."

"It's no trouble at all." Mrs. Buttonwood gave

Emily her own playful punch in the arm. "We rancher wives have to stick together." With that, she turned to her horse and mounted. "I hope we can plan that little get-together soon," she called from astride her saddle. "The others are dying to meet you." With a wave of her hand, she rode off, and the tension immediately left the air.

"Unprecedented heights?" Chase said, his eyes warm with humor, and for the first time since landing in Haywire, Emily couldn't help but laugh.

By the end of the day, Emily's mind was awhirl with the many sights she'd witnessed. Since she'd refused to mount a horse, Chase had made her walk to the roping pasture. It couldn't have been more than a quarter of a mile away from the main house. Even in her city shoes, the walk had offered no hardship, but one of the cowhands had chastised Chase for making his bride walk so far.

Emily thought it the strangest thing. The cowhands seemed to think nothing of sitting in a saddle for hours at a time but balked at having to walk even a short distance on foot.

Before witnessing the men at work, she'd had no idea that running a ranch required so much in the way of sweat and guts. Never again would she take a piece of meat on her plate for granted.

At first glance, the arid ground had looked dull and lifeless. What a false impression that had been! Under Chase's patient tutelage, she now knew that the land teemed with life, and the battle of survival against the forces of nature was in constant play.

Still, nothing had changed her mind about the ranch. She still hated the relentless dust and sickening smell. But given Chase's passion, she now understood why he would do anything to keep from losing the ranch. Why he would even endure their strange marriage.

The sun had dipped low in the sky by the time Emily returned to her room to catch her breath and freshen up for supper. There she found the housekeeper.

Peggy Sue jumped when Emily entered the room, and her face flared red. "Oh, I'm s-sorry," she stammered and quickly moved away from the full-length mirror. The wedding gown she'd been holding up to herself was now bunched in her arms. "I...I was just about to hang this up."

She looked so flustered and embarrassed that Emily felt sorry for her. Chances were she'd never seen a finer gown and was probably shocked to have found it so carelessly tossed on a chair.

"Thank you," Emily said. "That's very thoughtful."

Peggy Sue spread the gown neatly across the bed, smoothing out the full skirt. Though she appeared to be somewhere in her early twenties, she had the weary look of someone much older. Brown hair pulled into a severe bun did nothing to soften the sharp angles of her face. Nor did the shapeless gray frock and thick-soled shoes do anything to enhance her looks.

"It's beautiful," Peggy Sue said, her voice hushed in awe. She ran a finger along the lacy bodice. "I don't think it will fit into the wardrobe. Would you rather I boxed it up?"

"Yes, thank you." Since Peggy Sue still looked flustered and uncomfortable, Emily tried to put her at ease. "Have you worked here long?" she asked.

Peggy Sue shoved her hands in her apron pocket. "Ever since my daughter was a baby."

"Does your daughter live here too?" Earlier, Emily had spotted a young child but assumed she belonged to Cookie or one of the cowhands.

"Yes, ma'am."

"That must have been the little girl I saw earlier. What's her name?"

"Ginny. She's nine years old." Peggy Sue's eyes sought Emily's. "She won't give you any trouble."

"I'm sure she won't. Does your husband work on the ranch too?"

Peggy Sue hesitated, and her cheeks turned bright red. "I'm not married," she said.

"Oh, I'm sorry. I just assumed…" Emily felt bad for putting her on the spot and decided not to pry further.

Peggy Sue tossed a nod at the wedding gown. "I…I noticed that there's a small rip at the hem. I'm quite handy with a needle. If you'd like, I'd be happy to mend it."

Emily had no further use for the gown. If she never saw it again, that would be soon enough. Indeed, all it had done so far was bring her bad luck. But the housekeeper looked so eager to please that Emily didn't have the heart to turn down her offer.

"That would be very kind of you," she said.

With an audible sigh, Peggy Sue lifted the gown off

the bed, smoothed it carefully over her arm, and inched toward the door. "I'll have it back in a day or two."

"There's no hurry." Emily wanted to say more, but Peggy Sue had already left the room as if she couldn't leave fast enough.

9

EMILY HAD NO IDEA WHERE CHASE HAD SPENT THE night. Nor did she care. As long as it wasn't with her. All she knew was that he had left the house early that morning on urgent ranch business. In his stead, the affable cook insisted upon taking Emily to the bunkhouse and introducing her to the ranch hands while he delivered their noontime meal.

"Mind your manners," he called to the men as they entered the low-slung building. "There's a lady present."

The room was rustic and had an open-beamed ceiling and pitted plank floor. A rock fireplace commanded one entire wall, and bare, narrow windows took up another. Cots filled two-thirds of the room, and a long table surrounded by ladder-back chairs occupied the rest.

When introduced, the ranch hands rose from the table, shuffled their feet, and politely doffed their hats. Altogether there were seven ranch hands, and all were dressed in canvas pants and plain bib shirts.

Each man had a curious name that either described

his physical appearance or stated his place of origin. She'd already met Big-Foot Harry and Rusty, but there also were Kansas Pete, Beanpole Tom, Gabby, and the man they called Foxhound. The deep, gravelly voice belonged to the ranch foreman, Boomer.

The men varied in age from early twenties to midforties. All were wiry, had sun-bronzed skin, and spoke with either a twang or a lazy drawl. After an initial wariness at having a woman in their midst, the men began to relax.

"Nice to make your acquaintance, ma'am," the man who'd been introduced as Boomer said, speaking for the rest of them. "Anythin' me and the boys can do fer you, just give us a holler."

"Thank you," Emily said. She glanced at the steaming bowls on the table. "Please, don't let me keep you from your meal."

The men took their seats again and eagerly helped themselves to Cookie's son-of-a-gun stew. The man who'd been introduced as Kansas Pete spoke up. "Big-Foot Harry said you and the boss got married by accident."

Cookie looked appalled. "What's the matter with you, Kansas Pete? You ain't supposed to talk about that." He turned to Emily. "Let's go."

"It's all right," Emily said. "I'm sure no harm was meant." There was no sense denying what apparently was now common knowledge. Or would be once Mrs. Buttonwood learned the truth. Hoping to put the men at ease, Emily said, "The stampede caused a lot of confusion."

Boomer chuckled. "I'll say. Guess you could say the

stakes have never been so high." Laughing at his own pun, he lifted his spoon to his mouth and made a loud slurping sound.

Beanpole Tom reached across the table for a sour-dough biscuit. "If you ask me, the boss lucked out."

"That's what I *herd*." Big-Foot Harry laughed. When no one laughed with him, he spelled the word out. "*H-e-r-d*. Get it?"

Cookie rolled his eyes. "I think that's our cue to leave," he said, ushering Emily out the door. He waited until they were a distance from the bunkhouse before apologizing for the men. "Don't mind them. They're all talk, but they don't mean nothin' by it."

Actually, she liked the cowhands. They were nothing like the men back home with their tweed suits and uppity airs. Instead, the men here were much more down-to-earth and unassuming.

After Emily had visited the bunkhouse and met the friendly occupants, the main house seemed more remote and lonely than ever.

That was why she was disappointed to find the large dining room table set that night for only two. For some reason she couldn't quite name, the thought of being alone with the man who was her husband put her nerves on edge. Not that she'd seen that much of him since he'd shown her around the ranch.

Now he greeted her with a wary nod and held her chair for her until she was seated. He then took his place clear at the opposite end of the long table. It was their first meal together, and for once, he seemed to lack his usual self-confidence. Instead, he looked as uneasy as Emily felt.

Grateful for the distance between them, she glanced about the room. Accustomed to the noisy family gatherings she'd grown up with, she felt a wave of homesickness wash over her. It was only after her mother had died that things began to fall apart. Her grandparents, aunt, and uncle said it was too painful to visit the Beacon Hill mansion, and that put an end to the lush parties and festive dinners.

Perhaps if the family had been more supportive, her father might not have grieved himself to death. If he were still alive, she wouldn't be stuck on an isolated ranch miles away from anything, that's for certain. Nor would she be married to a stranger.

Emily heaved a sigh. It was hard to know what affected her more—thoughts of the past or the gloomy surroundings. Not even the soft glow of candlelight could make the room with its stark white walls, rough-hewn rafters, and austere furnishings feel warm or inviting.

As if sensing her troubled thoughts, Chase visually followed her gaze to one of the bare walls. "Something wrong?"

Shaking her head, she stared across the vast expanse of maple wood. Chase had removed his pearl-gray hat. His slightly disheveled brown hair gave him a boyish look. Twisted-wire garters held his shirtsleeves to his elbows.

"No, nothing," she murmured. *Everything*. She hated how her life had taken such an unexpected turn. This wasn't the kind of life she'd hoped for, had indeed planned for.

Chase studied her a moment before accepting her answer without further questioning. "I asked Cookie to serve us in here. Thought you'd feel more comfortable." He glanced around the room as if seeing it for the first time. "This room hasn't been used much since my grandmother died. She liked to entertain and would throw large dinner parties here."

Emily moistened her lips. "Where do you normally dine?"

"In my office," he said.

"And the others?"

He sat back in his chair. "The others?"

"Your men. Do they take all their meals in the bunkhouse?" The lack of a kitchen meant Cookie had to carry everything from the main house, and that seemed to her a needless chore.

The question seemed to surprise him. "That there's their livin' quarters."

"It just seems like a lot of extra work for Cookie," she said. "It would be easier if the men ate here."

If her interest in the domestic workings of the ranch surprised him, he didn't show it. "I'm fixin' to add a kitchen to the bunkhouse next year."

"I see," she said. "And Peggy Sue? Where does she dine?"

"Peggy Sue and her daughter take meals in their room."

She'd yet to make the child's acquaintance, but she already felt sorry for her. Growing up in such a somber place couldn't be much fun.

Cookie entered the room, and all at once, the tension in the room vanished. "And now for my famous son-of-a-gun roast beef," he announced and placed a steaming hot plate on the table in front of her. Cooked to perfection, the roast looked and smelled delicious and was surrounded by garden-fresh vegetables.

Whether it was that cold, sterile dining room or her husband's remote expression, she didn't know, but she suddenly had no appetite. Still, not wishing to hurt Cookie's feelings, Emily forced herself to eat, each bite feeling like a lump of coal in her mouth.

10

Later that night, Emily leaned her head against the rim of the metal tub with a sigh and tried to relax her tense body.

Filling the tub with water had required Peggy Sue to make several trips back and forth to the kitchen downstairs, and for that, Emily felt bad. The ranch had been built years earlier and didn't have the amenities many newer buildings had, such as a separate room for bathing. The ranch still relied on a galvanized tin tub for personal hygiene, though such a receptacle was better suited for its original purpose of washing clothes.

The housekeeper had stoically insisted that preparing Emily's bath was no trouble and had resisted all attempts to be drawn into friendly conversation. After making certain Emily had the necessary soap and towels at her disposal, Peggy Sue quietly left the room.

Emily closed her eyes and tried to relax her tense body. Fortunately, she'd agreed to stay married to Chase for only a year.

Her eyes flew open. Oh no, what was she thinking? Twelve months on a cattle ranch now seemed like an eternity. The mere thought made her feel faint. If the relentless heat, dust, and bugs weren't enough, every shift of the wind brought the sickening smell of cattle. There simply was no getting away from it.

But honestly, what choice did she have but to stay here? No one in town would hire her. Even more frustrating, not one person she'd approached for a job had been impressed with her Vassar College degree in liberal arts. Indeed, no one seemed to know what it was. The proprietress of the Feedbag Café had even said she wasn't looking for an artist, liberal or otherwise.

The degree that she had worked so hard to earn appeared to be as worthless here as last month's newspaper. Now that she knew her tuition had been paid for with ill-gotten funds, it seemed like retribution, however undeserved. The sins of the father or, in this case, her uncle...

She didn't know how long she'd soaked in that tub, ruminating over her situation, but she suddenly realized the bathwater had turned cold. Reluctantly, she reached for the towel on the nearby vanity stool. She felt pleasantly drowsy, so maybe the long soak had relaxed her enough to get a good night's sleep. If so, it would be the first real sleep she'd had since landing in Texas.

Standing, she stepped out of the tub onto the hardwood floor and dried herself off. Her wet hair fell down her back in tangled strands.

Just as she finished wrapping the towel around her middle, the door flew open, startling her. "Oh!"

Filling the doorway, Chase hesitated a moment, a look of apology on his face. He turned his head to address someone in the hall. "Good night," he said over his shoulder, and Emily heard the housekeeper wish him the same.

He then entered the room and closed the door firmly behind him.

Heart thumping madly, she clutched at the towel, making sure it was tightly tucked around her. "What do you think you're doing?" she demanded when at last she could find her voice.

The question seemed to surprise him. "Right now, I'm hoping to convince Peggy Sue and Cookie that we have a real marriage."

"You could have knocked," she said.

"They might have thought it strange, had they seen me knockin' on my wife's door." He arched an eyebrow. "Would you have let me in had I knocked?"

"Definitely not!" she seethed.

"There you have it," he said. "If word gets out that we're sleepin' in separate rooms, it will be hard to convince the executor of the will that we have a real marriage. You do remember our deal?"

Oh, she remembered it all right. Every last word. The question was, did he? "You're not sleeping in my bed! I told you—"

He cut her off with an abrupt wave of his hand. "I know what you told me."

His appraising look suggested he didn't miss a thing. Not the curve of her ivory shoulders or the swell of her firm breasts showing above the tightly clenched towel. Nor did he miss her shocking display of bare legs and feet.

Cheeks flaring, she gave her head a haughty toss and

lifted her chin with as much dignity as she could muster. "If you're done gawking, I must ask you to leave."

He raised a dark brow. "Don't worry," he said with a wry twist of his mouth. "Your virtue shall remain safe and secure. I'm fixin' to occupy the next room."

He inclined his head toward the arched doorway, leading to a small room adjacent to hers. Earlier, she had explored the space and decided that it had originally been used as a nursery. It had never occurred to her that Chase meant to sleep there.

He held her gaze. "Should you get the notion to climb into my bed, I shall put a stop to it at once."

Her mouth dropped open. "I shall never..." she sputtered.

The corner of his mouth quirked. "Never?" he asked. "More's the pity."

She glared at him. "If you don't mind, I wish to get dressed."

"Oh, I don't mind," he said with a lazy drawl. "Feel free to do whatever you need to do while we talk."

She stiffened. "We have nothing to talk about."

"Oh, but we do. Your ridin' lessons, for one." He tossed a previously unnoticed package on the bed. "Your ridin' outfit," he said. "Mrs. Buttonwood was as good as her word. I'll meet you at the stables first thing in the mornin', and we'll get started. Be ready."

"And if I'm not?"

"If'n you can't live up to your side of the bargain, then I shall be equally remiss in mine. In which case, you can say goodbye to your marital privileges."

She stared at him. "My what?"

"As my wife, you're entitled to my full support,

and that includes an allowance. I'm sure you'll find it quite generous."

Seeming to assume the matter settled, he walked across the room with long, easy strides. Irritated that her circumstances made her dependent on him, she kicked a slipper across the room.

Stopping at the entrance to his personal room, he tossed a look over his shoulder. His dark, smoldering eyes glanced at the slipper before meeting her gaze.

"Tomorrow, after your lesson, we'll discuss how to get you to town. You'll need some decent foot leather and"—he glanced at her feathered French hat on the dresser—"a more practical conk cover." He gave a slight nod. "Good night." Without waiting for a response, he ducked through the curtains leading into the tiny anteroom.

No door separated the two rooms, only curtains. *Thin* black curtains. That meant he could pop into her room any time he downright pleased and without so much as a warning.

Forcing herself to breathe, Emily pressed her hands against her heaving chest. Never had she met a haughtier, more conceited and arrogant man. *Ohhh.* Of all the men she could have married, why, oh why did it have to be Chase McKnight?

The thought of having to put up with his condescending attitude for a year left her feeling bereft. Not even his promise of a generous allowance made the situation easier to bear.

"You can get dressed now, Mrs. McKnight," he called from behind the curtains. "I won't look."

Seething, she reached on the bed for her linen

nightgown. "You can look all you want, *Mr.* McKnight, but you won't see a thing!" With that, she turned off the gas lamp, throwing the room into total darkness.

She quickly donned her nightgown and tried to ignore the warm chuckle floating from the other room.

∽

Chase lay on the small cot, staring at the dark ceiling. He wished he could have arranged for better sleeping accommodations, but that would have aroused Cookie or his housekeeper's suspicion. His father's will specifically stated that the marriage had to be real.

He'd have to make sure to leave the room as he found it in the morning. No one must ever know that he'd slept there.

The truth was, he had only himself to blame for this whole mess.

Chase had been sixteen when his brother died. Bent on punishing himself for Michael's death, Chase had spent more than a year in a drunken stupor. When that failed to relieve his crushing guilt, he lashed out with his fists and landed in jail.

When he'd finally come to his senses, he returned to the ranch, hoping to make up for what he had done and earn his father's forgiveness. The will proved that he'd never fully succeeded. Now he had to pay the penalty with a woman who had no business on a ranch.

None!

How he hated this, hated having to go through with this awkward charade just to keep what was rightfully his. His grandfather would turn over in his grave if he knew how his beloved ranch was now mired in such deception.

Pushing his thoughts aside, Chase rubbed his head and groaned. He shifted his body, and the straw mattress rustled beneath his weight. At least the bed was more comfortable than the floor of his office where he'd spent the previous night. But not by much.

He needed to get some shut-eye. Life on a ranch started early. If only his feet didn't hang off the end of the thin mattress. If only he could turn over without banging against the wall.

If only she hadn't been nearly naked…

The last thought popped into his head unbidden, and he sucked in his breath. He had no earthly reason to think of her creamy-white shoulders or the gentle swell of her breasts. She was his wife in name only. Theirs was but a temporary arrangement. It's what she wanted. What they'd agreed upon. What he wanted. It was the price he had to pay for his recklessness.

If and when he married for keeps, his wife of choice wouldn't be some prissy greenhorn, that was for certain and sure.

But even as he thought it, a vision of big blue eyes came to mind. He'd only heard her laugh the one time, but it had been enough to make him want to hear it again. At the very least, he'd like to see her smile.

What a puzzle she was. He couldn't help but be intrigued. Never had he met a woman of such extremes. She had startled at the sight of a mouse. Didn't even know how to ride a horse. Yet she had traveled halfway across the country to marry a stranger—a scary prospect in anyone's book.

But a mouse, for crying out loud! Heaven knows what she would do should a rattler or pack of wolves cross her path. What possible good was a woman like that on a ranch? The best he could hope for was that the two of them survived the length of their marriage without any serious mishap.

Turning over, he balled his hand and gave his pillow a good whack. Head on the plumped-up pillow, he closed his eyes. Blast it all, if he didn't picture her pretty, round face and expressive blue peepers. A man could get lost in eyes like those.

But it was the memory of the towel wrapped around her gentle curves that made him shrug off the blanket and toss the pillow across the room.

Sitting on the edge of the cot, he dropped his elbows on his lap and pressed his forehead into the palms of his hands. It wasn't just that she couldn't ride; she was an Easterner through and through. Like others of her ilk, she had no interest in the land. All those Eastern folks cared about was money. Like the carpetbaggers who had reaped high profits from the reconstruction of the South, the same sort of vultures benefited from the sweat of western cattlemen. They did it through exorbitant stockyard charges, commissions, and bad loans. As much as he hated putting Emily in that same group, he feared she too would try to bleed him dry at the end of their deal.

Oh yes. He had every reason to distrust her and not just moneywise. He couldn't imagine her getting her hands dirty. Or clothes soiled. Or sitting up all night with a distressed cow.

The only place he could imagine her was in his bed,

and that would never do. He had a very clear picture in his head of the kind of wife he wanted, the kind of wife the ranch needed. And his bride clearly didn't fit that mold.

He tried to think of the positive side. They would be together for only a short while. One year. Twelve months. Fifty-two weeks.

But the more the memory of her wrapped in a towel kept popping into his head, the more he worried. How fetching she'd looked. How utterly desirable.

He clamped down on his thoughts. For the love of Pete! What was the matter with him? She was off-limits. That was the promise made. She'd told him in no uncertain terms that should he cross the line, the deal was off.

The question was, how could he keep his side of the bargain for a full year when it was all he could do to get through one blasted night?

11

THE CROW OF A ROOSTER DRIFTED THROUGH THE OPEN windows as Emily stepped into the kitchen the following morning. The rising sun cast a ribbon of golden sunlight across the room, suggesting a cheeriness she didn't feel.

Still shaken by last night's encounter with Chase, she tried to make sense of her confused feelings. She wasn't afraid of him. Nor did she worry that he would demand his husbandly rights.

Her feelings for him were far more complex and unsettling, far more worrisome. It wasn't just that she found him attractive. At times, she'd felt a connection she hadn't felt with any other man. Like when they'd laughed over something Mrs. Buttonwood had said. Then there were instances when she'd wanted to throttle him. How could one man invoke such mixed emotions?

"Mornin," Cookie said, drawing her away from her thoughts. He looked her up and down. "Don't you look dashin'? All that Boston stuff cleaned off real nice, now didn't it?"

Feeling self-conscious but encouraged by his

approval, Emily smiled shyly and turned a full circle. "Are…are you sure I look okay?"

The divided skirt with its emancipated waist and lack of a cumbersome bustle couldn't have fit better had it been made special for her. But no matter what feminine name was used to describe it, the skirt still had the look and feel of men's trousers.

"You look like a proper rancher's wife. Or will when you put this on." He reached for a wide-brimmed hat on a wooden peg and handed it to her.

Fingering the felt hat, Emily raised her eyebrows. A proper rancher's wife? Who would have thought such a thing possible? None of her old friends in Boston would believe it.

She carefully arranged the hat on her head, and Cookie nodded.

"There you go," he said. He turned to the stove and scooped a toasted, round flapjack onto a plate. "When those cattle see you coming, they'll take notice. Mark my words."

Emily smiled, though it wasn't the cattle she'd hoped to impress. She hoped to show her arrogant husband that she wasn't just some Easterner he could boss around or rule with a generous allowance.

She did a quick check of the baseboards and, seeing no furry animals, asked, "Do you like living here? On the ranch?"

Cookie shrugged. "I'm just as happy where I am as where I'm not," he said. She was still puzzling over his answer when he handed her a plate. "Wait till you taste my son-of-a-gun flapjacks."

"Son of a gun, eh?" she said and laughed.

Emily wasn't a big breakfast eater, but then she'd never tasted flapjacks as light and airy as Cookie's. Surprisingly, she cleaned her plate.

Declining his offer of a second helping, she thanked him, carried her empty plate to the sink, and left.

She was about to leave the house when she noticed the housekeeper's daughter sitting on the parlor floor surrounded by wooden building blocks.

"And who do we have here?" Emily had caught several glimpses of the child the day before but had yet to be introduced.

"This is Ginny." Peggy Sue swiped a picture frame on the piano with her feather duster. "Say hello to Mrs. McKnight."

Emily smiled at the child, but all she got in return was a wary glance. Up close, Emily could see a family resemblance. Ginny's long, brown hair was tied with a blue ribbon and cascaded down her back in an abundance of curls. She was a pretty child, but there was something odd in the way she held her head, as if trying to pull something out of the air.

"Oh, please. Call me Emily. Mrs. McKnight is a mouthful," she said, thinking the child was shy or embarrassed as she failed to look her in the eye.

"Oh no, that will never do," Ginny's mother exclaimed. "You being the ranch owner's wife and all." To her daughter, she said, "Say 'hello, Mrs. McKnight.'"

"Hello, Mrs. Knight."

Before her mother could correct her, Emily laughed at the irony. As a young girl, she'd often dreamed of marrying a knight in shining armor. It appeared she'd done just that, if only in name. "Mrs. Knight it is."

As much as she wanted to get to know Ginny better, she knew she had to hurry. Chase was waiting for her. "Sorry, but I'm on the way to my riding lesson. Do you ride, Ginny?"

Her mother stopped dusting. "Oh, she can't ride."

Something in Peggy Sue's voice forbade further discussion. With a puzzled glance at the child, Emily took the hint and left.

Outside, she paused on the wraparound porch to check her divided skirt before heading to the stables. Despite Cookie's assurances, she felt a wave of insecurity. Her poor mother would turn over in her grave at the thought of her daughter in such masculine attire.

In Boston, a man or woman of breeding and means was expected to dress in a certain way. No such class distinction seemed to exist in Texas. Here, clothes were apparently chosen for comfort, durability, and practicality. Chase favored the same type of dark canvas trousers, plaid shirts, and vests as his ranch hands did.

Emily sighed. Texas and its way would take some getting used to.

Swallowing her apprehension, she took a deep breath and started down the steps. She wore her sturdiest high-button shoes, but the moment she stepped off the porch and into the glaring early-morning sun, it wasn't her footwear that earned her gratitude but rather the wide-brimmed Stetson hat Cookie had loaned her.

Nearing her destination, she stifled a yawn. It had still been dark when Chase had tiptoed past the foot of her bed and left the room that morning. She couldn't imagine why he'd been up so early, but maybe he'd had as much trouble sleeping as she did.

Rusty greeted her with a smile, bringing her out of her reverie. "'Morning, ma'am," he said politely.

"Good morning, Rusty," she replied, her curiosity peaked by the horse and buggy parked in front. Surely, it was too early for visitors. "Have you seen…Mr. McKnight?"

For answer, Rusty slanted his head to the side, indicating the barn-like stables. Thanking him, she stepped through the double doors and immediately heard a woman's voice.

Curious, she crept quietly along the straw-covered dirt floor, past the tack room and numerous box stalls.

One by one, horses peered over stall doors to stare at her. The sweet waft of fresh hay reached her nose, all but wiping out the smell of horseflesh and dung.

Emily was close enough now to recognize the visitor as Cassie Decker, the woman Chase was supposed to have wed.

The woman looked as if she were crying. His arm around her, Chase handed her a handkerchief. "How do you think I felt when I walked in and found you married to someone else?" the woman said.

Even in the shadows, Emily could see what looked like regret on Chase's face. "I never meant for that to happen."

"I counted on our marriage," Cassie continued. "My children…"

"I counted on it too. I hope you know, I never meant to hurt you. If you let me, I'll make it up to you."

Cassie dabbed her eyes with his handkerchief. "That's not necessary."

"I insist," he said. "I'm not one to back out of my

promises." Emily couldn't hear what he said next, but then he spoke louder. "Could you meet me in town on Friday?"

"I told you that wasn't necessary—" The last of her sentence was drowned out by a whinnying horse, and Emily failed to hear the next exchanged words.

Watching them, Emily chewed on a fingernail. Less than two days after they'd wed, Chase was already planning to rendezvous with another woman. Emily knew it shouldn't bother her. There was no reason for it to. What she had with Chase was a business arrangement, nothing more. Still, watching Chase and Mrs. Decker made her feel rejected and even more alone.

Cassie handed Chase his handkerchief, and he pulled his arm away from her.

"Friday," she said and turned.

Cassie's sun-battered skin and callused hands would be frowned upon in Boston, but they only added to Emily's guilt. Her unfortunate marriage had deprived the poor, hardworking woman and her children of a better life.

Emily stepped in her path, intent on apologizing. But before she could get a word out, Cassie darted around her with an icy glare and stormed out of the barn.

Emily felt bad for the woman and didn't blame Chase for wanting to do something to make amends. Still, for some unknown reason, his concern for another woman made Emily feel like an afterthought and even more alone.

After the scene with Cassie, she wouldn't blame Chase if he decided to cancel her lesson. If anything, she'd be grateful.

Instead, he gave his pocket watch a quick glance. "You're late."

Emily gaped at him a moment before finding her voice. "Late?" How could anyone be late so early in the morning? "It's only a little after seven. In any case, you appeared to have been occupied."

His dark expression told her he had no intention of discussing Mrs. Decker. "Like I said, late." He slipped his watch back into his pocket. "Things are done early around here. On account of the heat." He stalked past her with long, purposeful steps. "Follow me," he ordered in a clipped voice.

She stared after him. He'd made no mention of her attire. He might rue the day they had wed, but that was no excuse for him to take his frustrations out on her. He was equally at fault for what had happened. "Well?"

Chase stopped and turned, his stance wide as if to claim as much space as possible. Even in the dim light, it was hard not to notice his broad shoulders or even how his wide chest tapered to a narrow waist and slim hips. "Well, what?"

"Do I look like a proper rancher's wife, or don't I?"

He clamped down on his jaw, and his tight-lipped expression told her just how much he hated their arrangement. Maybe even hated her. He gave her a quick once-over. "You'll do."

"Is that all you can say?" Here she was, knocking herself out to play her part, and all he could say was she'd do? "Perhaps you'd prefer that I wore a towel."

It was a bold, even shocking thing to say, but she was still upset at the way he'd walked in on her last night—or rather how his heated gaze had made her tingle all over. Just as upsetting was the genuine concern he'd shown Cassie Decker. The least he could do was show a little of that same concern for his wife who was, after all, doing him a huge favor.

The hat shading his face hid his eyes, but his already straight back grew even more rigid, and his hands curled at his sides. "What I'd prefer is that you wore better footwear."

She glanced down at her high-button shoes. "These are the strongest ones I have."

"Then, like I said, you'll do." He whirled around. "You comin'?" he called from the open doorway, making even a simple question sound like an order.

Heaving a sigh, Emily followed. What a strange man he was, seeming to run hot and cold on a whim. How could anyone sound kind and caring one minute and so utterly distant the next?

She ran to catch up to him.

Without comment, he picked up his pace. Swallowing the bitter taste in her mouth, she hurried to keep up with him.

He led the way around the stables to the paddock in back where Daisy stood in the shade of a tree, saddled and waiting. The horse greeted them with a low nicker.

"Hello, girl." Chase patted the mare on the nose and reached in his pocket for a sugar cube. Palming the treat, he held his hand out flat, and Daisy grabbed the cube with thick velvet lips.

Irritated that Chase showed more humanity to the horse than he did to her, Emily watched him with glaring eyes.

Indicating he wanted her to pet the horse, he stepped aside. "The better you get to know and understand her, the better rider you'll be." The eyes meeting hers were dark, remote, letting nothing in and even less out.

Forgetting her irritation with Chase, Emily regarded the horse with reservations. "She...she doesn't bite, does she?"

He arched an eyebrow. "Who, Daisy? She's as gentle as a lamb."

Since there didn't seem to be any way to refrain from touching the horse without looking foolish, Emily cautiously held out her hand. The horse nuzzled her palm, and Emily jerked her hand back with a gasp.

Sensing Chase's disapproval, she cleared her throat. "It t-tickled," she stammered by way of explanation.

"Sudden movements can cause a hoss to bolt or cattle to stampede," he said.

Gritting her teeth, she stuck her hand out again. With sheer determination, she stiffened and let the mare nuzzle her palm.

When she pulled her hand away a second time, Chase handed her the rope and made her walk the horse slowly around the paddock.

He was a methodical teacher, leaving nothing to chance. Everything was about safety and care of the horse. Only after he was convinced she knew the basic commands did he allow her to mount.

Emily lifted her foot, but no sooner had she slid her high-button shoe into the stirrup than she lost her nerve. Pulling her foot back, she shook her head. "I-I can't do this. Maybe...maybe tomorrow."

"It's not gonna be any easier tomorrow."

That was what she was afraid of.

When his stern commands failed to convince her to mount, he changed tactics. "Come on, now," he coaxed. "You can do it. Just push off and swing your leg over the saddle."

Surprised by the thawing in his voice, Emily worked her foot into the stirrup a second time. Biting her lower lip, she pushed off but couldn't get enough momentum to clear the saddle with her leg.

After the third attempt, she was about to give up when he placed a hand on her behind and pushed her up.

The feel of his strong hand covering her buttocks was a shock that lasted for only as long as it took her to sit astride the saddle. Fear taking precedent over propriety, she squeezed the reins tight.

"I–It's so high," she stammered.

"What are you talkin' about, high? Like I said, the hoss is only fourteen and a half hands."

Heart pounding, she closed her eyes.

Seeming oblivious to the fact that she was frozen with fear, Chase led the horse slowly around the paddock. Eventually, Emily pried one eye open and then the other, forcing herself to breathe. Her death grip remained.

It took several turns around the paddock before her body relaxed of its own accord and began moving in rhythm with the mare. It was a pleasant feeling, making it seem like she was one with the horse.

Unfortunately, the feeling lasted but a short time.

Showing her how to use her hands and body to control the horse, Chase made her stop and start so many times that she wanted to scream. She was hot and thirsty, but that was only half of it. Her rump hurt, her thighs ached, a pain shot up her back, and her head felt ready to explode.

It did no good to complain, for it only gave him more reason to point out what she was doing wrong.

"You're grippin' the reins too tightly. That's why your hands are numb," he'd say. Or "You need to hold your back straight!"

Emily tried her best to do what he said, hoping he would end the lesson. But nothing she did passed muster, and Chase continued to find fault. "Point your toes up. Heels down." On and on he went, issuing orders like a wartime commander.

The sun rose higher in the sky, and the air grew more oppressive. Perspiration dripped off her forehead, and her mouth felt so dry that it could have been lined with cotton.

"Okay, you can dismount," he said finally, stepping to the side of her horse and raising his hands as if to catch her.

Not wanting to chance another intimate encounter, she shook her head. "I can do it!"

He stepped back, a doubtful look on his face. "Okay, take both feet out of the stirrups."

Swallowing hard, she glanced at the ground. Big mistake. She lifted her gaze to the sky and shifted her weight. Saying a silent prayer, she grabbed hold of the saddle horn, pulled her one foot free, and froze.

"Well?" he queried.

"Don't rush me. I want to do it right." Actually, she just wanted to keep from falling on her rear.

Grasping the saddle horn, she half slipped from the saddle. Her left foot still in the stirrup and her right leg draped over the leather seat, she dangled from the side of the horse like a flag at half-mast.

"Here, let me help you."

"No!"

Chase folded his arms across his chest and tried not to laugh, but the gleam in his eyes gave him away. Even the horse looked amused and nickered.

"Let me know when you're done hangin' like a possum," Chase said.

Emily would rather have died than ask him for help. Even so, she finally gave in, her face flaring with humiliation.

Chase grasped her around the waist with both hands and gently lifted her to the ground. After gaining her footing, she slumped against the fence and reached around to rub her sore backside.

Thinking the lesson over, she was surprised when he told her to mount again.

"Can't we stop?"

"Stop?" He stared at her, incredulous. "We're just gettin' started."

"We've been at this for a good long while." Hours. Or at least that's how it seemed.

He narrowed his gaze, and for one brief second, she imagined a look of sympathy in the depth of his eyes. But the look vanished as quickly as it had come, making her question if she'd seen it at all.

"Like I said. We're just gettin' started. The sooner you learn to ride, the sooner we can start your shootin' lessons."

She stared at him in wide-eyed horror. "S-shooting lessons?"

"The only sin in this land is inexperience," he said. "That's why you've gotta learn to ride and ride good. You also need to know how to handle a firearm for your own safety. You won't do me or anyone else any good dead."

Temper flaring, she planted her fists firmly on her hips and glared at him. "So that's what this is all about," she stormed. "You don't care about me. All you care about is your blasted ranch!" How foolish to think he had been teaching her to ride for her own benefit.

He reared back. "You knew what you were gettin' yourself into when you—"

"When I what?" Indignation shot up her spine like a steel rod. "Came crawling back? Is that what you were going to say?"

Frustration flitted across his face. "What I was about to say is when you agreed to stay."

She started to leave, but the muscles in her upper thighs hurt so much, she could hardly move. The most she could do was cling to the fence. Exertion made it hard to speak, but that didn't stop her.

"For your information, I did *not* come crawling back!" It wasn't like her to be argumentative. But she was hot and tired, and her body ached all over. She was done trying to please him. Done trying to be a "proper" rancher's wife! As far as she was concerned, their deal was off!

Taking Chase's lack of response as dissent, she flung up her hands. "Okay, that does it. I'm leaving, and it won't be on hands and knees." Or at least she hoped not.

12

Watching Emily stagger away like a drunken cowhand, Chase kicked himself mentally. Now he'd done it.

All he'd wanted to do was keep a safe distance from her emotionally. It was the only way he could keep from thinking things he had no business thinking. Things like how she'd looked in that blasted towel.

But he'd gone too far, and now it appeared he had pushed her away completely.

He hated thinking that he'd taken out the resentment toward his father on her. She wasn't to blame for any of this and was as much a victim of circumstances as he was.

Feeling lower than low, he watched her cross the yard for a moment before chasing after her. She might not admit it, but it was clear by the way she limped that she was hurting.

Emily stopped when he caught up to her. "Now what?" she demanded, eyes flashing.

"I just want to make sure you're okay."

If she was surprised by his interest in her welfare,

it didn't show. "I'm fine!" she snapped. "No thanks to you."

Yep, she was hurting all right. He could see the strain in her eyes. She also looked like she'd been through the wringer. She straightened her hat, but not much could be done for the abundance of yellow hair that had sprung free from its bun. The intriguing smudge on her cheek, however, called for a man's touch. *His* touch.

When he reached a finger to her smooth, silky skin to rub the spot away, her startled blue eyes met his. "Sorry," he said, pulling his hand away. "You had somethin' on your face."

Her hand flew to her cheek, and her already heated face turned another shade darker.

"It's gone now," he said.

Her mouth formed a perfect circle, and she lowered her hand to her side.

He felt bad for giving her a hard time. Lack of sleep had made him start the day out of sorts, and his encounter with Cassie Decker hadn't helped. Poor woman. She had counted on their marriage for her children's sakes.

His failure in keeping his promise to Cassie had made him more determined to do right by Emily. Or at least to see to her safety. He'd let one woman down; he sure in blazes didn't want to fail another.

Horses were dangerous. The land was dangerous. But a part of him knew there was more. A lot more. As long as they were at each other's throats, he could control his thoughts. Or at least keep from dwelling on such things as Emily's gold-tipped eyelashes. Or the little indentation on her cheek when she smiled. Or even the way her eyes flashed during their many confrontations.

Looking away, he reminded himself how unsuited she was for ranch life. How unequipped she was to deal with the harsh land. She was much more suited to the city.

"Tomorrow, we'll go a little easier with your lesson," he said, hoping to make amends for his bad behavior.

She lifted her chin, her face dark with anger. "There won't be any more lessons."

"Come on," he said gently. "You don't mean that. Look at you. You're fine." More than fine…

"No thanks to you!"

Surprised by the vehemence in her voice, he stepped back "Me? What did I do?"

Her blazing blue eyes met his. "You put me through hell, that's what!"

"By teachin' you the proper handlin' of a hoss?"

"By making me obey your every command like a helpless imbecile!"

He drew in his breath. He'd been rough on her, but he never meant to make her feel bad. "You have to admit your knowledge of hosses leaves much to be desired." Taking her silence to mean she agreed, he added, "Tomorrow, same time, same place."

She shot visual daggers at him. "If you expect to have your way with me a second time, you better think again." With that, she stormed away.

Her words struck a chord that was better left untouched. Still, he couldn't hold back the words that popped into his head. "Trust me," he called after. "If I wanted to have my way with you, it wouldn't be on a hoss!"

Emily's mouth dropped open, and her steps faltered. "Ohhhh!" There was simply no reasoning with the man.

Legs stiff, she forced herself to put one foot in front of the other and blinked back tears. When she'd agreed to stay married to Chase for a year, she certainly hadn't bargained on a life of torture!

Just as she reached the gate, a strange rattling sound stopped her in her tracks.

Her gaze darting to the sound, she gasped. A rattlesnake was poised within striking distance. Head rising from a coiled body, it flicked its fork-pointed tongue and hissed.

Staring in horror, she froze, her heart beating so fast, she could hardly breathe.

Poised ready to strike, the snake opened its mouth wide, revealing deadly fangs. The tail moved back and forth, making a loud buzzing sound.

"Don't move!" Chase said from behind her, his command followed by gunfire.

Emily jumped at the sound and almost fainted with relief when the now-headless reptile crumbled to the ground. Only then was she able to gasp for air.

Chase ran to her side and slipped his arm around her waist.

Ears still ringing from gunfire, she tried to act calm,

but her shaky limbs refused to cooperate. Much to her mortification, he pulled her into his arms and pressed her head against his chest. His manly fragrance offered a welcome respite from the smell of cattle, dust, horse-flesh, and gun smoke.

In the strength of his arms, she melted against him, eyes closed, and felt oddly, strangely safe. She pressed herself even closer to his corded chest, her soft curves molding against his. His hands explored the hollows of her back, and her eyes flew open.

Torn between staying in his protective arms and proving she wasn't as helpless as he seemed to think, she pushed him away. Now that the danger was over, she could pretend a bravery she didn't feel.

He studied her with furrowed brow. "You okay?"

She tugged at her sleeves and straightened her split skirt. "Of course I'm okay," she said, hoping her voice didn't give her away. As scared as she had been of the snake, being in Chase's arms was what had caused her the most anxiety.

With a quick glance toward the reptile to make sure it hadn't found a second life, she added, "It was just a snake."

He reared back. "Just?"

Intent on proving she wasn't some silly woman who jumped at her own shadow, she shrugged. "We have snakes in Boston." Poisonous snakes were known to live in the forested hillsides behind the house she'd shared with her aunt and uncle. Fortunately, she'd never had occasion to come across one.

He cocked his head as if trying to figure her out. "Is

it just the four-legged creatures that give you grief?" he asked in all seriousness.

"Not as much as some *two*-legged ones I've had occasion to meet," she said pointedly.

Much to her surprise, he laughed. It was a nice laugh, bubbling out of him like water from a spring.

Surprised at how much she liked him in this light-hearted mood, she turned and stalked away. But she kept a wary eye on the ground to make certain no other dangers lay in wait.

"Let me know when we can start your shootin' lessons," he called after her.

She gritted her teeth and kept walking.

13

CHUCKLING TO HIMSELF, CHASE WATCHED EMILY walk into the house with stiff dignity and slam the door shut.

Battling the temptation to follow her, he waited for several minutes before entering the house. With a quick glance at the stairs, he turned and headed for the kitchen. He was hot and thirsty, but the only thing that would clear his sleep-deprived head was coffee. The stronger, the better.

He walked into the kitchen and headed straight for the stove.

He only wished that holding Emily in his arms hadn't played such havoc with his senses. Even when she was fighting him, she had a way of getting under his skin. She was both intriguing and aggravating. Never had a woman confused him more. Never had his head been in such a tangle.

In the short time he'd known her, she'd taken over practically every thought. If he didn't watch out, she'd take over his lonely, vulnerable heart, and that could not be allowed to happen.

The last thing he needed was a greenhorn wife. Right now, he wasn't even certain she would last a week on the ranch, let alone a year.

It was only after he slammed the coffeepot on the stove that Cookie looked up from rolling out pie dough. "I take it the lesson didn't go well," he said.

Chase took a sip from his cup before answering. The hot, bitter brew was just how he liked it. "It went well enough."

"I saw you out there." Cookie sprinkled a handful of flour on the dough and kept rolling. "Don't you think you might have been a little rough on her?"

"It's for her own good." The broken, rutted ground was full of buffalo wallows and prairie-dog mounds. Armadillo and rabbit holes added to the problem. Cows and horses were constantly in danger of falling and breaking a leg. But it wasn't just the holes that worried Chase. Horses could easily be spooked by rattlers and other critters. Like it or not, he was responsible for her safety. "It's dangerous terrain out there."

Cookie lifted his rolling pin and set it aside. "So, we're still thinking of Michael, are we?"

Chase gripped his cup. Even after all these years, it still hurt to talk about his brother. Michael's death was a stain on his heart that couldn't be rubbed out. Chase had been only sixteen and his brother a full year younger that fateful day they'd raced their horses. Both had taken a fancy to the prettiest girl in all of Haywire and wanted to ask her to the Christmas dance. Since only one could be her escort, Michael had insisted they race to determine which one got the honor.

Without giving Chase a chance to decline, Michael

had taken off on his horse that long-ago day. Like a danged fool, Chase had followed in pursuit. His brother had gotten a head start and had been at least two horse lengths away when the unthinkable happened. His mount had stepped into a badger hole and broken its leg.

If Chase lived to be a hundred, he would never forget the horror of watching his brother take a dive over the gelding's head. He'd fallen hard onto the rocky ground, breaking his neck. Even now, all these years later, Chase could recall in heartbreaking detail the final seconds of his brother's short life.

Oddly enough, the ramifications of his brother's death continued to this day. Grief had shortened his mother's life and had driven his father to the gaming tables. Financial disaster had followed, which had almost cost his pa the ranch. Had Michael lived, things might have turned out a whole lot differently. Not only for his parents but for him as well. At the very least, he wouldn't be in this sham of a marriage and fighting to save the family legacy.

Chase grimaced. Trust Cookie to bring up the past he'd sooner forget. The old man knew too much, that's for certain. He'd been with the family for more than twenty years. He considered it his constitutional right not only to voice his opinion in family affairs but also to dole out unwanted advice.

Chase didn't want to talk about Michael. Not now, not ever. "It's dangerous out there," he reiterated, hoping to put an end to the discussion.

"All I can say is where cattle and women are concerned, the quicker you mend fences, the better."

Chase frowned. "For someone who never married, you sure profess to know a lot about women."

"It's because I know them that I never married," Cookie said.

With a shake of his head, Chase left the kitchen. He had enough problems without having to endure Cookie's advice. In any case, he was right to worry about Emily's safety.

She'd already had one close encounter with a belled snake. Fortunately, she'd escaped unharmed. Next time, she might not be so lucky.

∾

Later that afternoon, Emily made her way slowly, painfully down the stairs, rubbing her sore back. Every bone in her body ached; every muscle felt like it was on fire.

She paused at the foot of the stairs, surprised to see the little girl, Ginny, hadn't moved from her spot in front of the parlor fireplace since early that morning. It was incredible to think that a child that young could stay in one place for so long.

Why wasn't she in school? They did have schools here in Texas, didn't they?

The building blocks were now stacked high, the tower taller than the girl. Ginny had to stand on tiptoes to reach the top. Again, Emily noticed something strange in the way the child moved. Most children moved spontaneously, but not Ginny. Each action was slow, precise, and measured, like the movements of a rheumatic old woman.

Bending at the waist, Ginny walked her hands over the floor. Finding a block, she rose to her toes and carefully placed it atop the stack. She stood motionless for a moment as if expecting the tower to fall before bending over and repeating the process.

It suddenly dawned on Emily that Ginny was blind. That explained so much, including why she wasn't in school.

Ginny stopped and tilted her head upward. "Is that you, Mrs. Knight?"

"Yes, yes, it is," Emily said. Feeling remiss for not having announced herself, she moved toward the girl. "How did you know it was me?"

"I can see with my ears."

"Can you now?"

"Yes, and I knew it was you by the way you walk."

Hand on her back, Emily felt like she was limping more than walking. "I didn't know I walked in any special way."

"You walk like you have marshmallow feet," the girl said and laughed.

Emily laughed too. "I never heard of anyone having marshmallow feet."

"You smell good too." Ginny placed another block on the tower. "You smell like a flower garden."

"That's my perfume," Emily said.

Ginny picked up another block. "What do you look like? Mama said you look pretty, but she said the sunset looks pretty too. Do you look like a sunset?"

Enchanted by the child, Emily smiled. "'Pretty' just means that something is nice to look at." She picked up a block and placed it in Ginny's hand. "Like you."

Ginny rose on tiptoes to add the block to the top of the tower. "What color is your hair?"

Emily tried to think. How does one describe the world to a sightless child? "My hair is almost the same color as yours. Only a little lighter."

"I know what color that is," Ginny said proudly. "It's the color hot."

"Hot?"

"It's the same color as the sun, and the sun is hot. What color are your eyes?"

"My eyes are blue, same as yours."

"I don't know what blue looks like, but I know what it feels like. It feels like water. Mama said that water is blue if there's a lot of it."

"That's true," Emily said.

"I know what Cookie looks like cuz he let me touch his face. But Mama said it's not polite to touch other people on the face."

"You can touch my face," Emily said. "I won't mind."

"Really?"

Emily smiled at the child's enthusiasm. "Yes, really."

Kneeling, Emily guided Ginny's hand to her face. With a start, Emily recalled the feel of Chase's finger on her cheek. The tenderness of his touch. She must have reacted, for Ginny pulled her hand away.

"Did I hurt you?"

"No, no, of course not. I was thinking of…something else. Here, try again."

This time, she stayed perfectly still while the child ran her fingers the length of her face.

"Your skin feels smooth," Ginny said. "Like the ribbon in my hair. It's not fuzzy like Cookie's." She drew her hand away. "Mr. Knight makes the floor shake when he walks. Does he have a fuzzy face too?"

"You mean does he have a mustache or beard? No, he doesn't."

"Is he pretty like you?"

Emily was momentarily uncertain how to answer. She hadn't really given much thought to his good looks except in the most general terms. "Most men wouldn't like to be called pretty," she said. "They'd much rather be thought of as handsome."

"Is Mr. Knight handsome?" Ginny persisted.

"Oh yes," Emily said. "He is most handsome." Now that she thought about it, she had to admit he was the most handsome man she had ever known.

14

Emily wasn't sure if it was due to the snake episode or something else, but she and Chase seemed to have declared some sort of unspoken truce.

He now knocked before entering her bedchamber. For her part, she began arriving at the stables just after daybreak and didn't object to the long hours in the saddle or the rigorous training he put her through. Though God knew, she had plenty to complain about.

Her only break came on Fridays when Chase cut her lessons short. His reason was always the same—he had business in town.

Business that she suspected went by the name of Cassie Decker.

At first, it didn't bother her that he snuck away to spend time with another woman. Gradually, however, she found herself feeling at loose ends whenever he left the ranch. She wasn't jealous, of course. Jealousy would imply an emotional attachment, and that was out of the question. Her stay on the cattle ranch was temporary, and that was the way she wanted it. Ranch life wasn't the kind of life she'd bargained for. Not by a long shot.

Still, it was odd the way his absences from the ranch affected her. It felt as if he took the very air with him. But that wasn't the only change she'd noticed. Something else was afoot. Something she couldn't put her finger on.

Perhaps it was some sort of physical awareness that required them to keep a certain distance from each other, except in public. Or maybe it was the way their gazes met before one or both quickly looked away. Whatever it was, it kept Emily tense and on edge.

But while she puzzled over her riding instructor, she was surprised to find herself growing increasingly fond of the horse.

With Rusty's help, she had even taken over Daisy's grooming and enjoyed brushing the mare's coat until it was dust-free and shiny. She also liked combing Daisy's mane and tail and taking her horse treats. Never would she think of going to the stables without a carrot or sugar cube tucked in her pocket.

Saddling the horse was another matter. Mexican saddles weighed a ton, and Emily almost always needed help, though she was getting better at it.

After two weeks of lessons, she actually looked forward to the time spent in the saddle. It helped that Daisy was such a responsive horse and needed little prodding. It also helped that Emily had gained what Chase called her riding muscles, though she was still sore and required long hours in a hot tub to ease the pain.

By the third week, she was ready to do more than just ride around the paddock in circles, and she felt increasingly frustrated at Chase's restrictions. Something about the wide-open spaces called to her.

How she longed to ride the range with the wind in her hair and the sun at her back, but Chase was adamantly opposed.

"As you know, there are snakes out there," he'd said after she'd brought it up yet again. "Wolves and panthers are out there too. And bars."

"Bars?"

He looked at her all funny-like before raising curled hands and growling.

"Oh, bayahs," she said, pronouncing bears the Boston way. She was gradually getting used to the way Texans talked, but every so often, she was stumped.

Chase's eyebrows rose for a split second before he burst out laughing.

"What's so funny?" she asked.

"Nothin'," he said, lifting his gaze skyward.

She slanted her head. "Are you making fun of the way I talk?"

He shifted his gaze to her. "No more than you make fun of me."

"I never make fun of you," she said. There was no denying that his way with words had sometimes made her laugh, but never in a critical or unkind way.

Sunlight shimmered in his eyes, and something passed between them—a flame, a spark—catching her off guard. Feeling a quiver run down her spine, she quickly changed the subject.

"How long do I have to keep riding in circles?"

"Until you're ready."

Relieved that the worrisome moment had passed, she quickly resumed her role as difficult pupil. "And when will that be?" she demanded.

"When you have more wrinkles on your horns."

"What's that supposed to mean?"

He shot her a look of impatience. "It means when you have more experience."

She knuckled her waist and glared at him. This time, the eyes looking back held no soft lights or warm flames, only grim determination. Partly out of disappointment, she lashed out at him. "You're not my boss!"

She turned and stomped away.

"My brother died," he called after her.

She stopped midstep and turned. Not sure she'd heard right, she tilted her head. "What?"

"Out there." Chase indicated the area with a toss of his head. "His hoss stepped into a hole." He told her the rest in short, disjointed sentences, each word heavy with grief. "My brother was only fifteen, and I still miss him."

She felt his pain, and her heart went out to him. It was as if a window of his soul had been thrown open, revealing a hidden side of him. He'd seemed so strong, so self-possessed. So utterly in charge of his surroundings. Never had she imagined he kept such grief locked inside.

"I'm…I'm so sorry," she said. His brother's death explained a lot. No wonder Chase was so safety-conscious. Feeling guilty for giving him such a hard time, she moved toward him and placed a hand on his arm. He gazed at her hand for a moment before covering it with his own.

They had trouble at times understanding each other, but not now. The silence that followed was rife with the secret language of the heart.

"I'm sorry for being so difficult," she whispered at last. "I had no idea."

"I don't like to talk 'bout it," he said.

"I can understand that."

"I reckon you can." He studied her. "Are you ever gonna tell me what you're runnin' from?"

The unexpected question made her stiffen and pull her hand away. "I never said I was running."

He opened his mouth to say something, but the sound of a galloping horse drew his attention away from her.

Emily recognized the man as the foreman Boomer. His horse's front hooves left the ground as he shouted. "We lost a couple of calves. Looks like the work of a panther."

Chase didn't give him time to finish speaking before racing to his horse. In no time at all, the two men rode off together, Chase taking the lead.

Surprised by the loneliness that washed over her in the wake of Chase's departure, she sighed and led Daisy to her stall. After lugging the saddle off the horse and wiping her dry, Emily strode back to the main house on foot.

Moments later, she let herself in her room. Puzzled by the cardboard box on the bed, she quickly opened it. Inside was a pair of brown leather boots.

Gasping, she drew one out and ran a finger over the soft leather and examined the floral motif expertly etched onto the shaft.

Kicking off her shoe, she sat on the vanity stool and pulled on the boot. The ease with which her foot slid into the leather depths surprised her. After donning the second boot, she walked around the room. Staring at her feet, she nibbled on a nail. The boots were a perfect fit. How in the world had Chase managed that?

The thought of him measuring her foot while she slept gave her a jolt. He wouldn't!

Unfortunately, she had to wait until supper to question him. He was already seated at the table when she stormed into the dining room and tossed the boots on the floor by his chair.

He gazed at the boots for a moment before lifting his gaze to her. "You don't like them?"

"How did you know my size?"

He arched a dark brow. "How do you think…" He studied her. "Don't tell me you thought that I…" He laughed. "Sorry to disappoint you, but I borrowed one of your slippers."

She drew back. "You…took my slipper?"

He rubbed his chin. "It was either that or sneak into your bed."

Emily felt heat rise to her face. Chase never missed a chance to mention their sleeping arrangements, or lack thereof. Still, he'd done her a favor, and for that, she was grateful.

"Thank you," she said.

He arched an eyebrow. "Do you like them?"

"Yes. I like them. A lot."

He nodded. "No one makes better boots than Shoe-Fly Jones."

"You…you don't have to buy me gifts," she said.

He reached for her boots and handed them to her. "If it makes you feel better, we'll just call them part of our agreement."

The following morning, Emily felt more restless than usual. She wasn't used to having so much time on her hands. Each day seemed forty-eight hours long. Each night seemed endless.

She now understood Chase's refusal to let her ride outside the paddock, but that didn't make it any easier to accept. Had it not been for her lessons, she surely would have gone mad with boredom by now. There just didn't seem to be anything for her to do.

Cookie and Peggy Sue took care of the household chores, and the only books Emily could find in that large, rambling house were about raising cattle.

The one bright spot was Ginny. She was a bright child with a curious mind, and Emily looked forward to spending time with her each afternoon. Sometimes, they sat on the veranda, drinking lemonade and enjoying the shade. Other times, they'd take a walk and Emily would describe as best she could the world around them.

Today, she sought the child out earlier than usual and found her in the parlor with her building blocks. "Want to go for a walk?" she asked.

Ginny's face brightened. "How come you're walking funny?" she asked, jumping to her feet.

"I'm wearing new boots," Emily explained.

"What do they look like?" Ginny asked.

"Well, let's see. They have flowers and leaves etched on them. Here, feel." Emily guided Ginny's hand to her foot. "What do you think?"

"They feel soft," Ginny said. "Do you like them?"

"Yes, I do," Emily said, surprised at how much. The sturdy boots gave her surefooted confidence, and the heels kept her feet from slipping out of the stirrups.

She and Ginny left the house, walking hand in hand. Somehow, Ginny had learned to identify birds from their calls and never failed to amaze Emily with her knowledge. Today was no different.

"That's a warbler," Ginny said as they walked side by side through the prairie grass. After a while, she stopped. "Listen, do you hear it?"

"All I hear are cattle," Emily said. The lowing of cattle was almost constant, and she'd all but managed to tune out the sound.

"The one making all the noise is a Hereford," Ginny said.

"Oh? I thought the ranch ran longhorns."

"It does, but Boomer said they're trying to see how Herefords like it here."

"How do you know it's a Hereford?" Emily asked. "Don't all cattle sound the same?"

"Listen," Ginny said, cocking her head to the side. "A Hereford sounds like it has marbles in its throat."

"Marbles, huh?" Emily laughed.

Ginny lifted her face to the sky, and her mouth formed a perfect circle. "Oh, listen! There's the windmill."

Emily stilled and strained her ears. "I can't hear it. Your hearing must be better than mine."

Ginny looked surprised. "Really? You can't hear the arms turning in the wind?"

"No," Emily said. Shading her eyes, she stared at the stilted windmill in the distance. "It's too far away."

"I asked Beanpole Tom if he would take me up to the top of the windmill, and he said he would one day, when I'm older."

Emily studied Ginny with thoughtful regard. "I noticed that you seem to recognize the cowhands even before they speak."

"That's easy," Ginny said matter-of-factly. "Beanpole Tom smells of tobacco. And Kansas Pete walks funny. Mama says it's because he's bowlegged and his toes point in."

"What about Rusty?" Emily asked. "How do you recognize him?"

Ginny wrinkled her nose. "He smells like he fell in a bottle of perfume."

Emily laughed. "Actually, he smells of shaving lotion."

Ginny lowered her voice to a whisper. "That's because he likes my mama."

Emily's eyes widened in astonishment. "Now how do you know that?"

"I just do," Ginny said with a giggle. "He adds sounds to his words when he speaks to her."

"I believe that's called stuttering," Emily said.

"Why do people stutter?" Ginny asked.

"I guess some people stutter when they feel anxious or unsure of themselves."

Ginny giggled. "Or when they love someone."

Emily laughed. Never had she known someone so perceptive at such a young age. "And when they love someone."

"Sometimes you stutter when you talk to Mr. Knight."

Emily reared back. "Do I?"

"Is that cuz you love him?"

Emily opened her mouth in denial but quickly caught herself. Ginny was still of the age that believed in fairy tales, and Emily wasn't about to spoil it for her.

"He *is* my husband," she said instead and quickly changed the subject. "Let me guess. You recognize Boomer by his voice. But what about the new man, Gabby?"

"He doesn't talk much," Ginny said. "Cookie said he's short in speech and long in silences."

Emily laughed. "That sounds like something Cookie would say."

"I think he's just angry," Ginny said.

"Angry?" Emily stared at the child. "What makes you think that?"

"Mama doesn't speak when she's angry."

"Hmm. That's interesting. I'll have to think about that."

They walked in silence for a moment before Emily asked, "Why do you want to climb a windmill?"

"I want to climb high so I can touch the sky," Ginny said.

Emily smiled. "Right now, I want to touch the ground." She was enchanted by the wildflowers that spread beneath her feet for as far as the eye could see. Nearly overnight, it seemed that a floral carpet had appeared, stretching to the distant hills and beyond.

She picked a blue flower and handed it to Ginny. "Do you know what these flowers are called?"

Ginny didn't even hesitate. "They're called blue-bonnets. They're poisonous to eat, but Beanpole Tom said the cattle don't bother them."

"Bluebonnets," Emily repeated. "What a lovely name. And the blossoms do look like little bonnets. Here, help me pick some, and we'll take them back to the house."

"Hmm, smell," Ginny said, holding the one in her hand up to Emily. "It smells like honey."

Emily sniffed the blossom, surprised to find she could detect less scent than she had imagined.

"Can you smell it?" Ginny asked.

"A little," Emily said.

A short time later, they returned to the house, each with an armful of flowers, which they unloaded on the parlor hearth. Then Emily began the chore of tracking down enough vases to accommodate the cuttings.

"All we have is our fine crystal," Cookie said wryly and opened a cupboard filled with neckless whiskey bottles. "Take what you need."

Emily laughed. "Fine crystal, huh?" Everything on the ranch served a dual and even triple purpose. She took as many as she could carry. "I'll be careful," she said, making a show of handling the bottles as she would her aunt's fine china back home.

Returning to the parlor, she lined the glass containers on the mantel and filled each one with water from a pitcher. With Ginny's help, she arranged the flowers and set the bottles on every possible surface in the sterile parlor. The flowers added a much-needed feminine touch to a room heavy with leather, rough-hewn wood, and stuffed animals.

"It smells like we're still outside," Ginny said, sniffing. She knew somehow that her mother had entered the room even before Emily did. "Oh, look, Mama. Look what we did."

Peggy Sue's gaze lit on Emily, her expression dark. "If you didn't like how I take care of the house, I wish you'd have said something."

Emily blinked in confusion. "I am happy with your work. You do an amazing job." She wasn't just saying that to be kind. The Texas dust was relentless and found its way through even the smallest cracks and crevices. Keeping the house dust-free was a full-time job.

If there was anything Emily wasn't happy about, it was the woman's lack of concern for her child's education. Ginny couldn't count much past twenty, didn't know the alphabet, and couldn't even write her own name.

Now, however, didn't seem like the time to broach the subject. Not with Ginny in the room. Instead, Emily made one last attempt to soothe Peggy Sue's ruffled feathers.

"Please don't take offense. You keep a beautiful house. Mr. Knight…*Mc*Knight and I are most grateful. As for the flowers, I couldn't resist picking them. We don't have many wildflowers where I come from." Boston's gardens were much more formal, every flower carefully cultivated. Here in Texas, nature was permitted freedom to run wild.

Chase entered the room, bringing with him the smell of sunshine, leather, and sage. His piercing blue eyes shifted from Emily to the housekeeper and back again. "What's goin' on?"

"Just a…misunderstanding," Emily said.

He arched an eyebrow. "Oh?"

Peggy Sue lifted her chin. "If you'll excuse me, I

have work to do. Come along, Ginny." She turned, skirt swishing, and quickly left the room. With one hand extended in front, Ginny followed her mother close behind.

Chase waited until they were gone. "What was that about?"

"I'm afraid I got carried away with the flowers," she said, turning the mason jar on the piano to better display an arrangement. Her gaze fell on the daguerre-otype of a young boy, who she now suspected was Chase's late brother, Michael.

"And Peggy Sue didn't approve?" he asked.

Pulling her gaze away from the photograph, Emily turned from the piano. "She thought I was criticizing the way she keeps house."

"I'll talk to her."

"I'd rather you didn't," she said.

His questioning gaze met hers. "Why not?"

"Like I said, it was just a misunderstanding, and I believe we settled it." She didn't want to alienate Peggy Sue any more than she had already. Ginny was a perceptive child and would sense any hostility in the air.

"Very well. If she gives you any more trouble, let me know."

His response surprised her. It was what she would expect from a husband—a *real* husband—protecting his wife's interests.

His gaze drifted downward. "See you're still wearin' your boots."

"Yes, thank you. I l-love them." Catching herself midstutter, she drew in her breath. Thank God, Ginny wasn't around to hear her. She only wished the child hadn't linked stuttering with love.

Chase looked pleased, and the warm feeling that rushed through Emily was both exhilarating and worrisome. She had no intention of staying on the ranch one moment longer than necessary. Ranch life was not for her. It was too isolated. Too confining. Too intense.

Whatever crazy, mixed-up feelings she had for him had to stop.

15

MARCH DRIFTED INTO THE LONGER DAYS OF APRIL AND the second month of calving season.

Work demanded most of Chase's attention, and Emily saw little of him. It hadn't bothered her before, and she was surprised that it bothered her now.

How was it possible to miss someone for whom she had so little regard? But miss him, she did. It wasn't something she wanted to admit, but what else would explain the way he dominated her thoughts? Or why she constantly listened for his footsteps. His voice.

When asked why he spent so many evenings in his office, he told her he had bookkeeping to do, bills to pay, correspondence to catch up on. She didn't want to think that he was avoiding her, but it certainly seemed that way. Could a ranch really command that much paperwork?

Then, of course, there were his weekly trips into town. She tried not to picture him and Mrs. Decker together, but it was hard not to. It was harder still to reconcile her depression just thinking about it.

Many were the nights that she dined alone, and it

was often late before she heard Chase tiptoeing past the foot of her bed on the way to his own room.

Her loneliness might have been easier to bear had she not been subjected to sympathetic looks from Cookie.

Such were her thoughts that day as she left the stables, so she didn't notice the strange black horse tied to the railing until she reached the house. Did they have company? She got her answer the moment she climbed the steps to the porch and came face-to-face with Chase's stepbrother.

He sat on a wicker chair rolling a cigarette and greeted her with a sardonic look. The two men shared similar dark hair but otherwise looked nothing alike. Something about him made her think of a snake-oil salesman, and she quickly put up her guard.

"If you're looking for Chase, he won't be back until after sundown," she said.

"Actually, you're the one I came to see."

Eyebrows arched, Emily stared at him. "I can't imagine why."

"I have a proposition for you. A *business* proposition."

Curious now, Emily waited for him to explain.

"I know that this is not the marriage you planned. You expected to marry another," he said. "Just as Chase expected to marry Mrs. Decker."

She studied him with wary regard, and her mouth ran dry. She suspected that Chase still met Mrs. Decker in town every week, and it bothered her. She didn't want it to, but it did. "Go on."

"If you leave the marriage, I'll make certain you are well rewarded."

She frowned. "I don't know what you mean."

Turning his attention to the newly rolled cigarette in his hand, he licked the edge of the paper and sealed it before sticking it in his mouth. "I'm prepared to sell a fourth of the cattle to pay you to leave."

"Since the ranch belongs to my husband, I'd think you'd have a hard time selling his cattle."

Royce paused to strike a match and light his cigarette. He took a long drag and blew out a plume of smoke. "That's where you come in. You could end this sham of a marriage. As the only legitimately married heir, the ranch would then revert to me and... You know the rest."

"My marriage is not a sham," she said. "Chase and I...care for one another."

He scoffed. "You and I both know that's not true. You didn't even know each other before exchanging vows." He took another puff of his cigarette before continuing. "I ask that you give my offer careful consideration. End this marriage, and you'll be, if not a rich woman, a comfortable one."

Irritated that he thought she could be so easily manipulated, her nostrils flared. "Not interested."

His eyes glittered. "End this marriage, and I'll sell a third of the cattle to pay you."

"I must ask you to leave. Now!"

He took another drag of his cigarette. "You strike a hard bargain."

She turned toward the house and reached for the doorknob, glaring at him over her shoulder. "I believe I asked you to leave."

He stood, hat in hand. "You'll be sorry," he said. "Don't say you weren't warned."

Emily waited that night for Chase to enter her room to tell him of Royce's visit. It was late, almost eleven, and lines of exhaustion etched his face. He also seemed surprised to see her still awake.

He stood facing her from the other side of the bed, the mattress stretching between them like a vast desert that defied crossing.

"Your stepbrother offered me money to end the marriage," she said.

He stared at her, his face a mask of disbelief. "What?"

Though she doubted it needed repeating, she said it again. "He claims that he's now married too." She told him of Royce's plan to pay her from the sale of cattle. "I told him no."

His eyebrows shot up. "No! You said no?" He sounded incredulous. "Why would you turn down that much money?" His forehead creased. "You have no feelin' for the ranch. You and I both know you're not cut out to be a rancher's wife."

"I gave you my word I would stay for the allotted time, and that's what I intend to do."

His gaze bored into her. "Is that the only reason you turned Royce down?" he asked. "Because of your word?"

"Yes," she said and took a deep breath. "I own nothing of value. Not a dowry, nor any marketable skills." It still rankled that her college degree gained her no favors in landing a job. "The only thing they haven't taken…" She stopped herself and began again. "The only thing I have is my word."

He stared at her long and hard. "Who are 'they'?"

"What?"

"You said, there was one thing they hadn't taken."

She looked away. "It's not important."

"If'n it wasn't important, you wouldn't have mentioned it." His voice dropped. "Emily, look at me." He waited for her to lift her gaze before continuing. "I know you're runnin' from somethin'. I just want you to know that whatever it is, you're safe here for as long as you stay. I won't let anyone or anythin' harm you."

Both surprised and touched by his words, she felt a stirring in her chest. Her eyes burned with the threat of tears, and a lump rose in her throat. "T-thank you," she whispered and mentally kicked herself for the stutter.

He held her gaze for a full moment, the smoldering depths of his eyes stirring some yawning need within her. Clutching her hands to her pounding chest, she fought to maintain control.

"I'll always be grateful for your help," he said. "Because of you, my family legacy is safe." He shrugged in apology. "Not everyone understands why that's so important to me. My grandfather started this town. They even wanted to call the town McKnight, but he said it didn't sound Texan enough. He's the one who came up with the name Haywire."

She smiled at the fondness she heard in his voice. "I understand why you want to protect his memory."

"Even now? After all the trouble it's caused you?"

She moistened her lips, surprised at the sudden need to confide. "Someone…stole my family's good name," she said, choosing her words carefully so as not to reveal too much. "This…person turned everything that my father worked for into something bad, and there was nothing I could do about it. I know this makes no sense, but helping you save your family legacy helps with the pain of not being able to save my own."

His gaze softened. "It makes sense to me." He moved around the bed and held his hand out to her. "I'll always be indebted to you. If there's anythin' you need or want…?"

She stared at his offered hand, surprised that what she needed and wanted at that moment was to sink into his arms. But she knew—sensed—it wouldn't end there, and that was the danger. Already, the ranch was like a vine, entangling her in its tendrils. Leaving would not be easy. Consummating what was now only a shell of a marriage—and turning it into something more—would make leaving that much harder, if not altogether impossible.

It took every bit of strength she could muster to fight the temptation of placing her hand in his to embrace the comfort he offered. To hold and be held by him.

"That's very kind of you," she said, moving away.

If he was disappointed, he didn't let it show on his face. He simply dropped his hand to his side. "Anything you need, just ask."

She nodded her thanks and, not trusting herself in his presence a moment longer than necessary, murmured, "Good night."

He nodded once and crossed to his room. "I mean it, Emily," he said, pausing at the doorway. "You're safe here," he said again and ducked through the black curtains.

Sinking onto the edge of the bed, Emily clamped her mouth shut. His words echoed in her heart. *You're safe here.*

Oh God. She wanted so much to call him back but didn't dare. Theirs was a marriage of convenience, and she had best not forget it.

Before she gave herself fully and completely to a man, she wanted more than a business arrangement. Much more. She wanted to know without a doubt that the man she married for real loved her with his whole heart and soul.

She'd been hurt once—terribly, terribly hurt. Never would she allow herself to be hurt like that again. Whatever pleasure Chase's arms might have offered could never compensate for the pain that was bound to follow if she surrendered to one weak moment.

Tonight, she'd made the right choice. She'd passed on temporary comfort for long-term gain. She only wished she felt better about it.

In the privacy of his room, Chase pulled off a boot, cursing beneath his breath. He hadn't wanted to leave her. She'd opened up a bit about her past. Not much, but some. Enough to tell him that she trusted him—at least a little.

And that was what worried him. He'd been so close—so very, very close—to trying to turn this sham of a marriage into something real and meaningful. But that would have been an illusion at best.

Ranch life wasn't for her. She tried to make the best of things, but he could see how much she struggled at times. He could see it in her eyes whenever the subject of cattle came up, hear it in her voice.

Sometimes, he'd catch her staring into space as if she imagined living an entirely different life. At times, he'd hear her telling Ginny about the theater she had once attended, the fancy balls and parties she had once enjoyed.

Sure, after a rocky start, she'd learned to handle a horse. As for the rest, she had no interest. Not that he blamed her. Ranching wasn't for everyone. It was a tough life. Many had tried to raise cattle or horses and failed. One local rancher had married an Englishwoman who had grown so despondent that he'd had to send her back to her country. She couldn't handle the isolation.

Sighing, he pulled off his other boot. Knowing that Emily would never be happy here on the ranch—never be happy with him or their marriage—bothered him in ways he didn't fully understand. Nor did he know why the memory of her laugh, her voice, and her indomitable spirit followed him even out on the range.

She had turned down Royce's offer. That made Chase feel even more indebted to her, and that was a problem. He tossed his boot down. Gratitude was a lousy reason to want someone, but where Emily was concerned, it didn't take much to tempt him. A smile. The way she turned her head or wrinkled her nose. Anything would do.

Still, he didn't know what shocked him more—his stepbrother's underhanded offer or Emily's refusal to take it.

She said she was a woman of her word, and she'd proven it. It seemed only right that he show his appreciation in some way. But how?

After a few minutes of racking his brain, something occurred to him. She'd been cooped up on the ranch. No wonder she had seemed restless and bored of late. No doubt she missed the teas and parties she'd talked about. Missed whatever Bostonian women did to fill their days.

It was time to start socializing as husband and wife. Not only was it bound to please her, but it would send a message to Royce that any effort on his part to break them up would be a waste of time.

Convinced he was on the right trail, Chase decided that attending a worship service would be a good place to start.

He was tempted to tell her his plan at once but stopped short of ducking through the black curtains to her room. He didn't trust himself around her. The temptation to take her in his arms grew stronger with each passing day, but never had it been as strong as it had been tonight.

That was another reason why socializing might be a good idea. Having more people around might help defuse the tension he felt whenever they were alone.

For that reason, he forced himself to wait until the following morning when she arrived at the stables to tell her his plan. "It's time to introduce you to the townsfolk," he announced without preamble.

Once he'd formally introduced her around, invitations to social functions were bound to follow.

Certain she'd welcome the news, he continued

without waiting for her response. "On Sunday, we'll ride to the gospel...uh...church." He didn't trust her yet to ride that distance by herself, but he was relatively certain she could make the trip with him by her side.

Instead of looking pleased as he'd hoped, she stared at him with a look of dismay. "*Ride* to church," she gasped, as if he'd suggested some ghastly deed. "In my Sunday-go-to-meeting clothes?"

A vision popped into his head of her dressed in a fancy frock with a straight skirt and one of those ridiculous padded seats in back. What were they called? Bristles? Bustles? He much preferred her in her present attire, her feminine form left in its natural state the way the good Lord intended.

"What's wrong with what you're wearin'?" It seemed like a reasonable enough question. So why in blazes did she look so downright horrified?

"Wrong? You want me to go to church dressed like...like this?"

"This is Texas, not Boston. People here don't put that much stock in what a woman wears. Long as she's decent."

"Fortunately, we're more *civilized* in Boston," she said.

Chase burst out laughing. He couldn't help himself. Emily sure did have a way of turning the tables on him. Since she seemed disinclined to join him in mirth, he grew serious. "So, what are you sayin'?"

"I'm saying that I won't be attending church in men's trousers!"

His gaze traveled down the length of her. No men's trousers, as she called them, had ever looked so intriguing. "Then wear your stovepipe skirt," he said. "Just remember to yank it up to unprecedented heights, or you'll never get yourself in the saddle." With that, he turned and walked away, chuckling to himself.

16

FOLLOWING HER MORNING RIDE AROUND THE PAD-
dock, Emily headed for the kitchen for a cool drink,
her conversation with Chase very much on her mind.

She knew people did things differently in Texas,
but her dear, sweet mother would turn over in her
grave at the thought of her daughter walking into a
place of worship wearing something as scandalous as
a split skirt.

Cookie poured her a glass of lemonade. A rolled red
kerchief was tied around his forehead. Two gray plaits
ran down his back like train tracks.

She accepted the cool drink with murmured
thanks. The Texas heat and humidity made it hard to
quench her thirst.

He set the pitcher on the counter. "I happened to
see you talking to Royce yesterday. He giving you
trouble?" Before she had a chance to respond, he
answered for her. "Let me guess. He offered to pay
you to break up your marriage." He studied her. "So
whatcha tell him?"

His bold question surprised her. In Boston,

employees were much more circumspect. Here, the hired help acted more like family. "Actually, he offered to pay me for leaving. I told him I had no intention of doing such a thing," she said and took a sip of her beverage.

"That's my girl."

She studied Cookie over the brim of her glass. She doubted he was fooled by the little charade she and Chase played out for his benefit.

She set her empty glass on the counter, and he promptly refilled it.

"Heard you and Peggy Sue had a falling-out," he said.

She sighed. It seemed as though his curiosity had no end. "It was just a misunderstanding."

"Peggy Sue don't mean to be difficult. She's just set in her ways."

Emily raised an eyebrow. Peggy Sue was too young to be set in her ways. "What happened to her husband?" she asked.

Before answering her question, Cookie glanced at the open doorway as if to check for eavesdroppers. As an added precaution, he lowered his voice. "Well, it's like this. Ginny was a babe in the bushes."

Emily stared at him. "I'm sorry…"

"That's just a delicate way of saying the parents weren't hitched."

"Oh." Emily didn't know what to say. Such a thing would be cause for scandal in Boston. If Cookie's hushed voice was any indication, it was here too. No wonder Peggy Sue was so reticent. "Do you know who Ginny's father is?"

"His name is Joe Turner, and he worked here on

the ranch. Peggy Sue tracked him down to break the news. She marched into the bunkhouse like nobody's business and hauled him out of his cot. You never heard such a row in your life. The boss heard the commotion and was fit to be tied. He don't take kindly to a man shirking his responsibilities, so he gave Joe an ultimatum. Either he had to do what's right and take care of his family or lose his job."

"Chase did that?"

"He sure enough did. Unfortunately, by then, Ginny was already a couple of months old. When Joe found out his daughter was blind, he wanted to put her away in an asylum. He said that was the only way he'd marry Peggy Sue. When she refused to part with her daughter, he vanished quicker than a keg o' cider at a barn raisin'."

Emily felt bad for Peggy Sue and her daughter. "What kind of man would desert his family like that?"

Cookie shook his head. "No man I'd want to know, that's for sure. Fortunately, when the boss found out what Joe had done, he insisted Peggy Sue come work for him. That was nine years ago, and she's been here ever since."

"That was a nice thing Mr....my husband did."

Cookie leaned his back against the counter, arms folded across his chest. "That's just the way he is. He takes care of people. Most ranchers send all their good beef to market and feed their cowhands meat from their oldest cows. The boss don't think like that. He makes sure his men have only the best."

Cookie wasn't the only one who thought highly of Chase. She'd noticed that all the cowhands seemed to have the highest regard for him.

"Chase told me about his brother," she said. "How he died."

Cookie's gaze faded as if traveling back in time. "That was a sad day. Old Man McKnight was never the same after his son's death. Neither was his wife. If you ask me, grief hastened both their deaths. As for the boss…" He heaved a sigh.

"What about him?" Emily asked, surprised to find herself wanting to learn everything she could about the man she had accidentally married.

"He took it bad. Real bad. He left the ranch and went off on a yearlong bender. Spent more time in jail than not. That didn't sit right with his pa."

"The ranch means everything to Chase," she said. "I can't imagine him leaving it. Even for a short time."

Cookie shrugged. "Like I said, the boss took his brother's death hard. After that, Ole Man McKnight didn't trust him to do the right thing. That's why he wrote his will the way he done. He wanted to make sure that whoever inherited the ranch would stick around when the chips were down. Not run off like Chase done that one year."

Emily frowned. "But he was only what? Sixteen at the time. And he'd just lost his brother."

"'Round here, a boy is expected to act like a man by the time he's ten."

Emily shook her head. At ten, she was still playing with dolls. Would she ever get used to the ways of the west? She sipped her drink thoughtfully. "Why does Chase blame himself for his brother's death? He's not the one who started the race."

"Guilt is like one of those fancy hats some women

insist on wearin'." Hands over his head, he mimicked the feathers that made up fashionable headgear. "They get worn even if they make no sense."

Cookie's comparison of hats to guilt made her laugh.

He reached for the pitcher. "More lemonade?"

"No, thank you." She emptied her glass and carried it over to the sink. "About Ginny…" she said, changing the subject. "Why isn't she in school?"

"Peggy Sue tried that, but it didn't work out. The schoolmarm had no idea what to do with a blind child, and Ginny came home in tears more often than not."

"It must be tough raising a child like that alone," Emily said. "What about books?"

"Books?"

"I'd like to read to her, but the only books in the house are about cattle raising."

"I've gotta couple of cookbooks you can read to her, if you like."

Emily laughed. "I'm sure they all have thrilling plots."

"They do," Cookie said with a look of mischief. "You never know how one of them recipes is gonna turn out."

"I'm not sure that a nine-year-old would appreciate the suspense. Is there a lending library in town?"

"'Fraid not. Can't help you there."

Emily chewed on that a moment before a smile curved her mouth. "That's okay," she said with a mysterious smile. "I think I know who can."

Like a woman on a mission, Emily strode across the yard to the stables, anxious to get started. Daisy hung her head over the stall door in greeting, and Emily petted her velvet-soft muzzle.

She was just about to let herself into Daisy's stall when she noticed Rusty standing motionless by the barn's open window in back. Something in the way he held himself stoked her curiosity.

Moving closer, she stood on tiptoes and peered over his shoulder. From where he stood, he had a perfect view of the clothesline and Peggy Sue beating a rug.

"I'm taking—"

Rusty jumped at the sound of her voice, and she quickly apologized. "I'm sorry. I didn't mean to startle you."

"You didn't," he said, moving away from the window, his face red. Apparently thinking an explanation was in order, he added, "I was just...eh...getting some fresh air."

Smiling to herself, Emily took another glance at the housekeeper before following him. Ginny was right— Rusty had taken a fancy to her mother.

"I'm going for a ride," she said.

He stopped in front of Daisy's stall. "I'll go with you."

"That won't be necessary."

He frowned. "If anything happens to you, the boss will have my hide."

"Don't worry. I'll make sure he knows it was my idea and you had nothing to do with it." If Chase thought her good enough to ride to church, surely she could ride to town.

Rusty afforded her a worried look but didn't argue

or try to talk her out of it. Instead, he saddled Daisy and led the mare outside.

Emily grabbed the saddle horn and slipped her foot into the stirrup. With one smooth movement, she lifted herself astride the saddle. The ease by which she mounted made her smile. Now that she'd conquered her fear of horses, she felt like she could conquer anything.

Rusty handed her the reins. "If I didn't know better, ma'am, I'd think you were born in a saddle."

After enduring Chase's criticism for so long, she appreciated the compliment. "Thank you, Rusty," she said and scanned the terrain.

A couple of horsemen were rounding up cattle in the far distance on the sloping grasslands, but none appeared to be Chase. The air was still, and all looked calm and peaceful.

It was the perfect day for a ride.

There're snakes out there. Wolves and panthers are out there too. And bars.

With the thought came a sudden loss of confidence, and her hands tightened on the reins. "Is there a chance I might meet up with wild animals?" she asked.

Rusty shook his head. "Nah. They don't usually come out this time of day. Too hot."

"What about snakes?" The rattler she'd met up with hadn't seemed to be bothered by the heat.

"Belled snakes like to hide in rocks, so stay on open ground and they won't give you any trouble."

His assurances were encouraging, but still, she hesitated.

"Everything okay, ma'am?"

"Yes, yes. Everything's fine... Eh... I just need to know... Which way to Haywire?"

His eyebrows vanished beneath the brim of his hat. "You're riding all that way?"

She shushed him. "I am, but don't tell anyone." Giving him a knowing look, she added, "You keep my secret, and I'll keep yours."

"My se—" He stared at her, and his face turned scarlet. Without another word, he pointed a finger, indicating the way to town.

Chase adjusted his spyglass and scanned the terrain all the way to the rolling hills in the far distance. More cattle had been found missing, and he could ill afford to keep losing them. He and his men had tracked down the panther, but the rustlers defied capture.

Next to him, Foxhound held himself still as a statue. Intelligent brown eyes stared out from a square, rugged face. A headband was wrapped around his forehead, and his glossy black hair fell down his back to his waist.

His Cherokee name was Oukonunaka, meaning white owl. The cowhands had given him his current moniker, Foxhound, as a salute to his tracking skills. It was also a whole lot easier to remember.

"See anything?" Foxhound asked.

It was a joke between them. Foxhound had no need for a spyglass. His keen eyes never missed a thing, neither near nor far. He read nature like other people read books. A cropped piece of grass, an overturned leaf, a displaced pebble—all told a story that only he could interpret. It was a skill Chase had come to value and admire.

Chase closed the spyglass with a snap. "I'd say those hombres are long gone by now."

Foxhound dropped to his haunches, his sharp eyes focused on the mottled ground. Though he favored the usual cowboy uniform of California pants and bib-front shirts, he still preferred his flat-soled moccasins to the rawhide boots worn by Chase and the rest of his men.

"Looks like there were three of 'em," Foxhound said, pointing. "Two in high-heeled boots, one in low."

Chase followed Foxhound's finger, but all he saw were cattle tracks. "How long ago?"

Foxhound straightened and narrowed his gaze to the distance. "I'd say six, maybe eight hours ago. Since it's just the two of us, we could probably catch them in half that time."

"You said there were three of them," Chase said and swatted away a fly.

Foxhound grinned. "Sounds like a fair fight to me." He studied his boss. "So, what's the plan?"

Chase lifted his hat and swiped his damp forehead with the back of his hand. "Let's follow the trail a piece. Maybe you can pick up another clue or two. Somethin' we can give the sheriff."

Laughing, Foxhound shook his head.

"What's so funny?"

"You." Foxhound gave him a knowing look. "Wasn't that long ago you said that no woman could change you. Here, you've only been married what? A couple of weeks, and already you're a changed man."

Chase settled his hat in place. "Don't know what you're talkin' about."

"Time was that you would have followed those hombres to the four winds and back. It was only last year that you trailed the Davidson gang for days. We almost had to send a search party for you."

Chase shuddered at the memory. "Yeah, well, maybe I learned my lesson." For three days, he'd fought the wind, rain, and bitter cold. Still, the bad guys had gotten away. The last he'd heard, they were still creating havoc on the other side of the border. "My trackin' days are over."

"Maybe," Foxhound said, clearly unconvinced. "Or maybe you just don't want to give up that soft bed of yours in your lady's arms."

Chase spun around and headed for his horse. He didn't want to talk about a soft bed. And he sure in blazes didn't want to discuss Emily or her arms.

"Let's get goin'. Time's a-wastin.'"

"As you wish, *Nugvwayusadegi*."

Chase shook his head. In the Cherokee language, even a four-letter word like *boss* was a mouthful.

They rode in silence for an hour, stopping on occasion to allow Foxhound to dismount and check the ground. Squatting, he'd poke at a turd with a stick or check the remains of an old campfire.

When they reached a water hole, he grimaced. "Looks like they were joined by two more men."

"That's what I was afraid of," Chase said. Cow thieves were a lazy bunch. They didn't want the work of raising cattle. Their only interest was in making a fast buck. His beeves had probably already changed hands. "The rustlin' problem sure has gotten worse."

"Blame it on the stock raisers up north," Foxhound said in his thoughtful, slow way. "They got rid of their rustling problem by chasing the thieves down our way."

Chase scanned the horizon. Up ahead, the rugged terrain was covered with little more than sagebrush, prickly pear cacti, and limestone hills. "I'm headin' back."

"I'll catch up with you later," Foxhound said. "I just want to take a look ahead a piece."

Chase nodded. "Watch your step. See you back at the ranch." He turned his horse and cut across the arid ground to the road. The dirt road was quicker and kinder to his horse. Since he wasn't wearing chaps, it was kinder to his legs as well.

Around a mile later, something white in the middle of the road caught his eyes. He reined in his horse. It sure did appear to be a lady's handkerchief, and a closer look confirmed it. Only part of the embroidered initial was visible. Even so, it looked familiar. *Too* familiar.

Hoping he was wrong, Chase dismounted and swooped the handkerchief off the ground. It was a fine linen one edged in lace, but it was the embroidered *E* that made him suck in his breath. So how did Emily's handkerchief get way out here? Unless…

Tucking the handkerchief in his vest pocket, he quickly mounted and pressed his legs against his horse's side. "Giddup."

Less than a half hour later, he pulled up in front of

the ranch house. Tethering his horse to the hitching post, he ran up the porch steps and into the house.

"Emily!" he called. He took the stairs two at a time, only to find her bedroom empty. Racing down the stairs again, he was greeted by Cookie.

"What's goin' on?" Cookie asked, wiping his hands on his apron. "Where's the fire?"

"Have you seen my wife?"

"Not since mornin'." Cookie frowned. "Something wrong?"

"That's what I want to know." Chase stormed through the house, checking each room in turn. He found Peggy Sue and her daughter in the laundry room, but they hadn't seen Emily either.

The answer to his question came the moment he reached the stables. Even before he had a chance to question Rusty, he spotted Daisy's empty stall.

17

THE HAYWIRE BOOK AND SWEET SHOP WAS LARGER and better stocked than Emily could have imagined or even hoped for.

The sweet smell of candy had greeted her along with a riot of bells when she'd walked through the door. Bright and cheery as a circus, the colorful shop offered a startling contrast to the crudely built structures that made up the town. It was like walking into another world.

Whirligigs spun from the ceiling, and colorful signs plastered the walls. Tempting sweets of every color and description were artfully displayed behind a shiny glass counter.

The smell of chocolate, mint, and vanilla made Emily's mouth water. The only other customer in the shop glanced at her before turning his attention back to the dime novel in his hand.

A young woman with flaming-red hair greeted her from behind the counter. "Howdy, there," she said cheerfully. "You must be new in town."

"I am," Emily said and debated on how to introduce herself. She still had a hard time using her married name.

"My name's Kate," the proprietor said.

"Emily," she said, following Kate's example.

"Well, howdy, Emily. So, what brings you to Haywire?"

Emily hesitated. "I'm...actually...eh...Mrs. McKnight," she said.

Kate's face lit up. "Oh, I'm so happy to meet you. When I heard Chase had taken a wife, I couldn't believe my ears. Didn't think anyone could pull him away from his cattle. Congratulations. Don't know how you managed it, but I'm sure there are a lot of women in town who envy you."

Kate's friendly manner and lighthearted chatter reminded Emily how much she missed her female companions back home.

"So, what can I do for you today?" Kate asked.

Emily's gaze dropped to the tempting display of candy behind the glass case. "Do you have any children's books?"

Kate flashed a smile. "As a matter of fact, we just recently started stocking them." She walked around the counter and led Emily over to the book section.

The male customer glanced up from the book in his hand but said nothing. His frock coat and derby hat suggested he was from out of town, probably from somewhere back East.

"You'll like that," Kate told him approvingly, indicating the book he held. "You can't go wrong with a Kit Carson tale."

The man grunted and continued thumbing through his selection.

"Here we are," Kate said, drawing Emily's attention to the bookshelves. Dime novels took up most of the space, but one shelf was devoted to books for the young.

"Is there a special someone you wish to purchase a book for?" Kate asked.

"Yes, a young friend. Maybe you know her. Her name is Ginny."

Kate's smile brightened. "I know Ginny. Haven't seen her for a while. She used to come in with her class. She always asked for peppermint drops. How is she?"

"She's fine."

"Tell her I said hello." Kate fingered the covers as she scanned the books. "How old is she now? Eight?"

"She's nine."

"Nine, eh? Then she would probably love the illustrations in this book," Kate said, handing her a copy of *The Light Princess*.

Emily flipped through the pages. The illustrations were beautiful, no question. Unfortunately, Ginny would not be able to see them. "Were you aware that Ginny is blind?"

"Oh, that's right," Kate said with a look of apology. "I forgot. She never acted blind. I once started to fill her bag with the wrong candy, and somehow she knew."

"It's amazing how much she knows," Emily said.

Kate pulled another volume off the shelf and handed it to Emily. It was a copy of *The Swiss Family Robinson*. "I think she'll like this."

Emily smiled. "Oh, I remember this story! It made me want to live in a tree house."

Kate laughed. "Me too. I can hardly wait till my son is old enough for me to read it to him."

"You have children?" Emily asked.

"I have a son. That's one of the reasons the store now includes children's books."

"And you run this shop alone?"

"Oh, no. My husband and I run it together, and we have a part-time employee."

Emily had heard that women had more freedom in the west than they had back East. That was one of the reasons she'd chosen to come to Texas. In Boston, society frowned upon married women working outside the home. It was thought to reflect poorly on the husband. The man of the house was expected to be the sole provider for his family.

"Perhaps Ginny would also like this book," Kate said, picking up a copy of *Five Little Peppers and How They Grew*. "It's a customer favorite."

"I'll take all three," Emily said. She had grown up in a house full of books. Only now did she realize what a luxury that had been.

Kate gathered the books in her arms and walked behind the counter. While she wrapped the purchases, Emily perused the tempting sweets. "I'd also like a half pound of peppermint drops," she said.

"I'm running a special today on Chase's favorite rock candy," Kate said.

Aware, suddenly, of how little she knew about her husband, Emily felt remiss, though she didn't know why. As his wife in name only, she wasn't obligated to learn his likes and dislikes. Still, she couldn't deny that everything she learned about him made her want to learn more.

"I'll take some rock candy too." She hadn't planned on giving Chase a gift, but the friendly store proprietor might think it odd if she failed to do so.

Emily watched Kate fill her order. "Do you…know Chase well?"

"Oh, sure," Kate said, shoveling peppermint drops into a paper sack. "Our families go way back. His father and my uncle were good friends. Of course, he still stops by every Friday to say hello and pick up his favorite candy."

Emily's gaze sharpened as she studied Kate's face. Kate knew about Chase's trips to town each week? Did she also know about Mrs. Decker? Did everyone?

Clamping her mouth shut, Emily watched Kate add a scrap of paper into the bag. "What's that you added?"

A mysterious smile crossed Kate's face. "Just a few words of wisdom. It's done in fun, but maybe it will put a smile on your face. A new bride like you shouldn't look so…serious."

"Oh, I… It's just adjusting to a new life."

A look of sympathy crossed Kate's face. "Getting used to married life is hard enough, but you have it doubly hard. Having to get used to a new town and all. I'm sure you must find some of our ways rather…odd."

"Not odd. Just different. Women here seem to have so much more…freedom."

"Only because we demand it," Kate said and laughed.

Emily laughed too. She liked Kate, liked her a

lot, and wished they could be friends. Unfortunately, friendship required openness, and that was something Emily could ill afford. She had too many secrets, the terms of her marriage being just one of them.

Kate jotted numbers on an invoice and handed it over the counter. "Give my best to Chase."

"I will," Emily said and paid her with the exact right change.

"If you ever have need for some female company, let me know."

Emily gathered her packages. Wishing with all her heart she could take Kate up on the offer, she smiled. "Thank you."

Turning, Emily noticed the male customer watching her, an odd look on his face, though he tried not to look obvious. A cold shiver ran down her spine, and she quickly left the shop.

18

CHASE WAS HALFWAY TO TOWN BEFORE HE SPOTTED A horse in the distance. Reining in Rebel, he rose in the saddle and pulled out his spyglass.

It sure did look like Daisy, but he was too far away to be sure. One thing was clear: it was without a rider. Hoping it wasn't Daisy but fearing the worse, he returned his spyglass to his saddlebag and spurred his horse forward with a shout. The thought of Emily lying injured made his heart race with anxiety.

His worst fears were soon confirmed. It was Daisy, all right, and there was no sign of Emily.

Reaching his destination, he pulled on his reins and slid out of the saddle, calling her name. Frantic with worry, he failed to see her until she spoke.

"Are you trying to raise the dead?" she asked, sitting a short distance away in a spot of grass she'd managed to find in the shade of a windmill.

His relief at seeing her quickly turned to anger. "What the devil do you think you're doin'? I told you you weren't ready to ride alone."

"Don't worry! As you can see, I'm perfectly all right." Her eyes flashed. "Your *precious* ranch is safe."

Irritated that the ranch that brought them together remained a sore spot between them, he spoke through gritted teeth. "That doesn't make it right. It's dangerous out here. It's no place for a woman who's been mollycoddled and—"

"Mollycoddled," Emily gasped, shooting to her feet. "Is that what you think?"

"What else would you call a woman who refuses to follow simple directions?"

She glared at him, hands at her waist. "I may be many things, but *mollycoddled* isn't one of them!"

Grimacing, Chase drew in his breath and exhaled slowly. He hadn't meant to insult her. Never that. Nor did he want to argue. But he took any disregard of the ranch personally, and that made him want to strike back. It was unfair to expect her to share his feelings for the ranch, but he couldn't seem to help himself. Having poured blood and sweat into the land, he considered the ranch an extension of himself. Any rejection of it was a rejection of him.

Fighting for control, he lowered his voice. "So, what *are* you doin' out here?"

His question brought a frown to her forehead. "I'm waiting for Daisy to calm down."

Chase glanced at the grazing horse. If the mare was any more relaxed, she would topple over. "Calm down?"

"She's thrown a shoe. Naturally, she's upset."

Moving closer to Daisy, he noticed what looked like a white sock on a front hoof. A closer look revealed a lace bandage that could only have come from feminine underpinnings.

"I couldn't get the nail out," Emily explained. "I

went to ask for help at the house there, but it seems to be deserted."

He nodded. "That used to be the Circle R ranch, but the place went into foreclosure. It's one of many deserted ranches around here."

"Because of the drought?" she asked.

"That and a greedy loan company." Whenever he thought about the number of pioneer families that had lost properties due to bad loans, his anger flared. Now, however, was not the time to dwell on the past.

Crouching down, Chase ran his hand the length of Daisy's leg. The mare flinched when he touched the hoof.

Emily squatted by his side. "I wrapped her hoof so she wouldn't catch it on the other leg."

He nodded approval. "I thought you didn't know anythin' about horses."

"I know about injuries," she said, sounding defensive.

"You did good," he said.

"Whoa!" she said, standing. "Is that a compliment?"

He glanced up at her. "Yes, but don't make me regret it." Lately, Emily had looked pale and listless, but today, her eyes sparkled, and her cheeks were rosy as a ripe peach. The ride had done her a world of good. Or maybe it was just that she'd enjoyed going against his wishes. "You still haven't said what you're doin' out here."

"I rode to town to purchase books for Ginny."

"Books?" He raised an eyebrow. "You do know that she's—"

"I plan on reading to her."

He studied her for a moment before turning his

attention back to Daisy. As he unwound the strip of soft fabric from the mare's hoof, he caught a pleasant whiff of lavender that did nothing for his peace of mind.

Standing, he walked over to his horse and reached into his saddlebags for the pliers kept there for just such an occasion.

After pulling the nail out, he examined the hoof for other nails or chunks of metal. Finding none, he rewound the cloth around the horse's hoof.

Emily ran her hands along Daisy's neck. "Will she be okay?"

"She'll be fine, but I'd rather you didn't ride her. I'll pony her back." He tilted his head. "Don't worry. We still have my horse, and I'm willin' to share." Noticing her disproving frown, he added, "It's either that or you'll have to ride a shank's mare."

She glanced around. "I don't see any other horses."

He sighed. Talking to Emily was like talking to a foreigner. "A shank's mare means to walk."

Emily tossed her head. "And that's exactly what this mollycoddled woman intends to do!"

Chase raised an eyebrow. Apparently, his ill-advised comment had hit a nerve. Now it was up to him to make amends. "It's a couple of miles back to the house," he said gently. "Your boots aren't fully broken in yet. Trust me, you'll find sixteen hands preferable to two feet."

She stalked past him. "I'll take my chances," she called over her shoulder.

Watching her, he shook his head and muttered beneath his breath, "Stubborn woman."

He pulled the rope from his saddle and, after

attaching one end to Daisy's halter, mounted his own horse. Holding Rebel's reins with one hand and the lead rope with the other, he urged both horses forward.

Catching up to Emily, he again offered her a ride. As he expected, she again turned him down. At least this time, she sounded less obstinate about it.

Smiling to himself, he mentally gave her a mile at the most before she changed her mind and accepted his help. The midafternoon sun was relentless. Greenhorn that she was, she hadn't even thought to carry water. In Boston, she probably had a driver carry it for her.

"Would you care for some liquid refreshment?" he asked after they'd traveled for close to half an hour. He held out his canteen. It was a peace offering as much as a necessity.

This she took gratefully and, after gulping down a generous mouthful of water, handed the canteen back. "Thank you."

"My pleasure." Now they were getting somewhere. Or at least that was what he'd thought. But she relieved him of that notion the moment she took to walking again.

Shaking his head, he rode by her side. He looked for signs of her slowing down and saw none. Affording her his begrudging admiration, he tried to shade her with his horse as much as possible.

They traveled a total of two miles. Then three.

Noting her red face, he offered her another drink. Taking shallow breaths, she took a sip. Though he was dripping with sweat, her skin looked dry, and that was a worry.

"Emily, you need to ride with me." This time, it

wasn't a request or even an invitation. He meant business. Had he expected her to give in, he would have been sorely disappointed. But neither did she argue. She simply handed the canteen back and continued walking.

His breath rushed out of him. Having spent most of his time around the male species, he'd forgotten that women took everything to heart. "I'm sorry," he called after her. "I shouldn't have said you were mollycoddled."

Apologizing never came easy, but right now, he would do anything to get her on his horse.

Her steps faltered as her eyes met his. "Are you sorry you thought it?"

Now she was pushing it. "Okay, yeah. I'm sorry I said it, thought it, whatever!"

She tossed her head, and her chin jutted out in that determined way of hers. "You don't sound sorry."

He gritted his teeth. *Okay, Emily. You asked for it!*

Dismounting, he wrapped both the reins and lead rope around a bush and took off after her on foot. She whirled around to face him. "What—?"

"Sorry, sweetheart. But this is for your own good." With that, he picked her up and slung her over his shoulder. Fortunately, she was in no condition to fight him. At least no more than usual.

19

THAT NIGHT, EMILY STARED IN THE MIRROR AND hardly recognized herself. Though she always took care to wear Cookie's wide-brimmed hat outside, the strong Texas sun and wind had left its mark.

Her complexion was no longer the porcelain white prized by Bostonians. Instead, her skin was now a light-golden tan that enhanced the blue of her eyes. The color of her skin also made her hair look a lighter shade of blond.

No one in Boston would recognize her. But it wasn't just her outer appearance that had changed. Subtle changes had taken place within. Chief among them was the enjoyment and freedom derived from not wearing corsets and bustles.

Oddly enough, she'd even gotten used to the quiet and hardly noticed the cattle smells and dust anymore. Even more surprising was her newfound love of riding horseback. But that wasn't all; while in town earlier that day, she could hardly wait to get back to the ranch. She still couldn't believe it!

It wasn't just the physical and emotional changes on

her mind. It was also Chase. Their earlier argument still very much on her mind, she reached for her hairbrush and slowly worked it through her tangled, wet locks.

She wasn't proud of the way she'd acted. He was only trying to help, and she had made it as difficult as possible.

For some reason, he brought out the worst in her, and she didn't know why.

She'd fought him good and hard when he hauled her over his shoulder. But the moment he'd set her on his horse and climbed in the saddle behind her, she'd lost the will to fight. Instead, she'd relaxed against his muscular chest and melted into his arms. Fortunately, he'd blamed her sudden surrender on heat sickness, a notion she'd made no effort to correct.

When they had finally reached the ranch house, she even let him help her up the stairs to her room and shamelessly let him fuss over her. He'd lowered her gently to the bed and plied her with cool drinks. He'd then dabbed her heated face with a wet sponge and insisted she rest. It almost seemed…as if he cared for her.

No sooner had the thought occurred to her than she disregarded it with a shake of her head. His interest in her welfare had nothing to do with her personally. His only concern was retaining ownership of the ranch. She was nothing more than someone to be tolerated—just like their marriage.

She dropped the hairbrush on the dresser. He didn't care one whit about her personally, and that stung. She didn't want it to, but it did, and that was the biggest change of all.

Sighing, she opened the sack of candy purchased in town and peered inside. A sweet, sugary smell floated upward. Curious about the little strip of paper Kate had dropped in the bag, Emily pulled it out and unfolded it.

It was written in feminine handwriting and read:

A happily married couple shares everything—even their candy.

Emily sighed. Happily married? Was there really such a thing? She thought of all the married couples she'd known in Boston, including her parents, and *happy* wasn't the word that came to mind.

She thought of her uncle—a man she'd once idolized. But that was before she knew his greed and ambition came before all else. She'd vowed she would never marry a man who didn't put family first. That was why she could never stay married to a man like Chase. No woman could compete with his precious ranch, his precious cattle.

She dropped the slip of paper on the dresser with a sigh and refolded the sack. It wasn't the future that worried her. It was surviving day by day for the next several months. That would only happen if she and Chase could put their differences aside and make some sort of peace.

It wouldn't be easy, but it was the only way to make the duration of their agreement tolerable.

A plan forming in her head, she tied and retied the belt on her dressing gown, more out of nervousness than need. Inhaling, she reached for the bag of candy and let herself out of the room. At the top of the stairs, she stopped and listened. The quiet told her that the other household members had retired for the night.

Just before reaching Chase's office, she paused. A shiver of anticipation raced down her spine.

The glassy eyes of the stuffed wild cat stared down from the wall. The grandfather clock that loomed in the corner sighed and struck nine. Each bong echoing through the room seemed to sound a warning.

On the last note, she knocked on Chase's door.

"The door's unlocked."

The sound of his voice made her breath whoosh out of her, and she reached for the doorknob. Chase looked up from his desk as she entered, his gaze steady beneath a furrowed brow. A lock of brown hair had fallen across his forehead, giving him a rakish look. The glow of gaslight softened the hard lines of his features. Tonight, his face looked more sculpted than chiseled.

He stuck his pen into the penholder and sat back in his chair. On the desk in front of him, a ledger yawned open. "Feeling better?"

She nodded. "Yes, thank you."

He arched an eyebrow. "There a problem?"

She shook her head. "No. I just came to"—she cleared her throat—"apologize."

He ran a hand over the day-old whiskers at his chin. "Apologize?"

"I shouldn't have gone to town against your wishes. I thought I was prepared to handle myself. I never counted on Daisy throwing a shoe."

He folded his hands across his middle. "It happens."

She moistened her lips. "Will…will she be all right?"

"She'll be fine. Rusty will take good care of her. You won't find a better groom in all of Texas."

Relief washed over her. Should Daisy have suffered

permanent injury, Emily would never have forgiven herself. "I just want you to know how…sorry I am."

His eyebrows met and parted. "You don't sound sorry."

Taken aback by his comment, she was momentarily speechless until she saw the gleam of humor in his eyes. Reminded of her own response to his earlier apology, she blushed and held up the sack of candy.

"Maybe this will prove my sincerity," she said, wiggling the paper bag. She'd asked Peggy Sue to retrieve the books and candy from Daisy's saddlebags and bring them to the house. It had taken the housekeeper close to an hour to make the short trip to the stables and back, and Emily suspected that Rusty was to blame.

She crossed to Chase's desk and placed the offering next to the ledger.

He reached for the bag and peered inside. "Rock candy." He looked surprised and then pleased. "How did you know?"

"I had a little help from Kate."

"Ah, the candy lady."

"Is that what you call her?"

"It's what everyone calls her." He reached in the sack for a sugary lump and held it in the palm of his hand, grinning like a little boy. "These bring back a lot of childhood memories. I was only ten when I started workin' on the ranch."

"Ten?"

He shrugged. "We start young here. By the age of six, I could read every cattle brand within a hundred miles. I didn't know the alphabet, but I knew how to read brands."

"That's amazing," Emily said.

"My teacher didn't seem to think so. She objected to me writing my name with a rocking *M*."

Emily laughed. "Guess you can't blame her for that."

Chase laughed too. "Guess not." He studied the candy in his hand. "My first job was muckin' out the stables. Every Friday, my pa paid me in rock candy. If I did an especially good job, I got three pieces."

She tried to envision him as a ten-year-old child. "You must have felt rich."

"I did." He chuckled and popped the candy in his mouth. After a moment, he asked, "Care for a piece? You won't taste better."

The candy was too sweet for her taste, and normally, she would have said no. But something—and she refused to believe it was Kate's message about sharing—made her reach for the offered sweet. "Thank you," she said and popped the candy in her mouth.

He tucked the bag into a desk drawer.

She studied the thick ledger on his desk. "I could handle your bookkeeping. It would free up your time, and I'm good with numbers." It would also give her something to do to pass away the long, lonely hours.

He stuck the pen into the penholder. "Have you ever kept books?" He lifted his gaze to hers. "Or handled payroll?"

"No, but I have a college degree."

He sat back. "You went to college?"

The shock on his face rankled her. Just because she knew nothing of ranch life was no reason to think her dim-witted or incapable of working with numbers. "You don't have to look so surprised!"

"It's just…I've never met a woman who's gone to college," he said. "Come to think of it, I've never met anyone who's been."

Reminded of how little they knew of each other, Emily felt encouraged by the note of admiration she detected in his voice. "I'm quite good in chemistry and excelled at bookkeeping. I even know how to use a typing machine," she added, though it was apparent the ranch still relied on pen and ink. She didn't mean to brag, but she wanted to prove she wasn't the spoiled, inept woman he'd accused her of being.

"That's impressive," he said and looked like he meant it.

Irritated at being so easily placated by his praise, she lifted her chin. "So, what do you say? Do you want me to help with the books?"

"Let me think about it." He stood. "Right now, I say we get some shut-eye." He turned off the lamp, throwing the room in darkness. "Chemistry, eh?"

She smiled to herself. A lady was taught not to brag about her accomplishments, but in this case, it had paid off. "And did I mention calculus?" She hated the need to impress him but couldn't seem to help herself.

"Is that right?"

It was too dark to see his face, and it was hard to tell by his voice alone what he was thinking.

Together, they walked out of his office, through the parlor, and climbed the stairs. The closer they came to her room, the more nervous she became. Senses heightened, she was fully aware of his every move, his every breath, the very nearness of him.

Chase opened the door to her room with a flourish

and ushered her inside with a brush of his hand on her back. Had anyone been looking, she and Chase would have passed as a normal married couple. Only after the door had been firmly shut behind them did they drop the pretense and quickly move apart.

His height alone made him better suited to the great outdoors. In the confines of the room, he managed to dwarf everything around him except the bed.

Mouth dry, Emily increased the distance between them, but the bed still loomed large in front of her. Turning away, she caught his gaze in the mirror. Tension stretched across the room like a barbed-wire fence. His luminous eyes pierced the space between them as if to reach into her thoughts.

She turned to face him. Big mistake. Her securely tied dressing gown was a modest affair, but still, she felt naked beneath his studied gaze.

"Thank you for the candy," he said.

"Thank you for...coming to my rescue today."

There really was nothing more to say. Still, he lingered, and the tension between them threatened to snap.

"It's getting late," she said, hoping he'd get the message, even as she hoped he would not.

He stiffened visibly as if he'd suddenly caught himself staring. Back ramrod straight, like a soldier at attention, he strode toward the adjacent room.

"Good night," he said, his voice oddly thick. Casting a look over his shoulder, he ducked through the curtains separating their rooms. The black curtains fell in place, and it felt as if a door had slammed in her face.

Feeling very much alone, Emily sank onto the edge

of her bed. How was it that Chase McKnight managed to bring out the worst in her? At times, she'd felt like a stumbling fool, unable to have so much as a rational thought in his presence, let alone take care of herself.

But he also brought out another part of her. A softness she'd previously been unaware of. A recklessness that made her want to throw caution to the wind and see where it might take her. He had a way of making her feel more feminine than she had ever felt. More womanly. More needy in a way that was both exciting and alarming.

Oh yes, he brought out her worst, no question. But he also brought out so much more.

20

EMILY COULD HARDLY WAIT TO SHARE THE BOOKS she'd purchased with Ginny. The following morning, after visiting the stables to check on Daisy, she spotted Ginny waiting for her on the veranda.

"Hello, Mrs. Knight," Ginny called, waving.

The enthusiastic greeting made Emily smile. Ginny's uncanny ability to identify people, even from a distance, never failed to amaze her. "Hello, Ginny," she called back.

Picking up her pace, she stomped up the steps to the porch. "Guess what? I have something for you. Wait here, and I'll be right back."

It took but a few moments to race to her room, grab a book and bag of peppermint drops, and return.

Sitting on the wicker seat next to Ginny, she laid a copy of the *Five Little Peppers* on Ginny's lap. "I bought you something very special."

Ginny moved her fingers over the smooth cover, the serious look on her face melting into a bright smile. "Oh, it's a book," she said with awe, then impishly added, "A book about peppermint drops."

Emily laughed. "The peppermint drops are for later. I bought this book just for you."

Ginny's mouth turned down. "But I can't read. Blind people can't read."

"Some can," Emily said and quickly explained. "I once visited a special school in Boston that teaches blind people to read with their fingers. What do you think about that?"

Ginny ran her fingers back and forth across the cover. "But you can't feel words."

"Not with this book," Emily said. "But there are special books with raised letters that you can feel."

Ginny thought about that for a moment. "Are those special books hard to read?"

"Maybe at first. When I was your age, I had to work hard to learn to read. But it got easier with practice."

"I want to read with my fingers," Ginny said with a toss of her head.

"Maybe you can, one day. Then you could read to me. Right now, I'm going to read to you." Emily lifted the book off Ginny's lap. "This book is about a special family named Pepper."

Ginny giggled. "What a funny name for a family."

Flipping the book open to page one, Emily cleared her throat and began. "'The little old kitchen had quieted down from the bustle and confusion of midday…'"

Ginny was an attentive listener and hardly moved during the whole time Emily read, except to laugh at Joel Pepper's mischief. When at last Emily closed the book, Ginny protested.

"Oh, please. Can't you read more?"

"I'll read more tomorrow." Emily gave Ginny a quick hug. "How do you like it so far?"

"I like it a lot," Ginny said with a wistful sigh. "I wish I had a family."

Emily drew back. "But you do have a family."

"I only have Mama," Ginny said, the corners of her mouth turning down. "I don't have a pa."

"The Peppers don't have a pa either."

"But they have brothers and sisters."

Emily's heart went out to her. She'd never meant the book to make Ginny feel bad or lacking in any way. All she'd hoped was to open Ginny's heart and mind to the world around her.

"I'm part of your family now," Emily said. "So are Cookie and Kansas Pete." She named the other cowhands. "Mr. Knight is part of your family too." She'd noticed that Chase stopped to talk to Ginny whenever he had a chance.

Ginny's eyes brightened. "You mean I have a family even if I don't have brothers or sisters or a pa?"

"That's exactly what I mean."

Ginny thought for a moment. "Do you have a pa?"

Emily drew in her breath. "My pa's in heaven, and I miss him very much."

"What about your ma?"

"She's in heaven too." Emily missed her mother, but she had always been closer to her father. She still felt guilty for not taking over the family business as he'd wanted her to. Had she done so, her family's reputation would still be intact, and she wouldn't be hiding out on a Texas cattle ranch.

"Did they talk funny like you?" Ginny asked.

Emily laughed. "So you think I talk funny, do you?"

"That's okay. I like the way you talk. And I like that you're my family."

Emily brushed a wisp of hair away from Ginny's face. "If you ask me, you not only have a family but a special one at that."

Ginny flashed an impish grin. "Now can I have a peppermint drop?"

Emily laughed. "I guess you aren't going to let me forget those, are you?" She shook the bag of candy. "Let's go inside. I want to show you something."

Taking Ginny by the hand, Emily led her to the dining room and pulled out a chair for her at the table. She then dumped a handful of the hard candies on the polished surface.

Ginny's face lit up. "My favorite." She felt for the candy with her hand and popped a piece in her mouth. "Yum."

Emily set the empty paper sack on the table and arranged the sweets in a row. "These aren't to eat. They're for practicing how to count." Ginny's mouth drooped, and Emily quickly added, "Then we'll eat them."

Ginny rewarded Emily with a quick smile and immediately started counting. She stumbled when she reached the number nineteen.

Emily helped her count to thirty, then made her start all over again. Ginny was a fast learner. "Okay, you're at thirty. Thirty looks like this." She took Ginny's hand and helped her trace the number on the table with her forefinger. "Okay, what comes after zero?"

"One."

"So, what comes after thirty?"

"Thirty-one!" Ginny exclaimed.

It didn't take long after that for Ginny to count to a hundred. "Can I count to a million?" she asked, sneaking another peppermint sweet.

Emily smiled at the girl's enthusiasm. "Tomorrow," she said. Learning was best accomplished in short sessions.

Ginny grabbed a handful of candy from the table and made her way into the kitchen. "Cookie," she shouted. "Want to hear me count?"

Humming to herself, Emily picked up the rest of the candy pieces and dropped them into the paper sack.

Just as she finished clearing off the table, Emily noticed Peggy Sue watching from the doorway, a tight expression on her face. Pleased with Ginny's progress and thinking her mother would be equally delighted, Emily beckoned her into the room with a wave of her hand.

Much to Emily's surprise, Peggy Sue's frown only deepened. Instead of accepting Emily's friendly invitation, Ginny's mother turned abruptly and left.

21

CHASE CLUTCHED THE REINS OF HIS HORSE AND watched as the eighty-rod spools of barbed wire unwound from the back of the wagon. Kansas Pete drove the wagon slowly, while two men walked behind to make sure the strands of wire didn't tangle.

The devil's rope, as some called it, was thought to be superior to wooden fences and save time and money. That turned out to be a lot of hogwash. Between the free-range activists and cattle thieves, keeping the wire fence in good repair was a constant battle. Here it was, only April, and already Chase was over budget for the year.

This time, activists had cut a twenty-foot gap from the fence, allowing cattle to escape. Boomer had said he wouldn't know how many beeves they'd lost until he took a census.

No doubt his men would reclaim most, if not all, of the missing steers. But tracking them down would require hours away from the ranch, taking his men from other duties.

The cut fence, however, was only partly to blame

for Chase's dark mood. Emily bore the brunt of responsibility. The memory of holding her in his arms continued to plague him. Even when she was fighting him, he was drawn to her like a moth to light. Never had he been so attracted to a woman. Or so physically aware of her presence.

Like a smitten schoolboy, he lay in bed at night hoping to hear her sigh or catch a whiff of her sweet fragrance. Not even the wall between them could block out the nearness of her.

She'd made it perfectly clear that theirs was a marriage in name only, and he had no intention of doing anything that would jeopardize the ranch. Still, he couldn't help but wonder how it would feel to be married to Emily in every sense of the word.

The thought was as worrisome as it was surprising. She wasn't even his type. She was too independent for his taste. Too unsuited to ranch life. Too much of a spitfire. So why was he wasting time thinking of her when he had work to do? When did thoughts of a woman become more demanding than the call of duty?

Whatever hold she had on him had to stop. When working with cattle, a man had better keep his mind on the job or suffer the consequences. Cattle were unpredictable and spooked easily. One moment, they could be perfectly peaceful, the next, on a rampage.

His thoughts were interrupted by a cloud of dust, signaling a visitor. Narrowing his eyes against the bright morning sun, he watched the horseman head his way. It soon became clear it was his uncle. Considering the early hour, whatever Uncle Baxter had on his mind couldn't be good.

Hi uncle reined in his horse and greeted Chase with a nod. "Morning."

As usual, he was dressed for business in a dark suit, complete with a bow tie and a felt derby hat. Against the backdrop of cattle, the business attire looked absurd.

His uncle tossed a nod at the gaping hole in the fence. "Any idea who's responsible this time?"

"The usual activists."

His uncle scoffed. "If you ask me, it's that bloody Englishman. He's caused nothing but trouble."

Chase shook his head. "Fisher couldn't cut a lame cow from the shade of a tree, but that don't make him a fence cutter."

"Maybe not, but I still think he should go back to the old country to raise sheep and leave the cattle to us Texans. That's what the good Lord intended."

Chase raised his eyebrows. When had his uncle ever lifted a finger to help around the ranch? In no mood to argue, he shook the thought away. "What brings you all the way out here so early?"

"There's talk in town. Your brother—"

"*Step*brother."

Uncle Baxter's mouth thinned. "Royce has been shootin' off his mouth and telling folks your marriage is a farce."

Chase shrugged. "He can say what he wants."

"The will states the marriage has to be a real one. Your father was very clear on that."

"My marriage is real." It certainly had all the challenges of a real marriage. The only thing missing was some of the pleasures.

His uncle hesitated, his gaze on the men attaching the barbed wire to a post.

"What?" Chase asked, his voice edged with impatience. "Tell me."

His uncle's glittering eyes met his. "Word is that you and the missus haven't been to church or otherwise been seen together as a couple."

Chase moved his hat and swiped his forehead with the sleeve of his shirt. "Been busy. I'm trying to run a ranch here."

"If you don't watch your step, you might not have a ranch to run. You know as well as I do that Royce isn't about to give up what he thinks is rightfully his."

"He has no reason to think that. This ranch was started by the McKnights, and by God, it will die with them!"

Baxter's face darkened with disapproval. "I think you should take the threat from Royce seriously."

"He doesn't worry me. You know he's all hat and no cattle."

His uncle frowned. "I wouldn't be so sure of that. He's been making a lot of noise in town. He's sayin' your marriage is a farce, and he aims to prove it."

"Let him try."

Baxter stared him straight in the face. "A baby wouldn't hurt."

Chase stared at him. "What?"

"I said—"

"Forget it!" Not only had Emily made it clear that theirs was a marriage in name only, but bringing an innocent child into the world for such a selfish reason was wrong. Dead wrong. "Not gonna happen." Something is his uncle's face gave Chase pause. "What is it you're not tellin' me?"

His uncle let out his breath.

"Tell me!"

A pained expression crossed his uncle's face. "After Michael died, your father took to gamblin'."

"I know he enjoyed his card games."

"Oh, he enjoyed them all right. He almost lost the ranch because of them. That's why he took out that loan."

Chase's horse shifted restlessly beneath him. Leaning forward, he stroked Rebel's neck. "And?"

"When your father couldn't keep up the payments, he almost lost the ranch a second time."

None of this was a surprise to Chase. He remembered his father selling off cattle just to survive. None of the local ranchers could keep up with the exorbitant interest rates the loan company demanded. As a result, many local ranchers went into default. This allowed the loan company to sell some of the land at great profit to foreign investors and corporations.

Uncle Baxter continued. "Your father would have lost the ranch had Royce's mother not offered to pay off the loan. In return, he agreed to marry her and give her son equal consideration as his heir."

Chase drew back in his saddle, bile rising in his throat. "Pa told me he used his faro winnings to pay off the loan."

His uncle shrugged. "Guess he didn't want you to know the truth."

Chase frowned. "Are you saying that's the reason my father married Priscilla? To save the ranch?"

"I don't know that he had much choice. It was either agree to her terms or lose everything. Priscilla wanted him to split the property in half, but your father had reservations about dividin' the ranch. Especially since you and Royce never got along. He was also concerned about you runnin' off again like you did after Michael died. He believed runnin' away was a cowardly act and proved you lacked in character."

Chase's temper flared. No matter how hard he'd tried to make amends, his father had never forgiven him for that one crazy year. "So he gets back at me by forcing me into a sham marriage?"

"He believed marriage had a stabilizing influence. He hoped that would keep you from running away again, should things get tough."

"You don't think gamblin' was Pa's way of runnin' away?"

Baxter grimaced. "After Michael died and you took off, your father felt like he'd lost both sons. That's why he turned to gambling. That was his escape, though I don't think he saw it that way. Grief does funny things to people."

"I thought he blamed me for what happened to Michael. That's why I left." God knows, Chase had blamed himself.

Baxter shook his head. "He didn't blame you for the accident. He only blamed you for leaving."

Chase's jaw hardened. It had been wrong of him to run off as he'd done. He would regret it until his dying day. Still, he had spent the last ten years trying to make up for it. Why hadn't his father taken that into account? Why had one year carried so much more weight than ten?

"I'm surprised Priscilla went along with the way Pa wrote up the will."

His uncle shrugged. "She didn't want to, but that was the only way your pa agreed to marry her. He would rather have lost the ranch than split it between the two of you."

Chase could understand that. Sharing ownership with Royce would have been disastrous. "Why didn't Pa change the will after Priscilla died?"

"I don't know. Maybe he thought he owed her something for bailing him out when he most needed it."

Chase clamped down on his jaw. He had never been close to his father. Until now, he'd never understood why he'd remarried. Priscilla was nothing like his real mother, and Chase had never gotten along with her. Finding out the role she'd played in saving the ranch was a blow.

His uncle's pitying gaze didn't help. "I don't trust Royce. Never have."

Chase frowned. "I met the terms of the will. The ranch is safe."

"Just make sure it stays that way. Royce and his new bride are putting on quite a show as a happy couple. You might consider doing likewise." His uncle tugged on his reins and galloped off.

Watching him, Chase slapped on his hat and cursed beneath his breath. He was more concerned about Royce than he'd let on. The man refused to back down, and Chase sensed trouble ahead.

22

EMILY HARDLY SAW CHASE FOR DAYS ON END. MORE cattle were missing, and this time, rustlers were at fault. Trying to track down the thieves had taken up most of his time. Not having much confidence in the sheriff, Chase felt obliged to check out every lead himself.

Whenever Chase made an appearance, the two of them did their best to show a united front for Cookie and Peggy Sue. Yet there were times when Emily noticed Cookie staring at her like he knew more than he let on.

That Sunday morning, Emily left her room, wondering how to fill the long hours ahead. Much to her surprise, she found Chase waiting for her at the foot of the stairs.

"I have something to show you," he said, motioning her to follow.

He led her to a window and pointed to the buckboard parked out front. "Finally got it repaired," he said. "Get ready. We're going to the gospel mill... uh...church."

She stared at him. "Why?" It was hard to believe

he would drag himself away from the ranch, even for a few short hours.

He raised an eyebrow. "Why? Because it's Sunday, that's why. And it's nigh time I introduced my bride to friends and neighbors. Now go." He shooed her back toward the stairs. "You have a half hour to get ready."

Church. Emily couldn't believe it, and her heart pounded with excitement as she raced up the stairs to her room. How she missed the weekly outings to the little white chapel back home, missed the sense of community, the messages of hope. She didn't want to think that part of her excitement grew out of the prospect of spending time with Chase, though she had to admit the thought wasn't all that unpleasant.

Bursting into her room, she flung open the door to the chifforobe. After much consideration, she chose her favorite blue floral frock from among her neglected wardrobe and quickly set to work getting dressed. Her fingers fumbled with the hooks of her corset. She'd forgotten what a chore it was to dress the way Bostonian society deemed proper.

Strange as it seemed, she'd gotten used to the ease of slipping into a divided skirt and shirtwaist and not having to bother with corset, petticoats, and stockings. She'd even grown careless in arranging her hair. Instead of wearing it in a proper bun, she was now in the habit of tying it with a ribbon and letting it trail down her back, ponytail style.

After the necessary tugging, squeezing, and breath-holding that such attire necessitated, she was finally dressed. She stared at herself in the mirror and tried to breathe but had to settle for short little gasps of air.

A knight's armor couldn't have felt more confining. The steel corset ribs dug into her flesh like pincers, the bustle hung heavy, and her wool stockings felt scratchy and hot. If such fashion had been designed specifically to restrict a woman's movements, it succeeded on every level.

With a sigh, she reached for her fancy feathered hat.

Chase paced back and forth, his gaze shifting from the pocket watch in his hand to the top of the stairs. What in tarnation was taking Emily so long to get dressed? If they didn't leave soon, they'd be late.

Women!

He had just about decided to knock on her door when she appeared.

She stood at the top of the stairs looking down at him. It irritated him that the mere sight of her made his heart beat faster. So much so that it took him a moment to notice she was still dressed in her usual divided skirt and high-crown felt hat.

He drew his eyebrows together. "I thought you were getting ready for church."

She walked down the stairs. "I *am* ready." Reaching the ground floor, she turned a full circle. "Do I look like a proper rancher's wife?"

His already rapid beating heart surged at the word *wife*. As for *proper*, that seemed much too bland to describe her. The plain canvas skirt and shirtwaist enhanced rather than hid her small, shapely form in a way that no bustle or back staircase padding could do.

Reminded how that same figure looked wrapped in a towel, he drew in his breath.

"You'll do," he said, hiding his true feeling behind a curt reply. Not trusting himself to say more, he whirled around and held the door open for her. "Let's go."

Moments later, the two of them were seated side by side on the buckboard's horsehair seat. Studying her profile, Chase took the reins in hand. But before coaxing his horse forward, he thoughtfully regarded her rigid shoulders, firm chin, and set mouth. It didn't take a genius to figure out that he was the source of her sudden change of mood. Nor did it take much to figure out what he'd done wrong.

"You look…purty as a bald-face heifer," he said, hoping to make amends. It wouldn't do to arrive at church with that much tension between them. Instead of the smile he'd hoped for, her angry eyes lit into his and her nostrils flared.

"You don't have to insult me!"

He stared at her in utter confusion. "Insult you? I paid you a compliment."

"By comparing me to a cow?"

"Oh boy." He drew in his breath. "Here in Texas, that's the best compliment you can give a woman." He frowned. "How do men in Boston do it?" he asked. "Tell a woman she looks purty, I mean?"

Emily afforded him a sideways look as if to determine his sincerity. "They keep animals out of it."

He thought about that for a moment. "I might could do that," he said. Anything to keep the peace. "You look mighty…purty."

Much to his disappointment, even his Boston-like

compliment failed to win her favor. Instead, she folded her arms across her chest and stared straight ahead. "You don't have to pay me compliments. It's not part of the deal."

He clamped down on his jaw. It was easier to handle a herd of ornery cattle than one stubborn woman. "I said it because it happens to be true. No other reason."

When she failed to respond, he shook the reins, and his horse shuffled forward. A whiff of bacon fat floated up from the newly greased wagon wheels.

He slanted his gaze in Emily's direction, looking for some chink in her armor. "How come you didn't change into those fancy duds of yours?"

She swiped a wisp of hair away from her cheek before answering. "Thought it best not to call attention to myself."

He chuckled, which earned him an icy glare. "What's so funny?" she asked, her voice sharp.

"Mrs. Chase McKnight will command attention. Count on it."

They stared at each other for a full minute before they both looked away, he to focus on the bumpy dirt road ahead.

Just as he'd decided there was no use trying to draw her into conversation, she surprised him by breaking the silence. "Have you had any luck catching the rustlers?"

"Not yet," he said, recognizing her sudden interest in ranch business as an attempt at a truce. "But I will." He glanced her way and changed the subject. "Cookie said you've been workin' with Ginny."

This earned him the long-awaited smile, and it was all he could do not to reach over and finger her intriguing dimple. "I have. She's such a bright child and so eager to learn. I just wish there were other children for her to play with."

"Peggy Sue tends to be protective of her. Doesn't want to see Ginny get hurt. Can't blame her for that."

Their conversation ended when they drew up behind a long line of parked vehicles. Before they walked into the church, they were greeted by Mrs. Buttonwood.

"Oh, look at you," she said, eyeing Emily up and down with an appraising eye. "You look like one of us. Follow me. Everyone is dying to meet you."

Before Chase could stop her, the woman had effectively whisked Emily from his side and set to work introducing her to the other churchgoers.

Just as he'd predicted, Emily attracted much attention and quickly drew a crowd, including his neighbors, the Bentons and their twin boys.

"So, you finally decided to bring your…shall we say…pretend bride out of hidin'."

At the sound of his stepbrother's voice, Chase reluctantly pulled his gaze away from Emily and turned. Dark, glittering eyes met his. Church was the last place Chase had expected to bump into Royce.

Chase tried to sidestep him, but Royce barred his way.

Since this was neither the time nor place to air grievances, Chase fought to maintain control. "Where's your wife?"

"She's around," Royce said. "Unlike you, I have a *real* marriage." He tossed a nod at the knot of people gathered around Emily. "She's playing her role well, I see."

"Heard you tried to buy her off."

Royce shrugged. "Shouldn't have to buy what's rightfully mine."

Temper snapping, Chase fought to keep his voice low. "You have no right to the ranch."

"That's not how our *father* saw it."

Clamping down on his jaw, Chase balled his hands by his side. "Your *step*father, you mean."

Royce looked undaunted. "How do you think he'd feel if he knew who you'd married?"

Chase frowned. "Don't know what you're talkin' about."

"A visitor in town saw her in the bookstore and recognized her. He had some interesting things to say. Would you like to hear what they were?"

"I don't care what he said!" Chase raised a pointed finger. "Stay away from my wife. You hear? I mean it."

"Chase?" Emily suddenly appeared at his side. "Everything all right?"

Aware that all eyes were on them, Chase took Emily by the arm and moved her as far away from Royce as possible.

"Yes," he said, his calm voice belying his concerns. Royce was up to something; Chase could feel it in his bones. "Everything's…just dandy."

23

THE FOLLOWING WEEK PASSED QUICKLY FOR EMILY. Attending church had made her realize how much she missed a social life. To fill the void, she'd begun joining the ranch hands around their nightly campfires, and that helped pass the time. At least it made the long evening hours more bearable.

At first, the men seemed uneasy and reserved in her presence. Their constant "yes, ma'ams" and "no, ma'ams" made them sound like a bunch of schoolboys on their best behavior.

Fortunately, their mannerly behavior didn't last more than a day, and the flow of tall tales and bad jokes were unlike any that she'd ever heard. In Boston, female parlor talk invariably involved fashion and gossip, while the men discussed business.

She attended the campfire every night but Saturday. That was the night the cowhands rode into town and stayed until the wee hours of the morning.

She especially enjoying listening to Foxhound tell the stories of his people. The Cherokee Indians seemed to have an explanation for everything, from how a rabbit got a short tail to the great flood.

Boomer's tales always involved the weather in some way. One of his most outrageous tales involved a norther that blew his house clear off its foundation.

"So, what did you do?" the most gullible of the lot, Rusty, asked.

"Why I just waited for the wind to change direction and blow my house back," he said to appreciative laughter.

After listening to the men's tales for several nights, Emily decided to tell one of her own.

"I have one," she said with a wave of her hand.

The men exchanged glances before Boomer motioned her to take her place in front of the others. Conscious that all eyes were focused on her, she began the story of Tall Barney Beal.

"He's of such a towering height," she explained, "he has to stick his feet out the window at night to sleep."

She then went on to explain his strength. "He can drink from the bottom hole of a hundred-and-fifty-pound barrel." Beal was a real person, and his legend was well known on the East Coast, and some of what she said was true. But in the spirit of fun, she went on to exaggerate his other feats. By the time she had completed her tale, the men were practically eating out of her hand.

After telling her story, she tried yet again to draw the man they called Gabby out of his shell but to no avail. Instead of joining in the jovial banter, he sat silently braiding long strips of rawhide, his nimble fingers working them into a fine rope.

As much as she hated to admit Ginny was right, Gabby's demeanor could be interpreted as anger. He'd only worked on the ranch for a couple of months, and no one knew anything about his background. He was a compact, nondescript man. His only defining feature was his ears, which stuck straight out like handles on a sugar bowl.

What Gabby lacked in social skills, he made up for in artistry. He had a unique way of braiding, which made his ropes both beautiful and strong.

"Would you mind if I borrowed that rope?" she asked Gabby, pointing to a discarded length on the ground by his feet.

He looked surprised. "Why?"

Gratified that the man could talk, she explained how she was teaching Ginny vocabulary through touch. The braided piece of leather offered all sorts of possibilities.

He continued working on the rope in his hand. "Keep it."

Emily tucked the length in her pocket. "Thank you."

She moved away from Gabby just as Kansas Pete pulled out his fiddle. Beanpole Tom stepped to her side and asked her if she cared to "day-ins."

"Day-ins?" Emily asked, confused.

Moving his feet, Beanpole Tom showed her what he meant.

"Oh, you're asking me to *dense*," she said in proper Boston style.

This brought a roar of laughter from the men. Knowing that her accent was sometimes as difficult for them to understand as theirs was for her, she didn't take offense. Instead, she laughed with them.

Beanpole Tom planted his large, callused hand at her waist, and they did a quickstep around the

campfire while the others clapped their hands in time
to the music. Beanpole Tom had the dubious distinction of being the son of an undertaker. That and the
fact that he was more bones than flesh subjected him
to much good-natured ribbing.

Despite his lanky form and their differences in
height, Emily had no trouble keeping up with him,
and their rapid steps were in perfect sync.

It was only after the lively dance was over that
Emily noticed Chase watching from the shadows, and
her already-pounding heart skipped a beat. It was too
dark to see his expression. All she was able to make
out were his rigid shoulders as he turned and quickly
walked away.

Ginny was intrigued by Gabby's leather rope. She ran
her fingers along the intricate webbing as if playing
a musical instrument. "Could you braid my hair like
this?" she asked.

"I can braid your hair," Emily said. "But it won't be
as fancy as that. Gabby has a special way of braiding. I
guess you could say it's his trademark."

"Is a trademark like a cattle brand?" Ginny asked.

"Hmm. I guess you could say that."

"Do you think Gabby would braid my hair like this?"

The thought of the taciturn man braiding a child's
hair made Emily laugh. "I think Gabby would rather
stick to leather." She waited for Ginny to finish fingering the leather piece. "What words can you think of
to describe the rope?"

Before Ginny could reply, her mother called to her.

"You better go," Emily said. "We'll finish your lesson later."

After Ginny left, Emily felt restless. She wandered into the kitchen and found Cookie reaching on a shelf for a wire basket.

"Let me gather the eggs," Emily said.

He handed her the basket. "If you insist."

Grateful for having something to do, she walked outside with purposeful steps and headed straight for the chicken coop.

The sky was a deep azure blue. Today, the still air kept the cattle smells at bay, and Emily filled her lungs with the sweet fragrance of grass, wildflowers, and sage.

Chickens strutted around the enclosed yard, their heads bobbing up and down as they pecked at the ground. Hoping the wooden coop was empty, she reached over the fence to unlatch the gate.

The moment she stepped foot inside the fence, chickens squawked and flapped their wings, scattering feathers everywhere.

"Okay now, ladies. I'm not here to hurt you," she said.

Inside the coop, a white hen sat on its nest, staring at her with beady eyes. Moving cautiously, Emily quickly filled her basket with eggs from the deserted nests and stepped outside.

Just as she reached the gate to let herself out, a rooster flew at the back of her head.

Fighting off the slashing spurs and darting beak with flailing arms, she managed to let herself out of the pen and ran smack into a hard chest.

"Oh!" Confused, she looked up to find Chase grinning down at her.

"You really should stay away from two-legged troublemakers."

"I'm trying," she said and took a step back. The impact had caused two eggs to fall from her basket, and one had splattered his boots. "I'm sorry."

"Better egg on my shoes than my face," he said. He gazed at her with a look of concern. "I should have warned you. I'm afraid Oscar has the mistaken notion that he rules the roost. You have my sincere apologies."

"No harm done," she said.

"In that case…" He tossed a nod at the chickens that had escaped through the still open gate. "I'll return our friends to their pen and meet you in my office."

She flashed him a questioning look, but he'd already turned away to tend to the escaped chickens. Why did he want to meet with her? Was it because he'd caught her dancing? Did he object to how she spent her evenings? With these questions in mind, she turned and hurried to the house, her divided skirt flapping against her legs.

∞

Less than twenty minutes later, Emily paused in front of the door to Chase's office and quickly rehearsed the mental speech she'd prepared. Her nervousness surprised her. She felt like a schoolgirl summoned to the headmaster's office, and that would never do. A man like Chase respected strength, and that was what she intended to show him.

Chin up, she squared her shoulders and knocked.

"The door's unlocked."

She entered the room but hung back, not sure what to expect. Seated behind his desk, he motioned her closer with a wave of his hand.

She closed the door but kept her distance.

He arched a questioning brow. "I trust you're fully recovered from your bout with Oscar?"

"Yes, thank you," she said and decided to clear the air by taking the initiative. "About last night...I saw you watching." He was watching her now, and that made her nervous, but not in a bad way. "Under normal circumstances, it might seem improper for a woman to spend her time in such a way. But I think you'll agree that nothing about our marriage is normal."

Hands folded across his chest, Chase had an inscrutable look on his face. He had removed his hat, and a strand of mussed hair fell across his forehead.

"Is that why you think I asked you to come to my office?" he asked.

The question surprised her. "Isn't it?"

"I don't know how it is in Boston, but here if a husband dictates how a wife spends her time, he's likely to find himself full of lead." He picked the ledger off the desk. "The reason I asked to see you," he began with a droll smile, "is to take you up on your offer. You said you were willin' to handle the bookkeepin' chores."

She stared at him, speechless, before taking the offered ledger in hand. Never in a million years would she have thought he'd trust her to handle the books to his beloved ranch. "I d-did," she stammered.

He opened a drawer and pulled out a second tome. "I record expenditures in the daybook and enter them in the ledger later. I think you'll find the system self-explanatory." He dropped the second book on the desk and indicated the stack of bills that had yet to be recorded.

"That's it?" she asked. "You don't object to my dancing with Beanpole Tom?"

He lifted his eyebrows. "Why would I?" he asked.

"I just thought—"

He tossed a nod at the ledger in her arms. "Your taking over the books will free up some of my time."

"That's good," she said, her tone concealing her confusion. Was this his way of saying he planned on spending more time with her?

He hesitated. "I thought maybe…we could take a ride one night." He cleared his throat. "The ranch looks different in the moonlight."

Surprised by the unexpected invitation, she nodded. "I'd…like that."

"Well then." Standing, he moved away from the desk. "Feel free to use my office. That way, you won't be disturbed."

"Thank you."

They stared at each other for a moment. "I better get back to work," he said, though he made no effort to leave. "Unless you have any questions. About the books, I mean."

"No, no." Her gaze dropped to the heavy ledger in her arms. "I think I can manage."

"Okay then." He turned to the door. With a quick glance over his shoulder, he left.

Staring at the closed door, Emily hugged the ledger close to her chest. He hadn't objected to her spending time with the ranch hands, so that was good. He hadn't even said anything against her dancing. She was free to do whatever she wanted. So why did his lack of interest in her activities leave her feeling so despondent?

Leaving his office, Chase walked through the house with brisk, purposeful steps and let himself out the front door.

Why would Emily think he objected to her dancing with Beanpole Tom? Why would he? She was his wife in name only. He didn't own her. Long as she lived up to their agreement, she could do whatever she dang well pleased.

He only wished she hadn't looked so…carefree in another man's arms. So beguiling. Never had she ever laughed as heartily with him as she'd laughed with Beanpole Tom and the others.

Instead, she was always cautious around him, subdued. It was only when her dander was up or they were at loggerheads with each other that her eyes flashed and her stubborn streak flared.

He was surprised to realize, suddenly, how much he enjoyed such times. Enjoyed them even though it meant having to fight the temptation of taking her in his arms.

Clamping down on such wayward thoughts, he quickened his pace.

24

The following morning, Emily decided to give Ginny her lesson before tackling the ranch's financial books. In a short time, they had progressed from counting to adding and subtracting. They'd also touched upon history.

Today, Emily led Ginny to the world globe in the parlor and told her to put her hand on the orb. "You're touching a large body of water," she said.

"Is it the ocean?" Ginny asked.

"One of them. The one you're touching is called the Atlantic Ocean. It's more water than you could ever imagine."

"Is it as much water as in a rain barrel?" Ginny asked.

"Much more." Emily thought for a moment. "Do you know what a ship is?"

Ginny nodded. "Kansas Pete made a little wooden ship for me. Sometimes I float it in my bath."

"If that was a real ship, it would take a week or more to cross the ocean. That's twice as long as it takes a train to travel from New York to California."

Ginny's eyes widened as if trying to imagine such a thing. "Do you think I could cross the ocean one day?"

Emily smiled. "I think you can do anything you want to do." Her answer made Ginny beam. "Okay now. Keep moving your hand around the globe till you feel something."

As Ginny's hand circled the globe, Emily named the countries and told her a little about each one. Ginny soaked up facts and figures like a sponge soaked up water and couldn't seem to get enough.

Suddenly, Ginny gasped. "I feel something!"

Emily couldn't help but smile at Ginny's enthusiasm. Seen through Ginny's sightless eyes, the ranch had become a wonderland of amazing sounds, scents, and things to touch.

"What you feel is the United States," Emily explained. She had glued string along America's borders and around some of the states and territories.

After Ginny had followed the string around America twice with her finger, Emily guided her hand to the lower portion. "This is Texas. This is where we live."

"Is our house on the globe?" Ginny asked.

"No, but if it were, it would be about here," she said, moving Ginny's finger to the spot.

"I think it should be on the globe," Ginny said. "Don't you agree, Mr. Knight?"

"I quite agree," Chase said, joining them around the globe.

Emily turned to look at him. She hadn't even known he was in the room until Ginny addressed him by name.

He met Emily's surprised gaze with smiling eyes, and her heart lurched. Wondering how long he'd been standing at the doorway watching, she quickly looked away.

Chase reached for the ball of string on the end table, snipped off a tiny piece and glued it on the globe in the shape of an M. "There," he said. "The Rocking M Ranch."

Ginny followed the letter with the tip of her finger, a big smile on her face. "The horses are here," she said, moving her finger to indicate the stables. "And the mama cows and their babies are here." Her finger had moved from one end of Texas to the other.

Chase laughed and winked at Emily. "It looks like the Rocking M Ranch has taken over the entire state."

Feeling heat rush to her face, Emily looked away. Lately, just being in the same room as Chase made her feel all flustered and confused. It was unsettling, annoying, and more than anything, worrisome.

Emily didn't dare speak for fear Ginny would say something about stammering and love.

Fortunately, Ginny had other things on her mind. "Would you take me to see the newborn calves?" she asked Chase.

"I think you should ask your teacher to bring you," Chase said, seeking Emily's eyes.

"I think that's a great idea," Emily said, careful to control her voice. Ginny's use of the word *see* no longer surprised her. Sometimes, she could swear that the girl could see more than most sighted people. "I want to see the calves too."

Chase looked pleased. "I'll leave you two to your lessons."

He left the room, seeming to take some of the light and most of the oxygen with him. Shaking the thought away, Emily turned to Ginny.

"Tomorrow, we'll learn about the other states. Now it's time to read."

Ginny seemed reluctant to leave the globe, but she finally settled on the divan next to Emily and snuggled up to her.

"I'm glad Mr. Knight didn't marry the rancher lady."

Emily's breath caught in her throat. She had no idea that Ginny knew about Mrs. Decker. "Why…why do you say that?"

"I heard Kansas Pete say she was good with cattle and would have made Mr. Knight a fine wife. But I bet she wouldn't have read to me or taught me all the things you do."

Emily hugged Ginny close. "Reading to you gives me great pleasure."

"If you were working with the cattle, you wouldn't have time," Ginny said.

Emily smiled. "You're right. I wouldn't." Irritated that even the mere mention of Mrs. Decker made her feel inadequate, Emily released Ginny and reached for a book. "Since we finished *Five Little Peppers*, I thought you might like *Swiss Family Robinson*." Emily opened to the first page of the book and began to read. Ginny listened with rapt attention and was especially intrigued with the tree house. When at last Emily closed the book, Ginny's mouth dipped in disappointment.

"It's almost time for dinner," Emily said. Cookie always whipped up something special for the noon-time meal. "We'll read more tomorrow."

"I wish I lived in a tree house," Ginny said with a wistful sigh. "I would reach up and touch the sky. Would you come and visit me if I lived in a tree house?"

"Of course," Emily said and gave her a hug.

Peggy Sue's sharp voice rasped across the room. "Come along, Ginny!"

Ginny pulled out of Emily's arms. She looked puzzled, as if she didn't know what she had done to earn her mother's disfavor.

"Go," Emily whispered, giving Ginny a gentle pat on the back.

Without a word to Emily, Peggy Sue curtly turned away.

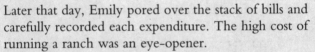

Later that day, Emily pored over the stack of bills and carefully recorded each expenditure. The high cost of running a ranch was an eye-opener.

As she'd expected, the payroll commanded most of the expenses. The younger ranch hands earned twenty dollars a month, and the more seasoned cowboys earned forty. After wages, the biggest expenses were barbed wire, freight charges, and cattle.

There were also bills for stirrups, spurs, collars, and saddles. The high price of pistols surprised her. How the average man could afford such a thing was a puzzle.

At first, it appeared that the ranch was hopelessly in debt. But after going over the books for the previous years, she realized that the ranch received its money in lump sums, mostly in the fall when cattle were driven to market. Bills were paid accordingly. For that reason, expenses were carried over from month to month.

She was so involved in what she was doing that she

failed to notice the late hour until Cookie knocked on the door and told her supper was served.

Carrying a copy of *American Cattle: Their History, Breeding and Management*, she found the dining room empty with only one place setting. It was no more than she'd expected, but still, she was disappointed. Evidently, Chase had found something else to occupy the time she'd saved him by taking over the books.

Emily stared at the steak on her plate and toyed with the peas with her fork. She couldn't explain why, but food just didn't seem to taste as good when dining alone.

She opened the book and began to read. The subject matter wasn't as boring as she'd previously thought. Some of it was even fascinating. She was surprised to learn that Christopher Columbus was credited with bringing the longhorn ancestors to the New World from Spain.

After completing her meal, she headed upstairs. She was tired and decided to skip the campfire and make it an early night. To her surprise, Peggy Sue stood waiting for her on the second-floor landing. "I need to talk to you," she said.

"I want to talk to you too," Emily said with a smile. "I have an idea that I hope you'll like."

Emily motioned the woman into her room and immediately explained. "At church, I met two local families, and they expressed interest in having their children come here for lessons. It would save them having to drive all the way to town. I think it would benefit Ginny to have children around her own age." Two were twin boys, and the girl was Ginny's age. "So what do you think?"

Peggy Sue shoved her hands into her apron pocket, her face serious.

"What is it?" Emily asked. "Ginny isn't sick, is she?"

"Ginny's fine. Or will be." Peggy Sue took a deep breath. "I'd rather that you didn't…pursue Ginny's lessons."

Not sure she'd heard right, Emily arched an eyebrow. "I'm sorry?"

"She's blind, and all you're doing is putting fancy ideas in her head." Peggy Sue rushed her words as if to speak her mind before losing courage.

Emily drew back. "I-I'm not sure what you mean."

"She now thinks she has a family."

"She does have a family. Chase…Mr. McKnight, me, the ranch hands…we're all family."

Peggy Sue discounted this with a shake of her head. "A family consists of a mother and father. Not an employer and"—her eyes grew misty, and her voice dropped—"his household."

"We're all very fond of Ginny," Emily said. "You know that, right?"

"I know you all mean well, but it's better that she learns to face reality. Now she wants to travel around the world. That's why I must insist that you stop teaching her things that will only end up frustrating her."

"I'm not sure I understand. What things?"

"Adding and subtracting. Writing her name. She has no use for such things, and that will only aggravate her."

Emily didn't want to tell Peggy Sue how to raise her daughter, but neither could she hold her tongue. "Ginny is a bright, intelligent child. She has great potential," Emily said gently. "I wish you would reconsider. Ginny deserves every opportunity that comes her way—"

"Opportunities?" Peggy Sue's face darkened. "The only opportunity for her is to beg in the streets!"

Peggy Sue's bitter tone made Emily cringe, but she refused to be deterred. If anything was holding Ginny back, it was her mother.

"That might have been true in the past, but not now. There's even a school for the blind in Boston. I've been there, and you'd be amazed at what they're doing. They're teaching people to read with their fingers. They start with children as young as Ginny and—"

"My mind's made up!" As if suddenly realizing she was talking to the mistress of the house, Peggy Sue's hand flew to her mouth. "I mean no disrespect. I'll…I'll tell her that you're busy and can no longer spend time with her. She'll understand."

Before Emily could further object, Peggy Sue whirled around in a circle of gray skirts and quickly left the room.

Emily sank onto the edge of the bed and stared at the closed door.

Ginny was still very much on Emily's mind the following morning. It worried her that the child wasn't in the usual places. The parlor was empty, as was the veranda.

Walking into the kitchen, Emily took an appreciative sniff of the savory smell rising from the steaming cast-iron Dutch oven on the stove. "Hmm, something smells good."

Grinning, Cookie rested his knife on the chopping board. "That's my famous son-of-a-gun chicken stew. And for dessert, we're having my famous son-of-a-gun peach cobbler."

Emily laughed. "My mouth is watering, already. Do you have any of your famous son-of-a-gun coffee?"

"Yep. Made fresh this mornin'."

She reached for a clean cup and poured herself coffee from the pot on the stove. "Have you seen Ginny?"

"No, ma'am. Can't say that I have." He pursed his lips. "Somethin' wrong?"

Sighing, Emily moved to the table, pulled out a chair, and sat. "Just that Peggy Sue doesn't want me working with her and told me to stop."

Cookie shook his head and proceeded to chop. The blade of his knife rapidly banged against the wooden board like the *rat-a-tat* tapping of a woodpecker. "Can't say that I'm surprised."

Emily scoffed. "Ginny's biggest handicap is her mother! Maybe Chase will talk some sense into her."

"I don't know." Cookie gathered up a handful of chopped carrots and added them to the Dutch oven. "The boss ain't one to put his nose where it don't belong."

"Somebody has to." Emily wasn't one to interfere either, but neither was she willing to give up. There had to be a way to make Peggy Sue understand the importance of allowing Ginny to learn and grow in every way possible.

She finished her coffee and left the kitchen. Since there was nothing to do around the house, she walked outside, intending to take a ride. Maybe it was time to get to know more about the workings of the ranch.

Just as she stepped off the veranda, she noticed a horse racing toward the stables. She narrowed her eyes for a closer look. The horse's reins dragged behind, and the empty stirrups flapped against the animal's side. It was Rebel—no question—but where was Chase?

Worried now, Emily raced to the stables. Rusty had managed to grab hold of the reins and was trying to calm the horse, his face dark with worry. Cold fear swept through her, and her stomach clenched tight.

Something was terribly wrong!

25

NOT WANTING TO TAKE THE TIME TO SADDLE HER OWN horse, Emily quickly mounted Rebel.

"Maybe you better wait here, ma'am," Rusty said. "I'll round up some of the boys, and we'll look for him. There could be trouble."

She didn't need Rusty to tell her that. Her head was already filled with frightening thoughts. Had Chase been attacked by animals? Been thrown? Fallen ill? What?

"That's what I intend to find out."

Too worried to be mindful of the horse's height or power, she pressed her legs against the animal's sides and yelled, "Find Chase!"

Rebel leaped forward, and she guided the horse back the way he had come.

She rode in one direction all the way to the barbed-wire fence on the northern end, calling Chase's name. Spotting a horseman in the distance, she yelled out. When he glanced her way, she recognized him as Kansas Pete.

"Something's happened to Chase," she shouted. "His horse returned without him."

Kansas Pete waved back. "I'll round up some of the boys," he called and galloped off.

With a tug of the reins, Emily urged Rebel in the opposite direction.

Eyes narrowed against the glare of the sun, she scanned the landscape. "Where is he, Rebel? Where's Chase?"

More than once, she spotted what looked like a man, only to find it was a cactus or stunted tree. A buzzard circled overhead, and her heart practically stopped. *Please, no, God!*

Several minutes passed, and still there was no sign of Chase. The buzzard had been joined by another, and they kept circling. Tears of frustration sprang to Emily's eyes. She only hoped that Kansas Pete had more luck than she was having.

She was just about to turn in another direction when a movement in the distance caught her eye. Praying it wasn't another false alarm, she reined her horse to a full stop and rose from the saddle for a better view. It sure did look like Chase on foot. Relief rushing through her, she spurred her mount into a full gallop.

Moments later, Chase greeted her with raised eyebrows. "You're riding my horse?"

"All sixteen and a half hands," she said, slipping out of the saddle. Overwhelmed with relief, she did something she'd never expected to do—she threw her arms around Chase's neck.

She felt him stiffen in surprise and then relax. "Whoa!" he said, his hands tightening around her waist. "If I didn't know better, I'd think you were glad to see me."

She looked up at him, their faces, their lips mere inches apart. The smoldering flames in his eyes startled her, and she quickly pulled away. Mortified at her own flagrant conduct, she wiped her damp hands on the sides of the skirt and fought for control.

"What happened?" she managed at last, aware that he was staring at her with a strange look on his face.

"My horse got spooked and threw me." He shrugged like it was no big deal. "It happens."

After he'd scared her half out of her mind, his nonchalant attitude annoyed her. "Didn't think things like that happened to you."

"I reckon there's not a horseman alive who didn't have to chew gravel on occasion."

From the distance came the crackle of rifle fire, the shots spaced at least twenty seconds apart.

"Sounds like they're lookin' for me," Chase said. He turned to his horse and pulled his rifle out of the saddle scabbard.

"I bumped into Kansas Pete and told him you were missing," Emily said.

"Cover your ears." He waited for Emily to do what he said, then fired his weapon into the air, letting his men know he was okay.

After replacing the rifle, he reached in his saddle for his canteen and took a quick swig of water. Wiping his mouth with the back of his hand, he tossed a nod at his horse. "Which of us gets to walk this time?"

Before she could reply, a shot rang out, this time from the nearby hills. The bullet bounced off the ground less than a foot from where Chase stood. Emily cried out, and Rebel whinnied and reared.

Before Chase could grab hold of his horse's reins, the startled animal frantically galloped away.

Another shot rang out, and suddenly Emily was on the ground with Chase on top of her.

"Stay still," he growled in her ear.

He had her pinned flat, and she wouldn't have been able to move even had she wanted to. All she could hear was his breath in her ear. All she could feel was his body on hers. His warmth and protection and care.

A minute passed. Then two.

Finally, he rolled off her, Peacemaker in hand. Body crouched low, he scanned the distant hills. In the deadly quiet that followed, Emily held her breath. Not even a bird or prairie dog dared break the silence that spread across the land like thick fog.

"Okay," Chase said, his voice hushed. "On the count of three, I want you to run behind those rocks. I'll cover for you."

She followed his gaze to an outcropping of boulders thirty or forty feet away, and her stomach knotted. "Chase—"

"Do it." His gaze falling on her trembling lips, he added in a softer voice, "I won't let anythin' happen to you. Honest."

He was asking her to trust him. After what had happened in Boston, she'd sworn never to depend on another man, but something in his eyes, his expression, his voice made her want to believe that trusting him was the right thing to do.

Seeming to take her silence for compliance, he pulled back the gun's hammer and took aim, pointing in the direction of the gunman. "All right then," he said, his voice but a murmur as he started counting.

Head low, she rose to her feet and sprang forward on the count of three. Heart pounding, she raced for cover. A barrage of gunfire split the air. No sooner had she ducked behind a large granite boulder than Chase joined her.

"Stay down," he ordered. Kneeling by her side, he quickly fed bullets into his gun's chamber.

Gasping for air, she asked, "Who's shooting at us?"

"Someone with bad judgment," he said. After reloading, he closed the cylinder and spun it hard. Resting his gun on top of a granite rock, he aimed in the direction of the shooter.

For several moments, neither of them moved. The air was still as if even nature held its breath. The only thing breaking the silence was the pounding of Emily's heart.

"Is he still there?" she whispered at last.

"Don't know."

At the sound of horses' hooves, she sensed Chase stiffen, and her already-taut nerves threatened to snap.

Chase surprised her by suddenly standing and waving. "Over here." In a softer voice, he explained. "It's okay. Come on."

Holstering his gun, he grabbed her by the hand and pulled her to her feet. Emily didn't think there could be a more welcome sight than Kansas Pete, Foxhound, Big-Foot Harry, and Boomer, all on horseback.

"Y'all okay?" Kansas Pete hollered from his saddle. "We heard gunfire."

Chase hollered back. "Someone started shootin' at us. The shots came from those hills."

Kansas Pete squinted against the sun to have a look. "Did you see who it was?"

"Nope."

Big-Foot Harry leaned over his saddle horn. "Think it was one of them there rustlers?"

"Dunno," Chase replied. "Take a look and see what you can find."

"What about you and the missus?" Kansas Pete asked. "How you gonna get back?"

"Don't worry about us. My wife is an expert at hoofin' it."

Kansas Pete gave Emily a doubtful look but shrugged in resignation. "Whatever you say, boss." With that, the men galloped off.

Emily watched them go. "Aren't you worried about them being shot at?"

"If anyone should be worried, it's the one they're after." Chase slapped his dusty hat against his leg and settled it on his head. "Now you know why I don't want you ridin' by yourself."

She slid him a sideways glance. "It seems that I get into the most trouble when I'm with you."

Squinting up at the yellow-white sun, Chase shook his head. "Funny you should say that. I was just thinkin' the same about you."

By the time Emily and Chase had made it back to the house, it was midafternoon. A breeze had begun to sweep across the land, bending the grass and stirring up funnels of dust. The light wind also brought with it the smell of cattle.

Emily was hot and tired. Nevertheless, she managed to drum up enough energy to race Chase to the rain barrel. They reached it at the same time, laughing.

They were both dripping wet when Cookie found them. "Boss, boss," he cried. "Come quick."

Emily exchanged a worried look with Chase. It wasn't like Cookie to show much in the way of emotion. He was usually so calm.

Chase handed Emily a dry towel and reached for his hat. "What's the matter? What's wrong?"

"Ginny's missin'."

Emily drew the towel away from her face and gasped. "What do you mean, missing?"

"We've looked everywhere for her. The barn, the stables. She's gone!"

"Oh no…" A whirl of frightening thoughts flooded Emily's head. First the gunman. Now this. Could there be a connection?

"She can't be far," Chase said. "We'll find her."

"Where's her mother?" Emily asked. No sooner were the words out of her mouth than Peggy Sue rushed toward them. Glaring at Emily, she looked fit to be tied.

"I'm so sorry…" Emily began.

Peggy Sue cut her off. "It's your fault that she's gone!" she stormed.

Emily reared back. "My fault?"

"Had you not put all those crazy ideas into her head, she wouldn't have—"

Chase stepped in front of his housekeeper, creating a protective barrier between the two women. "My wife is just as concerned for Ginny's welfare as we all are," he said, his voice thick with censure. "We're wastin' time. So think. When was the last time you saw her?"

"At b-breakfast," Peggy Sue stammered, looking deflated. "I told her there would be no more lessons, and she burst into tears and ran to our room. I've never seen her so upset, and it's all your wife's fault!"

Cookie handed Peggy Sue a clean handkerchief. "We didn't know the girl was missin' until the noon-time meal."

"We'll find her," Chase said. His voice left no doubt, but Emily could see that he was more concerned than he let on.

"I'll let the others know we need help," Chase added. He glanced at the western sky. The sun was low, and long shadows crept across the terrain.

Cookie nodded. "I'll send up the white flag."

"The white flag?" Emily asked.

"That's my signal that we have a problem back at the house," Cookie explained.

Anxious to start searching, Emily flung the towel on a hook and started toward the stables. "I'll saddle Daisy."

Chase stopped her with a hand to her arm. "If'n you want to help, hang a white sheet on the gate. That will let anyone passin' this way know we need help." He turned to Peggy Sue. "Stay here in case she shows up." With that, he spun around, calling to Rusty.

Cookie raced to the house with Emily at his heels. "Where do they keep the sheets?" she asked.

"Upstairs in the hall cupboard."

Just as they entered the house, Emily heard Chase sending a distress signal with three carefully spaced rifle shots. Between the flag, the sheet, and the gunfire, it was clear he didn't want to leave anything to chance. Knowing Chase was in charge helped calm her anxiety.

By the time she had located the closet, grabbed an armful of neatly folded sheets, and returned outside, Cookie had already raised the white flag on the flagpole, and it flapped briskly in the breeze.

Peggy Sue hadn't moved from the spot, and Emily couldn't help but feel for her.

The thought of Ginny out there alone and in danger made Emily cringe. How much harder it must be for her mother!

Emily handed Peggy Sue one of the sheets. Having something to do helped her, and she hoped it would help Peggy Sue as well. "Come on. Let's get to work."

Neither of them said a word as they made their way to the front gate. No sooner had they draped the sheet over the fence than a farmer driving a wagonload of hay stopped to inquire what the problem was.

"Thought I heard a signal for help," he said.

"A little girl is missing," Emily called over the gate. "She's nine, and her name is Ginny."

The farmer spat a stream of tobacco juice onto the ground. "I'll get my sons. I'll be back." He quickly took off, his wagon wheels leaving a trail of dust behind.

"We better go back to the house in case Ginny shows up," Emily said.

Arms folded, Peggy Sue glared at her. "I'd rather

that you weren't there when she comes home. You're the reason she's missing."

Emily bit her bottom lip. Ginny was missing because her mother had put a stop to the lessons, but it was no time to argue. The woman was half out of her mind with worry and, for that reason, deserved leniency.

"Chase will find Ginny," Emily said, her voice kind. "He won't rest till he does." If she knew anything about him, she knew that much. *Please, God, just make him find her soon.*

Already the sun had dipped behind the trees, and the long shadows were a grim reminder that only a couple hours of daylight remained. The thought filled Emily with dread.

She scanned the dry, arid land that spread as far as the eye could see. *Where are you, Ginny? Where are you?*

26

Night fell across the land like a lead weight, and still, there was no sign of Ginny. Emily stood in the yard in front of the house, watching the flickering torches of searchers in the distance. The lights looked like tiny lightning bugs, darting back and forth.

The gunman had been caught and said his name was Charlie Bunker. He claimed he had been tracking a deadly panther. That was what he thought he was shooting at. Since panthers killed calves and colts, it appeared that Bunker had tried to do the ranch a favor.

Chase doubted the man's story, but since there was no way to prove it one way or another, he let him go with a warning to stay away from the ranch.

Emily didn't know what was more worrisome: the thought of an outlaw on the loose or the possibility of a dangerous animal in the area.

The only comfort was knowing how many people were searching.

Word had spread quickly, and volunteers from neighboring farms and ranches had descended upon the Rocking M Ranch in droves.

Emily thought it the strangest thing. A person could travel for hours and not see a living soul. But when trouble came knocking, people seemingly crawled out of nowhere to help.

Shivering in the cool night air, she closed her eyes. *Oh God, why hadn't they found her?* What if someone had taken her?

Leaving her post, she hurried back to the house to get a wrap, taking the stairs two at a time and rushing into her room. In her hurry, she knocked a book off the bedside table. It was a copy of *The Swiss Family Robinson*.

Stooping to pick the book off the floor, she thought of the tree house, and a small voice echoed in her head. *I want to climb high, so I can touch the sky.*

Straightening, she stared down at the book cover. Was it possible...?

Maybe she was grasping at straws, but she had to know for sure. At the very least, it would give her something to do.

Tossing the book on the bed, she wrapped her shawl around her shoulders. She debated whether to let Peggy Sue know what she was thinking. Fearing it might give her false hope, Emily decided it best not to say anything. Instead, she quickly left her room and raced down the stairs.

She found a lantern and matches in the kitchen. After an anxious glance at the dark of night pressing against the window, she lit the wick with a shaking hand and let herself out the back door.

The lantern lighting her way, she circled around the vegetable garden. Fortunately, a near full moon had risen over the distant hills.

Stepping carefully through the tall grass and trying not to think about snakes, Emily headed for the water-pumping windmill. The wind had risen, and even from the distance, she could hear the windmill's steel blades turning.

Overhead, the stars winked as if enjoying a private joke at her expense. Even the heavens seemed to think she was on a wild-goose chase, but still, she kept going.

Reaching the windmill, she stood on the muddy ground and looked up at the tall wooden structure that towered over her. Her light failed to reach the top, and the platform above was still in shadows. The windmill's tail jutted out like a beak against the starlit sky, and the turning blades cast moving shadows, but there was nothing to suggest Ginny's presence.

Nonetheless, Emily set her lantern down and cupped her mouth to call Ginny's name, loud and clear. Holding her breath, she waited for a response, but all that could be heard were the whir of turning sails and the sound of water seeping over the sides of the large wooden storage tank.

"Ginny," she called again. She was just about to turn back when she thought she heard something, and her heart skipped a beat. "Ginny, is that you?"

The answer was slow in coming. "Mrs. Knight?" The voice was so soft, it was a miracle it could be heard above the swishing sound of air and water.

Tears of relief blurring her vision, Emily stumbled back a step. *Thank God!*

Blinking to clear her eyes, she reached for the lantern, lifting it high to study the tall, open structure and the flimsy ladder clinging to its side. The tiny platform was at least forty feet off the ground.

"Can you climb down?" she called, the wind seeming to snatch the words out of her mouth.

Ginny said something, but Emily couldn't hear what it was.

"You'll have to speak louder. I can't hear you."

"I said I can't."

"Are you hurt?"

"No."

"I'm right here. I won't let anything happen to you."

"I'm scared."

Emily tried to think. "Okay, don't move. I'm coming up," she said and slipped the lantern's wire handle over her wrist.

Blowing on her hands, she rubbed them together and grasped the sides of the narrow wooden ladder. She lifted a foot to the first rung, and the rickety ladder shook beneath her weight. Swallowing her fear of heights, she climbed. Reminding herself not to look down, she checked the sturdiness of each rung before stepping onto the next.

She'd seen Big-Foot Pete climb this ladder to oil or repair the blades, and he had made it look so easy.

Grateful that the light from the lantern stayed lit, she kept climbing. The wind together with the force of air from the moving blades slowed her progress, but at last, she reached the small platform.

Ginny was curled into a small ball. The windmill's blades swept frighteningly close to her huddled body. The platform was barely wide enough to hold a single man. Since Ginny's prone body took up most of the space, Emily remained on the uppermost rung of the ladder.

Reaching out, she touched Ginny's trembling arm. "It's okay. I'm here."

Ginny lifted her head, revealing a tear-streaked face. Her skin pale and lips blue, she looked cold. Her eyes were glazed with fear and exhaustion.

The lantern flickered, and the light went out, thrusting them in darkness. Kicking herself mentally for not thinking to bring matches with her, Emily set the lantern on the corner of the platform. Cast into darkness, she forced herself to breathe and took Ginny's icy-cold hand in her own.

"Okay, now move toward me. Keep your head down."

"I can't. I'm scared."

"I'm right here. Just move slowly, and I'll help you down the ladder."

"No!"

The child was clearly petrified, and Emily couldn't blame her. She was scared too. In the last few minutes, the wind had grown stronger. The windmill shuddered, and the paddles over their heads turned faster. The whirring of spinning blades sounded like the flapping wings of a giant bird ready to carry them off.

They needed help, but Emily didn't dare leave the child by herself. However, if they stayed, Ginny could well freeze to death. And Emily didn't want to think about the possibility of her falling. It was a long way to the ground.

"I'm letting go of your hand. Just for a moment. Don't move." She pulled her hand away and untied her shawl. The wind threatened to rip the wrap out of her hands as she held it toward the girl.

"Ginny, put out your hand. I want you to take my shawl and wrap it around yourself the best you can." She waited for Ginny to reach for the offered shawl. "Do you have it?"

"Yes."

"Hold on to it tight. It'll help keep you warm."

"I-I wanna go home," Ginny sobbed.

"I know, dear heart. I want to go home too." Never did she think to call the ranch home, but tonight, there was no place she would rather be.

Emily tried to think what to do. She didn't want to leave the frightened child on that dangerous platform, but she needed to get help—fast!

Hearing Ginny's sobs, her heart went out to her. Poor thing. "What are you doing way up here?" she asked. Perhaps if she distracted Ginny with silly talk, she could earn her trust. "Who do you think you are? The man in the moon?"

"I-I-I wanted to touch the sky," Ginny sobbed.

"You don't have to climb up to touch the sky," Emily said. "The sky reaches all the way to the ground. You can touch it from here, there, everywhere."

Ginny's sobs subsided. "What about the stars and the moon? Can those be touched from the ground too?"

"I'm afraid not. They're too high." Emily tried to think how to explain the heavens in a way Ginny could understand. It was hard enough for a sighted person to grasp such vast distances. "No ladder in the world is high enough to reach the moon, let alone the stars."

"Then I'll build one," Ginny said, sounding determined.

"That would have to be a very tall ladder, indeed. I'm not sure there's enough wood in all the world to build such a ladder."

"If I build it, will you climb it?"

Emily glanced at the moon. "Of course I'll climb it, and when I get to the moon, I'll make funny faces back to earth."

Ginny giggled. Seemingly satisfied, she stopped talking.

Emily was just about to pull her hand away when Ginny spoke again. "Mama said you can't read to me anymore." Ginny's plaintive tone nearly broke Emily's heart. "She said you're too busy."

Emily didn't know how to respond without placing the blame on Peggy Sue. "We'll talk about this later, okay?"

"But I missed you."

"I know, Ginny. I missed you too."

"When I'm with you, I feel like I can fly. Climbing the windmill made me feel like I was with you."

Tears sprang to Emily's eyes. "Oh, Ginny…"

"Are you crying?"

"I'm…just cold," Emily said. "We need to climb down so we can get warm."

Ginny failed to respond, and Emily's mind scrambled. She had to do something fast, or they would both freeze to death.

"I'm going to get help," she said gently, not wanting to upset the child more than she already was. "Don't move till I get back."

Ginny squeezed her hand tight. "I don't want you to leave!"

Emily didn't want to leave either. But what else could she do? "I know. But it will only be for a short while. Everyone is looking for you. Kansas Pete and Boomer and all the rest. I need to tell them where you are so they can help you."

"If you tell them, I'll get into trouble."

Emily opened her mouth to say something, but Ginny stopped her with a hushed voice. "I hear something."

Emily strained her ears, but all she could hear were the whooshing of blades, the creaking of the ladder beneath her weight, and the whistle of wind.

"Someone's coming," Ginny said after a while, and this time, Emily heard it too. The sound of a galloping horse.

Her heart leaping, Emily forced herself to look down. Even in the pale moonlight, she recognized Chase astride Rebel and never thought to see a more welcomed sight.

"Help," she cried. "Help!"

He slid from his saddle and rushed to the bottom of the ladder. "Emily, is that you?" he called, holding up a lantern.

"Yes. Ginny's up here, but I can't reach her."

"I don't think that ladder can hold both of us. Can you climb down?"

"I think so."

Ginny tightened her hold on Emily's hand. "Don't leave me."

"I'm not leaving you. I'm only going down so Mr. Knight can come up. He'll help you."

Emily pulled her hand from Ginny's clutching fingers and started to descend. This time, the ladder felt more stable but only because Chase was holding on to it.

Reaching the ground, Emily fell into the warm comfort of his arms. "You okay?" He waited for her to regain her footing before releasing her.

She nodded. "How...how did you know?"

"Thought I saw a light comin' from the windmill. I pointed it out to Kansas Pete, but by then, the light had gone out. He thought I was seein' things, but I decided to check it out anyhow."

"Thank God you did."

He thrust his lantern into her hands. "Hold that." Glancing upward, he grabbed the sides of the ladder and started to climb.

Emily stood at the foot and held the lantern high. She could hear his voice when he reached the top, but the wind snatched his words away.

After what seemed like forever but was probably only minutes, he started down, cradling Ginny in his arms.

He reached the ground with Ginny still clinging to him. Looking over the child's head, he held Emily's gaze, his eyes the color of liquid gold. "Let's get you two home."

27

It seemed that Emily had no sooner fallen into bed later that night when she woke to a knocking sound. Suddenly wide awake, she sat up. "Who is it?"

"It's me, Big-Foot Harry. I need to talk to the boss."

"Just a moment." Pushing the covers aside, she jumped out of bed and reached for her dressing gown. Shoving her arms into the sleeves, she raced across the room to Chase's room and plowed into him.

"Oomph!" she cried.

"Shh!" he whispered, steadying her.

Aware with a start that her hands were flat against his naked chest—and his at her waist—she gasped and pulled away.

"Are you folks okay?" Big-Foot Harry called.

"Yeah, hold on," Chase said aloud and then whispered, "You all right?"

"Yes," she murmured and backed away from him. Feeling for the gas lamp on the dresser, she found the matches and lit it. Yellow light flashed across Chase's broad, muscular chest before he crossed the room and ripped open the bedroom door. Much to her relief, he was only naked from the waist up. But it was enough to make her heart pound and her pulse feel like fire racing through her veins.

"What is it? What's wrong?" Chase asked.

Big-Foot Harry's urgent voice filled the room. "It's Kansas Pete. He's been shot. Took a bullet to the shoulder."

Hand on her mouth, Emily gasped. "Oh no!"

Chase glanced at her before turning back to his foreman. "How'd he get shot?"

"Rustlers." Big-Foot Harry made a face. "Turns out the man we let go was shootin' at no panther. When he heard you fire off your rifle, he must have thought you were firin' at him and his rustlin' friends."

Chase shook his head. "Where is Kansas Pete now?"

"At the bunkhouse. Foxhound went to fetch the doc."

"Give me a minute." Closing the door, Chase turned, his face grim. Worried eyes met hers before he crossed the room and ducked through the dark curtains.

By the time he emerged moments later fully dressed, Emily was dressed too.

"What are you doing?" he asked.

The question surprised her. "We have a man down. I'm going with you."

"This doesn't concern you."

She couldn't say why, but his words hurt. Still, it was no time to give in to such feelings. "Everything that happens here concerns me!"

Without another word, she turned and stomped out the door ahead of him.

Chase paused at the doorway of the bunkhouse sleeping quarters. Already, Emily was bent over Kansas Pete, her dainty soft hands cupping his pale face.

Chase clenched his jaw. They were the very same hands that had moments earlier pressed against his own bare chest. Somehow, her touch seemed to have left an imprint like a branding iron on his skin.

Irritated by the direction of his thoughts, he moved to the side of the injured man's cot.

Kansas Pete's face was twisted in pain. Someone had already cut away the sleeve of his shirt to his shoulder, and a blood-soaked kerchief covered the wound.

"Take off his boots," Chase ordered, "and bring another blanket."

While Rusty and Big-Foot Harry rushed to follow his orders, Chase gingerly pulled off the bloody kerchief. The slow-oozing wound told him that no main arteries had been hit.

Beanpole Pete handed him a clean kerchief. "We can't wait for old sawbones. That bullet's gotta come out now."

"We can wait," Chase said. More damage had been done by botched surgeries than caused by any bullet.

The sudden silence told him that his men didn't share his opinion, but only Boomer was willing to voice it. "Everyone knows that bullets must come out posthaste," he said.

"It can wait," Chase repeated.

Boomer opened his mouth to argue, but Emily stopped him with a hand on his arm. "My husband's right," she said. "The best thing we can do right now is make Kansas Pete comfortable until the doctor arrives."

Chase stared at her, surprised at hearing the word *husband* fall from her lips. He was even more stunned by how much it had affected him. For perhaps the first time, it seemed they were of a single mind—and bonded by more than just a legal document—and he liked it. He liked it a lot.

Pushing the thought away to be more thoroughly examined later, he turned to Boomer. The show of a united front between husband and wife had ended the discussion, and no further objections were made.

"Give him some whiskey. That should ease the pain." Lowering his voice for Emily's ears only, Chase said, "Go back to bed. I'll stay with him."

She lifted her chin in a way that had now become all too familiar. "I'm staying." She turned to Beanpole Tom and issued orders like an army general. "Fetch a basin of water and clean towels." Leaning over the patient, she removed the blood-soaked kerchief from the injured man's shoulder. "We need to clean the wound."

Beanpole Tom returned and set the basin and towels on the bedside table. Emily picked up a towel, dipped a corner into the water, and ever so gently dabbed Kansas Pete's wound.

After covering the bullet hole with a clean kerchief, she handed the basin of bloodied water to Beanpole Tom and took hold of Kansas Pete's hand in her own. "You'll be fine," she said softly. "It'll take more than that hole in your shoulder to keep you down."

Her assurances brought a glimmer of a smile from Kansas Pete before his eyelids drifted shut.

Chase arranged a chair next to Emily's and sat. "How does a nice girl like you know about bullet wounds?" he asked. Since some of the men were now stretched out on their cots, he kept his voice low.

Her blue eyes slanted toward him. "We have guns in Boston," she said.

"Oh? For some reason, I was under the impression that Boston was more...*civilized*." He was teasing her, of course, and the sudden dimple at her cheek told him she knew it.

"We are," she said. "There're only three reasons why a man gets shot in Boston. He loses a duel, cheats at cards, or helps himself to someone else's wife."

He chuckled. "If I ever have occasion to visit Boston, I'll remember that."

For the remainder of the night, he and Emily stayed by Kansas Pete's side and waited for the doctor.

Occasionally, Chase caught her glancing at him, a strange look on her face, and he couldn't help but wonder if she was thinking similar thoughts. Did she recall the feel of his bare chest? The feel of his hands at her waist? The way the two of them had worked together like a team?

It was past dawn before Foxhound returned with Doc Avery. An older man with gray hair and beard, the doctor adjusted his spectacles before setting his black bag on a chair and tuning to his patient. "Sorry it took me so long to get here," the doctor said. "I was delivering a baby." After probing the wound with a practiced finger, he pulled an extractor from his bag. He waited for Chase to pour a liberal amount of whiskey down the patient's throat and on the wound before setting to work.

Chase held Kansas Pete down with a hand on his chest while Big-Foot Harry clamped down on the poor man's legs. Uttering soothing words, Emily sponged the patient's head and seemed oblivious to the curses ripping from his mouth.

"Hey, we got a lady present," Boomer said out of habit.

Beanpole Tom shook his head. "She's no lady. She's a rancher's wife."

Chase met Emily's eyes for a split second before they both looked away.

Finally, Kansas Pete fell silent, and Doc Avery held the extractor up for all to see. The bloody bullet between the loop-shaped grips brought whoops and hollers from the men.

The bullet made a pinging sound when dropped into a metal bowl. "Give him a day or so, and he'll be his ornery self again," Doc Avery said, dabbing his damp forehead with a balled handkerchief.

"That's good news," Chase said and thanked the doctor. After making certain that Kansas Pete was comfortable, he left the bunkhouse ahead of Emily, surprised to find himself still reeling from the shock of having heard the word *husband* fall from her lips.

He had the uneasy feeling that Kansas Pete would recover from the night's ordeal faster than he ever would. A whole lot faster.

⌘

Later that same morning, Chase headed for the kitchen for coffee. Cookie insisted upon whipping him up something to eat. In short order, he ushered Chase into the dining room and placed a plate of scrambled eggs and bacon on the table in front of him.

Cookie filled his cup. "You look like you got one wheel down and your axle's dragging."

Chase rubbed his forehead. "Yeah, well, it was a tough night."

Cookie set the coffeepot on the stove. "All the more reason to get some grub under your belt." Food was the cook's cure-all for everything.

Chase picked up his fork and stabbed at the bacon. Tough night? More like a tough twenty-four hours, starting with getting thrown from his horse and being shot at. Then there was that frantic search for Ginny, topped off by Kansas Pete's run-in with a bullet. But none of that had anything to do with his present state of mind.

After making sure his man would live to see another day, he hadn't gone back to his room. Didn't trust himself to. Not after what had happened.

He drew in his breath. What was he thinking? Nothing had happened! He and Emily had collided in the dark was all. No reason to keep thinking of her hands on his bare chest. His hands at her slender waist. The sweet fragrance of her. No reason at all.

My husband's right…

The memory of her words affected him just as much today as they had when she'd uttered them. He told himself it was part of the charade. Part of the plan. She was simply play-acting as they had agreed. It was crazy to read something into a single word when there was so little chance it had been intended.

He clamped down on his thoughts only to be

confronted by another memory. *She's no lady; she's a rancher's wife.*

The sound of footsteps drew his attention to the doorway. Surprised to see his housekeeper up so early, he arched a questioning eyebrow. *God, don't let there be another problem.*

Stifling a yawn, he blinked to relieve the grit from his sleep-deprived eyes. It had been a long night in more ways than one. It promised to be an even longer day. "Ginny okay?"

"She's still asleep." Peggy Sue hesitated. "I just wanted to thank you for everything you did. Had you not found her—"

He set his fork down and dabbed at his mouth with his napkin. "I didn't find her. Emily…my…wife did."

"Yes…I know. And…I'm very grateful to her."

"We all are." He laid the napkin on the table. "Ginny is a special little girl and a brave one at that."

A rare smile crossed his housekeeper's face. "Yes, I quite agree."

He took a quick sip of coffee while considering his next words. "A girl like her needs…special care."

Worried eyes peered at him from a pale, round face. "I'm quite aware of that."

Hearing a defensive note in her voice, he set his cup down. He didn't want to make her feel bad, but neither did he want to miss the opportunity to help Ginny.

"My wife is concerned about her lack of formal education."

"You don't understand." Peggy Sue wrung her hands together, a look of despair on her face. "That will only put ideas into her head. Had Mrs. McKnight not—"

"The ideas are already in her head." Surprised by the fierce need to defend Emily, Chase began again in a gentler tone. "What my wife is tryin' to do is teach her how to put those ideas to good use. Left on her own…well…" He lifted his shoulders. "Ginny's likely to get into more trouble."

Peggy Sue clenched her hands to her chest. In the dim gaslight, she looked no more than a child herself. She had only been sixteen when she had Ginny, but her usual stoic demeanor often made her look older than her twenty-five years. This morning, she looked both young and scared.

"I…I don't know what to do," she said, her voice thick with despair.

Chase felt sorry for her. It couldn't be easy raising a child like Ginny by herself. He had given her a job and a place to live, but he felt guilty for not offering more in the way of support. Until Emily had mentioned it, he'd not given a thought to Ginny's education. At the very least, he should have insisted upon hiring a tutor.

"Let my wife help her," he said gently. "Don't try to do it alone."

Peggy Sue looked away, but not soon enough to hide her tears. "I…I'll let you finish your breakfast." With that, she turned, her rapid footsteps fading away.

Chase glanced up to find Cookie leaning against the doorjamb, arms crossed. "What?"

Cookie dropped his arms to his side. "Do you think she'll take your advice?"

"Don't know." Chase pushed his still unfinished breakfast away. "For Ginny's sake, I hope she does."

28

THE FOLLOWING WEEK PASSED UNEVENTFULLY. KANSAS Pete had made a full recovery. Ginny was back to her old self, and calving season was progressing on schedule.

Emily had resumed working with Ginny, with one significant change—she now had four pupils. The twins, Eddie and Adam Benton, were a year older than Ginny. Alice Riley was Ginny's same age.

At first, Peggy Sue had been opposed to the arrangement, but when she saw how much Ginny liked her new friends, her reservations vanished.

Between teaching and keeping the ranch's books, Emily's days began passing more swiftly. For that, she was grateful. She now had a purpose.

Still, doubts and worries haunted her. There really was no reason to feel unsettled and on edge, but she did. She felt like she was waiting for the next shoe to drop, and the feeling grew stronger with each passing day. Why she felt that way, she couldn't say.

Maybe it was because for the first time since coming to Texas, she now had something to lose if things went wrong.

When she'd first arrived in Haywire, she had no home, no friends, little money. All she had was a promise of marriage. She'd told herself that if it didn't work out, she would be no worse off than before. Knowing she had nothing left to lose gave her a sense of security, strange as it seemed.

Now, suddenly, everything had changed. She was surrounded by people she cared about, and oddly enough, the ranch had begun to feel like home. Much to her surprise, she'd also discovered how much she liked teaching. How much she liked working with children. How much she looked forward to her days.

To think that everything she now cared about could be gone in a blink of an eye scared her. It had happened before and could happen again. Sometimes lightning really did strike twice.

Now, as she sat at Chase's desk, she tried shaking away her uneasiness. She needed to focus on the stack of invoices waiting to be recorded.

It had been a dry winter and spring, and Chase worried about the continuing drought. For that reason, he'd ordered several factory-made windmills, an expense the ranch could ill afford. But if water didn't fall from the sky, it had to come out of the ground.

The cowhands spent a great deal of time talking about rain or, rather, the lack of it. Bostonians talked about the weather too, but never with such concern or urgency.

Here in Texas, every cloud was noted, every change in the wind analyzed. From Foxhound, Emily had learned that birds flew lower before a storm. He insisted that the low-flying birds spotted earlier that day meant rain was on the way. Beanpole Tom had disagreed, stating that rain was on the way only if his tobacco smelled stronger. Boomer had also taken issue with Foxhound, claiming there were too many spiderwebs.

"Spiders don't build webs when it's gonna rain."

Cookie's method of predicting rain was based on whether the drawers in his kitchen stuck. "Sad to say, but my drawers are loose," he'd said to uproarious laughter.

He'd taken a lot of ribbing about having "loose drawers," and Emily smiled at the memory. She was still smiling to herself when the door sprang open.

Chase walked in, seeming to fill the office with his presence. She had never been completely immune to his good looks, but lately, the mere sight of him ignited an awareness in her that was overwhelming. Recalling her hands on his bare chest, she sucked in her breath, and heat rushed to her face.

His eyebrows lifted. "I'm sorry. I didn't know you were working."

Hoping he hadn't noticed her reddening cheeks, she returned the pen to the penholder and closed the ledger. "If you need your office…" She stood.

"No, no. That's all right. Finish what you're doin'." He hesitated, his blue eyes seeming to pierce hers, and she found it impossible to look away. "I thought maybe you'd like to go on a calvin' check with me tonight."

Her breath caught. "A calving check?"

"We have to check the expectant mothers every three hours 'round the clock. I told the boys I'd take the nine o'clock shift. So, what do you say? Are you up for it?"

The thought of being out on the range at night made her nervous, and it had nothing to do with him. "I...I don't know..."

His eyes narrowed beneath a furrowed brow. "A rancher's wife is expected to take an interest in the ranch," he said.

In the past, her lack of interest had driven a wedge between them, but tonight, she heard something else in his voice. Resignation, perhaps, as if he no longer resented her lack of interest. She didn't want to think he no longer cared how she felt.

"A rancher's wife might also be concerned at being shot at," she said.

A look of apology fleeted across his face. "If'n that's what you're worried about—"

"If?" She stared at him. "I believe most *civilized* people *would* be worried about being shot at."

"While we're checkin' the calves, the boys will be on guard duty. You'll be perfectly safe."

"Like Kansas Pete was safe?"

"We're not goin' out that far." When she made no immediate reply, he added, "I would never ask you to go with me if'n I thought there was any danger. You know that, right?"

He studied her with concern-filled eyes, and she felt her resistance weaken. "Yes," she said. "I do know that."

"So? What do you say?"

She moistened her lips. Since it seemed important to him, she didn't have the heart to say no. "I say we check for calves," she said, managing a smile.

He flashed a crooked grin. "All right then. I'll

tell Rusty to have our horses ready." He hesitated a moment before adding, "Thank you."

Puzzled, she frowned. "For what?"

"For all that you've done for Ginny. For takin' care of Kansas Pete. For…" He cleared his voice and looked away.

"I haven't done all that much," she said.

"You have… More than you know." He turned and quickly left the room.

Staring at the closed door, Emily thought about the way her heart pounded at the sight of him, the way her breath caught in her lungs whenever he came into view. Lately, she couldn't fall asleep until she knew he was in the room next to hers.

If she didn't know better, she would think…

No, no, no! She could not, would not, must not fall in love with Chase McKnight. Life on a ranch was nothing like the one she'd envisioned for herself.

Not wanting to dwell on the alarming thought, she set to work adding figures to the ledger. But it was no good. Once the thought of love had entered her head, it was hard to think of anything else. After having to blot out a third mistake, she closed the record book.

Just as she opened the desk drawer to shove the ledger inside, a piece of paper fell from its pages. Stooping, she retrieved the paper and—thinking it was another receipt that had to be recorded—unfolded it.

The name on the letterhead pierced through her like a knife. Not wanting to believe her eyes, she stared at the signature at the bottom of the page.

The letter had been signed by her uncle.

The bad loan that had caused Chase's father to

almost lose the ranch and to marry Royce's mother had been borrowed from Fields & Fields!

How was that possible? Dropping the paper on the desk as if it had suddenly burst into flames, Emily pressed a hand to her mouth. She'd come all the way to Texas to escape her uncle's shadow, but it appeared she hadn't traveled far enough. Was there no place on earth where the long arm of Fields & Fields hadn't reached?

Now it threatened her very existence.

Oh no! What would Chase say if he knew she was related to the man who had caused the ranch so much trouble? Would he blame her? Hate her? Want nothing more to do with her?

Sickened to her stomach, she stuffed the letter into the ledger and fled from the room.

∞

"Mrs. McKnight, do you have a moment?"

At the sound of Peggy Sue's voice, Emily stopped at the bottom of the stairs, her hand on the brass railing. She'd been so eager to escape to her room that she'd failed to see Peggy Sue in the parlor.

"I'm sorry, I didn't see you." She didn't want to deal with the housekeeper at that moment, but neither did she want to appear rude. "Is everything all right? Ginny?"

"Yes, yes, she's fine. I just want to thank you." Peggy Sue curled her hands by her side. "Mr. McKnight said I should…uh…let you help me, and I'm glad I did."

Surprised and pleased that Chase had rallied to the

cause, Emily forced a smile. "I'm glad it's all working out. But...I can only teach her so much."

Now that she knew the part her uncle had played in the ranch's woes, she didn't know how much longer she could stay. "Perhaps we should try to find another tutor..."

Peggy Sue's face darkened in alarm. "Oh no! Ginny wouldn't want anyone else but you."

In no mood to argue or explain, Emily let the matter drop.

Peggy Sue blinked as if holding back tears. "I hate that my daughter can never fully experience life. You know, like other children."

"Ginny experiences life as fully anyone," Emily said. "She just does it in a different way." Through Ginny's eyes, Emily had learned to look beyond the obvious and see the merits of ranching life. "She sees things that most of us miss."

Peggy Sue lowered her gaze. "I apologize for the things I said."

"You were just concerned. I don't blame you for that, but I know a little about working with the blind. My mother did a lot of charity work and often took me with her. One of the places we visited was the Perkins Institution for the Blind, and I saw how they worked with children like Ginny. That's where I got the idea to glue string on the globe."

"It's not just that's she's blind," Peggy Sue said. "I guess you probably figured out I had her out of wedlock."

Emily didn't want to mention that she'd already heard that from Cookie. "That matters none to me and has nothing to do with her education."

"A lady like you can't know what it's like to live in shame. My own parents disowned me. No one would hire me. I didn't even feel welcomed in church." Tears filled Peggy Sue's eyes. "I'm afraid some of my disgrace has rubbed off on Ginny."

Emily didn't know what to say. Peggy Sue was wrong to think Emily knew nothing of shame. She knew, all right. Knew all too well how it felt to be shunned by society and have her family name met with curses. Almost overnight, she'd lost everything: home, respect—even the people she'd thought were her friends.

The memory of walking down the street amid icy stares would remain with her for the rest of her life. Emily knew firsthand what it meant to live under the shadow of her uncle's dishonest deeds. If word got out in Haywire that she was related to the owner of Fields & Fields, she might have to relive the nightmare all over again. Oh yes, she knew shame and humiliation. But of course, she couldn't tell Peggy Sue that. Didn't dare.

Peggy Sue did get one thing right, though; shame could rub off on Ginny, if it hadn't already. But there was still hope.

With this thought in mind, she took Peggy Sue's hand in her own. "I don't know everything you went through, but I do know this. You're a good, hard-working woman who loves her daughter. *That's* what will rub off on Ginny."

Emily had hoped to relieve Peggy Sue's worries and make her feel better. Instead, the housekeeper's tears flowed more freely. Releasing her hand, Emily pulled a handkerchief out of her sleeve and handed it to her.

Peggy Sue dabbed at her wet cheeks. "Had it not

been for Mr. McKnight, I don't know what would have happened to us." She was choked with emotion and her gratitude shimmered through her tears. "Thank you," she whispered. Taking Emily's hand, she shook it. "Thank you."

After Peggy Sue left, Emily walked up the stairs to her room with a heavy heart.

When she'd agreed to stay in the marriage, she'd felt like she could always leave if things got out of hand. Chase had even said as much.

Now, the thought of leaving the ranch seemed more like a nightmare than the answer to a prayer.

29

THAT NIGHT, EMILY MET CHASE AT THE STABLES AS planned. The horses were already saddled and ready to go.

Chase greeted her with a smile. He seemed relaxed. Certainly, more relaxed than she was. Since finding that letter in the ranch ledger, she hadn't been able to think of anything else.

Suddenly, all the secrets, lies, and half-truths felt like a heavy weight on her shoulders. She didn't know how much longer she could continue to keep everything bottled inside. Knowing the role her uncle had played in the ranch's troubles was almost more than she could bear.

Pushing her troubled thoughts aside, she tried to focus on her surroundings. It was a beautiful night, the velvety sky ablaze with dazzling stars. The full moon hung big and bright over the hills, giving the land shape and form. Knowing how much Chase loved this ranch, she felt as if she were riding through the channels of his heart.

She'd fallen into the habit lately of thinking up ways

to describe the world to Ginny. The very act made her study her surroundings as never before, and this helped her see things she might have previously missed or taken for granted. This more intense way of seeing enhanced her enjoyment and filled her with appreciation.

Tomorrow, she would tell Ginny that the land had looked like a counterpane spread far and wide. The hills were a giant's feet rising beneath the bed-covers. Moonlight trickled across the giant's bed like spilled cream.

Inhaling the brisk night air, she was surprised that the smell of cattle no longer bothered her. The truth was, she hardly noticed it anymore. Instead, she had learned to pick out other scents—pleasant scents. Tonight, the smell of laurel, sage, and freshly mowed grass created a fragrance sweeter than any perfume.

After riding in silence for several moments, Chase reined in his horse. "There they are," he called, a note of pride in his voice. "The heavies."

Emily guided her horse to his side. A wooden fence surrounded a pen, inside of which were perhaps fifty to a hundred cows. Almost all were lying down, their bulky bodies rising from the ground like dark mounds.

"These heifers are all expecting their first calves sometime in the next couple of days," he explained. "That's why we have to keep our eyes on them. During calving season, anything that can go wrong will go wrong. Count on it."

"Do you expect any to give birth tonight?" she asked.

"Maybe that one," he said, tossing a nod at a cow that couldn't seem to make up her mind whether to stand or lie down.

"What happens after the calf is born?"

"The good Lord willin',' the mother will take over its care. If not, it'll be up to us to see that she does. From time to time, we get an ornery cow who wants nothin' to do with her young. But that don't happen too often."

He went on to explain all the work that followed birthing. "Calves are watched to make sure they have full bellies. When they get older, they sometimes get separated from their mothers. That's when the mama cow and her babe wander around bawlin' until they find each other." He chuckled. "You never heard such a ruckus."

She smiled. It was easy to see that raising cattle wasn't just a business with him. "You really care for the cattle, don't you?"

The question seemed to surprise him. "Any rancher worth his salt knows to first care for the cattle, then his horse, and finally, himself."

She studied him. "That doesn't leave room for anyone else," she said.

"Sure it does," he said. "Takin' care of himself means takin' care of the people he cares about."

The tender note in his voice quickened her pulse, and she looked away.

"Cookie said you have the largest privately owned ranch around," she said, desperate to fill in the awkward silence that pulsed between them.

"That's true," he said. "The drought forced many local ranchers to take out loans they could ill afford. Many of my neighbors lost everythin'. The loan company sold the repossessed properties to English lords and German barons at great profit. Guess you could

say that foreigners now own a good portion of the
west." An edge of bitterness had crept into his voice.
"Outside investors have no feel for the land or even
the cattle."

Emily listened with growing dismay. Chase hadn't
mentioned the loan company by name, but she now
knew that he was talking about Fields & Fields. Her
father would turn over in his grave if he knew how the
company he'd founded had caused so many people to
lose their homes and livelihoods.

Nothing of the sort would have happened had she
taken over as her father had wished. Had her father
known all along what his brother was capable of? Is that
why he'd wanted her to take charge after his death?

Unfortunately, she'd had no interest in running a
loan company. Instead of complying with her father's
wishes, she'd gone away to college, leaving the family
business in her uncle's hands.

Had she not stubbornly and maybe even selfishly
followed her own dreams, things would have turned
out quite differently, of that she was certain. The
thought twisted inside her like a knife, and it was all
she could do to breathe.

On some level, she was conscious of Chase speaking,
but her frozen mind was unable to decipher his words.

"You okay?" he asked at length.

"What?" Snapping out of her inertia, she nodded.
"Oh, I'm fine. I was just...wondering why your
grandfather picked this particular piece of land."

"Grandpapa said it was where the sagebrush grew
the tallest."

His teeth flashed in the moonlight, and his eyes

shone bright as a sunlit sea. Grateful that she didn't have to describe the color of his eyes in a way that Ginny would understand, she returned his smile.

One of the cows made a lowing sound, and Chase's head swiveled in its direction before turning back to her. As if to guess her thoughts, he asked, "How are Ginny's lessons goin'?"

"They're going well. She has a quick mind. Sometimes I think she's teaching me more than I'm teaching her."

He chuckled. "Isn't that the way it's supposed to be?"

"I guess so, but…"

His gaze sharpened. "But?"

"I'm only here for a short while. After I'm gone—"

The ridges in his forehead deepened. "We'll cross that bridge when we come to it."

"You might have trouble finding a qualified tutor here," she said. "That's why I think Ginny would benefit from attending the school for the blind in Boston."

Chase shook his head. "I doubt you'd ever get Peggy Sue to agree to that."

Emily could hardly fault Peggy Sue for not wanting to leave the ranch and the protection it offered. Until finding that letter from her uncle, Emily had believed the ranch safe too. She now knew what a mistake that had been.

"How are your other students doing?" he asked, sounding genuinely interested.

"Better than I'd hoped. I don't think they notice Ginny's blindness anymore, and she likes having them around."

"That's good," he said. "I'm glad it's all workin' out."

Surprised by how much his approval meant to her, Emily chewed on her bottom lip and wished to God she'd never found that letter from her uncle's company.

Chase held her gaze for a long moment. "Last week…" he began, and something in his voice made her heart squeeze in her chest. "You called me husband."

She drew in her breath. The word had rolled off her tongue with such ease that she'd hardly noticed. "Was…was that a problem?"

"No, no problem. It's just…" She heard his intake of breath. "For a moment, it sounded like we were really married."

She frowned. "But we are married."

"I don't mean just legally. I mean…it sounded like we were together for real."

With a shock, she realized how much she wanted that, wanted them to be husband and wife in the way the good Lord intended. But the damage her uncle had done to the town, to the ranch, made that an impossible dream.

When she failed to respond, Chase let out an audible sigh. "I know you're not fond of cattle. Or the ranch." His voice rang with disappointment. "But I thought—"

"I'm glad I could help you keep the ranch," she said abruptly, her cool manner belying her misery. At first, she had hated the isolation of the ranch. But that was before. Before she'd met Cookie and the rest of the ranch family. Before she had experienced the joy of horseback riding. Before she had gotten to know and, yes, maybe even love the stranger she had married…

He'd turned his head away before she could read his

expression. Even so, she sensed—felt—his withdrawal. But it couldn't be helped. If she gave in to her feelings now, it would only make things more difficult, more painful, more unbearable when it came time to leave.

From the distance came a chorus of yipping animals. The sound was a grim reminder that the life she'd escaped could be slowly closing in on her, and she shuddered.

As if he'd sensed something, Chase's head snapped back in her direction. "Cold?" he asked.

"No. It's just…the wolves."

"Coyotes," he said. He guided his horse away from the fence. "Don't worry," he called over his shoulder. "They sound closer than they are."

"Not worried," she said, urging her horse to follow. It wasn't the coyotes that concerned her. It was the feeling she was more deeply involved in the ranch, its residents, and its owner than she'd ever intended, and certainly more deeply than was wise.

30

During the week that followed, Emily hardly saw Chase. He left long before she woke in the morning and didn't come back until late at night. That was if he came back at all.

Cookie had told her more than once that calving time required all hands on deck. Still, it bothered her that no matter what happened on the ranch, Chase never missed his Friday trips to town.

She tried not thinking of him and Mrs. Decker together, but she couldn't help it. Even Kansas Pete had said that the widow would have made Chase a fine wife. Emily could hardly blame him for thinking that. Mrs. Decker evidently knew all about cattle and running a ranch, skills that Emily knew nothing about.

Fortunately, her classes kept her busy. Still, she felt like she was always on alert. Always looking for Chase. Listening for him.

Last night was one of the nights that he'd failed to show. She'd stayed awake until the wee hours of the morn, listening for his tread. When it didn't come, she'd fallen into a restless sleep that left her feeling tired and out of sorts.

Hoping to take her mind off Chase and the vague yet unsettling feeling that something bad was about to happen, she tried to think what to do with her time.

The twins were needed at home that day, so no classes had been scheduled. Was that why she felt at loose ends? Why this nagging feeling of impending doom haunted her? Even the gray sky seemed to reflect her dark mood.

"Looks like rain," she said when Cookie joined her on the veranda.

"Nope," he said. "No loose drawers."

She laughed. Trust Cookie to make her laugh on a day when such a thing seemed unlikely. "Is calving always like this?" she asked.

"Like this?" Cookie studied her. "You mean are the boys usually gone so much?" he asked, and she got the feeling he purposely omitted mentioning Chase's name. "Yep, pretty much so. Heard they had a couple of difficult births, but so far, they've only lost a couple."

"Maybe I'll ride out and see if they can use more help," she said.

"They can always use an extra pair of hands," he said. "Just be prepared to fall in love."

She frowned. "What?"

He laughed at her expression. "Ever see a newborn calf?"

"No," she admitted.

"Well then. You're in for a real treat."

Ginny joined them, looking especially pretty in

a blue dress. Her hair fell down her back in a single braid. "Can I go and see the baby cows too?"

"That's up to your teacher here," Cookie said.

"Can I, Mrs. Knight? Can I?"

"It's *may I,* and yes, I think that can be arranged."

"May we go now?" Ginny asked.

Emily cast a glance at the threatening sky. "Yes, but we'd better hurry. We don't want to get caught in the rain."

Ginny couldn't stop talking the entire time it took them to walk the distance to the calving pen. She was so excited, she couldn't seem to get her words out fast enough.

It was a pleasant walk. The air was warm and humid, but the sun stayed hidden behind thick clouds.

The moment they reached the calf pen, Ginny's foot instinctively found the lower rung of the wooden fence. Climbing the fence as quickly as a monkey, she leaned over the top rail.

Worried that she might fall, Emily caught hold of the ties of her dress, ready to pull her back if necessary.

Ginny held her head in such a way as if to capture every sound and practically beamed from ear to ear.

Emily was just as captivated as Ginny. The calves with their white faces and wobbly legs were adorable. Cookie was right. Already she found herself falling in love.

"What are they doing?" Ginny asked.

"Well, let's see. Some of the calves are lying down, their brown bodies partially hidden by the tall grass. One little fellow is taking milk from its mother."

"Why is that one crying?" Ginny asked, pointing in the general direction of a bawling calf. "Is it hurt?"

Chase's voice floated from behind. "Not hurt. Just lookin' for his mother."

Surprised to hear his voice, Emily turned, and her heart jolted at sight of him. Sitting astride his horse, he looked down at them with a grin. Once again, she was reminded what a handsome man he was, and the thought brought a flush to her already heated face.

"How did he lose her?" Ginny asked.

Chase dismounted and, holding the reins in one hand, joined them by the fence. "That little fella is a curious one. The boys call him Tumbleweed."

Ginny frowned. "Is that cuz he has thorns?"

"No," Chase said. "It's because he keeps wanderin' off."

"Does he ever got lost?" Ginny asked.

"Sometimes," Chase said. "But don't worry. His mother always finds him. Do you know how she does it?"

Ginny thought for a moment. "She keeps looking till she sees him?"

"Nope," Chase said, flashing a grin. "She smells him. Cows have a keen sense of smell."

"Kind of like you do, Ginny," Emily said. "You can smell things that I can't."

"Can I touch one?" Ginny asked. "Can I touch Tumbleweed? Pleeeeeeease?"

Resisting the urge to correct Ginny's grammar, Emily gave Chase a beseeching look.

Chase tugged on the brim of his hat. "Well, it's like this. Mama cows are real protective of their young. They don't like strangers touchin' them."

"But I'm not a stranger," Ginny protested.

"Hmm. Okay, I'll tell you what. I'll let you touch one of the older cows in the barn. How's that?"

Ginny looked like she was about to burst with joy. "Oh, I can hardly wait."

Laughing at her enthusiasm, Chase tethered his horse. Taking Ginny by the hand, he helped her down from the fence. "This way, ladies," he said and led the way.

Chase spent a lot of time with Ginny, and his patience with her warmed Emily's heart. As if she didn't have enough to worry about, Emily felt herself becoming more and more attached to him and everything he cared about.

That afternoon, Emily found Ginny seated at the dining room table.

"Look," Ginny said, holding up a sheet of paper, a wide smile on her face. She had drawn a picture of a cow, and Emily was amazed. Chase had described the cow down to the patch on her forehead, and Ginny had accurately captured the image.

She still marveled at Chase's patience with Ginny and how he had allowed her to touch the cow from the tip of her nose all the way to the swishing tail.

"What a lovely picture," Emily said. "We must hang it on the wall."

Ginny laid the paper down and smoothed it flat with the palm of her hand.

A flash of light drew Emily's gaze to the window. Swirling clouds drifted over the distant hills, accompanied by a bright bolt of light. The storm was still too far away for the thunder to be heard.

"It's lightning, isn't it?" Ginny asked.

The child never failed to amaze her. "Now how do you know that?"

"The air feels different," Ginny said. "It feels heavy and tingly."

"It's dry lightning," Cookie said from the kitchen doorway. "The worst kind."

"I know what lightning looks like," Ginny said and made a zigzagging gesture with her finger.

A bright flash drew Emily's gaze back to the window. She worried about Chase. People were known to be struck by lightning. As always, his number one concern would be for the cattle, not himself. Even Cookie looked worried.

Leaving Ginny to her drawing, Emily walked outside and stood on the veranda to watch the dark sky. The air had taken on a greenish tint and had a sweet, pungent smell. The wind had picked up slightly. A thunderbolt stabbed the ground, followed by a bright upward flash and the low rumble of thunder. Nature was putting on quite a show.

After watching the northern sky for several minutes, Emily started back to the house, but something stopped her. Something had changed, but what?

She returned to the veranda railing and quickly spotted the column of smoke rising from the ground even before she smelled it.

Gasping, she clutched her hands to her chest and watched in horror as the smoke began to spread.

31

CHASE BEAT THE FLAMES WITH THE SHIRT OFF HIS BACK, his bare chest glistening with sweat. Fanned by the wind, the fire spread quickly across the dry grass.

Bolts of lightning zigzagged to the ground, followed by the crash of thunder.

Bright-orange tongues licked at a wagon, and the bales of hay stacked on the flatbed quickly caught fire.

Cattle had been moved away from the metal barbed-wire fences, but they were still in danger of being struck. Last year, the ranch had lost five cattle to lightning.

Chase's present worry was for the pen that housed the new mothers and their offspring. If the wind grew any stronger, the outbuildings might go up in flames, and fire could spread as far as the main house.

All around him, his cowhands slapped furiously at the ground with whatever they could get their hands on. Big-Foot Harry and Beanpole Tom pounded the flames with shovels. Faces streaked with soot and ashes, they looked like warriors on the warpath.

Rusty rode up on his horse and tossed burlap bags

to the men. Chase dropped his tattered shirt and grabbed a bag midair. Thick, scorching smoke burned his eyes, and a sharp, tangy smell seared his lungs, but there was no time to think of physical discomforts.

Loud bellows of panicky cows and frightened calves drowned out the shouts and curses of the cowhands beating the earth with frantic blows. Despite their efforts, the wind scattered the embers, and flames continued to spread.

Lightning forked the sky, followed by loud booms that jarred the earth. Rusty's startled horse reared up on its hind legs, throwing its rider.

Cursing beneath his breath, Chase ran toward the fallen man and dropped on his knees by his side. "Rusty!"

Rusty's eyes flickered, but he didn't speak. He looked dazed and had a nasty bump on his head.

"I'll take him back," Boomer said, waving Big-Foot Harry over. "We need a hand over here!"

While the two men struggled to lift Rusty off the ground, Chase picked up his burlap bag and set to work again. He was now down three men, and the fire continued to spread.

He beat the flames until his arms ached. Fire licked at his boots and the legs of his trousers. Sweat ran down his face and bare chest. Somehow, they had to keep the flames from reaching the taller grass next to the outbuildings. Gasping for air, he stopped to catch his breath. That was when he saw her.

Emily.

Only her small size allowed him to recognize her through the thick smoke. What in the name of Sam Hill…?

Fearing for her safety, he rushed to her side and snatched the burlap bag out of her hands.

"Go!" His throat was raw and his voice hoarse. Not giving her a chance to argue, he repeated his command. "I said, go!" The last thing he needed was to worry about her getting injured.

Her spine stiffened, and the stubborn look he'd come to dread suffused her face. "I'm not leaving."

His anger flared. He didn't have time to argue. "I mean it, Emily." He was yelling now but didn't care. "It's dangerous. Now go!"

"I'm not going," she yelled back. "This is my home too!"

Stunned by her words, he stared at her, speechless. It took him a full moment before he could find his voice again.

"Do...do you mean that?" he stammered. "About this being your home?"

She drew in her breath as if she too had been surprised, even moved, by the words that had fallen from her lips. "I mean it," she said, her voice thick with emotion.

Dropping the burlap bag, he cleared the distance between them. He took her in his arms and spun her around. "You'll never know how much I wanted to hear you say that." Setting her down, he gazed at her, his heart feeling as if it would burst with joy.

She looked up from his arms with swimming eyes. Her tears left white streaks on her ash-covered face.

God, she was beautiful. Lost in the depth of her eyes, he could see nothing but the warm glow he hoped—prayed—was for him. She lifted her hand to his cheek, and her touch ignited something inside. Pulling her close, he captured her lips with his own.

The feel of her mouth on his was every bit as sweet as he'd imagined, every bit as soft and as yielding as he'd envisioned.

Her warm breath mingled with his and chased away the acid taste in his mouth. He was lost in her embrace, his mind blank except for the feel of her. For a brief moment, nothing else seemed to exist. Certainly not the fire…

He might have stayed there forever had a sudden cloudburst not driven them apart.

The cowhands greeted the rain with whoops and hollers. A quick glance told Chase the worst was over. As joyful as he felt, he didn't move. He feared if he did, she would disappear as quickly as the flames had vanished beneath the pounding rain. Was she real? Or simply a vision, a dream? Had he only imagined her kiss? Her touch? The feel of her?

She lifted her face to the sky, her eyes closed against the battering rain. Laughter bubbled out of her like a song. "Thank you, thank you, God," she cried. Lowering her head, she looked straight at him and added in a softer voice, "Our home is safe."

He drew in his breath. Coming from her, they were the sweetest words he'd ever heard. He longed to take her in his arms again. Kiss her until they were both breathless and spent, kiss her until the next day, the next year. The next century.

He would have done exactly that had his foreman not appeared at his side and slapped him on the back. The man was soaking wet.

"Looks like somebody up there likes us," Boomer said. Throwing his head back, he laughed as water cascaded off his whiskered face.

Chase's gaze sought Emily's, and her soft eyes seemed to absorb him into their very depths. He longed to hug her and finish what they had started, but Boomer had reminded him their work was far from done.

"We'd better settle those mamas down, or we're gonna have a bunch of hungry calves on our hands," Boomer called, spurring the men into action.

As quickly as it started, the rain had stopped. It hadn't done much to quench the thirst of a parched ground, but the fire was out, and for now, that was enough.

Reminded that duty came before all else, Chase gave his men a thumbs-up. Boomer was right to worry. Frightened cows held their milk.

Water dripping off her hat, Emily's eyes sought his, and she looked equally surprised at what had transpired between them. "I'll bring you fresh clothes," she said.

He shook his head. Clothes were the least of his concern. "I need you to check on Rusty." He valued her nursing skills and knew the injured man could be in no better hands. "Would you do that for me?"

"Of course I will," she said. Her face and clothes were drenched and now splattered with mud. Yet never had she looked more beautiful, more desirable.

Her cheeks colored beneath his gaze, telling him she shared his thoughts. Fighting the impulse to take her in his arms again, he needed every bit of willpower he had to walk away and follow his men.

32

EMILY RAN INTO THE HOUSE CALLING PEGGY SUE'S NAME.

She had just come from the bunkhouse and was soaked to the skin. Water sloshed from her boots and dripped off her hat. She found the housekeeper cleaning silver in the dining room.

"Rusty's been hurt."

Peggy Sue gasped and dropped the spoon she'd been polishing.

Emily quickly assured her that he'd be all right. He was conscious but still dazed and had an egg-size bump on the back of his head. "I need you to sit with him just to make certain."

She would have stayed with him, but she had the feeling he would prefer Peggy Sue by his side.

Peggy Sue jumped to her feet. "Where is he?"

"In the bunkhouse." Emily caught Peggy Sue by the arm. "Try to keep him awake as much as possible."

Peggy Sue nodded and raced out of the room.

Satisfied that Rusty would be in good hands, Emily ran upstairs to change, her wet skirt flapping against her legs. Her hair was limp and her arms sore from fighting the fire. But that wasn't what caught her attention when she gazed at her image in the mirror.

Beneath her sopping-wet clothes, her body felt on fire. Her cheeks were flushed to a rosy pink, and a bright inner glow burned from the depths of her eyes. She touched her lips with her fingertips. Did she only imagine they were still swollen from Chase's kiss?

She couldn't believe it. He'd kissed her. He'd kissed her!

And she had kissed him back.

She filled the porcelain basin from the pitcher with shaky hands and splashed water on her heated face. Her lips still burned with the memory of his kiss, and a strange tingly feeling rushed through her limbs. Her body ached with a newly discovered need, and a knot of feelings whirled within. Was this how it felt to be in love? To be truly, fully, and completely in love? Nothing she had experienced in the past compared to how she felt at that moment.

She reached for the towel and buried her face in it. She had been in love before, but never had she felt quite like this.

His name was James Watkins. At the time, she'd thought she was the luckiest girl alive. He was handsome, successful, witty, and smart. She had been the envy of Boston's debutantes.

The day he'd placed the two-carat diamond betrothal ring on her finger, he'd promised her the moon. He'd vowed to love her forever, and fool that she was, she'd believed him.

Yet he'd been the first to bail out on her after the Fields & Fields scandal broke. He had political ambitions and said he couldn't afford to have his name linked with hers. Her uncle's arrest made her a liability. Those were his exact words. A liability.

Had he plunged a knife in her heart, he couldn't have hurt her more. It still hurt—though surprisingly, she hadn't thought about him in recent weeks. Even more surprising, she couldn't remember James's kisses affecting her as much as Chase's.

She drew in her breath. When had this happened? When had the man, the stranger she'd accidentally married, stolen her heart? When had the ranch she'd once had an aversion to become the home she now loved?

Pulling the towel away from her face, she tried to still her pounding heart. He'd kissed her, but the promise in his eyes, on his lips, in his voice, had made it clear he wouldn't stop there. He wanted her every bit as much as she wanted him, and her body shivered with anticipation.

Such was her joy that she didn't want to think about how she was living on the edge of an emotional cliff. If she acted on her feelings, she would have to tell him the truth, tell him that she was the niece of the man who had put his ranch in jeopardy. Tell him…

She closed her eyes. Tell him that she was as much to blame as her uncle. Knowing she was about to lose everything yet a second time, she sank to the floor on bended knee.

⁂

Chase came home late that night. Emily had just about given up on him when the bedroom door flew open. She jumped and dropped her hairbrush.

He closed the door behind him. "Sorry," he said. "I thought you'd be asleep by now. Didn't mean to startle you."

She clutched at the opening of her dressing gown. For the past several hours, she had rehearsed what to say to him. Before they took things any further, he had the right to know the truth of who she was. But the moment he'd stepped through the door, all reason and good intentions had left her. All she could think about was being back in his arms.

He was still bare-chested, and his bronzed skin gleamed beneath the gas lamp's soft light. Though she tried her best not to stare, her eyes had a mind of their own. Just his presence made her heart race. Her knees threatened to cave, and a quiver surged through her veins.

He appraised her, his eyes filled with longing. "Is Rusty—?"

"He's okay," she stammered.

A look of relief crossed his face. "Good to hear."

"Are…are the cattle all right?" she asked.

He nodded. "Took us a while, but we finally got them settled."

"That's…that's g-good news," she stammered.

He pulled off his hat and tossed it on a chair. "We need to talk."

Not sure what to make of his serious tone, Emily swallowed hard. Had she read too much into his kiss? Had she misinterpreted what had transpired between them?

"What happened…" he began slowly.

She held her breath, but he didn't complete his

sentence. Didn't utter the words *when we kissed,* and for that, she was grateful. Just being in his presence made it hard to think straight.

She searched his face. Did he regret what had happened? Was that it?

Gathering what little pride she had and feeling the need to save face, she said, "Things…happen during the heat of the moment." It was a question as much as a statement.

Beneath his furrowed forehead, Chase's eyes narrowed. "Is that what you think? I kissed you in the heat of the moment?"

She didn't know what to think, and they stood sizing each other up like two strangers meeting on a trail.

"I–I'm not blaming you," she stammered at last. "The fire… You could have lost everything. The cattle. The ranch…"

He cut her off with a wave of his hand. "And what you said? About this being your home. Was that in the heat of the moment too?"

"I meant what I said," she whispered. "But…" She turned her head away.

"Emily, look at me. Talk to me."

When she finally worked up the nerve to look at him, she had to blink away the tears to see him clearly.

He took a step closer. "Tell me to my face that what happened meant nothin'. That it was in the heat of the moment." He took another step forward. "Tell me you don't want to finish what we started." This time, he'd moved so close, she could feel his warm breath.

"I can't say that," she said. "Because…it would be a lie."

A spark flared in his eyes. He studied her as if to make certain he'd heard right before holding out his hand. Heart pounding, she gazed at his hand for a long moment before placing her hand in his. Groaning, he pulled her close and wrapped her in his arms. She laid her head on his bare shoulder and refused to think about anything but the feel of him. Palms pressed against his bare chest, she inhaled his manly scent and felt like she was floating on a cloud.

"God, Emily. I waited so long for this," he whispered in her hair.

Fingers on her chin, he lifted her face to his and nuzzled her on the forehead, nose, and cheek. Finally, he kissed her fully on the lips.

Standing on tiptoes, she worked her arms around his neck and kissed him back with the same intensity. The same sense of urgency. "I don't want you to hate me," she murmured between kisses.

"I could never hate you."

"When I came here, I had no idea that—"

"I know," he said. "I know."

"You don't know," she whispered back.

"Shh." He touched a finger to her lips and then cupped her face in his hands. "I know enough. What's important is where we go from here."

She gazed at him in awe and wonder. Why had it taken her so long to know what was now so utterly clear? She now knew without a doubt that she loved this man with her whole heart and soul. With the realization came dismay. For love required honesty. Openness.

"There's something you should know."

He shook his head. "The only thing I need to know

is that we care for each other and want to make this marriage work."

His words echoed through her until they reached the deepest regions of her heart. "I want that too, but—"

He cut off her words with his lips, and her mind went blank. She heard his intake of breath as his hands locked against her back. He drew her so close that she could hardly breathe. It was as if their hearts beat as one. The last of her rational thoughts dissolved into a mass of warm feelings. Her curves molded perfectly against his hard, lean body, as if they had been created for this very moment. Her head filled with the scent of him. The feel of him. The safe circle of his arms.

Cupping her chin gently, he ran his thumb over her trembling lips. "This is your home, Em. And if you let me, I'll be the best husband you could ever want."

He trailed heated kisses all the way to the hollow of her neck before covering her mouth once again with his own. Ripples of pure joy rushed through her as she kissed him back, giving as freely as she received.

When at last their lips parted, his smoldering eyes searched hers. The tenderness of his gaze made her senses spin, and she felt more alive than she'd ever thought possible.

Taking her by the hand, he pulled her slowly across the room, stopping just short of the bed. "Are you sure?" he asked, his voice gentle.

The question awakened feelings she hadn't even known existed. She'd never been so certain of anything in her life.

"Before you answer," he said, touching a finger

to her lips. "I think you should know that once you become fully mine, I'm never gonna let you go."

Her lips quivered beneath his touch. "The ranch," she whispered.

His eyes brimmed with tenderness. "This has nothing to do with the ranch." Sliding his hand up her arm, he drew in his breath.

She longed to hear the word *love* fall from his lips. Maybe it was too soon. Maybe she was rushing things.

"So I ask again," he said softly. "Are you sure?"

Sure? Oh yes, she couldn't be more certain. She wanted to be in his arms, in his bed, in his life. Unable to find her voice, she let her dressing gown fall from her shoulders to the floor. She stood before him completely naked, silently begging him to take her and fulfill the promise in his eyes.

The look on his face told her that was answer enough.

33

EMILY WOKE THE NEXT MORNING IN A WARM GLOW OF pleasant sensations and happy memories. She instinctively reached across the bed for Chase, but he was gone. Disappointment washing over her like a wave of cold water, she sat up.

She had wanted to wake in his arms. To feel the ecstasy of his touch, the joy of his kisses, the feel of his body next to hers. She'd wanted to know for certain that last night had really occurred and hadn't just been a dream.

Lying back on the pillow, she closed her eyes, and a vision of him quickly sprang to mind. Every curve of his nose, his jaw, his mouth had become so ingrained in her, it was almost as if he was still in the room with her.

Her body tingled with the memory of all that had happened between them, and she flushed anew.

Stretching, she counted the hours until she would be back in his arms and smiled. She was Chase McKnight's wife. He was her husband. Really and truly her husband.

The thought sent waves of happiness rushing through her. Not even the nagging feeling that something bad was about to happen could take away the pleasure she felt. Today was the day to bask in the lingering memories that filled her with such joy. The rest would have to wait.

⁂

Seated at his desk, Chase rubbed his bristly chin and stared at the newspaper his uncle had just thrust in his hands. After spending the night in Emily's arms, he was in no mood to deal with problems.

What he wanted was to go back to their room and wake Emily with his kisses. He wanted to crawl back in bed with her and—

His uncle's impatient voice cut through Chase's thoughts. "Well?"

Chase shook the vision of Emily from his head. "Why are you showing me this?"

His uncle stopped pacing, a puzzled look on his face. "What's wrong with you?"

"Nothing."

"Then read it!"

Chase scanned the headlines, and the name Fields & Fields snapped him to attention. The article was about Harry Fields, who was now serving time in the Charlestown State Prison in Massachusetts.

Chase dropped the paper on his desk. "It's about time he got what's coming to him." After the damage Fields and his company had done to local ranchers— had done to Chase's own ranch—no prison term would be long enough. Had it not been for Fields, his father would never have been forced to remarry, and Chase wouldn't have had to fight to keep the ranch. Of course, then he would never have met Emily…

Emily.

Just thinking her name made him marvel at the depth of his feelings. Though it was still only morning, already the minutes away from her seemed like an eternity. For once, he resented the chores that had pulled him from her bed. Resented the hours until he could hold her again.

"Read the rest," his uncle said, interrupting Chase's thoughts.

"Why?"

"Just do it."

Shaking his head, Chase scanned the article and was about to toss the paper aside when his gaze froze on his own name. Sitting forward, he read the paragraph below the boldly printed headline word for word.

Emily Fields, wife of local rancher Chase McKnight, testified that she knew nothing of her uncle's affairs, but her testimony was put in question when…

Feeling like he'd suddenly been tossed by a raging bull, Chase sat back. Mouth dry, he stared at his uncle, incredulous.

Baxter stopped pacing and lowered himself into the chair in front of Chase's desk. "I take it you had no knowledge of her true identity."

"No, none," Chase said, still in shock. *You know nothing about me,* she'd said.

I know enough.

"So what are you gonna do?"

Chase frowned. "Do?" He pinched his forehead and tried to think. "Emily's not responsible for her uncle's crimes." He dropped his hand. "She helped me save the ranch."

Uncle Baxter's mouth thinned beneath his mustache. "I wouldn't be so sure of that. The apple doesn't fall far from the tree. In case you hadn't noticed, the rustling problem has gotten worse—a lot worse—since your marriage."

Chase stared at his uncle. "You're not saying that Emily—"

"It wouldn't be the first time cattle thieves have worked with an insider. Now that her uncle is in prison, the woman is without means of her own. As an insider, she—"

Chase's temper snapped. "You're talking about my wife!"

He refused to believe that the woman he'd held in his arms, the woman who had murmured such sweet words in his ear, would try to harm him. Harm the ranch. It made no sense. "You don't know her."

His uncle's eyebrows shot up. "And you do? You didn't even know her true identity!"

"I know she would never purposely harm me!"

Baxter shook his head. "She's already done harm." He stabbed the desk with his finger. "That article could have serious consequences for the ranch."

"How?"

"I talked to the editor. That story was planted by your stepbrother."

Chase's nostrils flared. Royce again. He should have known. "How did he find out about Emily?"

"Apparently, a traveling salesman saw her in the sweets shop. Royce overheard him inquiring about her and was able to pull out enough information from Garvey to track down the rest."

Chase recalled Royce telling him about a visitor in town. *He had some interesting things to say. Would you like to hear what they were?*

"Knowing her true identity doesn't change a thing." Chase had always known she was running from something. At times, he'd sensed that her secret was a barrier between them. What a relief to know that nothing now stood between them!

His uncle's face darkened. "It might change a lot of things. If she's responsible for the rustling problem, she won't want to stick around once her cover is blown."

Chase slammed the desk with his fist. "I told you—"

"I know what you told me!" Baxter gave an impatient gesture with his hand. "If you're right, she might still have reason to leave." Palms on the desk, he leaned forward. "How do you think folks will react when they find out who she is? Do you think she'll stick around to find out? She ran away once. Royce is betting she'll do it again. It's what he's counting on."

Chase felt like all the blood had drained from his body. Elbows on the desk, he clasped his hands. "She won't leave. She knows how important the ranch is to me." She knew how it felt to be his bed, in his arms, in his heart.

"How can you be so sure?" Baxter asked.

That was the problem. Chase couldn't be sure. Last

night had meant everything to him, but how could he be certain it had meant the same to her?

Uncle Baxter straightened. "Royce is a gambler, just like your pa, and he's betting that Emily will either leave of her own free will or be forced to leave. There're a lot of angry people around here who could make her life hell."

"She won't leave," Chase repeated. *I won't let her.*

"She fled Boston," Uncle Baxter said stubbornly. He stood and donned his derby, a dubious look on his face. "You better make sure she doesn't run again. For the sake of the ranch."

The moment his uncle left, Chase stormed through the house calling Emily's name. It wasn't the ranch that worried him. He now knew he could lose so much more. He could lose the woman he loved!

"She rode into town," Cookie called from the kitchen.

"What?" Chase stopped in his tracks. "When?"

"About an hour ago. Said she needed to purchase more books." Cookie frowned. "Something wrong?"

"I sure in blazes hope not." Spinning around, Chase dashed outside and raced to the stables for his horse.

34

EMILY TOOK HER TIME RIDING TO TOWN AND SAVORED every moment. Seen through the eyes of love, the world had taken on magical qualities that made her heart sing. Today, the air seemed clearer, the sky bluer, and the wildflowers on the side of the road brighter than ever before.

She rode past a herd of mustangs grazing upon the knee-high grass, tails to the wind. The air vibrated with the sounds of nature. Insects buzzed, prairie dogs barked, and songbirds sang.

She couldn't remember ever feeling so happy. Even Daisy seemed to sense her good mood, and the mare was spunkier than usual.

She was Chase McKnight's wife. No more pretending. Her marriage was real.

Still, she had a hard time believing it. They'd started out two strangers who were worlds apart, and now it was as if they had merged as one.

The very thought filled her with such awe and wonder that she was certain her heart would burst with joy. She couldn't stop thinking of the night spent in Chase's arms. The sweet words whispered between them. The way he made her feel…

How was it possible to live so long and not know the thrill of loving someone like Chase?

Her exuberance lasted until she reached the deserted Circle R ranch. The broken windmill and fences, the tumbleweeds and deserted pens hit her with a stab of reality. *You'll find lots of deserted ranches around here.*

Her uncle's unethical business practices had come to light during the trial. But seeing the destruction he'd brought about with her own two eyes made it so much more real to her. So much more horrendous.

Panic welled inside her. Last night in Chase's arms, she had severed herself mentally from the past and pretended that it no longer mattered. But it did. Oh God, it did!

Forcing herself to breathe, Emily tried to think. Chase had the right to know she was the niece of a man who had caused him so much trouble. A man who everyone in Haywire probably hated. A man responsible for the sorry remains of the ghostlike ranch in front of her.

Would Chase still feel the same about her once the truth was known? The question felt like a rock in her heart, and a dark cloud of depression weighed down on her.

By the time she reached the outskirts of town, she knew what she had to do. In the secret recesses of her heart, she had always known.

Tonight, she would tell Chase who she was, who her uncle was. Why she blamed herself for some of the hardships caused by Fields & Fields.

She only hoped that the love she felt for Chase gave

her the strength to do the right thing. He was a fair man—that was one of the things she loved about him. He would listen, but would he hold her blameless? Or would he turn against her as so many others had?

Was a love as new and untested as theirs strong enough to survive the uncertainties of the future? That was the question that hammered at Emily's heart as she rode down Main Street.

The center of town buzzed with activity. Horse-drawn wagons were parked haphazardly, blocking traffic and soliciting curses from irate pedestrians.

Adding to the mayhem, snake-oil salesmen hawked their wares, while Mexican farmers and Indians worked side by side, joking among themselves as they unloaded fruits and vegetables.

A wagon piled high with blocks of compressed salt rolled to a stop in front of the Haywire Feed Shop.

Vying for what little space was left, Emily tethered her horse to a hitching post a good two blocks away from her destination. She hoped Kate was working at the candy shop that day. She could use a friend.

Just as she stepped up to the wooden sidewalk, she bumped into Mrs. Buttonwood. "How nice to see you," Emily said, pleased to see a familiar face.

Mrs. Buttonwood looked startled. "Oh yes. Eh… nice to see you too." She glanced around as if looking for a means of escape. "I'm sorry. No time to chat." With that, she scurried away like a cat with a mouse.

Puzzled, Emily watched Mrs. Buttonwood vanish around a corner as if she were being chased. Hoping nothing was seriously wrong, Emily shook her head and started for the candy shop.

A boy dressed in knee pants and a flat hat yelled in a high-pitched voice, "Readallaboutit!" Since the boy looked no older than seven or eight, Emily stopped to purchase a paper.

"Why aren't you in school?" she asked.

"Ain't got time. Gotta sell these papers."

Emily frowned. Massachusetts had a compulsory law requiring children to attend school. Apparently, the same was not true of Texas.

She paid the boy with an extra coin.

"Obliged, ma'am," the boy said, pocketing the money. He then continued his spiel.

Emily's heart practically stopped. It sure did sound like he'd said Fields & Fields. But between the boy's young voice and his Texas twang, she might have misunderstood.

Still, she quickly scanned the headline, and her breath caught in her chest. Oh God, no! Not wanting to believe her eyes, she read and reread the sentence. EMILY FIELDS, WIFE OF LOCAL RANCHER CHASE MCKNIGHT…

Gulping the bile that rose to her throat, Emily fought not to panic. She glanced around and tried to think. It seemed that all eyes were directed at her and there was no place to hide.

❦

The Wandering Dog saloon was nearly empty that afternoon when Chase shouldered his way through the batwing doors. For that reason, it was easy to pick out his stepbrother hunched over a corner table, nursing a half-filled glass.

Anger coiling inside, Chase rushed over to him.

Royce looked up. "Well, well," he said. "Look what the cat just dragged in."

It was all Chase could to keep from knocking the sneer off Royce's face. "You had no right draggin' my wife into our dispute!"

Royce's eyes looked as hard and lifeless as wood knots. "The town has a right to know who she is."

Temper snapping, Chase reached down and yanked Royce to his feet by his collar. "What you did to Emily... She's not leavin', if that's what you're hopin' for. My wife is here to stay."

An ugly smile crossed Royce's face. "If you really believed that, you wouldn't be here."

Chase hated Royce for knowing that. Emily had run from her past before. It was entirely possible she'd run again.

Afraid of what he was capable of, Chase released his hold, and Royce fell back. "You're not gettin' your hands on the ranch. You have no right."

Royce's eyes glittered. "My mother's life savings went to save that ranch. That gives me every right."

"How much?" Chase demanded. "How much will it cost to get rid of you once and for all?"

Royce straightened his shirt. "More than you can afford to pay."

Chase grimaced. Royce had that part right. The current price of beef had dropped to half the price it was two years previous, partly due to the drought, but that wasn't the only reason. Thought to be the new gold, the cattle business had been flooded with speculators, and that also made prices drop.

"I'll pay back your mother's loan. Every cent."

Royce scoffed. "Why would I settle for that when I can have the whole kit and caboodle?"

"That's my deal. Take it or leave it." Chase turned but not soon enough.

"Good luck," Royce called after him. "Convincin' your *wife* to stay, I mean."

Chase froze a moment before pushing his way out the swinging doors. Halfway down the block, he bumped into Mrs. Buttonwood.

"You're just the man I wanted to see," she said and flung a newspaper at him. "I had no idea your wife was related to that…that…awful man!"

"I can't talk about this right now."

She glared up at him. "Can't or won't?"

Chase shook his head and moved past her. He couldn't talk to anyone without first talking to Emily. Where was she? Had she left town? Had Royce gotten his way?

He glanced at his watch. Two fifty. That meant if he hoped to catch the three o'clock train before it left the station, he'd better hurry.

Picking up his pace, he raced across the busy road to where Rebel was hitched.

But before he could mount, a low rumble made him look up. The sky was still clear with not a cloud in sight.

A shout drew his attention to a man on horseback racing toward town and waving his hat. "Clear the road. Clear the road!" His way blocked by a milk wagon, the man pulled on his reins, and his horse rose on its hind legs.

The rumbling sound grew louder, and Chase cursed beneath his breath. Fisher again! "How many this time?" he called.

"A hundred or so."

Chase shook his head. Even a small herd could do much in the way of damage. Stampeding cattle had even been known to derail trains, and the thought turned his blood cold. All he could do was hope and pray the train left the station before the cattle could do any harm.

A woman's cry made him whirl about. Cassie Decker was frantically pushing her way through the crowd.

"Cassie!"

She ran up to him and practically collapsed in his arms. She was shaking.

Holding her steady, he asked, "Cassie, what's wrong?"

"It's little Johnny," she cried. "I can't find him."

Emily stepped out of the Feedbag Café and blinked against the glaring sunlight. Needing to be alone with her thoughts, she'd spent the last hour at a corner table, her back toward the other diners. It was time to go home.

Home.

Who would have thought that one day she would call the ranch home? Right now, she couldn't think of another thing she'd rather do than go home to her husband.

Would he hate her? Blame her for what her uncle had done? Rue the day they'd ever met? For her own peace of mind, she had to believe that the answer was no.

Still, there was no turning back now that her secret was out. She had to know how he felt, even though it could mean rejection and heartache.

Just as she stepped off the boardwalk to cross the street, someone yelled, "Stampede!"

She froze. *Oh, please, no!* Memories of her wedding day whirled in her head. How she wished she could do it all over again. Marry Chase. Only this time, it would be no accident. If she ever got another chance to say *I do*, she wanted to say it for one man and one man alone. For Chase.

"You better get out of the street, ma'am," a man yelled, bringing her out of her reverie.

She turned and raced up the three steps to the wooden sidewalk. People spilled out of shops and offices to view the onslaught of cattle. Curses rent the air as some rushed to release tethered horses.

Emily craned her neck, and that was when she saw him a short distance away. Chase. Never could she imagine a more welcome sight.

Calling his name, she started toward him, elbowing her way through the crowd. Realizing, suddenly, that he wasn't alone, she stopped. Upon seeing a woman in his arms, her heart shattered into a million pieces. Stunned, she stared, oblivious to the frantic chaos around her. It wasn't just any woman. It was Cassie Decker—the woman Chase was supposed to have wed.

Icy fear twisted inside Chase as he glanced over Cassie's head. There was no sign of her young son, but maybe that was a good thing. At least he wasn't in the street. If the boy stayed on the boardwalk, he should be fine. But then again, there was no telling what a two-year-old would do.

Chaos reigned throughout the town. Shopkeepers pulled their doors shut and inexplicably pulled down window shades. A woman screamed, picked her infant out of the wicker carriage, and ran. Horses whinnied and pawed at the ground. Dogs barked.

Chase's gaze traveled to the salt wagon, and an idea popped into his head. If he couldn't find the boy, the next best thing was to stop the stampede. He didn't know if such a thing was possible, but it was worth a try.

Releasing Cassie, he yelled to be heard. "Stay here!"

Racing across the street, he called to a group of men who had rushed out of a nearby saloon to see what all the commotion was about. "Give me a hand!"

Reaching the dray, he grabbed hold of a side railing and propelled himself into the back, his boots hitting the wagon bed with a thud. He then reached for a salt block.

The first man who ran to the wagon to help was Royce. Chase and his stepbrother locked eyes for a moment, and something like a silent truce passed between them. At stake was something larger than the ranch, something larger than the two of them. For now, their differences didn't matter.

Chase heaved a twenty-five-pound block of salt over the side and into Royce's waiting arms. Following Royce's lead, others rushed to help.

Chase hauled block after block over the side of the wagon, and the men hurled the salt bricks onto the road. Chips of salt broke loose as the blocks hit the ground, scattering snow-like flakes everywhere. Yelling instructions, Royce arranged the chunks to form a barrier. The wagon empty, Chase hopped over the side and ran to help.

"Think it'll work?" Royce yelled.

"Don't know," Chase yelled back as the two worked side by side.

The rumbling grew louder, and the wagon shook like a ship in a stormy sea. A solid wall of snorting longhorns came into view. Behind their clamoring hooves and tossing horns, dust roiled.

All Chase could do was pray the salt blocks did the trick. Cattle had a strong sense of smell and could pick up the scent of water five or six miles away. No doubt, the same was true of salt.

The faint sound of the train whistle signaled its imminent departure, and Chase's already taut nerves threatened to snap. It would soon be directly in the path of the panicked cattle. The thought of Emily being on that train drove what felt like a steel knife through his middle.

Hopping onto the boardwalk, Chase pushed his way through the milling crowd. He looked for Cassie but didn't see her. Nor did he see her son.

He held his breath as the rush of beeves thundered past the *Welcome to Haywire* sign and showed no sign of stopping.

One steer took the lead, followed by two others. Just when all looked lost, the leader reached the salt blocks and, at the last possible moment, set its hooves into a sliding stop.

The other cattle came to a standstill next to the leader, their dark, thick tongues all over the white, briny blocks.

A collective sigh of relief swept through the crowd. Chase turned and spotted Cassie with her little boy in her arms. Only then did he allow himself to breathe. Where the cattle were concerned, the worst was over.

Leaving the others to round up the beeves, he ran to his horse and threw himself into the saddle. "Giddup!"

Heart in his throat, he raced along Main, bypassing carts and wagons until he reached the train station, praying all the while that Emily wasn't on it. Or if she was, that the train had been delayed.

No such luck. Just as he'd feared, the three o'clock train had already pulled out of the station on time. All that remained was a dark dot on the horizon, beneath a thin column of curling smoke.

35

It was dark by the time Chase started for home, the way lit by the pale light of a waning moon. He'd turned the town upside down, hoping against hope to find Emily.

Everyone in town knew who she was by now, and old wounds had been opened anew. Some had a few choice words to say about Harry Fields. Others wondered aloud how Chase could have married his niece.

Not that Chase could blame anyone for asking such questions. Fields had preyed on desperate people like Chase's father, and all had paid dearly. Chase hated knowing that Emily was related to such a man. He'd let her into his house, his heart, and all this time, she had what?

Planned on hurting him? Been in cahoots with Royce all along? Chase didn't even want to consider his uncle's cattle-rustling theory. Had she made him fall in love only to break his heart?

God, he had to know; he had to know.

If his worst fears were true, it would kill him. But not knowing what was in her heart was killing him too.

Such were his thoughts that he almost missed the steer grazing peacefully just off the side of the road, the moonlight glancing off its hide. Fisher again?

Chase reined in his horse for a closer look. At first, he thought his eyes were playing tricks on him, but he was soon relieved of that notion. Much to his surprise, it was a Rocking M steer.

"Now what are you doing way out here?" he murmured beneath his breath.

Narrowing his eyes, he spotted the gaping hole in the barbed-wire fence and muttered a curse.

Urging Rebel forward, he chased the steer back where it belonged. He then reined in his horse and dismounted.

He reached into his vest pocket for the box of safety matches and hunkered down on his haunches. Striking a match, he held the flame close to the ground. The flickering spark illuminated the hoof marks of cattle mixed with the tracks of two, maybe three shod horses. Judging by the droppings, he guessed they had passed this way but a short time ago. No more than an hour or two.

Fishing pliers out of his saddlebags, Chase set to work repairing the fence the best he could. Cattle had an uncanny ability to spot an opening through which to escape. If he didn't repair the fence, most, if not all, of his cattle would be gone by morning.

After twisting the broken pieces of barbed wire together, he debated whether to summon his men or follow the trail alone. Not wanting to lose more time, he decided his best bet was to track the cattle himself. With Emily gone, he wasn't about to get much in the way of sleep anyhow, and riding helped him think.

Even in the pale moonlight, he could clearly see the tracks in the sandy soil. It would get harder ahead where the ground was rocky.

The mishmash of tracks in the sand suggested the thieves were in no hurry. They would probably hide the cattle in some remote canyon until morning. A ranch the size of his made a rustler's job easy. It often took days to notice cattle missing, and by then, there wasn't much that could be done. Tonight, luck had been on his side.

Mounting his horse, Chase headed northward, away from the main road. He expected the trail to lead to the distant river, but instead, it veered off toward the granite hills. Not much there but sagebrush and rock and an occasional stunted oak. He stopped from time to time to listen, but only the howl of a distant coyote and the whisper of the gentle wind broke the silence.

That and the muted cry of a broken heart.

Fighting the steel weight of despair that weighed down on him, Chase forced himself to keep going, but his heart wasn't in it. They could take his cattle, take his ranch. Nothing mattered now that Emily was gone.

Still, he kept going. He rode for an hour, maybe two. The tracks went up a hill. Unable to see the other side, he leaned forward, his senses alert, while his horse picked its way cautiously up the rocky slope.

On the top of a hill, he spotted the glow of a campfire nestled in a small canyon below. For several moments, he watched, careful to stay in the shadow of a stunted oak. He could see three horses below but no men. The cattle were bedded down, and he suspected the rustlers were too.

Making a quick decision, Chase hid his horse among a grove of trees and scrambled up the hill on foot. His plan was to get close enough to identity some, if not all, of the thieves. The sheriff suspected the rustlers were locals. If his theory was correct, identifying them would go a long way toward capturing them. Chase hoped and prayed that no one he knew was responsible.

His tall frame bent, he used whatever shrubbery he could find for cover. Dry leaves and twigs crunched beneath his feet, and he froze in place to listen.

Had they heard him? Seeing no movement below, he tested the ground with the toe of his boot before taking a cautious step forward.

As if sensing his presence, one of the thief's horses whickered. Chase ducked behind a granite boulder, crouching low. After several moments, he peered over the rock. Two men sat around the fire, but he was still too far away to identify them.

He didn't dare move closer. The moment he stepped into the clearing, his presence would be known. He was still considering his options when a sound from behind startled him. He turned just as a shadow swooped toward him. Instinctively, he reached for his gun. But before he could draw it out of the holster, everything went black.

36

CHASE STIRRED. IN HIS DREAMS, HE COULD HEAR Emily's voice, hear her saying his name.

He imagined himself reaching out to her, but she kept pulling away. Finally, she vanished altogether. He stood in the wilderness calling to her, demanding answers to his questions. *Why? Why did you make me fall in love with you? Why did you have to leave? Why wasn't I enough to make you stay?* But only the wind answered him. The cold, empty wind and the distant howling of a lone coyote.

His eyes flickered open. A fuzzy light hurt them, and he quickly closed them again. He tried moving, but something held him in place. He was vaguely aware that his head hurt.

A whispered voice in his head reminded him of something he didn't want to think about. She was gone. The one woman in all the world that he loved was gone.

He groaned inwardly and murmured her name. "Emily."

"Shh."

His eyes flew open. Emily's pale face floated inches above his own, and the faint smell of lavender engulfed him. Was he dreaming? He wanted to touch her, feel her, know that she was real, but he couldn't move. He felt as if he were frozen in a cake of ice.

"Have to get you out of here," she said, her voice low. "But I can't untie you."

His mind whirled. Either he was completely out of his head, or she was real. "I...I thought you'd left."

"Shh. We can't talk now. There's no time."

He tried to make sense of where they were. Why he couldn't move. Fighting the fog in his head, it finally dawned on him that he was bound with rope. "My...my boot."

"What?"

"There's an Arkansas toothpick. In my boot."

"A toothpick won't cut through these ropes," she whispered.

"A knife. It's a knife."

"Oh."

He felt her hand on his leg. "The other one."

She drew the dagger from his boot, and the blade glinted in the moonlight angling through the tree branches. It seemed to take forever for her to saw through the thick rope, but at last, his hands pulled free.

He rubbed his numbed wrists as she tackled the rope at his ankles. A worrisome thought crossed his mind, and he silently cursed his uncle for putting it there in the first place. As much as he didn't want to believe she was somehow involved in the recent surge of cattle thefts, he couldn't think of a legitimate reason for her being there.

"How...how did you find me?" he asked, unable to keep the suspicion out of his voice.

She tossed a nod at the campfire below. "I'll tell you later." She cut through the last of the rope.

"Are they asleep?" he asked, moving his feet.

She nodded. "Some more than others."

It took him a moment to absorb her meaning. "What...what did you do?" he asked, his voice hushed.

She answered beneath her breath. "Let's just say one of the men had an unfortunate meeting with a rock."

He stared at her. "You...you could have been hurt."

In the faint moonlight, her misty eyes sparkled like two gems. "I wasn't the one who got himself hog-tied."

"You got me there." Grimacing, he gingerly touched the back of head and felt an egg-size lump. Pulling his hand away, he reached for his hat and whispered, "I'm mighty obliged for what you did. Just don't do anythin' like that again."

She pursed her lips, but even that small gesture made him forget his pounding head, forget everything but the memory of her sweet lips on his.

"Are you saying that next time, I should just leave you tied up?"

"There's not gonna be a next time." He was better suited for raising cattle than tracking down bad guys. Staggering to his feet, he swayed slightly.

She grabbed him by the arm. "You okay?"

He nodded and donned his hat. "Yeah." She released his arm, and he reached for his gun. His holster was empty.

Together, they climbed to the top of the hill. The

going was frustratingly slow. Partly because of the terrain, but mostly because he still felt woozy.

He spotted a dark hump. With a glance at her, he ambled over to have a look.

Well, what do you know? If it wasn't Charlie Bunker, the man who had sworn up and down that he had mistaken Chase and Emily for a panther.

Dropping on his haunches, Chase pressed a finger to the hombre's thick neck. He was out cold but still breathing.

"Maybe I should tie him up," he whispered.

"Let's just leave," she whispered back and started for her horse.

Reaching for the man's gun, Chase shoved it in his holster.

His head still pounding, he gingerly started down the hill to where his horse was tethered and climbed into his saddle.

Not trusting himself to lead the way through the rough terrain, he motioned Emily to go first.

They traveled for miles without speaking. On occasion, he stopped to listen and make certain they weren't being followed.

Less than a mile from the ranch, he pulled on the reins, drawing his horse to a halt.

A fingernail moon hung overhead, and the stars shone bright, but the night was strangely quiet.

Emily doubled back and rode to his side. "Everything okay?"

"Yeah." He slipped from his mount and reached for his canteen. The bump on his head hurt like the dickens, but the questions in his head hurt even more.

He removed the cap from the canteen and took a long swallow. The water was warm and tasteless, but it soothed his dry mouth. Wiping his lips with the back of his hand, he offered her a drink before recapping the canteen.

"What were you doin' there?" he asked at last.

She hesitated before dismounting. "I saw a bunch of cattle being herded away from the ranch."

"Saw?"

She nodded. "I was on the way back from town and—"

"You were on the way back?" Without giving her a chance to answer, Chase asked, "Why didn't you go for help?"

"I didn't think there was time." Hesitating, she ran her hands up and down her arms as if to ward off the chill. "I wanted to prove to you...to everyone...that I wasn't like my uncle. I thought if I found who was behind the cattle rustling, it would help make up for some of the trouble my uncle caused."

"Blast it, Emily. You could have been killed!"

"You could have been too!"

His gaze sharpened. "Why, Emily? Why did you come here? Was it to hurt me?"

Had she been in cahoots with Royce? He hated that his uncle had put such thoughts in his head. But he had to know. He had to know.

"Hurt you? No, absolutely not! I came here to marry Garvey. You know that. How could you think I would want to hurt you?"

The pain in her voice, on her face, nearly killed him, but still, he persisted. "Why here, Emily? Why did you come to Haywire? Knowing what your uncle had done to the folks around here?"

"But that's just it. I didn't know. Not at first."

It was too dark to clearly see her expression. He wanted to believe the sincerity in her voice was real. His heart was willing, but the mind was harder to convince.

Turning his back, he slipped the canteen's leather straps over the horn of his saddle. "How did the cattle thieves not see you?"

"Guess I was better at hiding than you."

They stared at each other for a long moment, the air tense. "Did you recognize anyone?" he asked at last.

She shook her head. "No, but..."

"What?" he pressed. "Tell me."

For answer, she turned to her horse and reached into her saddlebag. She pulled something out, but it was too dark to see what it was. She handed it to him.

It was a piece of a leather rope. He frowned in puzzlement. "What is this?"

"That's what you were tied up with. Only one person I know makes a rope like that."

Chase fingered the braided leather strands, and a sick feeling washed over him. "Gabby," he said. Timewise, it made sense. The rustling problem had gotten worse since Gabby's hire.

She nodded. "Gabby."

He frowned. "You don't sound surprised."

"I was just thinking of something Ginny said. She insisted he was an angry man."

"Guess we should have listened to her."

"I'm sorry, Chase. What...what will you do?"

"Do?" he asked, not sure what she was asking of him.

She met his gaze with sympathetic eyes. "About Gabby?"

"Nothin'," he said. "It's the sheriff's job now." He didn't want to talk about Gabby. Didn't want to think about him. "I thought you'd left town." He wiped his mouth with the back of his hand. "That's what Royce hoped."

"I thought about it," she said. "But I couldn't bring myself to walk away from you, from the ranch. From Ginny."

"Why...why did you come to Haywire in the first place?"

When her answer finally came, her voice sounded strained, as if each word had been pulled from the deepest regions of the heart. "After my uncle's arrest and trial...things got difficult. I decided to leave Boston. To go someplace where no one knew me. That's when I saw Mr. Garvey's advertisement in the newspaper for a mail-order bride. I know it sounds crazy, but at the time, I thought it was an answer to a prayer. I had no idea that my uncle... I would never have come here had I known."

"And you didn't know Royce before you arrived?"

"How could I? I didn't even know my uncle had done business here until I found a letter in your desk. I couldn't believe it. I didn't know what to do. I tried to tell you..."

He studied her in the soft glow of the moon. "I know," he said softly.

"I was afraid you'd hate me."

He narrowed his eyes. "Why? Why would I? You aren't to blame for your uncle's crimes."

"That's just it. I am." She beseeched him with her eyes before continuing. "My father wanted me to take over the family business following his death. But I had other plans…"

"Other plans meanin' college?"

She nodded. "Had I done as my father wanted, you wouldn't be fighting to save your ranch."

"You can't blame yourself," Chase said.

"But I do. I now know why Papa pushed me so hard to take over for him. He didn't trust his brother. He never said as much, but the signs were all there. I was just too wrapped up in my own dreams to notice."

"You couldn't have known what your uncle would do," he said.

"What he did to you and the others…" Her voice wavered. "The town has every reason to hate me."

"They don't know you."

"They knew me in Boston and—" She shook her head.

He drew in his breath. "What…what about us?"

Her eyes widened. "Us?"

He frowned. "After last night, I thought—"

She looked away. "Last night was a mistake."

"Because of your uncle?"

"That and…" She shook her head.

"Emily." He reached for her hand, but she pulled away.

"I'll stay if you want me to. Like…like before."

"Like before?" He frowned. "You mean before last night?" Before he'd kissed and held her in his arms?

"I don't want you to lose the ranch. But...already it's started. The town... I'll stay as long as I can. I can't promise any more than that." Tears glittered in her eyes. "I can't go through what I went through in Boston. They even tried to set my uncle's house on fire. If it comes to that, I'll leave. I can't put the ranch in danger."

"I don't give a fiddle about the ranch! Without you—"

She held out the palm of her hand to stop him. "Don't say it," she whispered, and it sounded like a plea. She shook her head. "I-I saw you—"

He stared at her in confusion. "You saw me what?" He moved toward her. "Emily..."

She backed away and, without another word, threw herself into her horse's saddle and rode away.

37

TWO DAYS LATER, EMILY STOOD ON THE VERANDA waiting for Alice and the twins to arrive.

Never had she felt so miserable or had the future looked so bleak. How foolish of her to think that she and Chase could go back to the way things were. Go back to their marriage in name only. What an impossible task she had set for herself!

Keeping busy with classes and bookkeeping chores didn't help. Nothing she did could wipe out the memory of seeing Chase and Cassie together.

In her more rational moments, she hated Chase for what he'd done to her. For making her love him. For making her think that he loved her in return.

Somehow, he had left an indelible mark on her that made her feel restless and bereft. His absences commanded her thoughts every bit as much as his presence once did. When she wasn't staring out the window, hoping to catch a glimpse of him, she wandered through the house.

Ginny had taught her the importance of touch. For that reason, Emily habitually trailed her hands along furniture, doorknobs, and porch railings, hoping against hope that Chase had left something of himself behind.

The few times she'd accidentally run into him, the air had crackled between them with unspoken words and unvented feelings. Each encounter had left Emily feeling emotionally drained.

Chase had done his part to make their sham marriage work. He no longer slept in the little room next to hers. No longer teased her about her Boston accent. No longer asked her about her day. Instead, he left the house before dawn and didn't return until long after dark.

She'd tried telling herself that none of it mattered. She'd lived with an empty marriage once. Surely, she could live with it again. But that was before she had fallen madly and deeply in love. Before she had known the joys of a real marriage.

Before she had seen Cassie Decker in Chase's arms.

Neither Peggy Sue or Cookie seemed to think Chase's absences strange. "It's always like this during calving season," Cookie assured her. "Don't worry. It'll soon be over."

His assertion only made her wonder what excuse Chase would use then for staying away.

Her thoughts were dashed by the arrival of her students. Grateful for something to do, she called to Ginny and rushed down the porch steps to greet them.

Neither the twins' father nor Alice's mother had made mention of the newspaper article, but news traveled faster in town than it did out here in the backcountry. Sometimes it took several days before the newspaper reached the ranch.

Neither the cowhands nor Cookie had said a

word, but they had to know. They had gone to town Saturday night as usual, where local gossip ran rampant.

The morning went quickly as Emily led her charges through classes in arithmetic and reading. While the others took turns reading aloud, Ginny listened quietly and took an active part in the discussion that followed.

Since it was such a beautiful spring day—neither too hot nor too cold—Emily decided to continue the lessons outside in the shade of a sycamore tree.

"All right," she said, facing her students. "I want the girls to stand on this side and the boys on that side." She waited for Ginny and Alice Riley to take their places opposite the twins.

"Did you all practice your spelling words?" All four children nodded, and Emily unfolded the list in her hands. "Are you ready?" she asked.

"Ready," the children said in unison, though Eddie Benton looked less enthusiastic than the others.

Emily explained the spelling bee rules. She'd chosen simple words as a start. Since it was only the third lesson for Alice and the twins, she didn't want to scare them off by making things too difficult.

"When I give you a word, say it, spell it, and say it again. Any questions?" None of the four raised their hands. "All right, we'll start with Alice. Your word is 'yellow.'" Alice was a pretty child with red hair and green eyes. She was also smart as a whip and spelled the word without hesitation.

Eddie was better at arithmetic than spelling, but he managed to work his way through *seven* and *table*. His brother, Adam, correctly spelled the word *green* but forgot the *e* in the word *blue*.

Ginny giggled her way through the words *moon* and *earth* with no hesitation. After an initial curiosity, the others had accepted her blindness and the four had become fast friends. It did Emily's heart good to watch Ginny's confidence grow as the others cheered her on.

The girls eventually won the spelling bee.

Emily was just about to tell them to wash up for the noontime meal when she noticed a cloud of dust heading their way. Someone was in a hurry. It soon became clear that it wasn't just one wagon but two.

Leading the way was the twins' father, Fred Benton. The wagon following close behind was driven by Alice's mother.

Emily frowned. The children weren't scheduled to be picked up for another couple of hours. What could have happened to explain such urgency?

The first wagon pulled up to the front of the house, the second close behind.

The twins' father jumped to the ground and ordered his boys into the wagon. A compact man dressed in overalls, he sported a dark mustache and bushy eyebrows.

"What's wrong?" Emily asked.

"Wrong?" he sputtered, shaking the days-old newspaper in his hand. "I'll tell you what's wrong! You pretendin' to be a teacher, just so you can poison my sons' minds!"

Worried about scaring the children, Emily tried to calm the man, but he would have none of it. Instead, he accused her in no uncertain terms of coming to Haywire to finish her uncle's ghastly deeds.

He would have said more had Mrs. Riley's shrill voice not silenced him. "After what you and your family did, how dare you show your face around here!" she shouted.

Their angry faces made Emily feel like she was back in Boston. She glanced at her four pupils looking wide-eyed and frightened. "You're scaring the children," she said, but her pleas fell on deaf ears.

She didn't notice Chase's arrival until he spoke. "I think you'd better leave. Both of you." Chase's cool voice did nothing to dampen Mrs. Riley's fury.

Scowling at him, she sputtered. "I expected more from you. To bring this…this…"

Benton glared at Emily but addressed Chase. "Mark my words, she's up to no good. She'll hurt you like her uncle hurt us and—"

Chase's cold voice sliced off the rest of Benton's words. "I said, leave!" This time, his voice left no room for argument.

Mrs. Riley grabbed her daughter by the arm and practically dragged her to the wagon. Ginny made a step to follow, but Chase stopped her with an arm around her shoulder.

Fighting tears, Emily whirled around and ran to the house.

Chase came to her room a short time later, his dark eyes hooded. Tension had stretched between them before, but it was even more evident now. It was as if they each waited for the other to let down their guard.

In the end, Chase was the one to break the silence. "I don't know what to say, Emily. Except I'm sorry."

Emily stared at him before asking, "Is Ginny—?"

"She's upset, but I had Kansas Pete take her for a horseback ride."

"She'll like that." Riding was Chase's cure-all for whatever ailed a person. "I just wish she hadn't been there." Emily heaved a sigh. It nearly broke her heart to see the children looking confused and frightened.

"We can't always protect the ones we care about," Chase said, his voice thick.

She studied him. Was it thoughts of his late brother behind the haunted look in his eyes? Or Cassie Decker?

After seeing Cassie and Chase in the stables together, she'd suspected his affection for Cassie ran deep. But it wasn't until she had seen Cassie in his arms that she'd known just how deep.

"Are you okay?" he asked.

Hugging herself, she nodded. "When I left Boston, I thought I put everything that happened there behind me."

"Give it time. People here are still hurtin'."

"And you think I'm not?"

"That's not what I'm sayin'." He studied her with knitted brow. "The Rileys and Bentons were almost forced into bankruptcy. At the time, Mrs. Benton was in a family way, and...Fred blames the loss of the child on them nearly losin' the farm."

"Oh God." Emily lifted her eyes to the ceiling. "Will it ever stop?" Did her uncle's destruction know no end?

Chase reached out his hand but stopped short of

touching her. "I didn't tell you that to make you feel bad. I hoped that knowin' some of what happened would help you understand. It's not you they're mad at."

"It sure feels like it is."

"We Texans are simple folks. If someone does us wrong, justice is swift, and there's satisfaction in that. Folks here don't cotton to drawn-out trials and short prison terms."

"My uncle will spend ten years behind bars."

"Here, people hang for far less."

"I guess that makes Boston more civilized," she said. It was an old joke between them, but today, she made no attempt at humor.

"I'm not sayin' our way is right," he said. "It'll take folks a lot longer than ten years to recover from the financial burdens Fields & Fields created."

Emily covered her face with her hands.

Moving quickly, Chase wrapped her in his arms. Not with the passion he'd shown the other night, but ever so gently, as if consoling a child.

As comforting as his arms felt, Emily nonetheless pulled away. The memory of his arms around Cassie Decker was still too fresh, reminding her that the marriage had been thrust upon them by accident and was a mistake. The one night spent in his arms had been a mistake too.

He dropped his arms to his sides. "I don't think they'll bother you again."

His assurance brought her no comfort. She would miss Alice and the twins.

"What about the rest of the town?" she asked. It was a statement as much as a question. If what had happened earlier was any indication, Haywire wasn't all that much different from Boston.

"We'll deal with that when the time comes."

Suddenly, Emily felt tired. Weary. She had been dealing with the fallout from her uncle's arrest and drawn-out trial for almost three years. She didn't know if she had the stamina to keep going.

Regarding her with a look of sympathy, Chase backed away. "I'll let you get some rest," he said and turned.

She watched him go, Mr. Benton's accusations still ringing in her ears. "I didn't come here to hurt you."

He stopped short. "I know, Emily. I know."

The next day, Emily tried drawing Ginny out of her solemn mood by drilling her on the multiplication facts.

They sat outside on the veranda. It was a warm day, and the air was thick with the smell of sunbaked earth. "What's seven times three?" Emily asked.

Ginny pulled her gaze from the direction of a noisy scrub jay. "Will Alice come back?"

Emily sighed. "I don't know. Maybe…one day."

"Her pa said you were a bad person. I don't believe that. Mama doesn't believe it either."

Emily took Ginny's hand in hers. "Alice's pa was just angry. Sometimes when people are angry, they say things they don't mean."

"I hope I never do that," Ginny said. "I hope I never say things I don't mean."

"You know what?" Emily released Ginny's hand

with a squeeze. "It's almost noon, and I heard that Cookie was making your favorite chicken."

A mischievous smile curved Ginny's mouth. "You mean son-of-a-gun chicken."

Emily laughed. "Run along, and we'll practice some more later."

Ginny jumped up and made her way into the house. Emily was about to follow when she heard Kansas Pete call her name.

She waited as he shuffled bowlegged across the yard, hat in hand.

Reaching the porch, he nodded in greeting. "Don't mean to bother you, ma'am, but I'm what you might call the designated speaker."

Emily tilted her head. "Oh?"

"Yes, ma'am. The boys and me done drew straws, and I got the short end." He cleared his voice. "You haven't been comin' around our campfires, and the boys and me… Well, we miss you."

Touched by his words, Emily swallowed the lump in her throat. "That's very kind of you to say, Kansas Pete."

"Oh, I'm not sayin' it to be kind. It's true. When you're not there, I have to dance with Beanpole Tom, and all he does is crunch leather."

Emily laughed. Beanpole Tom did tend to step on his dance partner's feet. She grew serious. "I didn't think… you'd want me there, knowing my true identity."

"Shucks, ma'am. We don't care who you was. We just care who you is. You're the lady who saved the ole homestead, and for that, we're mighty obliged." He tilted his head. "So, what do you say about attendin' the campfire tonight?"

How could she turn down an offer like that? "It would be my pleasure."

A smile crinkled his whiskered face. "The boys will be mighty pleased to hear that, ma'am. And so will my feet."

Looking like a preacher who had made his first convert, he walked away whistling to himself.

The door opened behind her, followed by Cookie's voice. "Ready for some chow?"

She wasn't hungry, but not wanting to disappoint him, she nodded. "Can't wait."

Her attempt to sound enthusiastic apparently failed, for Cookie afforded her a look of sympathy. "I hope you're not still stewin' over what happened yesterday," he said.

There was no use denying it. Cookie wouldn't believe her even if she did. "When I came to Texas, I'd hoped to start over with a clean slate. I had no idea my uncle had such a long reach."

"In time, folks will disremember everythin' that happened here."

She heaved a sigh. Cookie was right; people did forget, but it could take a very long time. "So, what am I supposed to do meanwhile?"

"Lift your head and look 'em square in the eye."

"That's easy for you to say."

He shrugged. "Worked for me."

Her curiosity whetted, she studied him. "Worked for you how?"

"When Ole Man McKnight hired me, I was what you would call a hoodlum. I didn't break *all* the commandments, but it wasn't for want of tryin'. My downfall came when Chase's pa caught me stealin' his horse. Instead of hangin' me as he had the right to do, he hired me as a drover on his cattle drives. Let me tell you, I never worked so hard in my life. McKnight made me pay back every cent I'd ever stolen before I could keep a cent to myself. When folks saw me makin' amends, they decided maybe I weren't so bad after all."

"I can't believe you did those things," Emily said.

"Believe it." Cookie splayed his hands. "I was orphaned at a young age. Guess you could say I was mad at the world."

"My uncle hurt a lot of people," she said. He had also ruined the family's good name. Her poor father would turn over in his grave if he knew what his brother had done to the company that had been his life's work. "If there was a way of paying for what he did, I would, but…"

"Your uncle's debt to society ain't yours to pay. Nevertheless, what you're doin' for the boss is a good start. You're helping him keep the ranch. You're also helping Ginny."

"I'm not doing that much. Anyone could teach her the basics."

"Maybe so, but I doubt that anyone could make her smile the way you do. Or make her mama feel like she belongs. We all tried to do that, but only you succeeded."

"You're a good friend, Cookie. But not everyone feels as you do."

"The important ones do."

38

CHASE STOOD OUTSIDE EMILY'S DOOR FOR A LONG moment before knocking. Even after she'd called for him to enter, he hesitated before reaching for the doorknob.

She sat at the dressing table brushing her hair, and never had she looked more beautiful to him. He only wished he could tear down the barrier between them. He hated the way things stood. The polite talk. The awkward silences.

Even now, as she met his gaze in the mirror, he could see her put up her guard. She set her brush on the dressing table and swung around on her stool to face him. Only then did he notice the light shadows beneath her eyes. The past week had evidently been as difficult for her as it had been for him.

The sheriff had hauled Gabby to jail, and his band of rustlers was now under lock and key. As hard as it was to find out that one of Chase's men had betrayed his trust, it was nothing compared to watching the townsfolk turn against Emily.

Although no one dared speak up Sunday at church,

he saw the way the congregation looked at her. The way they whispered behind gloved hands. The way they went out of their way to avoid him and Emily. She saw it too. He could tell by the way the light faded from her eyes, the way her smile vanished from her lips, how much it hurt her.

The worst part had been when she was attacked outside the ranch house by Fred Benton and Maizie Riley. The surge of protectiveness that had swelled up inside him surprised Chase. He wasn't a violent man, but it was all he could do not to slam a fist into Fred's face.

Even now, he felt protective of her, which was why he had to do what he had come here to do. There was no other way. His first mistake had been marrying her; his second had been falling in love. It was his love for her that had brought him here tonight.

He drew in his breath. Entering the room had been torture. Everything in the room reminded him of the one glorious night they'd spent together. Did she think about that? Think about all that they'd had and lost? Did she wake in the morning and gaze at the empty pillow, the empty bed, wishing he was there?

Would he ever again be able to walk in this room without doubling over in pain?

Shaking the thought away, he pulled the check from his vest pocket. Without a word, he crossed to where she sat and laid the check on the dressing table.

Her gaze fell upon it before she lifted rounded eyes to his. "What's that for?"

"I told you I would pay your way back to Boston, if that's what you wanted. If not, it's yours to do whatever you want. After everythin' that's happened, I have no right to ask you to stay."

She sucked in her breath. "I said I would."

"I know what you said, but…I know how painful this has been for you." *For me…*

"You don't have to protect me," she said. "If that's what you're doing."

He knotted his hands by his sides. With a guilty start, he realized he wasn't just protecting her; he was also protecting himself. Living under the same roof and not being able to hold her was unbearable. He couldn't think of anything else, and he was no good to the ranch—to anyone—in his present condition. It had to end.

Aloud, he said, "Legally, you're still my wife, and that makes it my job to protect you." What he didn't say was that he would do anything to keep her safe. Even if it meant losing the ranch.

She bit her lower lip and looked away. "If I leave, what will happen to the Rocking M?"

"My uncle found someone interested in purchasin' half the land. It'll be enough to pay back the money my father borrowed from Royce's mother. I'll still have the ranch. It'll just be half the size it is now."

The thought brought a new pain to his heart. Splitting the ranch was the last thing he'd ever hoped to do. But nothing, *nothing*, was as painful as having to let Emily go.

"You can't do that," she said. "This land is your family legacy."

A muscle throbbed at his jaw. "It will still be McKnight land. There just won't be as much of it."

"And Royce agrees to this?" Emily looked surprised, and he couldn't blame her.

Chase nodded. "He does."

He wasn't sure why Royce had agreed to settle for so much less than he'd originally demanded. Perhaps the stampede in town had made his stepbrother realize what Chase had known all along—Royce wasn't cut out for life as a rancher. Or maybe it was simply Emily's refusal to leave.

"If I stayed," Emily began slowly, "the ranch would be yours, and you'd owe Royce nothing."

"Legally, no. But"—Chase rubbed his forehead—"his mother paid off my father's loan and helped him save the ranch. It's only right I pay Royce back."

The burden he'd taken upon his shoulders wasn't his to bear. But neither was Emily responsible for her uncle's actions, no matter how much she blamed herself.

"I'm sorry it didn't turn out the way you'd hoped," she said.

"Me too." He took a deep breath. "I just want you to know the annulment papers are ready. All you have to do is stop by the courthouse and sign them."

He searched her face for something—anything—that told him she didn't want to go. But she gave him no clue as to what she was thinking. He'd hoped—hoped in vain as it turned out—that forcing her hand would make her admit that she loved him.

She'd called him her husband, had called this her home, and he waited now to hear those same words again.

For several long moments, they stared at each other, the silence seeming to take up all the air in the room.

When the words he longed to hear didn't come, he cleared his throat. "I'll have Big-Foot Harry drive you to town tomorrow. The judge already questioned me, but he'll want to talk to you."

She moistened her lips and looked away. "Thank you."

Chase waited again. *Say something*, his heart cried. *Tell me you don't want to leave. Tell me that our love is real. Tell me that you long to hold me as I long—ache—to hold you.*

"Take care of yourself, Emily," he said at last.

He turned to leave, the heaviness in his heart slowing his steps.

"What are the grounds?" she asked.

He stopped, hand on the doorknob, and turned to look at her over his shoulder.

"What?"

"For annulment?" she asked, as calm and cool as if asking the time of day. "What are the grounds?"

"Coercion," he said. There weren't any other grounds—none.

∞

After Chase had left the room, Emily felt as if he'd taken her heart with him. For the longest while, she sat frozen in place, staring at the closed door and willing him to come back.

Once he'd found a way to save his ranch, or at least half of it, it hadn't taken him long to take steps to end the marriage. How foolish of her to think that his sweet words had meant something, that his kisses had been real.

Her eyes burned with the threat of tears. Nothing Mr. Benton or Mrs. Riley said had hurt as much as watching Chase walk out of the room.

She closed her eyes. Memories threatened to overwhelm her. Happy ones. Miserable ones. Chase holding Cassie Decker in his arms.

Emily tried to erase the image from her head. Once the annulment agreement was signed, Chase would be free to marry the woman he loved, the woman he had been meant to marry all along.

She stared at herself in the mirror. And she would be free…to do what?

She now knew she liked teaching and, more importantly, was good at it. Maybe she could find a teaching job in some remote area where the name Fields had never been heard.

The thought did nothing for her peace of mind. If anything, it only depressed her more, and that was when the tears came.

39

PEGGY SUE PULLED THE LAST OF EMILY'S DRESSES OUT of the wardrobe and spread it on the bed, next to the open travel case. "I wish you didn't have to go."

Emily finished folding her nightgown and tucked it into the valise. "I wish I didn't have to go either." She bit her lip to keep from choking up. "I'll miss you and Ginny." That was the least of it. Never could she have imagined how hard it would be to leave the ranch and its residents. Leave Chase…

"What you did for her…" Peggy Sue looked away as if to get her emotions under control. "I don't know how to thank you."

"There's no need," Emily said. "And you don't have to worry about Ginny. Chase has agreed to hire a tutor for her."

Peggy Sue clasped her hands to her chest. "I'm much obliged, but it won't be the same without you."

Since she looked about to cry, Emily reached for the dress on the bed. "Here, try this on. If it fits, it's yours."

"Oh no." Peggy Sue shook her head. "I couldn't."

"Of course you can. I insist."

Peggy Sue cast a look of longing at the frock. "What will a housekeeper like me do with a fancy dress like that?"

Emily gave her a knowing look. "Dazzle a certain young man, that's what."

Peggy Sue blushed and then giggled. She'd been spending a lot of time with Rusty lately, and Emily had seen the two of them walking hand in hand on several occasions. "Oh." Needing no further incentive, Peggy Sue quickly undressed and, with Emily's help, donned the dress.

Emily stepped back. The dress fit, but instead of enhancing Peggy Sue's complexion, the pink made her look pale.

Emily reached for a second dress. "Here, try this one on."

For the next hour, packing was forgotten as Peggy Sue tried on one dress after another. She was close to Emily in size and most fit her perfectly, but they both agreed that the brown print with the lace-trimmed bodice was the one she was meant to wear.

While Peggy Sue admired herself in the mirror, Emily reached for her hairbrush. She then set to work rearranging Peggy Sue's hair into a flattering braided chignon. Fluffy bangs were achieved with two snips from a pair of short-bladed scissors. The bangs softened Peggy Sue's features and made her eyes appear larger.

"Now for the finishing touch," Emily said, pulling out jars of tinted lip salve and carmine rouge.

"Oh no, I couldn't!" Peggy Sue looked aghast. "My mother said that only ladies of the night wore makeup."

Emily unscrewed one of the jars. "Only ladies of the night let it be known that they wear makeup. The rest of us keep it secret." With that, she dabbed Peggy Sue's lips with balm, turning them a pretty pink. After rubbing Peggy Sue's cheeks with a light coating of rouge, she stepped back.

"You look beautiful," Emily said.

Peggy Sue checked herself in the mirror, turning first one way and then another. "Oh my," she murmured. "I hardly recognize myself!"

Emily smiled. "The dress is yours to keep."

Peggy Sue bit her lip and took a deep breath. "I...I don't know how to thank you."

"I'm glad you like it." Emily watched Peggy Sue's face in the mirror and wished with all her heart that things would work out for her and her daughter.

Peggy Sue took another lingering look at herself before backing away. "I'd better change," she said with a sigh. "I have work to do."

"Wait. I need you to do something for me. I need you to go to the stables and tell Rusty to saddle my horse."

"You're going riding?" Peggy Sue asked, surprised. "What about your packing?"

"It's a beautiful day, and I think a little fresh air and sunshine will do me good," Emily said and added with a wink, "The packing can wait. But love can't. Now go."

That afternoon, Emily turned an anxious gaze out the parlor window. What could be keeping Big-Foot

Harry? He promised to have the buckboard ready an hour ago.

Ginny looked about to cry again. "I don't want you to go."

Emily exchanged a look with Cookie before wrapping Ginny in her arms. "I know, dear heart. I promise to write, and your mama said she'll read my letters to you. Also, Mr. Knight is hiring you a tutor."

Ginny pulled out of her arms. Her watery eyes looked like two blue pools. "But that's not the same as having you here. You said you were family, and that means you're not supposed to leave!" With that, Ginny turned and ran from the room.

"Ginny, wait!"

"Let her go," Cookie said. "There ain't nothing you can say that's gonna make her feel better."

Emily looked at him, surprised to see a suspicious gleam in his gray eyes.

"I'll miss you," she said. "You've been a good friend. And I'll especially miss your son-of-a-gun coffee."

"You sure you have to do this?"

She drew in her breath. "It's…what Chase…what we both want," she stammered. Never could she have imagined how hard it would be to leave. She'd lived at the ranch for only two months. Yet it felt like she was about to leave a lifetime of memories behind.

"Take care of yourself," Cookie said. Turning abruptly, he quickly left the room.

Swallowing the lump in her throat, Emily picked up her carpetbag. Big-Foot Harry would help her with the rest of her baggage. She was leaving with fewer belongings than she'd brought with her. In addition to the brown printed dress, she had given Peggy Sue her wedding dress. Maybe it would bring Peggy Sue better luck than it had brought her.

She walked outside and set her carpetbag on a wicker chair. What was taking Big-Foot Harry so long? She'd hoped to leave before Chase came back to the house. Seeing him would only make things that much harder.

After pacing the porch for several moments, she started down the steps. Maybe Rusty knew what was keeping Big-Foot Harry. Just as she reached the stables, Peggy Sue ran out of the double doors, tears rolling down her cheeks.

Alarmed, Emily stopped her. "Peggy Sue, what's wrong?"

Peggy Sue wrung her hands together. "It's Rusty," she sobbed. "He's leaving."

"Leaving? Why?"

Peggy Sue struggled to get the words out. "Mr. McKnight is selling half the ranch and said he would no longer need as many employees."

"Oh no!" Emily didn't think she could feel any worse.

"It's true," Peggy Sue said. "Rusty and I…" She bit her bottom lip and lowered her gaze.

"I know," Emily said. "I know."

Peggy Sue's lashes flew up, exposing fresh tears. "If he loses his job, he'll have to leave town. There aren't many ranches that can afford to hire a full-time groom."

"Oh, Peggy Sue… I wish there was something I could do."

"I don't know that there's anything." Peggy Sue picked up her skirts and ran sobbing to the house.

Emily curbed the impulse to chase after her. Nothing she could say would make things better.

Instead, she stood in the middle of the yard, staring at the cattle grazing peacefully on the rolling hills. At first, the vastness of the land had overwhelmed her, even frightened her, and made her feel small and insignificant. Now the spread seemed to make everything else seem small in comparison. It was easy to imagine that nothing existed outside of the McKnight ranch. Not Boston. Not anything.

Dividing the land in two as Chase had proposed would bring the rest of the world closer. What remained of the ranch would always be under the shadow of Fields & Fields. Future generations would never know the full extent of the McKnight legacy. But it wasn't just the ranch that would suffer from the split.

With Rusty gone, Peggy Sue and Ginny would suffer too.

The thought hit Emily like a sledgehammer. She curled her hands at her sides and tried to think. There was more at stake here than she knew.

Something had to be done. Thoughts spinning, she came to a quick decision. Not wanting to give herself a chance to change her mind, she raced to the stables.

40

EMILY RODE DAISY HARD. SHE DIDN'T KNOW WHERE Chase was, but she would find him. Had to find him.

Big-Foot Harry had driven up to the house just as she'd ridden away. She'd been in too much of a hurry to stop and explain.

Spotting Kansas Pete shoveling manure into the back of a wagon, she reined in her horse and called, "Have you seen Chase?"

Kansas Pete stuck his shovel in the ground, pulled off his hat, and wiped his forehead with the back of his hand before answering. "Last I saw, he was in the barn."

Thanking him, she clicked her tongue and rode to the large red building. Heart pounding, she dismounted and tethered her horse next to Chase's. She took a deep breath, said a quick prayer, and walked through the open double doors.

Chase looked up from where he was bottle-feeding a calf, and his eyes rounded at the sight of her. "I...I thought you'd left." He pulled the empty bottle from the calf's mouth and stood. "Is something wrong?"

She waited for him to let himself out of the stall

before answering. "Yes," she said. "There's plenty wrong. I'm not leaving!"

She heard his intake of breath as he stared at her. "If you stay, you could get hurt."

"I don't care!" Swallowing hard, she forged on. "The McKnight Ranch was meant to stay intact. That's what your grandfather would have wanted. This is where the sagebrush grows tallest and…"

As she spoke, his face grew still, and his eyes darkened with some emotion she couldn't define. Still, she kept going. She couldn't seem to stop herself.

"This is your family legacy, and it's worth fighting for. And if you won't fight for it, I will!" On and on she went, words tumbling out of her like rocks down a mountainside. She wasn't even sure she made sense. All she knew was that she could no longer keep her feelings bottled up inside.

"So don't think you can get rid of me, because I'm not going anywhere. Not until this ranch is safe, and Peggy Sue and Rusty—"

"I love you."

"This is my home too, and I'm not letting anyone run me off…"

"I love you."

"I don't care what anyone says. I'm not my uncle, and I'm not responsible for what he did. I would never hurt you or the ranch or—" She stopped midsentence and stared at him. "What…what did you say?"

"I said…I love you."

She stared at him in shock and disbelief. "Why? Why are you saying such a thing?"

He frowned. "Why? I'm saying it because I mean

it. I married you by accident. But loving you is by choice."

"But…" Her mind whirled. "What about Mrs. Decker?"

Pushing his hat to the back of his head, he frowned. "What about her?"

"She's the one you want." It hurt her to say it, but it was true. "She's the one you were meant to marry. The one you love."

"The one I…" Chase shook his head. "She and I had an arrangement. That's all. Just like you and Garvey."

Emily gaped at him. "You…you don't have to lie." God knows, he owed her nothing, not even consideration of her feelings. "I saw the two of you in town. I saw her in your arms."

He frowned as if trying to remember. "What you saw was me tryin' to comfort her. Her son had run off, and cattle were about to storm the town." He took two steps closer. "Emily, don't you know? You're the only one I love. The only one I've ever loved."

She swallowed hard. *Please don't let my mind be playing tricks on me.* "But…I heard you. That day in the stables. I heard you arrange to meet her in town. You said you'd make things right. Don't deny it."

"I don't know what you heard, but the only time I arranged to meet Cassie in town was to give her a check for her weddin' expenses. Didn't seem fair that she had to pay for her hotel room or weddin' dress."

She stared up at him. "That's it?"

He lifted his shoulders. "That's it."

"But what about all those trips to town every Friday?"

"That's when I do the banking, order supplies, and take care of other business." He angled his head. "You mean you thought I was with Cassie?"

"What else could I think?"

He lifted his eyebrows. "What else? What do I have to do to prove that you're the only one for me?"

"Do...do you mean it?"

He shook his head. "After the night we spent together, how can you ask that of me?"

"How?" she asked in disbelief. "You told me to leave. You arranged for an annulment."

He splayed his hands. "I thought that's what you wanted." He took a step closer. "After Fred and Mrs. Riley attacked you, I didn't want you to go through anythin' like that again." He moved closer still. "I don't know if I can protect you. Folks around here are pretty riled up."

"I just want you to love me. As...as I love you. That's all the protection I need."

"Don't you know?. Without you, the ranch means nothin'. Without you, life means nothin'. In the short time I've known you, you've become my world. My reason for livin'. My everythin'."

She gazed deep into his eyes. At times, she had trouble understanding him, but not tonight. Tonight, his words burrowed deep inside, pulling all the pieces of her broken heart together into one and making her feel whole again. They stared at each other for a moment before they fell into each other's arms. Secure in his warm embrace, she looked up at him, and the tenderness in his eyes made her feel more loved and wanted than she'd ever felt in her life.

"I don't know anything about cattle," she said. "And I still don't like mice. As for the chickens…"

He laughed. "How about you leave the wildlife to me? All I ask is that you keep on lovin' me."

Emily couldn't think of anything she would rather do. "Will that make me a real rancher's wife?" she asked.

"If that doesn't, this will," he said. He feather-touched her forehead with his lips before swooping down to capture her mouth with his. He kissed her until her head spun and her body tingled. Each heart-stopping, toe-curling, knee-weakening kiss filled a deep need even as it made her want more. A lot more.

Moaning softly, Chase tightened his hold on her. "Not only do I want you to be my wife for real, I want you to be my wife forever."

Tears welled in her eyes. "Forever," she whispered.

Now that she knew how it felt to be a rancher's wife, she had no desire to be anything else.

Epilogue

JUDGE GRAY LOOKED UP FROM HIS DESK AND GROANED. "Not you two again."

Emily squeezed her husband's arm and laughed. She'd been doing a lot of that lately—laughing. Everything had worked out better than she could have imagined. Once Royce learned that Emily was expecting Chase's baby and wasn't going anywhere, he'd agreed to accept Chase's offer.

Chase sold some of his cattle to square things with Royce, but the land was kept intact. It would take time for Chase to restock the herd, of course, but the McKnight legacy was secure, and the future looked bright.

Just as amazing, when word got out that Emily had identified the leader of the cattle-rustling ring and saved the ranch, the townspeople stopped blaming her for her uncle's misdeeds. She was now fully accepted as a rancher's wife.

The judge rifled through the stack of papers on his desk. "Don't tell me you're here for an annulment."

Chase winked at her. "We're not here for an annulment. We're here to get hitched."

"Hitched?" The judge's hand stilled. "If memory serves me right, you've already got your boots in a tangle."

"Yep," Chase said, "but we want to get married again."

The judge adjusted his spectacles. "Why?"

Chase gazed lovingly into Emily's eyes. "This time, I want to marry the woman I love."

"Are you sure about this?" Judge Gray asked.

"Couldn't be any surer," Chase said.

Gray directed his next question to Emily. "What about you?"

Emily ran a loving hand over her rounded stomach. "Oh yes!" She smiled up at Chase, and a warm glow rushed through her. "This is the man I intend to spend the rest of my born days with."

The judge glanced across the room at Rusty, Peggy Sue, and Ginny standing by the door. "I take it you're the witnesses."

"We are," the three of them said in tandem. Looking pretty as a picture in a blue floral dress, Ginny covered her mouth to hide her giggles.

Rusty wrapped one arm around Peggy Sue and the other arm around Ginny. "Then we want to make a date for you to marry us."

"He's gonna be my new pa," Ginny said.

Judge Gray nodded approval. "In that case, I'd say he's one lucky man."

The happy look on Ginny's face made Emily's heart swell with joy. Rusty had accepted a grooming job in Boston so that Ginny could attend Perkins Institution for the Blind.

The Rocking M school, as it was now known, would continue without her. When word got out how Emily had taught a little blind girl, local parents began clamoring for her help. Emily now had a total of six students, and more were on the way.

As much as Emily hated to see Ginny, Rusty, and Peggy Sue leave the ranch, the move would open up a whole new world for Ginny. She might never get her wish to touch the moon, but the school would certainly help her reach for the stars.

"All right, you two," the judge said, indicating with a pointed finger where he wanted Emily and Chase to stand. "You know the routine."

Tucking her hand in his own, Chase drew Emily into place by his side.

She barely remembered the fiasco of their first wedding, but she would never forget a single moment of the second.

This time, Emily wore a simple gingham dress she'd made herself. It was plainer than her first wedding dress, the simple lines more suited to the life she had now chosen. In keeping with her new lifestyle, no dainty slippers adorned her feet. This time, she chose to wed in her sturdy cowboy boots, just as a proper rancher's wife would do.

If their child should ever ask about their wedding day, this was the one Emily would describe. *Your father looked so handsome*, she would say. *And your mama was so happy, she couldn't stop smiling.*

At Chase's request, she wore no veil. He wanted to make sure he was marrying the right woman this time. Instead of a veil, Emily wore flowers in her hair.

"Let's get on with it," the judge said. He stood in front of Chase and Emily.

This time, no stampeding cattle drowned out his words. No veil came between her and Chase. This time, only tears of pure joy blurred her vision.

"Do you, Emily McKnight, take this man again…"

"Oh yes," she said, not giving the judge a chance to complete his sentence. "I do, I do, I do!"

Author's Note

Dear Readers,

I hope you enjoyed reading Emily and Chase's story as much as I enjoyed writing it. This is the second book in the Haywire Brides series, and I'm now writing the third.

I love reading and writing mail-order bride stories set in the Old West. It's hard to imagine a young woman traveling west to marry a man she'd never set eyes on.

The original catalog-bride business grew out of necessity. The lack of marriageable women in the west was partly responsible, but so was the Civil War. The war not only created thousands of widows but a shortage of men, especially in the South.

As a result, marriage brokers and heart-and-hand catalogs popped up all around the country. According to an article in the *Toledo Blade*, lonely men even wrote to the Sears catalog company asking for brides. (The latest such letter received by Sears was from a lonely marine during the Vietnam War.)

In those early days, advertisements cost five to

fifteen cents, and letters were exchanged along with photographs. Fortunately, the telegraph and train made communication easier.

Not all marriage brokers were legitimate, and many a disappointed client ended up with an empty bank account rather than a contracted mate.

For some mail-order couples, it was love (or lust) at first sight. In 1886, one man and his mail-order bride were so enamored with each other that they scandalized fellow passengers on the Union Pacific Railroad during their honeymoon.

Not every bride was so lucky. In her book *Hearts West*, Chris Enss tells the story of mail-order bride Eleanor Berry. On the way to her wedding, her stage was held up at gunpoint by four masked men. While signing the marriage license, she suddenly realized that her new husband was one of the outlaws who had robbed her.

No one seems to know how many mail-order brides there were during the 1800s, but the most successful matchmaker of all appears to be Fred Harvey. He wasn't in the mail-order bride business, but by the turn of the century, five thousand Harvey Girls had found husbands while working in his restaurants. Until next time,

Margaret

Acknowledgments

You would think that after publishing as many books as I have, the writing would get easier. It doesn't. If anything, it gets harder. After writing more than forty-five books, the biggest challenge for me is keeping my stories fresh and each couple's story unique.

I mention this because even old veterans like me need support and encouragement. Especially on the days when my characters refuse to talk to me and the writing stinks. That's when you need the most support. But there are other times too.

The one person who always stands ready to help is my wonderful agent, friend, mentor, and all-round adviser, Natasha Kern. She's been there for me during the many professional and personal ups and downs of this writer's life. I don't know how she does it, but I always feel better after talking to her, and I cherish our talks.

I also consider myself extremely lucky to write for Sourcebooks. I'm especially grateful that Mary Altman is my editor. She has some sort of sixth sense that can zero in on any weakness in a manuscript, and her comments are always right on target.

A special thank-you also goes to Chris Cocozza for *Cowboy Charm School*'s sweet, romantic cover. That's just how I pictured my couple!

I'm also grateful to my dear family and friends who think my habit of talking to myself weird but love me anyway. Finally, a great big thank-you to you, my readers. You make it all worthwhile.

Enjoy your return to Two Time, Texas, where tempers burn hot, love runs deep, and a single marriage can unite a feuding town...or tear it apart for good.

LEFT
at the
ALTAR

One

"FIFTY-FOUR MINUTES."

Her father's booming voice made Meg Lockwood want to scream. But airing her lungs in church wasn't an option, and thanks to the whalebone corset beneath her wedding gown, neither was breathing.

"Mama, make him stop."

Her mother straightened the garland of daisies in Meg's hair for perhaps the hundredth time so far that day before turning to her husband. "Henry, must you?"

Papa kept his gaze glued to his gold pocket watch rather than answer, his wagging finger ready to drop the instant the minute hand moved. Not by any means a formal man, he'd battled with Mama over his wedding attire until, like a defeated general, he'd thrown up his arms in surrender. Unfortunately, the knee-length coat Mama had chosen emphasized Papa's ungainly shape, which bore a striking resemblance to a pickle barrel.

The finger came down. "He is now fifty-five minutes late."

Meg's hands curled around the satin fabric of her skirt. Where *was* her bridegroom? She hated to keep the wedding guests waiting, but she didn't know what to do. Time meant nothing to her erstwhile fiancé, but he'd promised not to be late for their wedding. She'd trusted him to keep his word.

Just you wait, Tommy Farrell!

When he finally did show up, she wouldn't be responsible for her actions.

Tommy wasn't the only reason for her ill temper. As if her too-tight corset wasn't bad enough, the ruffled lace at her neck made her skin itch, and the butterfly bustle hung like a brick at the small of her back. Worse, the torture chambers disguised as dainty white slippers were killing her feet.

The church organ in the nearby sanctuary moaned louder, as if even the organist's patience was spent. The somber chords now rattled the walls of the tiny anteroom, threatening the framed picture and forcing the glass beads on the kerosene lamp to jiggle in protest.

She met her mother's worried gaze in the beveled-glass mirror. At forty-five, Elizabeth Lockwood still moved with the ease and grace of a woman half her age. The green velvet gown showed off her still-tiny waist and slim hips.

A wistful look smoothed the lines of worry on her mother's face. "You look beautiful."

Meg forced a smile. "So do you, Mama."

Meg had inherited her mother's honey-blond hair,

turquoise eyes, and dainty features, but her restless countenance was clearly thanks to her father's side.

"Fifty-*six* minutes late," her father exclaimed, and Meg's already taut nerves threatened to snap.

Clenching her hands tightly, she spun around to face him. "You never change!"

"Change? Change!" Papa looked indignant as a self-righteous preacher. "Why would I? Someone has to maintain a healthy respect for time."

The door swung open. *Thank goodness.* Meg whirled about again, ready to give her errant fiancé a piece of her mind, but it was only her older sister. The worried frown on Josie's face told Meg everything she needed to know, but still she had to ask.

"Anything?"

Josie shook her head. At twenty-three, she was two years older than Meg, and at five foot ten, stood a good six inches taller. Today she wore a dusky-rose gown that complemented her dark hair and gave her complexion a pretty pink glow. She took after Papa's side in looks, but of the three Lockwood girls, she was most like Mama in calm disposition.

"Ralph looked all over town." Ralph Johnson was Josie's husband, and he owned the saddle shop at the end of Two-Time's main street. "You don't suppose something might have happened to Tommy, do you? An accident?"

"It better have," Meg muttered.

Gasping, Mama looked up from straightening Meg's gown. "Of all the things to say!"

"Sorry, Mama." Hands balled at her sides, Meg gritted her teeth. Her mother was right, of course; such uncharitable thoughts didn't belong in church.

Neither did thoughts of murder.

"Fifty-eight minutes," her father announced.

"I'm sure he'll be here soon, Papa." Josie always tried to see the bright side of things, but even she couldn't hide the doubt in her voice.

Papa's gaze remained on his watch. "Soon's already come and gone. Now he'll have to answer to me for keeping my daughter waiting!"

Her father didn't fool Meg one whit—he'd been against the marriage from the start. If she didn't know better, she would suspect him of causing her fiancé's absence just to prove he was right.

"Fifty-nine minutes!"

"Henry, please," her mother cajoled. "You're upsetting her."

"She *should* be upset. The boy's irresponsible and will never amount to a hill of beans. He's like a blister; he never shows up till the work's all done. Doesn't even know whether to wind his watch or bark at the moon. I should never have agreed to this marriage."

"You didn't agree to anything, Henry."

"And for good reason! Furthermore—"

A knock sounded, but before anyone could answer it, the door cracked open and Reverend Wellmaker popped his head into the room. "Is everything all right?" he asked, eyes round behind his spectacles. "We're almost twenty minutes late."

"*Fifty-nine* minutes late!" her father roared.

The difference in times raised no eyebrows, since no standard time existed in Two-Time. It was common practice for communities to set watches by the local jeweler, but unfortunately, their town had two—Meg's father and Tommy's pa. Both stubbornly insisted they alone had the right time.

The feud dividing the town for more than fifteen years was expected to end the minute the two families were joined by marriage. Both fathers had agreed—albeit reluctantly—to standardize time once the deed was done.

"Shh, Henry, not here." Her mother gave the minister an apologetic smile. "Soon."

Josie left with the pastor, and Papa continued his sonorous count until interrupted by another knock on the door.

"Meg, it's me, Tommy."

"It's about time!" She hiked her skirt above her ankles and started across the room.

Her mother grabbed her by the arm. "It's bad luck for the groom to see you in your wedding gown," she whispered.

"It's worse luck for the groom to be an hour late for his own wedding." Meg pulled free from her mother's grasp and ripped open the door. "Where have you been? You agreed to get married on Lockwood time and—" Suddenly aware that something was terribly wrong, she bit back the rest of her sentence.

Tommy looked as sober as an owl in a barn. Even more worrisome was his attire—old canvas trousers held up by blue suspenders. He appeared haggard, as if he hadn't slept, and his unruly red hair stood on end like a rooster's comb.

"We have to talk." He grabbed her by the hand and pulled her out of the room and down the hall.

She held back. "Thomas James Farrell, stop right now. You hear me? I said *stop*!"

But he didn't stop, not until they reached the cemetery behind the church. It took a moment for Meg's eyes to adjust to the bright autumn sun.

Tall, granite grave markers stood at attention like pieces on a chessboard waiting for someone to make the first move.

She snatched her hand from his. "What do you think you're doing? What's going on?"

Tommy grimaced. "Meg, I'm sorry, but I can't do this. I can't marry you."

She stared at him, dumbfounded. *This can't be happening.* "What are you saying?"

"I'm sayin' I can't be the husband you want. I can't spend the rest of my life workin' on watches in my father's shop. All those hairsprings and gears and stems and—"

"*This* is how you give me the news?" She gave him an angry shove. "Tommy Farrell, I've known you nearly all my life, and you've caused me plenty of grief along the way, but this takes the cake!"

"I'm sorry." He slapped his hand to his forehead. "I'm goin' about this all wrong. It's not that I don't want to marry you. I just can't."

"And you waited for our wedding day to tell me this?"

"I feel bad, I do."

"*You* feel bad? How do you suppose our guests feel after being kept waiting all this time? And what about the town? Our fathers promised to end their feud—"

"I know, I know." He grimaced. "Right now, I'm only thinkin' of you."

"By humiliating me in front of the entire world?" She stared at him as if seeing him for the first time. For years, she'd made excuses for his lackadaisical ways and had even defended him to his own father. She'd forgiven him for forgetting her birthday—not once but twice! But this…this was by far the worst thing he'd ever done.

"I'd make you miserable," he continued, his Texas twang even more pronounced than usual. "I'm not ready to settle down. I want to see the world. To travel to Europe and Asia and…and the Pacific Islands. I read somewhere that they're real nice."

"You've said some mighty dumb things in your life, but this has got to be the dumbest."

"I knew you wouldn't understand."

"No, I don't understand," she cried. "I don't understand how you could wait till today to throw me over for a bunch of islands!" She backed away from him, fists at her side. "I should have listened to Pa."

"Meg, don't look at me like that. It really is for the best. Maybe in a year, or two or three, I'll be ready to marry and settle down. Maybe then we can—"

"Don't you dare say it, Tommy Farrell. Don't you even think it! I'd sooner die a spinster than marry the likes of you."

"You don't mean that…"

"I mean every word. I don't ever want to see you again. Not ever!"

"Meg, please."

"Just…just go!"

He stared at her as if making certain she wouldn't change her mind. Then he swung around and rushed along the narrow dirt path leading out of the cemetery as if he couldn't escape fast enough.

Watching him flee, Meg felt numb. Today was supposed to be the happiest day of her life, but instead, it had turned into a nightmare. How would she break the news to her family? To the guests? To the folks counting on this marriage to bring peace to the town? She pulled the garland from her hair, threw it on the ground, and stomped on it.

A movement caught her eye, and a tall figure stepped from behind an equally tall grave marker. Her gaze froze on the man's long, lean form. A look of sympathy—or maybe even pity—had settled on his square-jawed face, crushing any hope that the humiliating scene had somehow escaped his notice. Her cheeks flared with heat. Could this day possibly get any worse?

He pulled off his derby and nodded at her as if apologizing for his presence.

"Sorry, ma'am. Forgive me. I couldn't help but overhear." If his dark trousers, coat, and vest hadn't already marked him as an easterner, the way he pronounced his words surely did.

In no mood to forgive a man—any man, even one as tall and good-looking as this one—she grabbed a handful of satin, turned, and rushed to the church's open door, snagging her wedding gown on the doorframe. She glanced over her shoulder to find him still watching her. In her haste to escape, she yanked at her skirt, and it ripped. The tearing sound might as well have been her heart.

Inside, the thundering organ music rang like a death knell. Hands over her ears, she kicked off her murderous slippers and ran down the hall in stocking feet.

two

GRANT GARRISON LEFT HIS BOARDINGHOUSE AND rode his mount down Peaceful Lane. Two-story brick residences lined the street, the boardinghouse where he lodged among them. Either the street name was a misnomer or someone had once had a strange sense of humor, because the street was anything but peaceful.

Even now, angry voices filled the morning air, the loudest coming from Mr. Crawford, who took regular issue with his next-door neighbor's bagpipes. But he wasn't the only one airing his lungs.

Mr. Sloan was yelling at the Johnson boy for stealing his pecans; Mrs. Conrad could be heard expressing her disapproval at the goat eating her flowers. Next door to her, Mr. Quincy was arguing with the paperboy, who had thrown the morning newspaper on the roof for the second time that week.

Grant tipped his hat to the two women gossiping over a fence and steered his horse around the wagon belonging to the dogcatcher. A terrible commotion drew Grant's attention to an alleyway, and the dog-catcher emerged running, chased by a big yellow hound.

A half block away, the widow Rockwell walked out of her tiny house carrying a lamp. Compared to the other buildings on the street, the two tiny residences she owned looked like dollhouses. She waved at Grant, and he tipped his hat in greeting.

"Need any help?" he called. He'd already helped her move twice that week.

"No, not today."

The widow's two houses were located directly across from each other. Almost identical in size and style, they were called Sunday houses and had originally been built so that immigrant farmers could stay in town during weekends to run errands and attend church.

The problem was, the widow could never make up her mind which one to live in. No sooner would she haul her belongings to one side of the street than she decided to live on the other. So back and forth she traipsed from house to house, moving, always moving.

It had rained the night before, and puddles of mud dotted the dirt-packed road, causing the widow to pick her way across the street with care.

Except for a few lingering clouds, the sky was clear, and the air smelled fresh with just a hint of fall.

It was a normal day on Peaceful Lane—except for one thing. In the middle of the roadway, a woman was fighting with a pushcart.

Grant reined in his horse and narrowed his eyes against the bright morning sun. Did he know her? He didn't think so. Still, something about her small, trim frame struck a familiar chord.

The lady pushed the cart one way and jerked it

the other. A trunk or chest of some kind was perched precariously on top of the hand wagon, and it teetered back and forth like a child's seesaw.

Apparently seeing the futility of her efforts, she leaned over to examine one of the wheels stuck in the mud. This afforded him an intriguing glimpse of a white lace petticoat beneath an otherwise somber blue dress. She surprised him by giving the pushcart a good kick with a well-aimed boot.

Hands folded on the pommel of his saddle, he leaned forward. "So what do you think, Chester? Should we offer to help before the lady does injury to her foot?"

For answer, his horse lowered his head and whickered.

"I quite agree."

Urging his horse forward in a short gallop, Grant called, "May I be of service, ma'am?" He tugged on the reins. "Whoa, boy."

She whirled around, eyes wide as she met his gaze. Two red spots stained her cheeks, but whether from exertion or embarrassment at being caught in a less-than-ladylike predicament, he couldn't tell.

"Thank you kindly," she said with a soft southern lilt.

"My pleasure."

Her face looked vaguely familiar, but he still couldn't place her, which struck him as odd. Her big turquoise eyes should not be easily forgotten. Hatless, she wore her honey-blond hair piled on top of her head, but a couple of soft ends had fallen loose. The carefree curls didn't seem to belong to the stern, young face.

He dismounted and tethered his horse to a wooden

fence. He guessed the woman lived nearby, but that still didn't tell him where they might have met.

He tipped his hat. "Name's Grant Garrison."

She studied him with a sharp-eyed gaze. "You!"

Since she looked fit to be tied, he stepped back. At that point, the flashing blue-green eyes jarred his memory.

"You're the"—he almost said *jilted*—"bride." He hardly recognized her out of her wedding gown. According to local tongue-waggers, her name was Meg Lockwood. Best not to let on how last week's disastrous nonwedding was still the talk of the town.

She glared at him, eyes filled with accusations. "That day at the church…you had no right to eavesdrop on a private conversation."

He extended his arms, palms out. "Please accept my apologies. I can assure you the intrusion was purely unintentional. I was visiting my sister's grave."

Uncertainty crept into her expression, but her combative stance remained. "You…you could have announced yourself."

He also could have stayed hidden, which might have been the better choice. "I considered doing just that. I'm afraid that had I done so, I might have flattened your bridegroom's nose."

This failed to bring the smile he hoped for, but at least she looked less likely to do him harm. She glanced up and down the street as if trying to decide whether to accept his help.

"I would be most obliged if you didn't mention… what you heard."

Her request confused him. Everyone in town knew the wedding had been called off.

"About the Pacific Islands," she added.

Never would he profess to understand the way a woman's mind worked, but her concern was indeed a puzzle. Would she *rather* her fiancé had left her for another woman, as some people in town suspected?

"I promise." He pretended to turn a lock on his mouth. "Not a word."

She let his promise hang between them for a moment before asking, "What brings you to Two-Time, Mr. Garrison?"

He hesitated. "I'm a lawyer. Since the East Coast is overrun with them, I decided to try my luck here. I just opened an office off Main." He replaced his hat and tossed a nod at the cart. "Where are you taking that?"

"To my sister's house." Her gaze shifted to the end of the street. "She lives in the corner house with the green shutters."

"Well, then." He grabbed hold of the handle and yanked the cart back and forth before giving it a firm push. The wheels gave a reluctant turn and finally pulled free of the gooey sludge with a *slurp*. But just as it cleared the mudhole, the cart tipped to one side and the chest shot to the ground, splashing mud everywhere.

Miss Lockwood jumped back, but not soon enough to prevent mud from splattering on her skirt. "Oh no!"

Muttering an apology, Grant quickly turned the chest upright, leaving an intriguing assortment of corsets, petticoats, and camisoles scattered on the ground. He never expected to see such a fancy display in a rough-and-tumble town like Two-Time.

While she examined the chest for damage, he quickly swooped up the satin and lace dainties and shook off as much mud as possible. Did women actually need this many corsets?

"I have to say, ma'am," he began in an effort to make light of the situation, "there are enough underpinnings here to fill an entire Montgomery Ward catalogue." He couldn't help but look at her curiously before dumping the garments back into the chest.

Checks blazing, she slammed the lid shut and double-checked the lock.

He offered her his clean handkerchief, which she turned down with a shake of her head. Silence as brittle as glass stretched between them, and Grant couldn't help but feel sorry for her. They seemed doomed to meet under trying, if not altogether embarrassing circumstances.

Since the lady seemed more concerned about the wooden chest than the corsets…uh…contents, he studied it more closely. It was obviously old but had been well cared for. Intricate engravings of birds, flowers, and a ship graced the top and sides, along with several carefully carved initials.

"No damage done," she said, her voice thick with relief. The red on her cheeks had faded to a most becoming pink. "My family would kill me if something happened to it."

"A family heirloom?" he asked.

She nodded. "All the way from Ireland. It's called a hope chest."

Grant knew about such things, of course, from his sisters. But never before had he been privy to a hope chest's contents. It was hard to know what disconcerted him more—manhandling Miss Lockwood's intimate garments, or the possibility that something of a similar nature filled his sisters' hope chests. Whatever happened to filling a hope chest with household goods?

Tucking the handkerchief into his trouser pocket, he struggled to lift the chest off the ground. He set it atop the cart and wiggled it back and forth to make sure it was balanced just right. "I'm afraid the contents may be ruined."

"Th-they'll wash," Miss Lockwood stammered, refusing to meet his gaze.

He brushed off his hands and grabbed hold of the cart's handles. This time, the wheels turned with ease, and he pushed it slowly down the road. She fell in step by his side, and a pleasant whiff of lavender soap wafted toward him. With heightened awareness, he noticed her every move, heard her every intake of breath.

"You said you were visiting your sister's grave," she said in a hesitant voice, as if she wasn't certain whether to broach the subject.

He nodded, and the familiar heaviness of grief rose in his chest. "Mary died in childbirth a month ago. Her husband owns a cattle ranch outside of town."

They had reached the gate leading to the two-story brick house with the green shutters. The rail fence enclosed a small but well-cared-for garden. A hen pecked at the ground next to a row of sprouting squash plants.

Miss Lockwood afforded him a look of sympathy. "I'm sorry for your loss," she said.

"And I'm sorry for yours." In danger of drowning

in the blue-green depths of her eyes, he averted his gaze. "Where would you like me to put it?"

"Put it?"

He shot her a sideways glance. "The corset...uh"—he grimaced—"hope chest."

She lowered her lashes. "The porch would be just fine," she murmured.

Since the cart wouldn't fit through the gate, he had no choice but to haul the chest by hand. Fortunately, only two steps led up to the wraparound porch. Even so, he was out of breath by the time he set the heavy chest next to a wicker rocking chair.

She'd followed him up the porch steps. "I'm much obliged." Her prettily curving lips made the sadness in the depth of her eyes all the more touching.

"My pleasure." He studied her. "I hope you don't mind my saying this, but...if I had someone like you waiting at the altar, I would never walk away. Not in a million years." The expression on her face softened, and he was tempted to say more but decided against it. Better stop while he was ahead.

With a tip of his hat, he jogged down the steps and headed back to his horse. The memory of all that silk and lace remained, as did the shadow of her pretty smile.

❦

Meg stood on her sister's porch, surprised to find herself shaking. *If I had someone like you...*

Never had anyone said anything like that to her, not even Tommy. Just thinking of Mr. Garrison's soft-spoken words sent a shiver racing though her, one that ended in a sigh.

Pushing such thoughts away, she knocked and the door sprang open almost instantly.

Josie greeted her with a questioning look. "Who's that man I saw you with?"

"Just...someone passing by. He stopped to help me." Meg seldom kept anything from her older sister, but she didn't want to discuss Mr. Garrison. Not in her confused state.

Josie looked her up and down. "Oh dear. You're covered in mud. What happened?"

Meg glanced down at her skirt. "I had a little accident."

"I told you to wait for Ralph," Josie scolded. "That hope chest is far too heavy for a woman to manage alone."

Meg hadn't wanted to ask her brother-in-law for help. Not with the way he'd been coughing lately.

"It's a good thing I have you to help me, then." Meg cleaned the sludge off the soles of her high-button shoes on the iron boot scraper, then shook as much of the mud off her skirt as possible. Satisfied that her sister's pristine carpets would not be soiled, she circled the hope chest. "Grab hold of the other side."

Carved by her great-grandfather, the wooden piece had been handed down to family members for generations. Each bride carved her initials into the old wood before passing it on to the next woman in line. Mama had passed it down to Josie who, after her own wedding, had handed it over to Meg during a ritual that had made all three Lockwood sisters roll on the floor with laughter.

Today, however, no such happy ritual was in play as she and Josie struggled to carry the massive chest inside the house and into the small but tidy parlor. They set it on the brick hearth so as not to get mud on the carpet.

"Whew! I forgot how heavy it was," Josie said.

Meg brushed a hand over her forehead. Good riddance. The hope chest that once held her girlish dreams was now a dismal reminder of a day she'd sooner forget.

"I don't know why Amanda refuses to take it. It's only fair. You and I both had our turn."

Josie frowned, as she was inclined to do whenever their younger sister's name came up. "Amanda's too independent to get married. She's only interested in stirring up trouble."

By trouble, Josie referred to Amanda's many causes. One—her campaign to close saloons during Sunday worship—had almost created a riot. Their youngest sister was the black sheep of the family and was always on the warpath about one thing or another.

"Poor Mama," Meg said. "All she ever wanted was to see the three of us married and bouncing rosy-cheeked babies on our laps." She gasped and quickly covered her mouth. "Oh, Josie, I'm so sorry."

"It's all right." Josie patted her on the arm. "I haven't given up hope that one day I'll have a child of my own. Some things just take time."

Meg flung her arms around her sister's shoulders and squeezed tight. "I wish I had your patience."

Josie hugged her back. "I love you just the way you are."

Meg pulled away and smiled. Spending time with Josie always made her feel better. "Thank you for taking the hope chest off my hands. If I have to look at it one more day, I'll scream." She and Josie had spent hours working on her trousseau—and for what?

"I'm afraid the clothes inside are a mess. The chest tipped over, and everything is covered in mud." Just thinking about that handsome new lawyer's hands all over them made her cheeks blaze.

Josie opened the hope chest to check the contents. She lifted the carefully sewn garments one by one and examined them.

While her sister inventoried the damage, Meg glanced out the parlor window and froze. There rode Mr. Garrison on his fine black horse. Her breath caught, and she quickly stepped behind the draperies so as not to be seen gaping. Did she only imagine him staring at the house? *If I had someone like you...*

Josie's insistent voice brought her out of her reverie. "I'm sorry?"

"I said I'll wash and press the garments, and they'll be as good as new." Josie studied her a moment, and her expression softened. "Are you okay?"

Meg moistened her dry lips. "I'm fine."

Josie lowered the hope chest's lid and stood. "It's been nearly a month. You can't keep hiding. Papa misses you at the shop. You know what a terrible bookkeeper he is, and with Christmas just around the corner..."

Guilt surged through Meg like molten steel. How selfish of her. Staying hidden like a common criminal had done nothing but place an extra burden on Papa's shoulders. It was her job to keep the shop records, order supplies, and serve the customers, thus freeing her father to spend his time repairing watches and clocks. And yet...

"I don't know that I'll ever be able to show my face in public again."

"Meg, that's ridiculous. No one blames you."

Taking the blame wasn't what bothered Meg; it was the feeling that she had let everyone down. Papa had promised to make peace with Mr. Farrell as a wedding present. Now that the wedding had been called off, the feud between the two men had resumed. If anything, their animosity toward each other had grown worse, each blaming the other for the disastrous affair.

"Go and clean up while I fix us something to eat."

Meg nodded and started down the hall, but not before taking another quick glance out the window. The deserted road looked as forlorn and lonely as she felt.

Moments later, Meg joined her sister in the sun-filled kitchen, her skirt still damp where she'd washed off the mud.

Josie's kitchen table had become the sisters' sounding board. Everything that happened—good, bad, or otherwise; every crisis, every problem—was hashed out, analyzed, resolved, or left to die upon that maple table.

Meg pulled out a chair, plopped down, and rested her elbows on the smooth-polished surface. "I don't understand why Papa and Mr. Farrell continue to fight." For as long as she could remember, bad blood had existed between the two men. Mama blamed it on professional differences, but Meg was almost certain their warfare had more personal roots.

Josie filled the kettle and placed it on the cookstove. "Sometimes I wonder if even they remember what started it. It happened so many years ago." She wiped her hands on her spotless white apron and pulled a bread knife out of a drawer.

Through the open window over the sink came the sound of bells pealing out the noon hour for the residents living and working north of Main. The rest of the town, including her father, had stopped for the noontime meal a good forty minutes earlier.

"Josie...how did you know you were in love with Ralph?"

Josie gave her an odd look. "What a strange question."

"I'm serious. How did you know?"

Josie thought a moment, cheeks tinged a pretty pink. "It was the way he made me feel. The way my heart leaped whenever he came into sight."

Meg chewed on a fingernail. She had known Tommy nearly all her life. Next to her two sisters, he was the best friend she'd ever had.

In school, he'd dipped her braids in ink and helped her with geography and science. In turn, she'd teased him about his red hair, drilled him on his numbers, and made him read aloud until he became proficient.

Knowing how their fathers disapproved of their friendship only strengthened the bond between them and forced them to meet in secret. It had been Romeo and Juliet all over again. Still, during all those years she'd spent in Tommy's company, never once had her heart leaped at the sight of him.

Josie dumped a loaf of bread out of a baking tin and proceeded to slice it. "I know you're still hurting, Meg, but I never did think you and Tommy belonged together."

A month ago, Meg would have argued with her sister, but now she only nodded. "I guess there're worse things than being jilted for the Pacific Islands."

Josie laughed. "I hope we never find out what those things are."

Meg laughed too, and for the first time in weeks, her spirits lifted.

About the Author

Bestselling author Margaret Brownley has penned more than forty-five novels and novellas. Her books have won numerous awards, including the National Readers' Choice and *Romantic Times* Pioneer awards. She's a two-time Romance Writers of America RITA finalist and has written for a TV soap. Not bad for someone who flunked eighth-grade English. Just don't ask her to diagram a sentence. You can find Margaret at margaret-brownley.com.

ALSO BY MARGARET BROWNLEY

A Match Made in Texas
Left at the Altar
A Match Made in Texas

The Haywire Brides
Cowboy Charm School
The Cowboy Meets His Match

Christmas in a Cowboy's Arms anthology